Lim the Swift

Becca Edney

DEDICATION

For my friends

CONTENTS

Little Archer

Chapter One   1

Chapter Two   13

Chapter Three   51

Chapter Four   78

Chapter Five   102

Chapter Six   126

Swift

Chapter One   1

Chapter Two   19

Chapter Three   43

Chapter Four   70

Chapter Five   88

Chapter Six   99

Little Archer

Book 5

CHAPTER ONE

Lord Caleb, king of Duamelti, looked from the letter in his hand to the messenger who had brought it. The young Wood-elf was standing in the middle of the empty receiving room, a respectful distance from Caleb's chair. He didn't seem to notice Caleb's gaze; he kept staring at the floor.

Caleb looked back at the letter, paying particular attention to the part about the messenger.

I would consider it a personal favour if you could find a place in Duamelti for the elf who bears this letter. He is the orphaned son of a ladies' maid of my wife, but for reasons I would prefer not to discuss in a letter he can no longer remain here in Silvren. Rest assured that this banishment is for his safety, not through any fault of his.

The letter was from Taffilelti, the king of the Wood-elven realm of Silvren.

"What is your name, child?" Caleb asked. He'd not normally have used such a term of address, but the elf barely looked of age.

The elf looked up, dark eyes wide. "Lim, my Lord," he said quietly.

Caleb waited a moment for the usual patronym, but Lim didn't seem about to give him one, so he looked back down at the letter. He could guess from that and the odd way that Taffilelti described his ancestry that Lim had been begotten on the wrong side of the sheets. A moment's cheekiness made Caleb smile as he considered the possibility that Taffilelti was afraid of his wife finding out who the lad's father was.

The smile passed as Caleb turned to the serious problem of what to do with Lim. He didn't want to turn him away; strife in the royal household of Silvren would serve nobody and he didn't want to offend Taffilelti. In any case, he only had a guess that that was the reason Lim had been sent. Maybe he was actually in danger for some reason.

"Have you eaten today, Lim?" he asked after a moment.

"No, my Lord," said Lim, a hopeful note entering his voice for a moment.

Caleb rang for a servant and instructed him to take Lim down to the kitchen and get him a meal. When they were gone, Caleb sat for a while, drumming his fingers on the arm of his chair. The sound of a movement beside him made him look round and he smiled at his honour guard, Ekehart, who stood beside him.

"Sorry, my Lord, I didn't mean to disturb you," said Ekehart.

"Not at all." Caleb stood up and hitched his shoulders. "Do you know where Master Kerin is? Or Nairion?"

Ekehart frowned. "I believe Nairion was going to spend the day putting some tax records in order."

Caleb nodded. "Let's see if we can find one of them; I need some advice."

Ekehart nodded and followed him out of the room.

Caleb found his brother, Kerin, first, sitting with a book and a slate in a window alcove. When he saw Caleb coming he put them both down gratefully.

"I hope I don't interrupt?" asked Caleb, nodding towards the slate, which was covered with scribbled writing and columns of numbers.

"It's necessary, but I'd be glad of a rest from looking at figures." Kerin untied his ponytail with a sigh. Like Caleb, and most Valley-elves, he had let his hair grow to his waist. "You look worried, though," he said.

Caleb showed him the letter, pointing to the paragraph about Lim. "I'm not sure what to do about him," he said.

Kerin frowned as he read. "Is this all you have?"

"And his name. Lim. Just Lim."

"Fatherless?"

"It looks like it. He's very quiet; I don't believe I've had a sentence more than twelve words long out of him."

Kerin frowned a little. "Difficult to know without a better idea of what he can do," he said, "but I'm sure there's something. He's a Wood-elf, after all; he must be good with animals."

Caleb nodded. "I sent him down to the kitchen to get something to eat." He smiled a little. "In part to buy myself some time to think."

Kerin also grinned. "I'd suggest you talk to him a little more before making any decisions." He looked back at the letter, the smile fading. "And maybe see if he'll tell you why he's been sent here. Lord knows I trust Taffilelti, but..." He trailed off there and they stood in silence for a while. Suddenly, Kerin suggested, "Do you want me to go and talk to him? He might be less shy with me."

"That's not a bad idea," said Caleb thoughtfully. It was possible that Lim had simply been overawed by him, and Kerin was naturally less of an imposing figure. "I imagine the cook will have sent him to the lower hall to eat."

"I'll go and speak to him now," said Kerin. "Where will I find you?"

"I have some other work to do," said Caleb with a sigh. "Check my study first."

Kerin nodded and headed off towards the lower hall.

When he arrived, Kerin immediately spotted Lim; his long braid made him distinctive. He was sitting alone at a rough table at one end of the hall, hungrily devouring some bread and cheese. There were a few servants in the room eyeing him curiously, but they went about their business as they saw Kerin enter. Nonetheless, they didn't leave the room. Kerin nodded to them and went to sit opposite Lim. The young Wood-elf looked up warily and didn't say anything, leaving it to the newcomer to introduce himself. Kerin considered him for a long moment before he spoke. He was short even for a Wood-elf and there was still a childish softness about the line of his jaw and his large dark-grey eyes

"My name's Kerin," he said at last. "I'm Lord Caleb's brother."

At that, Lim immediately started to scramble up. "I'm sorry," he said, "I didn't realise…"

Kerin shook his head. "Sit down," he said softly. "I'm not here to interrupt your meal; you look hungry."

Lim nodded. "I am," he admitted as he gingerly sat down again. "It was kind of Lord Caleb to give me this."

Kerin smiled a little. "We'd not send one of Lord Taffilelti's messengers away hungry."

Lim looked up and swallowed. "Send away?" he asked tentatively.

"That's what I came to talk to you about. I take it you know Lord Taffilelti asked for you to be allowed to live here?"

Lim nodded. "It was very kind of him," he said softly, his eyes on the table. He seemed to have lost his appetite and Kerin gestured towards his plate.

"I meant it: I don't want to interrupt you."

Lim glanced up, then quickly picked up the food and took another bite.

"But before my brother can give permission, we need to know a little more about you, and your circumstances."

Again, Lim paused, looking up, wide-eyed.

"Can you tell me why you were sent here?"

Lim looked down again. "It… it wasn't safe for me to stay," he said hesitantly. There was a slight tremble in his voice, as if he was choking back tears. "I probably should have… but it wasn't safe any more and Lord Taffilelti said I must leave." He looked up. "I'm sure —" he began, but then seemed to catch himself.

Kerin waited patiently.

At last, Lim continued, "I'm not running from the law," he said softly. "And... but... Lord Taffilelti is wise, and he said I could not stay, that I might be killed if I did."

Kerin frowned. That was stronger than his first impression: that Lim was an orphan Taffilelti had taken under his wing. "By whom?"

Lim shook his head. "I'm sorry," he said, his voice catching. "I can't..." He looked up and there were tears in his eyes. "Will you send me away?"

"It doesn't sound like you wanted to leave your home."

Lim shook his head. "But I don't want to die, and I trust Lord Taffilelti. He knows better than I do, and he says I was in danger there."

"Do you know why you were in such danger?"

Lim hesitated. "I... I can't say," he said softly, after a moment.

Kerin sighed, and again gestured encouragingly to the food. "Eat," he said.

Lim smiled a little, wiping the tears away with the back of his hand. His right hand, Kerin noticed suddenly. Throughout the conversation he'd kept the left one hidden under the table, though judging by his slightly clumsy movements, he was left-hand-dominant. Of course, it was possible that he was just clumsy.

After watching him take a few more mouthfuls, Kerin asked, "So what can you do?"

Lim looked up and hesitated. After a moment, he said softly, "Well, I have some skills with animals" – a note of pride entered his voice – "and the bow, and... I can run. I've been told I can outrun the west wind."

Kerin raised an eyebrow at that. It was an odd skill, but he was relieved to hear something other than nervous subservience in Lim's tone.

"Did you have an apprenticeship of any sort back in Silvren? Have you any craft you could continue to practice here?"

Lim shook his head. "I wasn't much use to anyone," he said in a very small voice. "I practiced my archery, and..." He shook his head.

That was a surprise. Apparently Lim was not low-born, if he'd never had to learn a craft.

"What did your parents do?"

Lim stiffened for a moment as though something had hit him, but then he shook his head a little. "My mother is dead and my father was a member of Lord Taffilelti's court," he said quickly.

Kerin noted the 'was'. Perhaps Lim's father had recently died?

"How old are you?" he asked.

"Forty-three."

Still an adolescent, as Kerin had suspected from looking at him. He didn't think he was going to get anything more from him; he was obviously nervous.

Kerin got up. "Is there anything else you want to tell me?" he asked.

Lim bit his lower lip. After a moment, he said, "I can learn. Please give me a chance."

"You want to stay here in Duamelti, then?"

Lim looked down, still chewing his lip. After a moment he said, "I... y-yes."

Kerin nodded. "We'll see," he said. "Stay here so we know where to find you, all right?"

Lim nodded, looking relieved and Kerin could feel his eyes on him as he left.

Caleb was in his study with Ekehart waiting outside, and he glanced up as Kerin entered.

"With you in a moment," he said and Kerin nodded, waiting while Caleb finished reading the paper in his hands, then signed it.

"He didn't have a lot to say for himself," he said when Caleb was able to pay attention. "I asked him why he'd been sent here but he was obviously distressed and I decided not to press the matter. I gather that Taffilelti believed he was in danger, though, and that he has his doubts but was disinclined to argue. He seems honest enough. I think Taffilelti really did send him, and at least told him that that was the reason. He's high-born; he said his father was a member of Taffilelti's court – 'was', mark you – but didn't give any details. I'm guessing from the fact that he's forty-three and hasn't begun to learn a trade."

"So young?"

"Yes. It makes me more inclined to say there's nothing dangerous about him. Perhaps his father made powerful enemies."

Caleb sighed. "We don't need them coming here after him, if so." He smiled a little as Kerin arched an eyebrow at him. "Don't worry, I'll not send him away if he's not a threat to us."

Kerin nodded. "So what do you want to do with him? Apparently he has some skill with animals, but he seemed proudest when he said that he could use a bow and that he's a fast runner."

Caleb paused a moment, staring into the distance and drumming his fingers on the desk. Suddenly, he smiled. "We could always send him over to Seregei."

A smile flashed across Kerin's face too, but then he sighed. "He could do with a trainee," he said.

Caleb shrugged slightly. "Some of our ancestors would disagree."

"Some of our ancestors were willing to let a Valley-elf die without a healer because he went to become a Swordmaster," said Kerin curtly. "I really don't think we should be modelling ourselves on them. Besides, I thought you liked Seregei?"

"Sometimes," Caleb admitted. Kerin knew that Captain Seregei of the Swordmasters was a loyal friend and a great warrior, but Caleb had never denied that from time to time he found that sharing a kingdom with him became insufferable. After a moment, just as Kerin expected, Caleb added, "When he's not being a cheeky, sarcastic pain in my neck."

"Well, do you at least agree he needs some company over in the Guardhouse?"

Caleb nodded. "You know," he said thoughtfully after a moment, "I think I *will* take him down to the Guardhouse. Apart from anything else, Seregei will keep an eye on him."

Kerin nodded. "That might be best," he said. "I told him to wait in the hall, so he'll be there when you're ready, I expect."

Caleb nodded and Kerin went back to retrieve his book and go on working on the supply inventory of the healing house.

It was into the afternoon before Caleb was able to escort Lim over to the Guardhouse. He'd have sent someone else in another situation, but he felt he owed it to Seregei to explain in person; the other elf would probably resent having a complete stranger foisted on him and Caleb would rather explain straight away than have to face Seregei bursting into his own study later. Besides, as Swordmaster Captain Seregei technically warranted the same level of respect Caleb would have given to another king; he was the nominal ruler of the Duamelti Mixed-bloods, after all.

Lim had been waiting in the lower hall, as Kerin had said. Caleb wondered if he'd been bored, sitting down there with nothing to do for several hours, but if so there'd been no sign of it when he arrived with the servant Caleb had sent to fetch him. Lim didn't ask any questions as they went. He kept about a pace behind Caleb, level with Ekehart, who kept shooting curious glances at him but had given up trying to talk to him.

As Lim walked, he kept his head down. He had shown a little interest in the news that he was hopefully going to become a Swordmaster, but had quickly gone back to being quiet and subservient.

"I think you'll like Seregei," said Caleb, in an attempt at making conversation. It wasn't true – he'd spoken to Lim so little that he had no idea who he might like – but he felt he had to say something.

Lim looked up. "I'll try, my lord," he said.

"If you don't, or he doesn't like you, I'm sure we'll be able to find you somewhere else to go."

"Thank you."

It seemed that there was still going to be no conversation there. Caleb sighed and shook his head a little.

At last, they arrived at the Guardhouse. Seregei was outside, practicing with his long sword on the clear, grassy space in front of the building. Caleb waited for him to finish, having long been taught not to interrupt weapons practice.

Seregei saw them standing there and stopped the sword's swing with a grunt, then lowered it.

"Hello, Caleb," he said, sounding a little breathless.

"You're out of practice," said Caleb.

"Longer drill than usual, and the weather's warm," said Seregei, wiping his brow with the back of one hand and brushing away wayward strands of shoulder-length hair. He glanced at Lim. "Hello," he said.

"This is Lim," said Caleb, stepping aside so Lim wasn't standing slightly behind him any more.

There was a pause, then Seregei smiled a little. "Well," he said, "I'm always happy to meet new people." He swapped the sword to his left hand and held out his right. "What brings you here, Lim?"

"Lord Taffileiti sent me," said Lim, hesitantly taking Seregei's offered hand, which almost entirely enclosed his smaller hand. "And... Lord Caleb brought me to become a Swordmaster."

Seregei's eyes widened in surprise, then he shot Caleb a glare. Lim visibly tensed and Seregei apparently noticed, for he let go of his hand.

"Sorry, sir," said Lim, looking down again. He started biting a fingertip.

"It's not your fault," said Seregei, still looking at Caleb. "You're an archer?"

"Yes, sir," said Lim, his voice rising a little. A smile appeared on his face for a moment.

"Well, why don't you run and get a bow and I'll see how you shoot."

Lim glanced at Caleb, who nodded. "Ask someone at the palace how to get to the armoury," he said.

Lim nodded and ran off. Caleb could see what Kerin had meant about Lim's speed: he'd not seen anyone run like that in years.

After a moment, he asked Seregei, "How did you know he is an archer?"

"I could feel the calluses on his hand," said Seregei curtly.

"Apparently he's very skilled; that was one of the few things he told Kerin about himself."

Seregei just nodded. He waited a while for Lim to get clear out of earshot, then said, "What's going on?"

Caleb sighed, gesturing to Ekehart to withdraw a little way. When the guard had taken a few steps back, Caleb said, "Taffileiti sent him here, as he said, with a letter that asked me to let him stay because it wasn't safe for him to stay in Silvren."

Seregei grunted as he slid his sword back into the sheath on his back. "So you brought him to me?"

"He's an orphan with nowhere else to go." Caleb tilted his head a little as he looked up at Seregei. "Have you a better suggestion?"

Seregei shook his head. The irritation was tempered by tiredness as he said, "Well, you might try sending him somewhere he actually wants to go."

Caleb wasn't sure what he meant by that. "I can't send him back to Silvren, and I don't know where else –"

Seregei shook his head firmly. "I meant that you just have to take one look at him to know he didn't want to be here. He looked like he was afraid I was going to eat him!"

"You're seven feet tall and look like you could break him in half!" Caleb protested, but then sighed. "That's how he's been looking at everyone. Honestly, I think you've got the best chance of keeping an eye on him and keeping him safe." After a moment, he added, "And of getting him to talk about himself a little. I would very much like to know why Taffileti sent him."

Seregei scowled for a moment, but then sighed. "Well… I'll see. If he's willing to stay, I can see how he gets on for a few months. But, Caleb…" – he frowned – "you don't have the right to pick trainees for me. Next time you want to find somewhere to put someone, ask first, do we have an understanding?"

Caleb frowned back. "I thought you might appreciate some company," he said, "and you didn't seem to be getting anywhere with choosing someone for yourself. Am I supposed to just let you mope?"

Seregei hesitated a moment, a wince crossing his face. "I'm all right," he said at last, with an effort.

Caleb shook his head. "You clearly aren't. Do us all a favour and at least try him."

Seregei smiled. "I'd have thought you'd be happy to see the end of the Swordmasters," he said dryly. "If I die…"

Caleb cut him off. "Well, you'd be wrong."

Seregei's response was interrupted by Lim's return. He looked hot and out of breath, but not as if he'd just sprinted all the way to the palace and back.

"Well," said Caleb, looking from one to the other, "Now we're agreed, I'm going home." He beckoned to Ekehart. "If you have anything else to say, Seregei, let me know." He smiled at Lim. "Good luck."

"Thank you, my lord," said Lim softly, while Seregei simply waved.

Once Caleb and Ekehart had left, Seregei pointed to a target set up near the Guardhouse, midway between the low building and the trees. "There you are," he said. "There's no-one else in the building, so don't worry."

Lim bit his lip. "It's a little far from here, sir," he said uncertainly.

"I just want to see how you shoot." Or, more importantly, if he had just been boasting about his skill as an archer. "And please call me Seregei; everyone else does."

Lim nodded uncertainly and took the bow in his left hand, finally shaking aside the cloak that had hung over it.

Seregei choked a little as he saw Lim's hand. A jagged scar ran from his knuckles to his wrist. The fingers seemed oddly angled even as they curved around the bow, with the smallest one visibly bent to the side.

"What the...?" he gasped.

Lim hastily withdrew his hand under the cloak. "I'm sorry," he said, watching Seregei with wide eyes.

Seregei shook his head. "Just... all right. You can still use that hand? I don't want you hurting yourself."

Lim nodded. "It's fine," he said. "It wasn't so bad."

"Not so bad? What *happened* to it?"

"I shut it in a door," said Lim quickly. "I'm clumsy sometimes."

Seregei forced a smile. "Well, I'm sure I'm safe giving you a bow, then."

Lim looked crestfallen. "I... I can use it," he said softly.

"Well... go on, then."

Lim hesitantly drew his hand back out, but he got into stance in a fluid motion, almost becoming a different elf as he raised the bow, nocked and loosed in one easy, natural movement. Seregei watched as the arrow flew, arcing down to land short. He could tell that was just because it was indeed too far a shot for the small bow.

"That looked good," he said. "Move within range and let me see you hit the target now."

Lim nodded and went to stand at the end of the bow's range, presumably judging by how far the arrow had flown. Again he nocked, drew and loosed, and this time the arrow arced up and down again to quiver in the centre of the target.

Seregei let out a soft whistle. That display made him feel like he should go and work on his own archery. Lim had evidently been telling the truth when he told Kerin he was skilled.

"That was impressive," he said softly. "I'll show you a room and we'll see what else you can do tomorrow."

***

A month went by and Seregei felt he was no closer to understanding Lim, or even forming a relationship with him. The best impression he had was that Lim liked him a little better than he liked anyone else. Given that he didn't seem to like anyone, though, that wasn't saying much. Dealing with him was frustrating; it had taken a week to get him to address Seregei by name, and he still spoke as little as possible, mostly looking down as he did so. Seregei's empathic power didn't work on Lim yet, but he didn't need it to see that the young elf was unhappy.

But every time Seregei seriously considered going to Caleb and telling him that this wasn't working and he'd just have to find something else to do with this young exile, he thought of how Lim looked when he was using a bow.

9

He was practising now, for example. For once, he seemed entirely unaware that Seregei was watching him and his expression was distant, contented, as he stood holding his bow ready to loose. Seregei knew the exercise: Lim was building up the strength in his arm and hand so that he could hold a shot for longer, as well as preparing to move to a stronger bow.

Seregei shook his head with a small sigh. No, there was definitely more there than met the eye. Besides, Lim had really given him very little cause for complaint; he was painstakingly polite, listened to everything he was told and worked hard. It was just... he seemed so unhappy.

After another minute Lim loosed the arrow. It landed a little off the centre of the target and Lim lowered his arm with a sigh.

"Bad luck," said Seregei. "Pretty good for the length of the hold, though."

Lim had startled a little as he spoke, but smiled at the praise and went to fetch the arrow.

"Tell me, Lim," said Seregei when he returned, "are you happy here?"

Lim looked at the ground, all the confidence gone like water running out of a cracked jar. "You've been very kind to me, sir," he mumbled.

Seregei shook his head. "That doesn't answer my question. Are you happy?"

Lim shifted on his feet. "I miss my home," he said after a long pause.

"Would you prefer to go back?"

Lim looked up in clear alarm. "I can't."

Seregei frowned. "Why?"

Lim looked at his hands, his shoulders slightly hunched. "It's dangerous; Lord Taffilelti sent me away."

"So Caleb mentioned, but neither you nor he has ever told me what was so dangerous."

Lim didn't reply. He started to chew the tip of one finger.

"Well, are you happy here at the Guardhouse? Or would you prefer to go somewhere else in Duamelti?"

Lim looked pitiful. "I... I can try harder," he said. "I'm sorry..."

"What?"

"If I'm not good enough..." He trailed off, fiddling with his bowstring. "You and Lord Caleb have both been very kind. I'll try harder."

"Lim, you've worked very hard and done very well." Seregei went over and gently put a hand on the younger elf's shoulder. "But I don't want to keep you here if you're *not happy*."

Lim had started biting his finger again, but at that he looked up. "I am happy," he said.

Seregei sighed. "That's a lie."

Lim bit his finger again, cringing. "Please don't send me away," he begged. "I don't want to have to go somewhere else."

Seregei sighed. "All right," he said slowly. "We'll keep seeing how this goes."

"Thank you." He sounded genuinely grateful and Seregei sighed, but smiled a little.

"Just..." He squeezed Lim's shoulder a little. "You always seem miserable."

"I'm not. Truly, I'm not." Lim looked down. "You've... given me everything I could have dreamed of: I can... can practice my archery in peace. I have my own room, my own space. You teach me and are patient even when I'm slow to learn... truly, Seregei" – he looked up – "I'm happy here. It's just..." He sighed. "I miss my home. I can't go back, but..." He sighed again and fell silent. Seregei waited patiently for him to finish and at last he said, "My father will be missing me."

Seregei blinked. Caleb had said Lim was an orphan. "Does he know where you are?"

Lim looked away, tears suddenly starting in his eyes, and Seregei instinctively went to hug him.

To his surprise, though, Lim pulled away, quickly blinking away the tears. "Sorry... I shouldn't cry."

"Why not?" asked Seregei. "You're homesick; there's nothing wrong with that."

"But it's not right for me to trouble you with it. I... I'm acting like a child. I'm sorry."

Seregei sighed. "I asked if you were happy, why wouldn't I want to know about something that was making you unhappy?"

Apparently he wasn't getting anywhere with this, though, and decided to drop it. Instead, he just stepped away and waited for Lim to compose himself.

After a while, he said, "How good is your sense of direction?"

Lim looked around. "I can navigate fairly well in Silvren," he said softly.

Seregei nodded. "Let's go for a walk, and I'll see how you are at navigating here."

Lim nodded. "I'll do my best," he said, with a wan smile. He unstrung his bow and slung it on his back, then they set off.

"You should write home, if you think your father will be missing you," said Seregei as they walked.

Lim looked quickly at him, but then sighed. "Lord Taffilelti said no-one should know where I am," he said softly.

Seregei frowned. "Why?" he asked.

"It would be dangerous," mumbled Lim.

Seregei's frown deepened. He was starting to grow tired of that explanation. "Do you actually know why you were in so much danger in

Silvren?"

Lim had started biting his finger again, and he refused to look at Seregei as he said, "No."

Seregei gritted his teeth. He did not like being lied to, especially when the lie came from someone he had to trust.

Lim apparently noticed his anger, for he shifted away, looking warily at him. "I'm sorry," he said miserably. "But I can't talk about it."

"Can't or won't?"

Lim sighed. "It hurts."

"For pity's sake, Lim, what am I supposed to think?"

"I… I didn't do anything wrong…" He sounded uncertain, but that fact actually made Seregei feel a little better than if he'd been vehement about it, given that Lim had never spoken strongly on anything.

"Did you offend someone?"

Lim nodded a little, awkwardly. "Someone… with a lot of power," he said slowly.

Seregei wasn't sure why *this* was the best way for Taffileti to protect Lim from someone within his own kingdom, but he could accept that and nodded. "And you're afraid – or Taffilelti's afraid – that if you write home to your father with news of what's happening, the letter might be intercepted?"

Lim nodded. "So I can't write anything," he said miserably, his eyes on the floor. "He said so."

Seregei sighed a little. "Well, I'll mention it to Caleb next time I talk to him, and ask him to slip something into his next letter to Taffilelti. I'm sure he can pass the news on that you're doing well."

Lim looked at him in silence for a moment, then nodded, though he didn't seem entirely happy. "Thank you."

Seregei nodded. He suspected there was nowhere else to go down that line of conversation. "All right. Which way is North?"

CHAPTER TWO

Almost a year had passed since Lim had first come to Duamelti. It was spring and Seregei had taken him outside the valley to practice tracking in unfamiliar territory. He sat perched on a fallen log, fiddling with his bow and watching the progress of the shadow cast by a stick Seregei had thrust into the ground. He was to wait an hour, then try to follow the older elf's tracks.

He sighed, looking up at the trees. They bore soft, new leaves and he could hear birds calling for mates. An early pair already had chicks; he could hear them cheeping. It reminded him of Silvren and all its bittersweet associations, though when he took a deep breath the smell of the air alone reminded him of how far away he was.

Another sigh. He missed his home, and he knew his father would be unhappy; he loved Lim, for all his faults. Lim never felt worthy of that love, and now he felt that he would have deserved hate; he had agreed to flee and leave his father alone.

He reminded himself that Lord Taffilelti had said it was best; it was the only way he would be safe. He couldn't think that was untrue. Nonetheless, doubt did creep in, especially in moments of solitude when he had time to sit in silence and wonder. After all, he knew why everything had happened. It was his own fault and if he could only learn from his mistakes, surely it would never happen again. His father loved him. That was all he should need, and surely...

He shook his head firmly, putting the thoughts aside as best he could, and got up to pace to and fro. He entertained himself by listening to the birdsong, picking out the different species of birds and trying to make out what they were saying. There was the ever-changing twitter of a goldfinch calling for a mate, and there the quick chittering of an angry chiffchaff. He could just make out the little brown-green bird chasing another bird, which he identified as a wren as it crossed his clearing. He smiled a little, wishing the tiny fugitive luck. It was probably safe enough once it was out of the chiffchaff's territory.

He sat back down with a heavy sigh, glancing at the shadow of the stick. He didn't have that much longer to wait, and he found himself looking forward to this new challenge. He had to admit that he loved hearing praise from Seregei, though there were times when it made him feel guilty; the older elf wouldn't be so free with his praise if he knew what sort of person Lim was.

He sighed again, his thoughts once more going back to his home, once more doubting. He was happy to be here, but he had no right to be; he had left those that had been kind to him, who had only ever hurt him because he did something to deserve it, back in Silvren. How could he now sit here on a warm spring day and feel joy? Or take pleasure in someone else's words of praise when he should have been at home trying to earn that praise from his father?

Again, he did his best to push the thoughts away and sat still and silent, watching the shadow of the stick moving slowly across the ground until the full hour had passed, then got up and started along the path Seregei had taken.

It was easy to follow; the ground was soft and Seregei's boots left clear prints. From time to time he had passed over grass and Lim had to stop for a while and make sure he was still following the right trail, but he began to feel pleased with himself; he never lost his way.

The confidence drained out of him like water from a basin, however, as he followed the trail into a small stand of pines. Seregei's prints vanished utterly. Lim paused, looking over the ground, suddenly at a loss. He felt a momentary pang of fear as he took a deep breath and smelled the pines, but he shook his head and began to go back and forth over the area under the trees, checking carefully for even the slightest scuff in the needles. Seregei had clearly taken deliberate care and Lim wondered if he'd even climbed a tree to get off the ground. There were no marks on the bark that would indicate such a thing, though, and at last he found a print in the dirt leading away from the patch of needles. He followed that path with a sigh of relief.

After that check the footprints were a little harder to see, but he was able to follow them with care until he reached some rocks beside a stream. Once more, Seregei's prints vanished.

This was a little easier, though; a few minutes' careful search revealed a scuff of mud over one side, down towards the stream. Lim scrambled down to the stream himself and began looking along the bank to see if he could make out where Seregei had crossed. He couldn't see any disturbance to the muddy bed, though, and there was no sign that someone had climbed out again on the other side. He swiped his braid back behind his shoulder, aware of time passing. He didn't want to fail…

Maybe Seregei had climbed down into the stream and walked along it a little way? But surely there'd be some marks in the mud? Water couldn't smooth over footprints that quickly.

With that thought he began searching around the rocks again and he almost shouted aloud in joy as he found another print. Now he was off again.

He cast a worried look up at the sun, trying to judge how long it had been. Longer than an hour, he thought, and cringed. Seregei would surely be angry with him.

The fear distracted him and he suddenly realised that there were more prints on the ground in front of him. He looked back and forth, his heart in his mouth. Had he lost the trail? He continued to stare helplessly at the ground for several seconds, then shook his head. Better not make it any worse. He needed to hurry, he needed to find tracks that were definitely Seregei's, he needed to get back as fast as he could…

Panicking, he began casting about on the path, eventually spotting a footprint leading off it. He frowned over it, biting his lip as he reflected on the fact that he wasn't actually sure what Seregei's prints *looked* like; he'd just been following footprints.

Still, he made it back to the previous set and looked at them, then compared the new print. It looked the same, so he'd either been wrong the whole time or he'd found the trail again, and he followed it with a sigh of relief and resignation, trying not to bite his finger; he'd noticed that Seregei frowned when he did that.

The tracks were plain and easy to follow now, and Lim watched them very carefully, frowning deeply and concentrating on the ground in front of him. He was determined not to lose them again. He was in enough trouble already.

He barely realised he was at the end of the trail until he heard a laugh and looked up, his heart in his mouth. He gaped as he realised he was back in the same clearing. Seregei was sitting off to the side, tending a small campfire.

"Welcome back," said the older elf with a grin.

Lim's glance went to the stick still standing in the ground. He gulped. By the look of it, he'd been gone for almost two hours.

"That was slow," he said, bracing himself. "I'm sorry, Seregei."

Seregei didn't speak for a moment, but then he said, "For what? I was expecting to have to go and retrieve you, since this is your first time somewhere entirely new, and I put a couple of decoys down for you." He grinned and gestured Lim over. "Come and have some tea, then we'll go over the trail again and you can talk me through what you did."

Lim went over hesitantly, expecting trouble. A cheerful reception didn't necessarily mean anything. "I missed a couple. I took wrong turns because I couldn't see the tracks, or I got confused with other tracks."

"You were well within the time I'd have expected. If it had taken another hour I'd have gone to see if you needed to be pulled out of any ditches, but it always takes longer to follow a trail than to lay it." Seregei poured out two cups of tea and handed one to Lim, then raised his own in salute.

Lim did the same, but the fear wasn't gone; Seregei's smile didn't look entirely real.

Some weeks after Seregei and Lim returned from their training trip, Seregei was at one of his regular meetings with Caleb. It was one of the reminders that, while Caleb claimed the title 'king of Duamelti' and for most purposes was the ruler, his jurisdiction was really only over Valley-elves. As Swordmaster captain, Seregei ruled the larger Mixed-blood population. They had to meet regularly to discuss matters of importance to their twin realm and ensure everything continued to run smoothly.

They had finally hashed out an agreement in favour of Mixed-blood merchants who wished to trade with clans who would have absolutely nothing to do with Valley-elves. Despite the rivalry, Caleb hadn't wanted to admit that his own people were barred from pursuing the opportunity. Seregei was tired and more than willing to turn the conversation to something lighter.

"Are you courting someone?" he asked, stretching and tilting his chair to balance on its back legs.

Caleb looked like he'd rather the subject had been something else. "How is that your business?"

Seregei shrugged. "I'm curious. Rumour has it you've been walking out with Helid."

A smile spread across Caleb's face at her name, but his tone remained careless. "She and I have been friends for some time."

Seregei raised an eyebrow at him. "Well, far be it from me to nose into your private life —"

"Indeed."

"— but from what I've heard, she's a very nice girl."

"I think so." Caleb smiled a little. "How's Lim?"

Seregei sighed. "You're interested in his progress, aren't you?" he asked to put off answering the question.

"Taffilelti clearly takes an interest in him or he'd not have sent him, so if he or one of his ambassadors asks I want to have an answer."

Seregei nodded. "Has he mentioned who Lim's father is?"

"No." The corner of Caleb's mouth twitched a little. "Were it not for what you told me, I'd still be convinced that *he* was Lim's father."

Seregei sighed. "Well, I hope he at least passes messages back. Lim's still homesick and I wish I had something to tell him."

Caleb sighed, looking down at the notes on his desk. After a moment, he asked, "He's still just as unhappy?"

"Miserable. And still scared of me." Seregei waved an arm in frustration. "I don't know what the *matter* is! Am I really that frightening? I know I'm taller than him, and stronger, but I've never made a move to hurt him and yet after a *year* he still seems convinced I'm going to. Every time he makes a mistake he apologises for it almost as if he's asking me to be angry and seems confused when I'm not. Do I really give *that* bad an impression?"

Caleb looked sympathetic throughout the rant, but didn't really seem to have anything to say about it.

"So, to answer your question..." Seregei sighed. "It's not going very well." He checked himself and added, "That's not fair; he's learning fast and works hard, and seems to care about making sure he gets things right. I just get the impression it's because he's afraid I'll punish him if he does otherwise, rather than because he actually wants to learn." An idea struck him. "I'd love to meet his father, actually. Maybe he can shed some light on it."

Caleb nodded. "Well, depending on what happens, you might be going to Silvren before Taffilelti comes here."

"Is something going on?"

"No, but his next visit isn't for another year."

"Well, maybe if you could mention it..." Seregei smiled a little. "It might be good for Lim to see his father again, as well."

Caleb nodded. "I'll see what happens. But do you think you can carry on like this, or is it entirely unmanageable?"

"Unmanageable would be if he couldn't or wouldn't be taught." Seregei sighed. "I'll persevere. It's strange: every time I start to seriously think this isn't going to work, he does something that makes me think it will. There's something going on there."

"You're still thinking about how he is with a bow in his hands?"

Seregei nodded. "I know I've talked about it before, but it's true. He's a different elf. I just wish I could see that elf a little more."

"Well, maybe it just takes more time than you'd expect to bring it out of him." Caleb shrugged. "Maybe he's afraid most of the time because he thinks if he doesn't work hard you'll stop training him and he'll lose your protection, if he really is convinced that he's in some sort of danger."

Seregei frowned. He had his doubts about how convinced Lim really was. "It's true. I just... don't like it."

Caleb nodded. "I understand that, but keep trying. Let me know if you really can't handle him, but keep trying."

Seregei nodded. "And you can tell Taffilelti if he asks that I'd appreciate knowing what went on back in Silvren, if Lim's so terrified of being made to go back."

"I will." Caleb shuffled some papers together. "Oh, I forgot to mention this: there's been a complaint from one of the human settlements that their river is running low despite the rains we've had recently. They're accusing us of damming it."

Seregei frowned. "It would be outside the border, to be running to a human town." The border of Duamelti ran around the watershed at the tops of the surrounding hills, after all.

"That's one of the reasons I mention it to you: one of the clans might have something to do with it."

Seregei nodded. "I'll have a look. Which river?"

Caleb pulled out a map, frowned over it for a moment, then pointed. "This one. It would have to be a bit lower down the hill to really make a difference."

"All right. I'll go in the next couple of days, and take Lim with me; it'll be good for him to start meeting some of the clans. If it is a dam, I'll see about finding out who put it there, and then we can work out what to do next."

Caleb smiled. "I appreciate it."

***

As Seregei had promised, he took Lim out towards the northern border of Duamelti a couple of days after his meeting with Caleb. The rain seemed to have stopped for a while and the sun appeared from time to time between the clouds as they rode up into the hills from the Guardhouse. Lim rode in silence, his eyes fixed dully ahead as though he were lost in his own thoughts. Seregei asked him questions about navigation from time to time, and Lim's answers satisfied him that he was learning well, but not that Lim was any more comfortable. At last, he sighed and fell silent, looking thoughtfully up at the clouds.

"What would you say the weather's going to do today, Lim?" he asked.

Lim looked up. "I... I think it might rain again. The clouds look very low and grey; that means they're full of rain."

Seregei nodded, smiling a little. "I'd like you to lead the way for a bit," he said. "Pick a good path, given how much rain we've had recently. I'll keep an eye on you."

Lim nodded and steered his horse – Wilwarin – in front of Seregei. Seregei hung back, looking carefully from Lim to the horse and also keeping half an eye on the weather. He agreed about the threat of rain, but didn't think that would be a problem; they could ride in the rain and he didn't think there was likely to be a storm.

Ahead of him, Lim had given Wilwarin her head and was apparently steering with his knees, encouraging her around muddier patches but otherwise letting her pick her own route. Seregei smiled. He had Menel on a tighter rein, but she seemed happy to follow Wilwarin's lead until they got to the top of the pass. Then Seregei drew up beside Lim again.

"Good work," he said with a smile.

Lim smiled back fleetingly, then went back to looking at the view.

"We're looking for some sign of a blockage to one of the rivers," Seregei reminded him. He frowned as he recalled the map Caleb had shown him, then pointed. "That one."

Lim nodded. "I'm afraid I can't see anything from here."

Seregei shook his head. "There's a mortal settlement just there." He pointed to a distant gap in the trees, in which houses and farmland could vaguely be seen. "We're looking at the river that's supposed to run to it."

Lim nodded again. Seregei waited for a moment in case he was going to say something, then sighed and rode on, letting Menel pick a path much as Lim had done with Wilwarin. They would need to go across the hillside to get to the river they wanted and it would take time and care; Seregei wasn't sure if all the paths could be trusted in such wet weather and they couldn't risk cutting across country.

They reached the river at around noon and paused to eat some of the bread, cheese and dried meat they'd brought with them. Seregei watched the water as he ate. It looked high and he couldn't tell how quickly it was flowing. Probably quite fast, judging by the mud it had stirred up.

"Lim, how would we go about crossing this?"

Lim stared at him, then said uncertainly. "I... sorry, but... I really don't think that's a good idea." He watched Seregei closely as he spoke.

Seregei nodded. "Right. We'd find somewhere else – safer – to cross. How did you know?"

"The water looks deep and fast."

Seregei smiled. "There you are. Well done. There's also the fact that the bottom's probably mud – look at the colour of the water – which is dangerous because you'll probably end up stuck. You've got the right instinct, though."

Again, Lim smiled for a moment, and then went back to his lunch.

***

The next day, after a long, slow ride down the bank, they finally found the blockage in the river. Seregei reined in Menel and stared at it thoughtfully while Lim dithered beside him, wide-eyed. The river was choked with what looked like a couple of fallen trees and all the debris that had piled against them. The resulting pool had spread some distance though folds in the ground and only a fraction of the water was actually making its way down the channel.

Seregei frowned. There was certainly nothing he and Lim could do on their own about this. They'd need to find help, and the best place was probably in the human settlement that had been complaining. That meant they could see it was a natural occurrence, and also that Seregei would not have to locate an elven clan and ask them to help clear something that had nothing to do with them.

"Do you speak the human language, Lim?" he asked as he wheeled Menel round and began to skirt around the pool.

"No," said Lim, sounding worried. "Sorry."

"I didn't really expect you to" – Seregei paused a moment as he encouraged Menel through a shallow outcrop of water – "but that does mean I'll have to do the talking." He glanced over his shoulder and saw Lim's expression: he looked confused and still worried, so Seregei explained about seeking help at the mortal settlement.

"The easiest way to get there is probably to follow the line of the river course, once we're around this pool..." Another pause as he looked for a way around a fallen tree. A few drops of water fell on his head and he looked up. It was starting to rain again.

As they rode, the rain got heavier. They pulled up their hoods, but the water soon soaked through the fabric of their cloaks and soaked them to the skin. Seregei wiped some water out of his eyes, glancing over towards Lim. The young Wood-elf looked miserable. Seregei considered suggesting that they should find shelter until the rain stopped, but hesitated. He wanted to see if Lim would be able to tell when they should seek shelter. It might also be a way to finally wring a complaint out of him.

"Let me know if you want to stop and look for shelter," he said casually.

Lim glanced at him and nodded.

It took about an hour, and the rain was showing no sign of letting up. Eventually, Lim said quietly, "I'm sorry, Seregei, but I think we should stop."

Seregei sighed in relief. "Indeed," he said. He half-noticed Lim's apprehensive expression, but dismissed it; he always looked rather like that. "Let's look for somewhere fairly out of the rain. A cave facing downhill would probably be best, but a thick-branched stand of trees – conifers for preference – would work."

Lim nodded and began looking around. Seregei did the same. Visibility was poor with the heavy rain and it didn't look like they were likely to find anything nearby. He sighed. Perhaps they should have started earlier. He leaned forward to pat Menel's neck in apology and she shook her head, sending drops of water flying from her mane in all directions. Seregei chuckled, but his laughter died on his lips as he heard something from behind them, upstream.

A loud crack, then a crashing noise. Then creaking and ripping, and a terrible roar.

"The dam's gone!" he yelled, his voice ringing shrill. "Uphill! Ride!"

Lim stared at him, frozen. Seregei leaned over and grabbed Wilwarin's reins as he wheeled Menel. Lim let go at once.

Too late. Even as they raced away from the river course, the flood was on them.

The force of the water bowled Menel over. Seregei lost his grip on Wilwarin's rein as he hit the water. It was too late to leap clear. As she fell he was dashed against the ground. He lost consciousness instantly.

Lim had managed to get clear from Wilwarin just before their horses were knocked down, but he was still swept under. He struck out desperately for the surface. Finally, he broke it with a splash and a gasp. He blinked the water from his eyes and looked around as he struggled to stay afloat. Where was Seregei? Had he been swept further downstream?

"Seregei!" he shouted breathlessly.

He couldn't see the horses either. Had Seregei managed to get clear of Menel? Was he still underwater?

Suddenly, he spotted something: a glimpse of fabric on the surface. A cloak? It was gone almost at once. He swam towards it, fighting the current. When he reached the spot he took a gasp of air and dived, groping with his eyes shut. His fist closed on a handful of cloth. He pulled. There was a definite weight attached to it. He kicked towards the surface.

Something struck him in the side. He felt it rip across his flank and screamed, grabbing at the spot with his right hand. His left couldn't grip well enough. He felt the cloth slip from between his fingers. He started after it, but his lungs were burning for air. He had to surface.

As he broke the surface and gasped, he looked down and saw blood in the water. The sight made the pain redouble and he whimpered, but he had to ignore it. Another breath and he dived again, gritting his teeth. Left hand on the wound, he snatched about with his right. Relief as he once again seized Seregei's cloak and headed for the surface.

This time they made it and Lim managed to pull Seregei up with him. The other elf was unconscious. He didn't seem to be breathing and another shock of panic went through Lim. Surely he wasn't dead?

Holding Seregei made it difficult for Lim to stay afloat. Kicking made his side hurt. He gasped, tears springing into his eyes, and spat as he almost inhaled some water.

However, he noticed that the current was slackening, and he thought he was getting closer to the shore. After a moment, he realised that the water level was falling. Soon his feet were on the ground. He wasn't sure if it was easier to walk or swim, but he stumbled through the mud and water until he had dragged Seregei onto the riverbank.

He collapsed for a moment, his head on Seregei's side, and realised with a dizzying thrill of relief that he could hear a heartbeat and Seregei was breathing. The sudden release from tension made the tears overflow and he burst into near-hysterical sobs, unable to control himself.

He was still crying when Seregei shifted, and he immediately jerked back, sniffing and trying desperately to get the tears under control. His sudden movement had disturbed his side and that made it harder, but he tried to ignore it.

Seregei was coughing as though he was choking on his own lungs, and after a minute or two the coughing turned to retching. Lim felt useless; all he could do was support the other elf on his side and hope.

At last, though, Seregei seemed to have recovered. He started to roll onto his back, then suddenly tensed and screamed in pain.

"Seregei?" asked Lim, his heart in his mouth.

"My leg…" Seregei's breath caught in a gasp

Lim looked at Seregei's legs. One did look oddly angled. "I…"

"Can you tell what's wrong?"

Once again, Lim felt scared of the possible consequences of failure, especially as this wasn't a training exercise; this was horribly real. He shifted to hide his own wound and look more closely at Seregei's leg. He didn't really know what to look for.

"There… there's no blood. I don't know what else is wrong. I'm sorry," he said softly.

Seregei just balled his hands into fists in the mud and started to push himself up.

"Hold my legs still," he said through his teeth, and Lim hastened to obey, though he grimaced as he moved his hand from his own wound.

Seregei pushed himself upright and twisted to look down at his legs. After a moment, he sighed and hung his head. Lim bit his lip.

"My leg's broken," said Seregei with forced calm, lowering himself to the ground again. For a moment he stared into space, frowning, then bit out a curse. Lim flinched and whimpered in pain, his hand going back to his side. At least the bleeding seemed to have stopped.

"That wasn't aimed at you, sorry," said Seregei. "Just…" He said a few more words that Lim didn't understand. He guessed they were more curses.

"Is… is there anything I can do?" Lim asked nervously. He was starting to shiver, noticing the cold and wet for the first time.

Seregei sighed. "I don't know." He tried to move and grimaced. "We need to find shelter, find the horses and find some way of getting home. I should have asked before: how did you come through that? Are you hurt at all?"

Lim pressed his hand a little closer to his side. "No." He didn't want to add his own problems to Seregei's.

Seregei smiled. "I'm glad."

"Shall I look for shelter?" If nothing else, Lim knew Seregei would need somewhere out of the rain.

Seregei nodded. "The closer the better. I'll work on moving."

Lim struggled up. His legs felt wobbly, but he didn't collapse again. "I'll be back soon."

He put conscious effort into walking normally as he went into the forest, but once he was out of sight he leaned on a tree for a moment and whimpered. He'd not hurt this badly since the last night he'd seen his father.

The thought made him whimper again and he rubbed his eyes, fighting down the memory. There was no time to think of that now. He had to find shelter. At some point he would also have to bandage his wound, especially if he was to keep it hidden. He didn't want to lie to Seregei, but it didn't feel right to add to his troubles.

He was steadily getting colder and the shivering was getting worse, but he wrapped his free arm around himself and did his best to ignore it, making for a low cliff that he could see ahead.

It wasn't far, and he sighed in relief as he found a small cave, dug back into the cliff face. Its roof was about chest-high, but there would be room to sit in it, and it was dry. He went back as quickly as he could to tell Seregei.

Seregei had managed to edge himself about a foot closer to the forest, but he looked relieved as Lim approached. The small smile turned to a frown, however, as he looked at him a little more closely.

"Are you sure you're not hurt?" he asked.

Lim nodded. "I'm fine."

"You look very pale."

Lim knelt down beside him, drawing his cloak around himself. "It's cold, that's all."

Seregei nodded. "It certainly is." He was also shivering, though not as badly as Lim. Despite his agreement, he still looked suspicious.

"I found a cave," said Lim quickly, glad to have some good news.

Seregei smiled. "Good. And it's not too far?"

Lim shook his head. "But... I don't know how you're going to get there..."

Seregei nodded. "We're going to splint my leg, and I'm going to hop," he said curtly.

Lim bit his lip, torn between worry, shame that he'd had no ideas, and horror at how much that would probably hurt Seregei.

"We should set it, but the circumstances aren't ideal." Seregei swallowed hard. "I'm going to need you to find a strong, straight stick, about the length of my lower leg."

As soon as Lim was out of sight he once again pressed a hand firmly to his side, ignoring the resulting sharp pain as best he could. Still, he couldn't help a small whimper and stumbled against a tree as his head swam. There had to be an easier way of stopping and hiding the bleeding…

A thought occurred to him and he laughed to himself, groping at a pouch on his belt. It contained a little food and a bandage: good enough for an emergency, and he was glad Seregei had insisted he carry it. He took out the bandage and finally looked down at his wound. The sight almost made him faint: a raw, bloody gash with dirt clinging to the edges. He swallowed hard, looking away, but he had to look again to position the bandage properly.

This time, he was sick.

At last, he'd managed to bandage his wound. There was nothing to be done about the bloodstains on his clothes, but he smeared mud over them to cover them. Finally, he could begin the search for a suitable stick.

He moved as quickly as he could, looking for a branch lying on the muddy ground. The rain was still plastering his clothes to his body and he was shaking with cold by the time he found a solid length of branch. When he returned to the riverbank, Seregei was sitting up and looking around.

"Lim!" he exclaimed. Lim tensed, trying to read his tone. After a moment, Seregei continued, "Sorry, you took longer than I expected. Was it hard to find one?"

Grateful for the excuse, Lim nodded. "Will this do?" he asked, holding out his stick.

Seregei frowned at it, then nodded. "That should work," he said. "Have you ever splinted a bone before?"

Lim shook his head, instinctively clenching his left hand as best he could.

"Well" – Seregei winced as he shifted a little – "I won't ask you to set it, though we should… Let's have that stick?"

Lim handed him the stick and, on his instructions, helped him steady it against his leg while he tied it in place with the straps that had held his daggers. He tucked those into his belt.

"Now help me up."

Lim did his best, but Seregei was much taller than him, and heavier. It took considerable effort to get him to his feet, and Lim could feel his own wound starting to bleed again. He looked away to hide the tears.

"What's wrong?" asked Seregei, tilting his head to see Lim's face.

"Nothing."

"Lim, that's a lie." His tone was curt again and Lim instinctively tensed.

"I… I'm sorry…"

"Tell me what's wrong."

"You're… heavy," said Lim hesitantly.

Seregei sighed. "Sorry," he said. "Let's" – he groaned – "get this over, shall we? I'll try not to lean on you more than I can help."

Lim nodded.

Every time Seregei hopped, he had to lean on Lim. The extra weight and twisting motion sent a stabbing feeling up Lim's side and he could only just repress small sounds of pain. Seregei didn't seem to notice; his eyes were closed and his teeth gritted as they went. Fortunately, neither one of them overbalanced as they made their way between the trees to the cave Lim had found.

"There it is," said Lim as they approached.

Seregei opened his eyes for a moment. "That... looks good," he panted.

Lim nodded, his teeth gritted. "Thanks."

The cave wasn't high enough for them to walk in, so Lim helped Seregei sit down and shuffle into it backwards, then crept in himself. He sat against the wall with his knees drawn up, hiding his face and hoping that the tears of pain could be mistaken for rain.

It took some time for Seregei to get comfortable, lying on the ground, and for the fire chasing up his leg to fade, but then he once again took a deep breath and looked over at Lim. The younger elf was sitting curled up against the wall, shivering. Seregei sighed, wondering if there was any way to build a fire; he was cold and Lim was thinner than he was. They didn't have any firewood, though, and he wasn't sending his poor trainee out in the rain again if he could avoid it.

"Lim?"

Lim looked up. He looked dreadful: pale as death, and his eyes were bloodshot. Seregei sighed a little.

"I just wanted to say 'well done'."

A faint smile, then Lim laid his head on his knees, side-on. He still looked like he was in pain.

"Did you hit something in the water?"

Lim curled up a little tighter and shook his head, watching Seregei's expression. His finger crept towards his mouth and he just snatched it away before he started to bite it.

Seregei sighed, letting his head fall back and closing his eyes. He was tired. There was only so long he could keep himself calm and collected, and his strength was running out. He didn't feel up to an argument.

"This would be a really stupid time to try to make yourself look tough, Lim."

"I'm not," said Lim softly. "N-nothing of the kind."

Seregei sighed again. He was also starting to shiver and shifted awkwardly to pull his cloak around himself a little more closely. Wet as it was, it probably wouldn't help, but it made him feel better. He was trying to remember what had happened after the flood had hit, but it was all a blur. He must have fallen into the water, and at some point he had been separated from Menel, but the next thing he could remember was vomiting up the water he'd swallowed on the bank.

"Lim... did you pull me out of the river?" he asked. Lim looked up again and nodded slowly. Seregei blinked. Even now, he looked almost ashamed of his actions. "You saved my life."

"But... you still got hurt."

Seregei pushed himself up on his elbows, doing his best not to move his legs. "Why do you always act as if I'm about to *punish* you for something?"

Lim looked bewildered. "Because I fail."

"And? You're a trainee; I don't expect you to be able to act as a fully-trained Swordmaster!" Seregei's arms were getting tired and he lay down again. "Listen: I'm not angry with you because my leg's broken. That's not your fault. Given that I don't remember how it happened, I assume I was knocked out at some point. That means that I'd have drowned if you'd not pulled me out."

Lim didn't say anything for a long moment. Finally, though, he murmured, "I didn't want you to die."

Well, that was something, and Seregei nodded. "Thank you."

Lim smiled, then curled up again. Seregei sighed, looking out of the entrance to the cave. The rain was as heavy as ever. No chance of a fire, even if they had wood. He pushed himself upright and shuffled round to sit against the wall, moving with wincing care. A glance over at Lim showed that he was still curled up; he seemed oblivious to the outside world. Seregei frowned. There was something wrong. He knew there was, but he couldn't quite tell what and it was clear that Lim didn't trust him enough to explain.

"Lim?" he called softly, and was relieved when Lim looked up. "Come and sit beside me; it'll be warmer."

Lim didn't even hesitate. He crept over and sat down beside Seregei, but tensed as Seregei put an arm and a fold of his cloak around his shoulders.

"I'm not going to hurt you."

Lim sighed. "I know. I just..." He paused. When he spoke again, it was as if the words were being forced out of him. "I don't... like being touched."

Seregei frowned a little, but didn't ask for a reason; if Lim wanted to share, he would. He just withdrew his arm, moving carefully so that the cloak remained in place.

After some time, the rain was showing no sign of abating, but Lim didn't seem so cold. At least, he was no longer actually shivering.

"Do you know where the horses went?" Seregei asked him, more for want of something to say than any other reason.

Lim shook his head. "I couldn't see them when I surfaced," he said in a small voice.

Seregei nodded slowly. The horses had their supplies, and with his broken leg they were also the only realistic way home. When the rain stopped, they'd have to try to find something he could use for crutches; leaning on Lim wouldn't work over any distance.

Lim had curled up again, his own cloak hugged tightly around himself. Though he didn't seem as cold, he was still pale. Seregei patted him gently on the shoulder.

"It'll be all right," he said, smiling. "We'll get home." He wasn't sure how it would be done, but Lim looked like he needed some encouragement. "For now, let's just stay warm and wait for the rain to stop."

Lim smiled a little, a wistful look in his eyes. "I..." He sighed and didn't continue.

"What?"

"Sorry, it's just... it still doesn't really... seem like home."

"You'd rather go back to Silvren?"

Lim looked away sadly. "I'm sorry; you've been very kind to me, but..." Another long pause.

"But what? If you're homesick, you can tell me." It was one of the few things about Lim that Seregei actually understood.

Lim nodded, but didn't say anything else.

"Would you like your father to be here?"

To his surprise, Lim didn't answer at once; he seemed unsure what to say. After a moment's stammering, he hid his face again, beginning to shiver. Seregei sighed and just shifted to tuck the cloak around him a little more closely. He began to ask about Lim's silence, but didn't finish the question. Perhaps asking about Lim's father had simply served to remind him that he *wasn't* there.

Seregei sighed. "I'm sorry. You must miss him."

Lim looked up for a moment, tearfully. "I..." He shook his head, then nodded. "I do miss him."

"But... you wouldn't want him here?" Seregei prodded gently.

Lim shook his head and looked away again.

Seregei stifled the next question at once, but he still wondered about it: why would Lim *not* want his beloved father there? He knew it would be a bad idea to ask, though; Lim was already upset enough. After a while, he said, "When we get back to Duamelti, I'll ask if next time Taffilelti comes to Duamelti he might bring your father to visit you." He smiled. "A little bit of- what's wrong?"

Lim had curled up more tightly, shuddering.

"Lim, what's the matter?"

"Nothing... just homesickness."

Seregei was about to put his arm around Lim's shoulders, but remembered what he had said about being touched.

"You're doing well," he said softly. "This is a lot to drop on you so soon, so you're not doing anything wrong if it's overwhelming."

Lim looked up with a small smile, then lowered his head again with a sigh. Seregei nodded a little and turned his attention back to the rain, concentrating on the sound and trying to see if it was getting any lighter. He felt Lim stir and looked round, but the other elf had just turned his head so that he was looking towards the back of the cave. Seregei took the opportunity to grit his teeth in pain, keeping silent with an effort. It made him feel a little better.

The rain began to let up as night fell and Seregei sighed with relief. Beside him, Lim had apparently fallen asleep, leaning slightly on Seregei's shoulder. Even had he been inclined to try to get up, that would have stopped him. He glanced over with a small smile. Lim looked even younger when he slept and the worried lines were smoothed away; Seregei hadn't seen him asleep, since they slept in different rooms in the Guardhouse.

Hopefully things would get a little drier soon, and maybe they'd be able to find firewood and food. That would help. Seregei sighed, looking down at his leg. Perhaps something suitable for crutches.

He looked round again as Lim stirred. He frowned and gritted his teeth, then suddenly startled up with a small cry.

"Lim?"

"I'm sorry," said Lim groggily, shaking his head. "It wasn't... I didn't mean to..."

Seregei put a hand on his shoulder. "Lim!"

Lim flinched away and Seregei remembered he didn't like being touched. At once, he removed his hand. "Lim, it's all right."

Lim had wrapped his arm around his waist and was still watching Seregei warily. "I didn't mean to fall asleep. Sorry."

Seregei shook his head. "It's all right. Do you feel better? Warmer?"

Lim nodded and glanced at the door. "It's getting dark," he said softly.

"Yes. I think we're going to have to spend the night here."

Lim bit his lip. "How... how will we get back?"

Seregei sighed. "If we can't find the horses, that's going to be a problem," he admitted. "I think the first thing to do" – he glanced at his leg again – "is to find some crutches."

Lim nodded. He looked as though he wanted to add something to that, but didn't actually speak. After a long moment, Seregei sighed and rubbed his eyes. They felt gritty with tiredness and his head was starting to ache.

"Lim, if you want to tell me something, please just say it. I can't play guessing games at the moment."

"Sorry." Lim shifted uncomfortably. "I... I'm hungry."

Seregei sighed a little; he was too. "Understandably. Do you still have your emergency pouch?"

Lim's eyes lit up and he patted the pouch on his belt.

"Don't eat too much of it," said Seregei, opening his own. "It may have to be breakfast as well." He carefully rationed himself to a couple of mouthfuls of the fruit chips and nuts. It wasn't enough, but it was something.

Lim was carefully nibbling a piece at a time, making them last, and Seregei smiled in approval. The smile turned to a frown, though, as Lim took out another piece of fruit and Seregei saw that the bandage that should also have been in the pouch was gone.

"Lim, where's your bandage?"

Lim tensed and quickly closed the pouch, like a boy caught in mischief. Seregei's eyes narrowed as he glimpsed the bandage wrapped around Lim's waist.

"Are you sure you're not hurt?" If Lim was hiding something serious, he was an idiot, but Seregei wanted to know so that he could do something about it.

Lim shook his head. "I'm not," he said, drawing his cloak around himself.

"Then why the bandage?"

"Well…" Lim looked away, rubbing his eyes. "Maybe a little, but it's not bad; I just wanted to keep it clean. Was… was that wrong?"

Seregei shook his head. "No, but you should have told me when I asked if you were hurt. Let me see it."

Lim drew away, creeping towards the other side of the small cave, still holding his cloak close around himself.

"Lim, if you're badly hurt, hiding it puts us both in danger. Tell me: is it bad?"

Lim shook his head. "It's all right," he said. "I'm sorry; I don't want to cause trouble…"

"Telling me when you're hurt isn't causing trouble."

"I don't want to…" he whimpered, tears starting to appear in his eyes.

Seregei sighed. "For pity's sake, Lim, tell me honestly. Are you hurt?"

Lim didn't know what to do. His side was throbbing in time with his heartbeat and felt like it was burning him from the inside. He couldn't think straight enough to decide. What should he do? He felt a few more tears make their way down his cheeks, to his shame, and shook his head.

Seregei sighed. "Not badly?"

"No." He flinched from the lie, but it was the best he could think of. He didn't want to lie to Seregei, but, even apart from not wanting to cause any more trouble to the other elf, he was afraid of the consequences of starting the lie. Surely Seregei, as kind as he was, would punish him for lying. Even his father, who loved him so much, was angry when he lied. When they got back he could take care of it.

He couldn't help a few more sobs, despite his best efforts. His father would be ashamed of him, but he wanted him there; he'd take care of him as he always had.

The thought didn't make it any easier to stop the crying. Without thinking, he bit his finger to make himself think about something else.

He was distracted, though, at a sudden cry of pain and thump of a body hitting the ground. He looked up, snatching his hand from his mouth, and saw that Seregei had overbalanced.

"Seregei?" He crept back over as fast as he could and helped Seregei sit back up.

"Thanks." Seregei grinned wanly and put a hand on Lim's shoulder. He just managed to restrain the flinch; Seregei's grip was gentle. "This was what I was trying to do. It'll be all right. We'll get home."

Thinking of home almost made Lim break down again, but he managed to sniff the tears back this time.

"I'll go and see if I can call Wilwarin," he said at last, when he had himself under control.

"Can you do that?" asked Seregei. "I mean... I know Wood-elves can talk to animals, but you've learned?"

Lim blinked. He had been born with the ability; it came as naturally as speech. "Yes."

It was still just light enough for him to see Seregei smile. "All right. Be careful."

He left the cave and splashed a little way away, until he was out of sight. Then he sat down against a tree and tried to get a look at his wound. The light was bad and the mud had done a lot to hide the bloodstains, but he didn't think it was still bleeding. He wondered whether to unwrap the bandage and decided against it; he didn't want to see what it looked like. It hurt.

He sighed and got up, pressing a hand against his side. It was getting darker and he knew he should hurry back, but first he whistled as loud as he could to call Wilwarin. He hoped she was still alive. He whistled once more, then closed his eyes and pictured her standing beside him, sending the message to her. Fortunately, she was his horse and he had a closer relationship with her than with any other, so he didn't need to be touching her to communicate with her. The mental call still wouldn't carry as far as the whistle, but would probably be more effective. He whistled again and tried to call Menel, then turned and trudged back to the cave.

"Has it stopped raining?" asked Seregei.

"Yes." Lim felt too tired to say much more than that, but added, "I called both of them."

"I heard." Seregei sighed. "Hopefully they'll arrive soon. For the time being, though, I think the best thing for us to do is rest. We'll see where we are in the morning."

Lim nodded.

"We'll sit side-by-side again, if you're willing; it was warmer."

That was certainly true and Lim went over to sit beside Seregei. Even there, he felt chilled, but he was tired and quickly fell asleep once more.

***

When Lim woke up, he felt stiff and still tired. He was still leaning on Seregei's shoulder and the other elf looked like he was also asleep. He felt chilled and his clothes were still damp, but he seemed to be handling the cold better than Lim himself; he couldn't seem to stop shivering. At least the rain had stopped; watery sunlight was shining into their cave.

He very carefully moved away and got up, gritting his teeth. He needed to go and have a look at the wound, which was throbbing horribly in time with his heartbeat. He didn't want to leave Seregei alone, though, without telling him where he was.

Still, he stepped outside and called out again for Wilwarin. He didn't hold out much hope; if she hadn't found them overnight, there was little chance that she was close enough to hear him, assuming she was still alive. At the thought, his heart squeezed in grief, but he called again.

He gasped as he heard an answering whinny and he whistled as loud as he could. After a few minutes, she came trotting towards him between the trees and he went to greet her with a sigh of relief. She was muddy and looked bedraggled, her saddle was askew, and she had lost one of the saddlebags, she didn't seem to be hurt and he sighed again as he went over to her and flung his arms around her neck. "I'm so glad to see you," he murmured into her ear. For a moment he stood still, leaning on her. His head was spinning and it was nice to have something relatively warm to lean on while he recovered.

She snorted and nudged him, fortunately missing his wound. Still, he bit his lip and had to lean on her a moment longer, his knees wobbling slightly. Once he'd recovered, he set about removing her saddle, knowing that it would make her more comfortable.

"Lim?" called Seregei, a worried note in his voice.

"I'm outside!" Lim shouted back. "Wilwarin's here!" He slid the saddle and remaining saddlebag to the ground and stayed there himself a moment, gasping. He could feel sweat starting to run down his face, though he didn't feel warm.

"How is she?" asked Seregei.

Lim started running his hands down Wilwarin's legs, checking for injuries. There was no sign of any swelling or heat, so he nodded. "She seems fine."

She nudged him again, knocking him over, and he lay still for a moment. His side was still throbbing, worse now from the sudden movement, but he

31

couldn't wallow in misery for long. He forced himself to get up and take the saddle and bag back to the cave. Wilwarin followed him and he smiled, pausing to pat her affectionately on the nose as he went in.

Seregei grinned. "Good to see her," he said. "Is there… any sign of Menel?"

Lim shook his head. Apparently Menel hadn't heard him call, assuming she had come through the flood unhurt. He set the bag down beside Seregei and sat against the opposite wall, his knees drawn up; that seemed to help with the pain.

Seregei frowned. "You really don't look well."

Lim shook his head. "It's still cold." Though he felt ill, he was still determined not to let Seregei know.

Seregei sighed and nodded. "Hopefully this sun will warm us a little," he said, "and we can have a fire tonight."

"Will we be able to get back to the Guardhouse tonight?"

"Probably not; it took us a day in total to get to where the flood hit us, after all." Seregei sounded remarkably calm. "But we can start making our way back."

Lim remained silent, wondering what Seregei could be planning. Whatever it was, he was sure it was a good idea, but he couldn't think what to do. His heart sank as he realised that in his state he couldn't even run for help.

"Do you think Wilwarin would be able to drag a hurdle?"

Lim blinked. "I expect so," he said, his eyes straying to the horse.

"Well, the first thing to do is to build one. That's how I'll have to travel." He sighed. "At least it'll be quicker and easier than crutches."

Lim couldn't help a small smile as he recognised a way he could help. "I can build one," he said. Once or twice he'd helped to build hurdles for dragging things back in Silvren. It would just be different dimensions. "At least… I could." He looked at his left hand. It was far weaker and clumsier than it had been, and he still hadn't quite learned to use his right for anything delicate.

Seregei grinned. "Good. I'll help, of course, but it'll be up to you to find what we need to make it. We should eat first, though." He glanced at the saddlebag. "Do you mind if I look in here?"

Lim shook his head.

Seeing his expression, Seregei smiled. "It's your bag, after all," he said, opening it. "Let's see what survived the flood."

The bag contained a couple of wet blankets, a small bundle containing bandages and another which had held food. Seregei unwrapped it, looking hopeful, and sighed. The bread was soaked and disintegrating, useless, and water had evidently got into the packet of dried meat. The older elf shook his head and set the bundle aside.

"Emergency rations again, I suppose," he said distantly, still frowning.

Lim bit his lip and nodded. He wasn't hungry, but nibbled a couple of pieces of fruit from his pouch. Seregei also ate sparingly, frowning, his eyes on the ground. Lim watched him, biting his lip and wondering if his leg hurt. If so, he showed very little sign of it; he was pale, but there was nothing more.

Lim quickly looked away as Seregei looked up; he'd probably not like being stared at. If he was angry, he showed no sign of it, but glanced out of the cave and sighed. "At least the sun's still out. Looks like it'll be a nice day." He glanced over at Lim. "You've finished your breakfast?"

Lim nodded.

"Right. We should start on that hurdle. I imagine there'll be dead wood lying about. Do you know what you need?"

Lim nodded again.

"Right. You go find it and bring it back here, and then I'll do what I can to help." Seregei sighed, looking down at his leg.

"All right." Lim started out of the cave at once. He'd find the branches, cording and brush they needed and hopefully also be able to check on his own wound. Thankfully, Seregei didn't seem to have realised he was hurt.

Seregei watched Lim go with a frown. Something was definitely wrong, and he was beginning to come to the conclusion that Lim was never going to tell him that much, let alone what it was. He was clearly injured somehow – the bandage was proof of that – but how seriously? How much of his weakness was due to it and how much genuinely was cold and weariness? Not to mention hunger; Seregei hadn't missed the fact that Lim had barely eaten. He sighed. Perhaps his own worry about food had rubbed off on Lim, and the younger elf was now trying to ration what he had. He sighed again and shook his head. He should have tried to avoid that, at least.

The thought drew him back to the matter of food. Indeed, they had very little and perhaps it was for the best that Lim was trying to ration it; their supplies had been with the horses, and what they had recovered… Seregei glanced over at the soggy mess, lying apart from the blankets and bandages. Those things, at least, would probably come in handy once they'd dried. He picked up a blanket and tried to spread it in the sunshine by the cave mouth, but he couldn't move enough to do it properly.

A sudden flash of pain as he tried to lean over made him stiffen and swear, gritting his teeth and clenching his fists. Frustrated, he swore a few more times and slammed one fist into the ground. It didn't make him feel much better, but it let off some of the stress, and he'd not be able to do that when Lim returned. Until then, there really was nothing he could do.

He sighed, tilting his head back against the wall. He didn't like being helpless and having to send Lim to do everything. He hoped this would do the lad some good, though: let him see that he was capable and that Seregei did trust him, as well as distracting him from the situation and making him feel useful.

That thought, in turn, led back to the worry that Lim was hiding something serious. He shook his head. It might not be so bad, and Lim surely had the sense to tell him if it were. It bothered him, though; not only was Lim potentially in danger from some untreated injury, but this was another piece of strange behaviour: another sign that Lim was frightened of him and refused to trust him.

He shook his head with a sigh. Perhaps it was like the delay before finding shelter: Lim felt he had to prove something. Well, he'd leave it a little longer, as long as it wasn't obviously bad.

It was a little while before Lim returned, and Seregei spent the time edging closer to the cave entrance, trying to get into the sunshine. He had just made it and was enjoying the relative warmth when Lim arrived, dragging two long branches and carrying a bundle of shorter ones under his arm. Seregei almost got up to help him, but fell back with a hiss and a growing sense of frustration. Lim bit his lip, going, if possible, even paler.

"My fault," said Seregei, guessing what was worrying him. "I tried to get up. Let's get started, shall we?" Building the hurdle would take his mind off the pain and continue his attempts to keep Lim occupied.

It took them a couple of hours, tying four branches into a frame and then adding cross-pieces between them. Seregei was impressed to note that Lim really did seem to know what he was doing, and the young elf relaxed as he worked, looking happier, though he was still shivering. Seregei touched the blanket he'd laid out to see how dry it was and found it still damp. He sighed. To offer it to Lim would do more harm than good.

"Are you still cold?" he asked.

Lim looked up quickly. "A little," he said apologetically.

Seregei nodded. "It'll be better once you're on Wilwarin. She'll help keep you warm."

Lim smiled a little, though the expression didn't quite reach his eyes.

At last, the hurdle was finished. Seregei fervently hoped it would bear his weight; not only did he not want it to collapse with him on it, but he didn't want to see Lim's expression if it did. He was fairly confident, though.

"How will she draw it?" asked Lim, looking from the hurdle to Wilwarin.

Seregei frowned. "If you can attach the longer branches to her saddle and something across her chest to keep it from sliding back, that should work."

Lim nodded and got up. Seregei noticed that he went pale again as he did so, and his hand strayed to his side.

"Are you sure there's nothing wrong?" he asked, knowing what the answer would be.

Lim nodded, removing his hand from his side with an almost guilty gesture.

"You're not hurt?"

"No... not badly."

Seregei sighed. "You know you can tell me and I won't think any less of you."

"I'm fine, really."

Seregei shook his head again. "All right," he said, and watched as Lim went to tack up Wilwarin and attach the hurdle. He gritted his teeth as he looked at it. Well, at least getting onto it couldn't be much more painful than getting up to this cave. Lim would have to help him again, but then they could move without it being too much worse...

As Lim tightened Wilwarin's girth, he suddenly hissed and stumbled, grabbing his side as he had earlier.

"Lim?"

"I'm fine," said Lim, sounding guilty. He didn't look at Seregei as he spoke.

"Sweet Lady, Lim, just tell me!"

"There's nothing wrong. Really!"

Seregei buried his face in his hands. "Lim, please don't lie to me. I don't want to have to pull authority on you."

When he looked up, what colour was in Lim's face had left it, and the younger elf was leaning on Wilwarin, biting his fingers. From where Seregei was sitting, it looked rather like cowering. He sighed.

"I'm not going to eat you."

Lim nodded and went back to harnessing the hurdle to Wilwarin. "I know... I'm sorry."

"For what?"

Lim glanced at him. "Upsetting you."

Seregei narrowed his eyes at him, but then sighed and closed them. He was already tired, and his leg was aching even though he wasn't trying to move it. Getting over to the hurdle was going to *hurt*.

When Lim had finished attaching the hurdle he came back over and, on Seregei's instructions, helped him to get up. Seregei leaned heavily on him as he hopped, doing his best to avoid jarring his leg or touching Lim's injured side. Lim was obviously having trouble; he was sweating and even his lips lost their colour. Once or twice Seregei was afraid the younger elf was about to faint, but they made it over to the hurdle and Seregei lay down on it, shifting to try to get comfortable. Lim went back to the cave and returned with the blanket Seregei had laid out to dry.

"Ah…" Seregei frowned. "We probably should have put that on here before I lay down."

Lim bit his lip. "Sorry," he said softly.

"It's not your fault. Just a moment…" Seregei slid down the hurdle a little way and gestured to Lim to lay the blanket where he'd been lying, then accepted his help to slide up it again. "Have we any more rope?"

"I think there's some in the saddlebags."

"Good; if I'm not going to slide down this thing as soon as we start moving, you'll need to tie me to it."

Lim blinked, looking highly uncomfortable at that idea.

"I can't do it from this angle…" Seregei sighed at the expression on Lim's face. "All right, I'll do what I can. Pass me the rope?"

Lim handed it over and Seregei tied his own shoulders loosely to the top of the hurdle. It would do; at least it made him less likely to fall off, even if it wasn't entirely secure.

Lim, meanwhile, picked up the few things that they'd left in the cave and put them back in the saddlebags, then proceeded to scramble up onto Wilwarin's back as if he was climbing a haystack.

Seregei frowned. He'd never seen anything that undignified, especially not from Lim, who normally vaulted neatly into the saddle.

"Lim?"

Lim obviously knew what had caught his attention. "I'm stiff."

Seregei sighed. "Let me know when you want to stop."

"I will." Lim's voice sounded faint, as if he was already tired, but he clicked his tongue at Wilwarin to urge her on and they began to move.

For some time, Seregei was too distracted by his own pain to pay much attention to anything else. Every rough patch in the ground jarred his leg and sent shocks like lightning all the way up his side. He gritted his teeth and bit his lip, determined that he wasn't going to let Lim know he was in pain; the younger elf would feel far too guilty about that to keep going.

At last, though, he began to get used to it. Maybe he was just losing feeling below the waist, but it was more bearable and he was able to look up and try to check on Lim.

He frowned; he couldn't see Lim from this angle. A little twisting and wriggling cost him in pain, but he managed to glimpse Lim's leg and see that he was leaning over Wilwarin's neck, hugging himself with one arm.

"Lim?"

There was no reply at first.

"Lim!"

"Huh?" It sounded like he'd been startled out of sleep. "Fa- Seregei?"

"Are you all right? Didn't you hear me the first time?"

"I'm sorry! I wasn't paying attention…"

Seregei felt as if something had snapped inside him. Enough was enough. He was not going to sit and watch any longer. "Next suitable place you see, we're going to stop and rest," he said firmly.

"All right," said Lim with a mixture of trepidation and exhaustion.

Seregei frowned and folded his arms. He was going to get to the bottom of this.

They stopped at a stand of pines and Lim unharnessed Wilwarin while Seregei untied himself from the hurdle and dragged himself over to sit against a tree. Seeing what he was doing, Lim hurried over to help, but Seregei had made it before he got there and he stopped. Seregei noticed that he was dragging his feet, almost stumbling as he started to move away.

"No," he said, grabbing Lim's outstretched hand. "Sit down."

Lim obeyed at once, looking grateful not to have to support his own weight any more. His skin was hot and somehow clammy to the touch and his breathing didn't sound good.

Seregei frowned. "Lim, what's wrong? And don't insult my intelligence by telling me 'nothing'."

Lim looked at him like an animal caught in a trap: a mixture of hopelessness and fear. Then he whispered something.

"What?"

"Please don't be angry," mumbled Lim.

Seregei frowned. "I'm not angry. Just tell me what's wrong."

Shivering, Lim pulled his cloak aside and touched the bandage wound around his waist. "Something… hit me. In the flood."

"Let me see it?"

Lim nodded a little and stayed still while Seregei began to unwrap the bandage. At the first turn, it stuck and Seregei realised that blood had soaked right through. There was some yellow on the cloth as well and he frowned.

"This looks bad," he muttered.

"I'm sorry."

Seregei shook his head absently. "I think I'm going to have to cut the bandage off and peel it away. I'm afraid it'll hurt." He glanced at Lim's face, but the younger elf just nodded vaguely.

As soon as Seregei produced a knife, though, Lim tensed. He watched it carefully as it approached and twitched when it apparently got too close. Seregei sighed.

"Here," he said, holding it out hilt-first. "Do you want to do it yourself?"

Lim nodded. "Thanks." He took the knife and carefully slid it under the bandage, sawing through it with careful movements. Even when he'd cut it, it didn't come free. Seregei nodded.

"I'm afraid this'll hurt," he repeated, and quickly pulled off the bandage.

Lim yelped and shied away, shielding his side with one hand, his shoulder protectively hunched, crying softly. Seregei waited until he'd recovered a little, then patted him gently on the shoulder, blinking as he moved away.

"It's all right."

"Sorry," gasped Lim, still hiding his side.

"Let me see it."

Lim nodded, but Seregei had to almost force his hand away. Upon pulling up Lim's shirt and seeing the wound, his eyes widened in shock, then narrowed. The gash had been long and deep to start with, and had festered. It had begun to bleed again when the cloth was ripped away.

"Lim, what the... what were you *thinking?*" Seregei's voice rang loud and he raised a hand to run it through his hair.

To his shock, Lim flinched, raising an arm to defend his face. Seregei hadn't seen that gesture often, but he still knew what it meant.

"I'm not going to hit you," he said, his voice dropping to a whisper.

Lim bit his lip. "I know," he said quickly, lowering the arm. "I know that you wouldn't..."

"But... why did you flinch?"

Lim looked away, raising a hand to his mouth.

"Has someone hit you before?"

There was no reply.

"Is that why you didn't tell me about the wound? Someone punished you for complaining in the past?"

"No, I just didn't want... you're already hurt, you didn't... you didn't need to have me to worry about as well."

That was infuriating, but in light of what he'd just seen Seregei made a particular effort to calm down before he spoke. "A lesson for the future, Lim: do *not* lie to me about injuries. It's not selfless; it's stupid. Are we clear?"

Lim nodded, looking stricken.

"Good." Seregei looked at the wound again. "I... I'm not a healer, but I'll do my best to clean it." His water bottle was still about half full and he picked it up. "You'll need to pull your shirt away from the wound and come close enough, though."

Lim gulped and obeyed.

Seregei was as gentle as he could be as he washed the wound, mopping away the dirt and blood as best he could with his handkerchief. Nonetheless, he could tell he was hurting Lim. He also kept half an eye on the weather and the light. He wanted to make a little more progress today, but he knew he couldn't push Lim too hard. This had probably halved their speed.

"Thank you," Lim murmured, breaking the silence.

Seregei paused in his work. "For what?"

"You're so kind to me…" Lim sighed. "Kinder than I deserve."

Seregei frowned. "Than you deserve? What have you done that you wouldn't deserve to be looked after?"

Lim shook his head hard, as if to wake himself. "I… nothing. I shouldn't have said that; I'm sorry."

Seregei frowned, but decided not to push the matter. "How do you feel?" he asked. "Tell me honestly; I need to know."

Lim hesitated, then said, "I… don't feel well. I'm so cold, and I feel tired even though I've hardly done anything."

Seregei reached out to put a hand on his forehead, but hesitated before touching him. "Do you mind?"

Lim looked curiously at him.

"If I touch you. I remember you said you didn't like it." And if someone had hurt him in the past, Seregei was especially determined to respect his wishes on the subject.

Lim smiled wanly. "It's all right," he said softly, though he still didn't seem entirely comfortable as Seregei laid a hand on his brow. As he'd expected, it was hot and sweaty to the touch.

"You've a fever," he explained. "That's probably most of it."

Lim nodded. "Can I still ride?" he asked hesitantly.

Seregei sighed. There wasn't much choice if they were to get home. "Yes, if you can get on Wilwarin." He got out his own emergency bandage and wrapped it around Lim's waist, under his shirt this time, making sure the wound was properly covered. "That should keep it clean."

"I'll do my best," said Lim, smiling a little. "Thank you."

Seregei nodded, but didn't smile. "You didn't have much breakfast, did you?"

Lim shook his head. "I… wasn't hungry."

"You should eat something before we go on."

Lim looked like he was about to say something, then obediently nibbled a few pieces of fruit, glancing at Seregei as he did so. Seregei looked away, trying not to let Lim see how worried he was. Lim couldn't ride far at a time, even had Seregei been inclined to ask it of him when he was in this state. They'd just have to do what they could: go as fast as possible with frequent rests.

"We'll set off again as soon as you're ready," he said with a sigh.

Lim nodded and finished the piece he was holding. Seregei still didn't think he'd eaten enough, but didn't press the matter apart from saying, "Eat a little every now and then as we go. It'll make matters worse if you starve yourself."

Lim nodded.

Once again, they got Seregei onto the hurdle and Lim struggled onto Wilwarin's back. Then they set off.

Lim felt ill. There was no other word for it; he couldn't pin down exactly what was wrong any more, but he felt ill. He alternately shook with chills and wiped sweat from his brow. His muscles twitched and ached. He couldn't concentrate on anything; his head was full of fog.

A sudden wave of dizziness made him lean forward on Wilwarin's neck, gasping. The movement disturbed his wound and the sudden pain made him whimper. The ordeal of having it unbandaged and cleaned had made it hurt much more, though he knew it was for the best.

Seregei's words about hiding the wound rang in his ears. He'd done the wrong thing and now Seregei was angry with him. Truly angry, he knew. Yet... he didn't seem to be in real *trouble*. He wished he'd not flinched when Seregei raised a hand, though; he wouldn't hit him. Of course not. Even though he was angry...

Lim whimpered again, his thoughts spinning off into words he couldn't follow, barely forming themselves into sentences. He could make out that Seregei clearly didn't think he deserved to be punished, despite lying about the wound. For the moment, he was content with that. He didn't want any more pain.

Perhaps he'd fallen asleep. The next thing he knew, Seregei was calling his name. He startled up, resisting the urge to turn round.

"I'm awake," he slurred, trying to shake the fog from his head. His tongue felt swollen and dry.

"Lim, drink something," Seregei ordered.

Lim blinked until his vision cleared and grabbed his waterskin, fumbling at the stopper. His fingers felt numb, moving in slow motion, but he managed it at last and took a mouthful of water. Gradually, his head cleared a little and he continued to sip until he no longer felt thirsty.

"Better?" asked Seregei. His voice sounded tense.

"Y-yes."

"Good. It'll be getting dark before long; you'll need to stop soon, especially if we're to have light to – ack!"

The cry of pain scared Lim. "Seregei?"

"I... I'm all right. Hurdle went over a rock... jarred my leg." Seregei groaned, then took a deep breath and continued, "If we're to have light to look at that wound again. And we..." he sighed. "You'll need to find some water."

Lim nodded. "All right," he said. "I'll look for somewhere."

It felt odd that Seregei was relying on him, but he had to admit that perhaps he was doing well. He squashed the feeling, though. He wasn't the one to decide that, and they weren't home yet. A sudden feeling of responsibility made him bite his lip. If he failed – and that was by no means impossible – he wouldn't be the only one to suffer for it. Seregei was relying on him.

Lim realised that he'd nodded again and shook his head, trying to focus his gaze on his surroundings. He couldn't fall asleep again. He had to find some shelter first. Then he had to find water, and then… then he would ask Seregei if he could sleep.

At last he saw a clump of trees whose branches formed a canopy overhead and he turned aside. He fell more than dismounted and leaned on Wilwarin while he waited for his head to stop spinning. He was starting to feel really cold again and huddled against her body, knowing she was warm. She didn't feel it, though.

"Lim? Are you all right?"

He looked round guiltily. Once more, Seregei had dragged himself off the hurdle. He was leaning on a tree, looking pale and tired. Lim knew he himself probably didn't look much better.

"I don't know if there's water near here," he apologised as he instinctively fumbled at the buckles of Wilwarin's tack. He couldn't grip the saddle properly and all but dropped it, but dragged the saddlebags to within Seregei's reach.

Seregei nodded. "In this weather, there probably is. The only question is if it's clean."

"I'll go and look."

"Don't go far, and reply if I call." Seregei sighed a little. "If you need to rest, sit down, but try to stay awake until you're back here."

Lim nodded. "I will."

Seregei held out his water bottle without another word. Lim took it and set off, moving from tree to tree and leaning on the trunks for support. The shivering was getting worse and he couldn't concentrate; he had to keep muttering the word "Water" to himself just to remember what he was looking for. A couple of times he heard Seregei call his name and shouted back, but it took him a long time to find a swollen stream. He fell to his knees beside it and splashed his face with the icy water. Hopefully it would wake and refresh him a little.

It mostly served to make him feel colder, and he shuddered as he filled the bottles. His side felt better, at least; the pain was less than it had been. Still, he pressed a hand to it as he stood up and the pain spiked, sending spots dancing across his vision for a moment. He only just managed to keep his feet.

He didn't know how he made it back, but suddenly he was in their shelter again. He weaved on his feet for a moment, then half-collapsed beside Seregei. The older elf immediately put an arm around him and he was too tired and sick to shrug it off.

"Thank you," Seregei said softly.

"I'm so cold," whispered Lim.

Seregei nodded. "You've a bad fever; it'll make you feel cold. You're doing very well, though."

"I keep almost falling asleep. I'm sorry…"

"I know, and it's not your fault. You're sick. Have a bite to eat, then you can rest."

Lim wasn't hungry, but he ate a piece of fruit. His pouch was getting rather empty. "What happens when we run out?" he asked.

"We'll be home by then," said Seregei firmly. "You get some sleep. I'll have another look at that wound in the morning."

Lim nodded and began to move away; he shouldn't sleep on Seregei; his patience probably wouldn't stretch to that.

"You can stay where you are if you're comfortable."

Or maybe it would. Lim didn't question the offer; he just settled back down, murmuring thanks, and soon fell asleep.

Seregei sighed a little, drawing his cloak a little closer around them both. It was more to make Lim feel protected than for warmth; the poor little elf was burning with fever. He ate a few pieces of fruit, gazing towards Duamelti. Not too much further. He did his best to hold onto that.

Wilwarin stamped a foot and Seregei sighed, reaching a hand towards her. He smiled as she came over and nuzzled his fingers. Would search parties be out looking for them? Probably not; they weren't expected back for a couple of days yet, unless it was known that they might have been caught in that flood. He wondered whether sending Wilwarin home would prompt people to look for her rider, but he couldn't talk to her and, in any case, it might still be a couple of days before they were found. He looked down at Lim's face and wiped away a bead of sweat that was working its way down his cheek. He had a feeling that Lim didn't have days.

He sighed, but took some comfort in the fact that he'd not been lying: if they made the same progress tomorrow as they had today, they'd make it home. At least, they'd make it to somewhere they would be found. He nodded a little to himself and tilted his head back against the tree. Though not as exhausted as Lim, he was tired and soon fell asleep.

***

Seregei was woken when Lim twitched and whimpered in his sleep. For a moment he was disoriented, but then he remembered what had happened and looked around with a sigh. He was hungry and thirsty, but limited himself to a swallow of water.

Lim was still huddled against him, and whatever had been troubling him seemed to have passed. He looked terrible, though; his face was flushed and his lips were cracked and dry. Seregei didn't want to wake him, but he needed to drink something and then they needed to set off again. He hoped Lim could stand.

"Lim?" he called, shaking him gently. "Lim, it's time to wake up."

Lim stirred, then tensed, gasping.

"It's all right. Here." Seregei offered him a water bottle and he drank greedily. Seregei quickly put a hand on his. "Not too much at once; you'll make yourself sick."

Lim nodded. "Sorry," he whispered.

"You've nothing to apologise for. How do you feel?"

"All r–" Lim shot Seregei a worried look. "I... not very well..." He looked down.

"Better or worse than yesterday?"

"Worse," whispered Lim.

Seregei sighed. "If we make the same progress today as yesterday, we'll make it over the border. Then it's likely someone will find us."

Lim nodded.

"Can I have a look at it?"

Another nod and Lim drew away enough for Seregei to unwrap the bandage and expose his wound. Once again, the bandage stuck, but fortunately it wasn't as bad and they didn't have to cut it off.

The wound itself, though, was no better. It was still swollen and red, and there was pus visible at the edges. Seregei wrinkled his nose and did his best to clean it off, then bandaged it again. He hoped Lim couldn't tell from his expression how bad it was.

"I'm sorry," said Lim.

"For what?"

"I..." Lim sniffed and continued haltingly, "I don't know if I can ride much further, but I don't want to let you down."

Seregei sighed. "You're hurt. That fact isn't your fault. I'd not push you if we didn't need to, and you're a tough elf." He smiled. "I'm sure you can make it further than you think." That was a lie, but Lim didn't really look up to realising that.

Lim still looked unhappy. "I never... I never do anything right," he said distantly, still sniffing from time to time. "Not by my father and not by you."

Seregei frowned. "That isn't true."

"That's why he used to get so angry with me. Now you're angry too because –"

"Lim, I'm *not* angry with you. When we get home, you and I are going to discuss the fact that you hid this wound, but at the moment I just want to get you home, all right?"

Lim looked at him pathetically. "I don't think I can..."

"Once you're up on Wilwarin you just have to sit there; she knows the way home. Even sick, you can do that. You've done very well so far; I'm sure you can keep going a little longer."

Lim sniffed and nodded.

"Think about it," said Seregei with a smile, squeezing Lim's shoulder. "This time tomorrow you'll be lying in a warm bed with something to eat and your side properly cleaned and bandaged. And everyone – including me – will be proud of you."

Lim sighed. He didn't look entirely convinced, but nodded. "I'll do my best," he whispered.

His movements were slow and weak as he tacked up Wilwarin and set up the hurdle. Seregei refused his offer of help and dragged himself over. He had to actually push himself up and gritted his teeth to try to hide the pain of putting pressure on his leg, despite his efforts to keep his weight off it.

"Can you mount?" he asked.

Lim nodded and whispered something into Wilwarin's ear, pressing a hand against her forehead, then scrambled onto her back. Seregei winced; it was even worse than the day before. Wilwarin stood stock still, though, which was a blessing.

Once Lim was up there was a long pause. Seregei could hear him whimpering brokenly, presumably in pain, and bit his lip. He felt utterly helpless; he couldn't even say anything to make the situation better.

At last, though, Lim urged Wilwarin on and they began to move.

***

They didn't stop to rest at noon and Seregei didn't suggest it; he doubted that Lim would be able to get back on Wilwarin. He heard Lim drink once or twice and was glad he'd remembered, but apart from that they both remained silent. Twisting round, Seregei could see that Lim was lying on Wilwarin's neck, resting. It was sensible and he nodded to himself.

At last, as the afternoon was wearing on, they crossed the border and began to head downhill into the valley. Seregei breathed a sigh of relief and called, "Almost there, Lim! There's a guard post just a little further on!"

Lim mumbled something. At least it sounded like he was still conscious. Seregei bit his lip and regretted it as the hurdle went over a bump and his teeth drew blood. He swore and pinched his lip.

After only a little longer, though, Lim stopped even trying to respond to Seregei's comments.

"Lim!" Seregei shouted, hoping Lim had just fallen asleep.

Lim didn't reply, and after a moment he slipped off Wilwarin's back to land in a heap on the road. Wilwarin sidestepped a little and stopped.

Seregei swore, tearing at the rope holding him to the hurdle. He cursed his own clumsy knot but forced himself to relax and untie it slowly. Then he slid carefully off the hurdle and crawled over to Lim. He had to drag his leg. The effort sent lightning up the whole of that side of his body, but he made it and sat beside Lim. His heart in his mouth, he rolled the younger elf onto his back and laid a hand on his chest to look for a heartbeat.

For a moment he couldn't feel anything and began to really panic, but he moved his hand a little and sighed in relief. Lim's heartbeat was fast and shallow, but there.

Seregei shifted again to pat Lim gently on the cheek, calling his name. His skin was hot and sweaty to the touch. Fortunately, Seregei's water bottle was clipped to his belt and he was able to splash some on Lim's face, but there was still no reaction.

Seregei swore again and looked around. They were within Duamelti, and he thought they were close enough to the guard post that a shout would carry. He hadn't many other options; he couldn't go anywhere.

He took a deep breath and bellowed, "Help!" at the top of his voice. Then he took another breath and shouted again, and then a third time.

Even all of that hadn't woken Lim, and Seregei once again felt for his heartbeat. It was still there, and no longer as shallow. Hopefully, that was a good sign.

Just as he was beginning to consider shouting again, he heard hoofbeats from further up the road. Wilwarin raised her head and whinnied.

Seregei sighed in relief. "Hie!" he shouted, and he waved as he saw a rider come around the corner. The rider shouted over his shoulder and spurred his horse into a canter. A few others joined him and they hurried towards Seregei and Lim.

"Captain Seregei!" the leader exclaimed, dismounting almost as soon as he arrived. "What happened?"

"We were caught in a flood. Lim needs a healer."

The other members of the patrol had arrived now and heard what he'd said.

"I can take him," said one. "I'm lightest, so he'll be least burden."

"You'll need to lift him," Seregei told the others. "I can't stand; my leg's broken."

There were a few shocked looks, but before anything else they worked on getting Lim onto the horse and Seregei blessed them for it. The elf carrying Lim wheeled round and cantered off as soon as he could and Seregei watched him go with a sigh of relief. The healers of Duamelti were very gifted, and he thought they'd arrived in time. Lim would be all right now.

"I'll send for a litter," said the patrol leader, eyeing Seregei's leg. "How much does it hurt?"

Seregei shook his head a little. "It's fine if I don't move it too much. I think I could sit on Wilwarin if someone would lead her." He didn't especially want to be carried through half the valley on a litter if it could possibly be avoided. Not only would it be undignified, but he didn't want any rumours that he was severely injured or dead. He knew such things could spread like wildfire.

The patrol leader looked sceptical.

"Honestly, I think I'll be all right if you can get me back to the Guardhouse and find someone who can set my leg." That was closer, at least.

"It's not set?"

"Lim doesn't know how and I wasn't about to make this his first lesson."

The patrol leader shook his head. "I'm not risking it," he said. "I think you should really go to the healing house."

"I can ride there, though."

"I don't think you should jostle it any more, especially given everything that being dragged on that" – he nodded towards the hurdle – "will have done to it."

Seregei frowned. "I really don't think I need to be carried."

"As far as the Guardhouse, and then we'll leave it to the healers to decide."

That seemed a fair compromise, and Seregei nodded. "All right."

Kerin had been about to go off duty from one of his occasional shifts at the healing house when he heard a clatter of hooves in the courtyard. He started towards the door, then broke into a run as a voice yelled, "Healer!"

A couple of others got out before he did, and when he arrived they were helping the rider to lower a limp body to the ground. Kerin turned in the doorway to call for a stretcher.

Once the unconscious elf was on the stretcher and being carried in, Kerin finally recognised him.

"Lim?" he gasped. He turned to the rider, who had just dismounted. "What happened? Where's Captain Seregei?"

"We found them just inside the border. Captain Seregei said they'd been caught in a flood. His leg's broken. I imagine they'll be bringing him after me."

Kerin breathed a sigh of relief. "Thank you," he said, and went in after Lim.

They'd laid him on a table in one of the side rooms. Most had left, but one of the two remaining was carefully cutting away Lim's shirt and the bandage wound around his waist.

Kerin swore as he saw the wound: a long laceration that had been left to infect. There was dirt in it despite the bandage, presumably from Lim's clothes, alongside the dried blood and pus.

"How fevered is he?" he asked as he washed his hands.

"Pretty bad," said the second healer, who was sponging Lim's face to try to cool him.

"All right. Let's get his shirt off so we can see what we're doing."

They cut the shirt off completely so that they moved him as little as possible, then set about washing the wound. Kerin heard someone enter the room behind him as he lanced an abscess, but made sure he'd removed the piece of wood at its centre before he looked round. It was another border guard.

"Did you bring Captain Seregei?"

"No, my Lord," the guard said awkwardly. "He insisted on being taken to the Guardhouse instead."

"Isn't his leg broken?"

"Yes, but he refused to be carried through the city on a litter."

Kerin sighed, glancing at the healer who was helping him. "Can you take over?" Apparently it would take some time to deal with this.

The other elf nodded and moved to go on with treating Lim's wound. Kerin turned back to the guard.

"How has he treated it?"

"It's splinted, but not set, and he was being dragged on a hurdle."

Kerin resisted the urge to rub his eyes. "He should be brought here," he said. "Go back and tell him that, and that if he really insists on staying there he should know it'll probably be a couple of hours before anyone can be spared and he's to lie still until they arrive. Otherwise he should be brought here, moving his leg as little as possible."

The guard nodded. "I'll tell him, my Lord."

Kerin smiled a little and dismissed him with a wave, then turned back to Lim. The other healer had finished cleaning the wound and Kerin inspected it carefully, wondering whether to stitch it. He decided against it; they might have to clean it out again. Instead, he packed it with marsh woundwort and comfrey with a bandage to hold them in place.

He'd have felt a lot better were it not for the fact that Lim had remained deeply unconscious throughout. He was glad the young elf had been spared pain, but it was worrying nonetheless.

"Lim?" he called softly, gently shaking Lim's shoulder. There was no response at first, but when he called Lim's name again he stirred a little, whimpering. "Lim, it's all right."

Lim's eyes fluttered open for a moment, then he apparently lost consciousness again. Kerin sighed. Well, a momentary recovery was a hopeful sign. He went to wash his hands and gave instructions for Lim to be moved to one of the small rooms.

"Have someone stay with him," he said, "And call me if he wakes or there's any sign of trouble. Keep him cool; it'll probably help revive him." He knew that sleep would help Lim to heal, but wanted to make sure he was well enough to speak. He himself would wait until he had news of Seregei, and preferably until he'd seen him; he wanted to have something to tell Caleb. With another sigh, Kerin went to sit by the door of the healing house, waiting for news.

Before long, the same rider arrived. Kerin got up to greet him as he dismounted.

"Is he coming?"

"Yes; I told him what you'd said and he agreed to be brought here."

Kerin nodded, relieved. "All right. I'll wait until he gets here, at least."

At last, a pony-litter arrived. Seregei was sitting bolt upright on it, looking uncomfortable.

Kerin rolled his eyes as he got up. "You couldn't just be carried, could you?"

Seregei half-heartedly glared at him. "Caleb wouldn't want to either," he said softly, "I imagine there are enough rumours already going round that something terrible has happened to me."

That was a fair point and Kerin nodded. Behind him, two assistants had already brought out a stretcher and he glanced at it.

"You'll lie on this one, though," he said firmly.

"All right," said Seregei, looking away. "How's Lim?"

"We cleaned and bandaged the wound, and he woke up briefly. We're keeping an eye on him."

"Will he be all right?"

"I think so."

Seregei sighed in relief and nodded, then accepted help to get off the pony-litter. Kerin saw him go suddenly pale as his leg was disturbed and immediately went to grab his hand.

"Are you all right?" he asked.

Seregei nodded. "It hurts, is all."

"I imagine so." Kerin helped Seregei lie down on the stretcher. "Ready?"

Seregei smiled a little. "When you are."

Kerin escorted him inside and gave him some painkillers in preparation for having his leg set. "How did it happen?" he asked as they waited for the drug to take effect.

"I don't really remember. The flood hit us and Menel fell, but the next thing I remember is being on the bank, and my leg was broken by then."

Kerin frowned. It might be any kind of break, then. He was tempted to stay and work on it himself, but mentally shook his head. His subordinates were perfectly capable.

Seregei was starting to look groggy and Kerin's frown deepened. "When did you last have a real meal?"

"The day after the day we set off." Seregei smiled wanly. "We lost almost all our supplies."

"Almost?"

Seregei patted a pouch at his waist. "I insisted we carry these."

Kerin nodded. At least he'd not given Seregei anything strong. It might knock him out, given that he was already weak, but it wouldn't do him any harm.

"Make sure you eat when you recover from the drug."

"Oh, I intend to. Same goes for Lim: he wasn't hungry but I tried to make sure he ate *something*."

Kerin nodded. "I'll leave instructions for him to have something simple when he wakes up."

Seregei nodded, looking distant. Kerin couldn't tell whether or not it was the drug. "Is something wrong?"

Seregei sighed. "Just... I need to think it over when I'm not distracted. Something's going on, though, with Lim. There's some really nasty reason why he's here, I'm sure of it."

"What?" Kerin leaned a little closer before catching himself and backing off again. "What's happening?"

Seregei shook his head. "I'm not sure, but I've not had a moment to think these last couple of days."

"What should I tell Caleb?"

"Nothing yet. I don't think you're in danger. Either of you."

"And Lim?"

"That's what I'm worried about." Seregei sighed, his eyes falling closed. "Head's getting fuzzy now, though. I'll talk to you later."

Kerin nodded. "All right," he said, and watched as Seregei fell asleep. Then he left the other healers to work and went to check on Lim.

The younger elf was awake when Kerin went in, and he nodded a little in approval as he saw that the assistant sitting with him had sent for some soup. Lim was sitting up and eating listlessly. He still looked terrible, but he glanced up as Kerin looked round the door.

"I can leave if you like, Master Kerin," said the assistant, getting up.

"Please," said Kerin. "I won't be long."

She left and Kerin took her seat. Lim looked sadly at him for a moment, then went back to toying with his soup.

"Not hungry?" asked Kerin.

Lim shook his head. "I'm sorry."

"How's your side?"

"It... it hurts. And I feel sick."

There was a basin beside the bed and Kerin moved it to be within easy reach.

"I don't remember what happened," said Lim. "One moment I was on Wilwarin, and then..." He rubbed his eyes. "I just felt so dizzy..."

Kerin shook his head a little. "I imagine you fainted and I'm not surprised. You'll be all right, though; we can take care of the wound properly here."

Lim nodded. "Thank you."

Kerin looked at him in silence for a moment, pondering what Seregei had said. He wouldn't ask Lim about it, though; it would be wrong to distress him.

"I left Seregei getting his leg set," he said. "I imagine he'll come and visit you when he can."

Lim looked up, a flash of fear crossing his face. Kerin frowned.

"Is something wrong?"

"N-no, just... please tell him I'm sorry? I tried, I really did!" Lim started chewing his fingertips.

Kerin's frown deepened. "I'm... sure you did," he said, confused. "No-one's saying you didn't and I'm sure he understands that; he'll just want to see for himself that you're all right."

Lim was looking at his soup again, shivering. Kerin gently touched his hand and found it was still too warm.

"I think you need some more rest," he said. "I'll have someone bring you some elder tea, which will help with the fever, and then you'll feel better."

Lim nodded. "Thank you," he said again.

Kerin pressed his hand. "Is there anything else I should know?"

Lim shook his head, squeezing his eyes shut.

"All right." Kerin took the half-eaten bowl of soup and put it to the side. "That can be reheated," he said, smiling, then helped Lim to lie down. "I'll send for that tea, then you can sleep."

"All right. Thank you."

Kerin nodded and left, glancing over his shoulder as he went. Lim didn't say anything else.

As he'd promised, he told the assistant who had been sitting with Lim to heat some elder tea and take it to him. He himself went to see Caleb.

CHAPTER THREE

Caleb was meeting with an extremely agitated human representative and Kerin slipped into his study as quietly as possible.

"And so you flooded us!" cried the human, waving his arms.

Caleb had noticed Kerin come in and gestured at him slightly to wait.

"As I've said, neither the blockage nor the flood had anything to do with us. It wasn't even on our side of the border. I passed on your complaint to a friend of mine and he went to check on what was happening, but... he and his companion haven't returned."

Kerin shifted on his feet and Caleb looked at him again. "Excuse me," he said to the human, then asked, "Is it important, Kerin?"

Kerin nodded, stepping forward. "I'm sorry to interrupt you, but Seregei and Lim just arrived back."

Caleb sighed in relief. "Praise the Lady," he said softly, then explained to the human, "Those are the elves I mentioned." He turned back to Kerin. "How are they?"

"Injured, but alive, and they should recover well."

"What happened?"

"They were caught in a flood and it was difficult for them to get back due to their injuries."

Caleb glanced at the human. "I doubt they set it off," he said mildly. "And I hope you don't think I'd unleash a flood with my friends in its path, even though you apparently *do* believe me capable of toying with your village like this."

"Well, then, how did it happen?" asked the human, only sounding slightly mollified.

"Hopefully Seregei will be able to tell us. What state is he in, Kerin?"

"Unconscious when I left, I'm afraid. It would be best to wait until morning." Seregei would probably have come round before it was too late in the evening, but Kerin thought he could do with some rest.

Caleb nodded. "If you'd like to speak to him, we can put you up for the night and see how he is in the morning."

The man sighed. "What about the other elf? Leem?"

Kerin shook his head at once. "Lim's worse. No-one should visit him unnecessarily for a few days at least."

The human sighed. "Very well, then. If it's all right with you, Lord Caleb, I would like to speak to Seregei in the morning."

Caleb nodded. "I'll have a room prepared for you," he said.

The human nodded, bowed a little and left.

Caleb turned to Kerin. "How badly-off are they?"

"Seregei's leg is broken and Lim has a badly-infected wound and is feverish. They're both tired and hungry, but should recover well given some time."

Again, Caleb sighed in relief.

Kerin smiled. "Seregei's a grumpy pain in the neck, isn't he?"

Caleb shot him a look. "I'd rather he didn't die," he said, smiling himself.

Kerin wondered for a moment whether to mention what Seregei had said. The other elf had asked him not to tell Caleb yet, and said that there was nothing serious to worry about, but...

Caleb was frowning. "What's wrong?"

Kerin shook his head slightly. "Something Seregei said worried me."

"What?"

"He said he suspected there was something dark behind Lim's being here."

Caleb frowned, tensing slightly. "Did he say what?"

"No. He wasn't sure, but he said we're not in any danger."

Caleb frowned bitterly. "I don't like the sound of that. Could I speak to him sooner?"

"He said he needed time to think when he wasn't distracted."

Caleb sighed. "All right. Tomorrow, though, I'm talking to him."

Seregei's leg ached and felt heavy and clumsy, especially splinted, but he was determined not to stay in bed. As soon as a healer had told him he could try using crutches on the morning after he and Lim arrived home, he asked for a pair.

Arani smiled a little. "Try a short distance first," he advised. "I'll stay to keep an eye on you."

Seregei wasn't good on crutches, but he managed to get to the outer door and turned to Arani with a grin. "How was that?"

Arani smiled back. "Not bad, but how far are you planning to go?"

"I'd like to visit Lim. How is he?"

"I believe he's awake, and a little better than yesterday."

Seregei nodded. "Would he like a visit, do you think?"

Arani frowned. "He seemed unnerved by the idea of talking to anyone yesterday… especially you."

"What?" Seregei turned to face him. He could both see and sense that the healer was worried.

Arani shook his head a moment. "He seemed frightened."

"Why?" asked Seregei, the question coming out more like a demand.

Arani raised an eyebrow and Seregei apologised. He knew he shouldn't have been surprised; Lim always seemed frightened, but given all they'd just been through he had thought that fear was a little less.

"Well, he wanted us to assure you that he'd tried his hardest to get home."

"I know that." Seregei leaned on the wall beside him.

Arani smiled wanly. "I thought you might, and I told him as much."

Seregei nodded. After a moment, he asked, "Arani, can I ask your opinion?"

"Of course."

"What do you think of Lim?"

Arani looked hard at Seregei. "Well, you're his captain and mentor. I'd expect you to know him better than me."

"Maybe I'm too used to him."

Arani nodded. "Well… he's frightened. I think he really thinks you're going to hurt him."

Seregei bit his lip. "But why?"

"I don't really know. Not without knowing him better."

Seregei shook his head a little. "I should go see him."

"Speak softly."

Seregei nodded. "Thanks," he said as Arani held the door for him.

"Of course." Arani grinned. "You'll need someone to let you into Lim's room as well."

Seregei smiled. "Well, I meant for the warning as well, but I'd appreciate it."

It wasn't far to hop, fortunately – Seregei still wasn't used to the crutches – and if Arani noticed that he was having trouble he didn't mention it. He just opened the outer door of Lim's room, then told the younger elf he had a visitor and left.

Lim didn't look well, but he tried to push himself upright as Seregei went over to sit beside his bed.

"You can stay lying down if it's more comfortable," Seregei told him as he carefully sat down.

Lim lay back with a sigh. "Sorry," he said softly. "But… it is."

Seregei nodded. "How do you feel?"

"Sick." Lim sighed. After a moment, he asked, "Are... you angry?"

Seregei stared at him. Even though he'd had some warning, the words still came as something of a shock.

Lim bit his lip. "I just couldn't go on any longer. You were relying on me..."

"You pushed yourself to the end of your strength. That's all I could ask."

Lim fidgeted with the edge of a sheet, watching Seregei out of the corner of his eye.

Seregei sighed. "Can I ask you something?"

Lim looked up. "Yes?"

"Do you trust me?"

Lim blinked. "Well... yes?"

Seregei shook his head with a sigh "You clearly don't; you're convinced I'm going to do something to hurt you no matter how many times I tell you I'm not."

"But I let you down. You *were* upset with me." Lim's hand twitched and he went back to playing with the sheet.

Seregei sighed. "When you'd repeatedly told me that you were all right and unhurt, and then I discovered you were hiding a large and badly infected wound, *yes*. I *was* upset with you."

Lim's full attention was now on Seregei's face.

"Because you lied to me repeatedly in a dangerous situation where I needed to know how fit you were. You're right: I was relying on you to help me get home; without you to help me away from the river, call and guide Wilwarin, fetch the material for the litter and help build it and find water... I don't know how I would have got home. But for the first part of that, I thought you were all right. I didn't know you were hurt. Knowing what happened with us taking care of that wound for the last couple of days, do you see how much worse things might have been had we *not* taken care of it?"

Lim nodded. "I'm sorry."

"I know – you've told me that – but do you understand why that was *very* stupid?"

Lim nodded again. "I could have got you killed," he said in a very small voice.

"Me and yourself."

"But..." Lim trailed off and bit his lip, looking away. "I don't matter."

Seregei stared at him, totally lost for words. After a moment, he managed to find his tongue and blurted, "Who in the Hells told you *that*?"

Lim blinked. "I... it's true, isn't it?"

"*No!*" Seregei once more went to run his hand through his hair, and Lim once more flinched away. Seregei froze, glancing at his still-raised hand.

For a long moment, they stared at each other in silence. Lim relaxed first, looking away and biting his lip. Finally, Seregei lowered his hand again.

"You've been hit," he said bluntly.

"I know you'd not hurt me," said Lim quickly, looking at Seregei with wide eyes.

"Then why flinch?"

"I don't know." Lim fiddled with the edge of a blanket.

Seregei took a moment to calm himself again. He knew he mustn't snap. "I do: even if you weren't aware of it, you expected me to hit you."

Lim's grip on the blanket tightened and tears started to appear in his eyes.

"I've seen elves who've been beaten bloody who don't flinch from a raised hand the way you do."

"I... I can't..."

Seregei was only a little surprised when Lim outright burst into tears. He sighed and took the younger elf's hand. "Sorry," he said. "I didn't mean to make you cry."

Lim whimpered, looking away. He was still crying, despite his attempts to hide it. Seregei sighed.

"If I'm going to protect you, I need to know what I'm protecting you from," he explained gently. "Or who," he added.

"I can't," said Lim again, wiping his eyes with his free hand: his left.

Seregei sighed. "You're tired," he said quietly. "I'll leave you to get some rest."

Lim hiccupped. "I'm sorry."

"For what?"

"I just... can't tell you." He sniffed. "Or go back, or..." – his voice started to go shrill – "even write because I can't say where I *am*."

"At least news of you will have reached home, even if it's just to say you're safe." Seregei squeezed Lim's hand, but he sniffed and looked away, his shoulders hunched. Seregei shook his head a little. "I'm going to let you get some sleep. We'll talk again soon."

Lim looked round, wiping his eyes again. "Are you going to send me away?" he whispered.

Seregei hesitated. It was starting to look like it might be best; Lim would probably make a good Swordmaster, but he didn't think he could train him any more. "I don't know," he said at last. "We need to talk again first. Why do you think I would?"

"I've not been a good trainee."

Seregei managed to restrain himself to a slow movement as he pushed his hair back from his face. "You've been an excellent trainee, Lim. You learn fast, you listen and you're a gifted archer. Given a few differences, the last few days would have sealed it for me. Guess again."

Lim sighed. "I lied about being wounded."

Seregei nodded. "At least you've now given me a reason why you did that, though… it's a bad one."

Lim looked like he was about to say something, but then stopped.

"What is it?"

"It's… nothing."

"If you want to say it, I want to hear it."

Lim hunched his shoulders again. "I don't; it upset you."

Seregei raised an eyebrow. "The fact that you think your life is inherently worthless *does* upset me, yes."

Lim looked about to protest, but once again caught himself. Seregei shook his head a little and squeezed his hand.

"That isn't true, Lim. No matter who told it you, it's not true." He released Lim's hand. "Get some rest. We'll talk again later."

Lim nodded. "I'm sorry."

"Don't be. I just want you to understand why I'm disappointed and why I keep questioning you."

Lim nodded, though Seregei didn't think it very likely that he did understand.

"And thank you again," he added as he sorted out the crutches and got up.

Lim looked up. "For what?"

Seregei shook his head; he couldn't quite believe this. "For saving my life," he said wearily, and hopped towards the door.

As he was heading back down the corridor towards his room, he heard a voice call, "Captain Seregei!" behind him. He looked round to see an elf in Caleb's livery, accompanied by a human.

"Hello," he said, turning carefully. "Is everything all right?"

"This is Liran," said the elf, gesturing to the human. "He's from a town just outside the border, and would like a word with you."

Seregei nodded. "Here probably isn't the best place. Shall we go outside?"

Liran nodded. "If you'd prefer it."

"And Lord Caleb would also like to speak to you later," said the elf.

"Very well." Seregei adjusted his crutches carefully and hopped over to them. "I should probably go back to my room before that, though." He was genuinely tired.

"I'll tell him to find you there, sir," said the elf, then inclined his head to both of them and left.

"Shall we?" said Seregei, starting towards the door out into the courtyard. Liran fell awkwardly into step beside him. "Is it private?" asked Seregei as he went.

"Not very, I suppose."

"Right. There's a bench just outside."

They didn't speak again until they'd reached the bench and Seregei had lowered himself carefully onto it.

"Lord, I hate crutches," he muttered. "Now, Liran, what did you want to speak to me about?" He gestured to the bench.

Liran shifted uncomfortably, then firmed his spine and sat down beside Seregei. "I'm from a town outside the border. We complained recently that the river that supplies all our water was running dry, and then..." Liran was getting more agitated as he spoke and he began to gesture wildly, twisting slightly to face Seregei. "Then the other day all the water we'd been waiting for came at once! I came to ask what the elves had to do with it!"

Seregei frowned. "Nothing," he said shortly, then shook his head with a small sigh. "My trainee and I went to investigate when Lord Caleb told me about your complaint, since if any elves were involved it would be those outside his kingdom. We found that the river had been blocked by a couple of fallen trees."

Liran nodded a little. "That does explain the fact that the water stopped," he muttered.

Seregei wondered why no-one from the town had been to investigate themselves, but put the thought aside. "We were on our way to your town to tell you and seek help with clearing it when it burst. We were caught in the flood."

Liran's eyes flicked to Seregei's splinted leg. "Lord Kerin mentioned you'd been caught in a flood. That's when Lord Caleb said I should speak to you."

Seregei nodded. "Well, that's all I know." He shrugged a little. "These things happen. I hope no-one in your town was hurt?"

"Not hurt. There was some damage, but not to any people."

"Then it looks like Lim and I took the worst of it." Seregei sighed.

"How is he?"

"Recovering well. Given time and tending, he'll be fine."

"I'm glad to hear that." Liran sighed. "Thanks for telling me what happened." He got up. "I'll leave you to rest. Do you need help getting back inside?"

Seregei eyed his crutches uncertainly, but managed to struggle back to his feet. "I think I'm all right," he said once he was there.

Liran nodded and walked away. Seregei sighed, then turned and hopped back to his room. Once there, he lay down with a sigh, wincing as all the aches and pains caught up with him. It had been a long time since he had last used crutches, and his back and shoulders hurt.

Arani visited briefly to check his leg and assured him that it would probably heal well. Seregei was most worried that he'd end up with a limp, but Arani said there shouldn't be a problem as long as he rested properly while he was healing. After Arani left, Seregei supposed that he'd fallen asleep, since he was woken by the sound of the door opening again.

He blinked the sleep from his eyes and smiled as he saw one of the assistants bow Caleb into the room.

Caleb came over and looked down at Seregei, smiling a little.

"How do you feel?" he asked.

"Not bad." Seregei pushed himself up carefully. "I've felt worse, and Healer Arani says it'll heal cleanly."

"That's good." Caleb sat down. "Kerin told me basically what happened. Is there anything you'd like to add?"

Seregei smiled wryly. "I've told the story a few times now, but I'm willing to tell it again, since you came to hear it."

Caleb shook his head. "Unless there's something more, that's not what I came to talk about."

Seregei blinked. "Then what did you come for?"

"Kerin said something about Lim."

"He did?" Seregei frowned. "I told him I needed some time to think about it."

"If there's something going on here, I need to know about it."

"As I said to him, I don't think there's any danger to you."

"And to you? And to Duamelti?"

"To any of us." Seregei sighed. "Just to Lim."

"But it might overflow; I can't assume all is well, and neither can Kerin. He did the right thing. Please tell me what it is that you suspect."

Seregei frowned. "It's not solid enough to be a suspicion. It's more of an uncomfortable feeling."

"Then please tell me about that." Caleb sat forward, his elbows on his knees.

"It's poor form to question someone confined to a healer's bed."

"If that's where he is, that's where I must question him. Stop avoiding the subject."

Seregei scowled at him, then looked away with a sigh. "Honestly, Caleb, I think he's the only one in danger," he said softly. "I think... someone hurt him. Taffilelti didn't send him because he feared he was in danger; he *was* in danger."

"What do you mean?" asked Caleb, leaning forwards.

Seregei scowled. "A couple of times, now, I've raised a hand and he's flinched."

Caleb raised an eyebrow. "He's scared of you, I'm not surprised."

"There's no reason for him to be," said Seregei, nettled. "And this is more than being nervous. He acts as if he actually thinks I'll hit him."

"So you think someone has in the past?"

"I'm certain."

Caleb sighed. "But you are sure that it's not going to affect anything else."

Seregei nodded. "If I thought it would cause any serious problems for you, I'd have told you."

Caleb smiled a little and got up. "You can't blame me for being concerned. Shall I ask Taffilelti next time I write?"

Seregei sighed. "Best not until I'm more sure. Before, he seemed worried about word of his whereabouts getting back to someone, and I think I agree with him. Besides... I can't really back this up. Keep it quiet until I know more."

Caleb nodded. "I'll leave you to your rest, then," he said. "Let me know if there's anything else you think you should tell me."

"I will," said Seregei, inclining his head a little in response to Caleb's nod. Then the other elf left. Seregei sighed, looking up at the ceiling. He didn't think there was much more he could do without more information from Lim. He already had the rough idea; now he needed details.

***

As time went by, Lim began to seem a little more comfortable when Seregei visited, but not as much as he'd have liked. The younger elf still watched him carefully and never seemed even as relaxed as he had been before their trip. Seregei sighed as he knocked on the door of Lim's room.

"Come in?"

He pushed the door open and hobbled in. "No, you stay there," he said as Lim looked like he was about to get up and help with the door. "I can manage." He'd had some practice at getting through doors on crutches, after all.

Lim sat back against the headboard, looking a little relieved.

"How do you feel today?" asked Seregei, sitting down beside him.

"Much better, thank you."

"That's good." Seregei stretched. "The healers here are very skilled."

"Indeed." Lim fidgeted. "I'm grateful for their help."

Seregei smiled. "You'll be all right; you just need time now."

Lim bit his lip. "I... I don't wish to complain – I'm very grateful and they're treating me very well here – but... when can I go back to the Guardhouse?"

The request rather surprised Seregei. "I didn't think you much liked it there."

Lim continued to fidget as he said, "Please don't think I'm ungrateful, but I like having my own space."

Seregei shook his head. "I don't think you're ungrateful – staying in the healing houses always makes me nervous and I've done it far more often than you – but I didn't think you thought of the Guardhouse as your home, much though I'd like you to."

Lim looked down, chewing his lip. "It's not... home. I'm sorry. But I truly am happy there."

"Well, I'm glad to hear that, at least." Seregei reached out carefully to pat Lim's shoulder. To his relief, Lim didn't flinch. "I'm afraid there's nothing I can do, though. You have to stay here until the healers say you can leave."

Lim shot him a miserable look, but then looked down again. "Do you know when that will be?" he asked in a small voice.

"If you're healing well, I can't imagine it'll be too much longer, but they have to be sure you won't have to come back tomorrow worse, and that you'll be able to take care of yourself at least a little. They won't keep you any longer than they have to, trust me, and I'll do my best to look after you."

"But... you're hurt too, it wouldn't be fair."

Seregei shot a rueful look at his splinted leg. "Well... I'll do my best. I can't claim that'll be much."

Lim smiled shyly. "It's more than I'd have asked," he said softly. "Thank you."

Seregei nodded. "Well, you don't have to ask. I'll look after you." After a moment's hesitation, he asked, "Are you sure you don't want me to write to your father?"

Lim looked tempted for a moment, but then sighed and nodded. "It's kind of you, but I'm sure."

"All right." Seregei stretched.

"Does it... does it hurt?"

"My leg? It aches sometimes, but that's all right. It's better than it was."

Lim nodded, rubbing absently at his broken hand. Seregei wanted to say something about it, but he didn't think this was really the time. Besides, Lim seemed to have made the connection for himself. Seregei patted him on the shoulder again.

"How's your side?"

"It's better. It doesn't hurt any more except when I move suddenly."

"That's good. I expect you will be able to come back soon."

"I hope so," said Lim forlornly. Then he looked worried again. "I don't mean —"

"I know you appreciate the care you're given here." Seregei squeezed his shoulder. "No-one could think otherwise."

Lim looked back down at the blanket edge.

"I'm afraid I've been sent home," said Seregei softly. "I'll come back and visit you, though, in case you're not tired of my company yet." He smiled.

Lim shook his head. "I appreciate it."

Seregei squeezed his shoulder. "Do you want me to bring you anything from home? From the Guardhouse, I mean."

Lim had glanced at him at the word 'home', a look of mingled hope and fear flashing across his face. It was gone almost at once, though, and he shook his head. "Thank you."

Seregei nodded. "Just let me know if you think of anything."

Lim smiled, but then looked away. "You don't have to…"

"No, but I want to." Seregei settled back in his chair, refraining from asking any of the questions that came to mind. He'd done his best to stay off the subject of Lim's past and his – in Seregei's opinion – twisted view of the world and his place in it. That was not what the younger elf needed when he was trying to heal.

He pushed himself up with a sigh. "I should go," he said, once he had his balance. "A friend is taking me back to the Guardhouse. I may not be able to get back tomorrow, but if not I will come the next day."

Lim smiled, looking wistful. "I'll see you then."

"Get some rest and get better. Hopefully you'll be able to join me soon."

Lim nodded and waved a little as Seregei left.

A week after Seregei had returned home, Arani thought Lim was almost ready to join him. The young elf was obviously keen to go, after all, and he was getting stronger. However, he still needed someone to take care of him and Seregei couldn't even walk. Arani was not looking forward to explaining this to Lim; he always looked pitiful.

He knocked on the door before going in, and smiled at Lim.

Lim smiled back. "Good morning," he said softly, sitting up.

"How do you feel?"

"Better. Thank you."

Arani put down the teapot and mug he'd brought. "Can I see your side?"

Lim hesitated before nodding slowly. Unlike most of Arani's patients, even time hadn't made Lim more inclined to submit to treatment.

"I need to see it."

Lim nodded again and sat up a little straighter to let Arani unwrap the bandage around his waist. The wound was closing, but it still looked red and angry. Lim tensed as Arani touched him.

"Let me know if I'm hurting you."

Lim nodded. "Is it any better?" he asked.

"A little. You want to go back, don't you?"

Lim bit his lip. "You've been very kind, I don't mean to say otherwise, but…"

"It's all right – no-one wants to stay in the healing wing any longer than they have to." Arani replaced the bandage with a fresh one. "It is healing well, but you're not ready to go home yet."

Lim sighed, his lower lip jutting a little.

"You still need someone to look after you, and Seregei can't do it."

"But…" Lim caught himself and nodded. "I shouldn't impose on him when he's already hurt," he said sadly.

"Why are you so keen to go back? Wanting to get home is one thing, but… I don't think that's what it is for you." Arani finished tying off the bandage and laid a hand on Lim's head to feel his temperature.

Lim watched his movements, but then looked away, starting to bite one fingertip. "It's not home, but… it's more… more like it."

"You must feel a bit at home there?" Arani poured him a cup of tea. "Here. It's camomile; it'll make you feel better."

Lim accepted the cup with thanks.

"I've known Seregei for years. I'm sure he's doing his best."

"So am I," said Lim quickly, "But…" He looked away again. "I don't make things easier for him."

"What do you mean? He seems to me to be generally pleased with you."

Lim blinked.

"He's told me that you're an excellent trainee."

"If I weren't so bad," said Lim with a resigned sigh.

"If he could persuade you to trust him," said Arani as if he'd not spoken. "For my part…" He sighed, looking at Lim and trying to decide how far he could push this. "I think it's because you're so unhappy with it."

"I'm *not* unhappy," insisted Lim.

"Tell me: if I said that you could stay here in Duamelti, safe from whoever was hounding you, doing some other work – as an apprentice healer, for example – would you still want to stay at the Guardhouse?"

Lim hesitated, then said, "But… I like Seregei."

Arani was startled at that. "You seem to be scared of him," he said bluntly, raising an eyebrow.

"He gives me choices and…" Lim looked away. "I know he'll not hurt me."

That was probably a lie, but Arani knew better than to push it. "Why, then? Why do you seem scared? You were afraid of the very thought of him when you first came here, after you woke up."

Lim sniffed and said in a small voice, "I thought he'd be angry with me. I didn't want him to be angry."

Arani had tried to persuade Lim that his eventual collapse was not his fault, and knew it was hopeless. The young elf remained convinced that it was a sign of weakness and worthlessness that made him unfit to be a Swordmaster.

Lim sniffed again. "I don't want to disappoint him any more. I just… I didn't think… I was wrong, but I thought I was doing the right thing by not telling him. I thought it was more important to get him home, and he didn't need to be worrying about me too."

Arani sighed. "He's told you this, I know, and I know you're aware of it: you did the wrong thing. Do you understand why?"

"I could have got him killed."

"You could have died."

Lim nodded, tears starting to well in his eyes. "I didn't really think about that."

"Self-sacrifice can be noble, but only as a last resort. Your life is valuable. Don't throw it away."

Lim sighed. "I suppose… I didn't realise it might kill me. It hurt, but…" He fell silent.

Arani patted his hand. "I understand that."

Lim shot him a grateful look. "I couldn't really think about what I was doing after a while."

"That'll be the results of the fever."

Lim nodded. "And it hurt."

Arani smiled. "And now it's healing. You'll be fine in a little while, and then you can go home."

Lim sighed, but nodded. "Thank you," he said again.

Seregei was tempted to try walking without crutches. It had only been two weeks since the flood, but he was already thoroughly tired of the sight of them. His leg was wasting away and he felt ready to start building its strength again, other than by the exercises the healers had told him to do. He knew he couldn't do that, even though it no longer hurt as much. Not until the healers had given him permission. He was still afraid that the break wouldn't heal cleanly and he'd end up with one leg shorter than the other.

He was halfway through stretching out his leg muscles when someone knocked at the door. He had to admit he was grateful for the interruption.

"Coming!" he called, fumbling for the crutches. It took an embarrassing length of time before he was able to open the door, but he smiled at the elf standing outside.

"Sorry to disturb you, Captain Seregei," said the elf quickly. "We need an arbitrator…"

"What's the dispute?"

"Our neighbour claims that my father has been moving the boundary stones."

Seregei nodded. "Is it far?"

The elf shot a look at the crutches. "I can go back and fetch a pony…"

Seregei sighed. Not only was it annoying that he'd have to ride, but he couldn't help his continuing worry about Menel; he was starting to suspect that he was never going to know what had happened to her. "It might be best," he said, bringing himself back to the present, "if only for speed."

The elf nodded. "I'll be back soon," he said, and hurried off before Seregei could say anything else. Seregei watched him go, then shook his head a little and hopped back inside. He would have to change into slightly more presentable clothes, if he was to play the part of judge.

Now that summer was coming on, the weather had turned warm and dry and he had been wearing shorts, but that couldn't be helped; none of his trousers would go over the splint still strapped to his leg. He sighed as he looked at it. He couldn't wait to be rid of it.

"Not too much longer," he muttered to himself. "And the more careful you are, the better it will heal." He put on sandals and a clean shirt and tunic, then went back out to await the elf's return.

Apparently it wasn't too far; the young elf soon arrived, leading a sturdy pony, rather smaller than Seregei had anticipated. Seregei hid a grimace. It was humiliating to have to be carried everywhere he went, but he sighed and got up. It really couldn't be helped, and at least it was better than having to ride on a litter.

There was only one problem that he could see. "Will he bear my weight?"

The elf's face fell as he looked from Seregei – heavy-set and tall – to his pony – also heavy, but a pony nonetheless. Seregei smiled a little. "It evidently isn't far; you came back too quickly. I'll go as far as I can on crutches, and then we'll see."

***

He made it all the way to the field where the dispute was taking place, but Seregei didn't think he'd ever been so sore. He did what he could to hide the fact, but gratefully accepted a chair when it was offered.

"Right," he said, once he was comfortable. "Let's begin."

First, the two elves involved in the dispute – Sarin accusing and Lomel defending – made their arguments. Seregei didn't think that this was entirely about the moving of boundary stones, given the dirty looks they gave one another and the occasional references to each other's manners and ability to plough a straight line. Still, he didn't say anything, letting them get the whole thing off their chests.

At last, they were finished and stood glaring at one another. Seregei hid a smile.

"Has the field been measured?" he asked.

"They're oddly-shaped, sir," said Lomel. "Measuring either side doesn't mean anything for the boundary line." He shot Sarin a nasty look.

Sarin scowled back. "That made it easier, right?"

"Aye, for you to miss –"

"That's enough," said Seregei before any more insults could be exchanged. He had the impression that Sarin was bad at ploughing into corners and tended to leave the fallow areas to grow creeping weeds.

The two elves fell silent, though they continued to glare.

Seregei sighed. "Where's the field? I'll have a look at the boundary myself." He groped for his crutches.

"Would you like help, sir?" asked Sarin, looking stricken as he looked at Seregei's splinted leg.

"How far is it?"

"Not far."

"I'll hop, then." Seregei smiled to cover the twinge that went though his back as he settled the crutches back under his arms.

Indeed, it wasn't far to the disputed boundary, and Seregei looked carefully up and down the grassy line between the two fields. Boulders had been placed at intervals to make it clearer. It didn't look like they'd been touched for centuries

"What stones do you say Lomel moved, Sarin?" he asked, sitting down again; someone had brought the chair.

"These ones," said Sarin, pointing to the two nearest.

"I never *touched* them. I can just plough closer to them than he can."

"He's been edging them sideways for *years*. Every season..." Sarin held up his hands and moved one an inch away from the other. "Just a little bit. That's why the grass doesn't show it."

"Then how do you know?"

Sarin pointed at an elf-woman who was waiting shyly at the back of the group. "Alassei saw him the night before last."

Lomel made an angry noise. "Alassei, you liar!"

The woman shifted nervously on her feet. "I..."

Seregei sighed a little, then gestured to her to come forward. "Would you prefer to tell the story in private, Alassei?" he asked, seeing the nervous looks she was shooting at both Lomel and Sarin.

She nodded.

"Is there anywhere handy where we can talk?" he asked those around them.

"You can use my house," said another elf.

Seregei thanked him and asked him to lead the way.

Once there, he sat down again with a sigh – he wondered absently if he could find somewhere here to fall over until he felt better – and smiled at Alassei.

"Right," he said. "Why don't you tell me what you saw?"

She wrung her hands awkwardly. "Well, it was dark – there wasn't much moon – but I'm sure I saw Lomel messing with one of the boundary stones."

"Could you tell what he was doing?"

"I thought he was rolling it a little."

"But you're not sure?"

She shook her head.

"Why did you tell Sarin you'd seen him moving the stone? It's a serious accusation."

"I know, but he was so convinced someone had moved it and I only said I thought I'd seen someone there, and he kept on at me so…" her voice caught a little and she rubbed her eyes.

Seregei sighed. "Do you know if anyone else saw Lomel by that stone?"

"No, I don't."

"You're sure it was him?"

She nodded. "I'm sure."

"Right. I think I'd better speak to him." Seregei smiled a little. "Thanks."

She nodded and left. Seregei leaned down with a sigh to rub carefully at his leg, wondering if he'd have to get up and find Lomel or if he could stay sitting down and give his muscles a rest.

"Captain? Are you all right?"

He looked up and sighed in relief as he saw Lomel standing in the doorway.

"Alassei said you wanted to talk to me," he said, throwing a glance back out of the door as he said her name.

Seregei nodded, sitting up. "Were you doing something to that stone?"

He shook his head. "I think I know what you're talking about, though. You remember I said Sarin let weeds grow along the boundary and they were seeding into my field?"

Seregei nodded.

"I went out the night before last to try and clear some."

"Why in the middle of the night?"

Lomel scratched his head absently. "It had slipped my mind earlier – I had a lot to do – and I wanted to get it done before morning, so I thought there was *just* enough moon…"

Seregei nodded. "Did you manage to get the boundary clear?"

"Far enough back, anyway."

"Is there anyone I can talk to who would have noticed the difference?"

After talking to about a dozen more elves, Seregei was pretty certain he could see what had happened. No-one else from the settlement seemed to think that Lomel was likely to have moved the boundary stones. While normally good people, Lomel and Sarin had apparently been rivals since childhood and their neighbours thought that this was just an especially nasty manifestation of an old quarrel. He also spoke privately to Sarin, who was absolutely adamant about his claims, and when pressed on the matter became slightly hysterical.

At last, he left the house to talk to the gathered elves. "I've made my decision," he announced. The muttering and whispering fell silent. Seregei shifted a little, trying to ignore the itch in his leg. "I don't believe that Lomel has been moving boundary stones. There seems to have been a misunderstanding over what Alassei saw." He looked over at Sarin. "Don't pressure other elves to give false evidence."

Sarin looked about to protest, but Seregei cut him off.

"*Both* of you need to calm down and stop letting an old rivalry get out of control like this. The claim is dismissed."

Sarin looked upset, but nodded. Lomel sighed in relief and smiled as his son gave him a hug. The two elves glared at each other for a moment, then shook hands. Seregei sighed in relief, shifting slightly to ease his shoulders.

"I've got a larger horse," said Alassei, eyeing his crutches. "Would you prefer to ride back?"

Seregei smiled gratefully. "If it's large enough for me to ride, I would appreciate it."

Mounting was not easy, but Seregei eventually managed to scramble onto the heavy plough-horse and pretended to be dignified. It was a credit to them that none of the elves who had gathered to see him off cracked a smile.

"Ready, Captain Seregei?" asked Alassei's brother, who was leading the horse.

Seregei nodded, grinning. "Let's go," he said.

The ride back was much more comfortable than the walk there, as well as being much faster. It was also easier to dismount than to mount, and Seregei managed not to fall as he landed on one foot.

"Thanks," he said as Alassei's brother handed him his crutches.

"Thank you for coming," the elf said with a warm smile, then nodded past him towards the Guardhouse and led the horse away.

Seregei glanced over his shoulder and grinned as he saw Lim hovering in the doorway. He looked pale and was leaning on the doorframe, his hand near his mouth, but standing was an improvement.

"Hello," said Seregei, going over. "When did you get back?"

Lim lowered the hand quickly. "Just a little while ago."

"Sorry I wasn't here to welcome you; I was called away."

Lim nodded. "I should have sent more warning..."

"Not at all." Seregei grinned. "Come in and sit down. It's good to have you back."

Lim smiled a little. "It's good to be back," he said as he quickly made way for Seregei to go in. "I much prefer it here." He added, "They were very good to me, but..."

Seregei nodded. "As I say, no-one likes to be stuck in the healing house."

"Shall I take the crutches?" asked Lim as Seregei sat down.

"No, no. I prefer to keep them with me. You sit down."

Lim nodded, settling gratefully on a couch.

"How are you?" asked Seregei.

"Much better, thank you."

"You look it. You're still pale, but you seem much stronger." Seregei smiled. "Take it easy for a while longer, and I'll be doing the same. I expect you'll be back to full strength before I am, but you'll just have to wait for me."

Lim shifted uncomfortably. "I'll do what I can to help."

"Likewise." Seregei grinned at him. "Seriously, though, how do you feel?"

Lim looked at him for a moment, but then nodded. "I do feel better. My side hurts less, and I feel stronger." He smiled a little. "It's good to be able to walk again. Sorry," he added, looking at Seregei's leg.

"Oh, I'm sure I'll be saying the same thing in a few weeks." Seregei shifted, trying to ease the ache in his back. "I'll be glad to be off the crutches. Have you ever had to go on them?"

Lim nodded. "Once. I'd sprained my ankle. I tripped."

Seregei winced in sympathy. "That's always painful."

Lim nodded again. "A broken leg is worse, though," he said softly.

"It lasts longer, that's all." Seregei shifted again. "We'll take it easy for a while, so you can keep resting."

"Thank you."

Seregei nodded. It made sense in another way: so far he'd mostly been concentrating on the more practical aspects of being a Swordmaster: fighting, survival and so forth. Now was a good opportunity to teach their more ceremonial roles. "There are things we can do that don't involve too much activity. For example, what I was called away for: I was being a judge in a land dispute."

Lim looked a little surprised and Seregei smiled.

"Sometimes we do get called to handle problems among the mixed-bloods in Duamelti or among the clans just outside. Occasionally further afield, but that tends to only be when something really serious happens: inter-clan disputes, for example. Smaller things are handled by the thanes."

Lim nodded.

"How much do you know about the Mixed-blood clans in and around Silvren?"

"Very little, I'm afraid. I've seen representatives once or twice when they come to court, but they tend to keep to themselves."

"How about the Wild Elves?"

"I've seen them…" Lim shifted in his seat.

"That's rare enough. Even I don't have much say over them."

Lim looked like he was about to say something, but stopped.

"Go on."

"I... thought you were the lord of all Mixed-bloods? High Thane, I think you said?"

"I am, as Swordmaster captain, but the Wild Elves don't recognise any thane."

Lim fidgeted. "I'm a pure-blooded Wood-elf. Would... anyone mind if I were to end up as captain?" He raised his hands. "I don't think it'll happen, but..."

"Why don't you think it'll happen?" Seregei asked softly.

Lim blinked. "You're so much stronger than me, and so much better trained, and..."

"And none of that makes me immortal," said Seregei softly, remembering with an inward shudder how the Swordmasters before him had died.

Lim shifted, pressing a hand absently to his side.

Seregei sighed. "I was trained as one of five Swordmasters. All four above me were killed in one incident. Don't fool yourself into thinking it can't happen." He chuckled bitterly, thinking back over the lonely intervening years. "Caleb was right. I did need to find a trainee."

"You... weren't happy with me, though."

"I thought foisting you off on me without so much as a by-your-leave was rude and something he had no right to do, but that wasn't *your* fault."

Lim looked at the floor, fidgeting.

"Is that why you've been so keen to prove yourself?" Seregei guessed.

Lim shook his head quickly, then caught himself, looking unsure what to say. "I wanted to try hard and... make you proud of me," he said, his voice dropping to a mumble at the end.

Seregei nodded. "You've done a good job so far." He moved forward a little on his seat. "Now let's see how you do after some lectures."

Lim actually smiled and leaned forward to listen.

***

Some weeks after Lim had been released from the healing house, he seemed to be fully healed and recovered. His strength had returned and he was able to use his bow, run and climb trees again. He also seemed in better spirits, though he was still nervous and very eager to please. Seregei had to admit he appreciated having someone around who was happy to help him as his leg healed. He was still on one crutch, but his leg would take some weight and he had Arani's permission to start exercising it again on increasingly long walks. Lim accompanied him, both for the company and so that Seregei could continue to talk to him and point out landmarks as they went.

"Do you remember that training exercise we did a bit before the flood?" asked Seregei as they walked. "The one where you had to track me?"

Lim nodded. "I remember."

Seregei sat down carefully on a stump by the path. "How much do you know about hiding your tracks?"

Lim shifted awkwardly on his feet. "Not very much," he said, looking at the floor.

"Well, I want you to try it. Do things that make sense and I'll come after you and see how you do."

Lim didn't look too sure, but nodded. "How far should I go?"

"No more than a mile." Seregei patted his crutch. "I can only go so far on this thing. Perhaps loop round to meet me back here. You should know the land well enough to do that by now."

Lim nodded and dithered a moment longer.

"Go on," said Seregei, waving at him, and he hurried off.

Lim walked down a path between the fields for a while, looking for a good place to turn off it. He was mindful of Seregei's crutch as well as the need to hide his tracks, so he'd have to keep off soft ground. Fortunately, the weather had turned fairly dry.

He wondered if it would be cheating to just stay on paths; surely it would be hard to see his footprints among the many already there. He didn't think there were any routes back to where he'd left Seregei that were less than a mile long and only on paths, though. He'd have to take a short cut at some point, and he looked around. The fields on either side were full of standing wheat and he didn't want to risk causing any damage, so he couldn't leave the path until it reached the forest.

He paused and bit his lip, looking around. He wanted to do well. This was the first serious exercise Seregei had sent him on since the flood, and he didn't want to disappoint him again.

He began walking again, still looking about hopefully. He reckoned he'd gone less than half a mile, so he'd be able to make it to the woods. He could try to hide his tracks more thoroughly there.

His tracks weren't clearly visible on the path, at least. He smiled a little, daring to feel proud. It really would be cheating to stay on the path, though, even putting distance aside. That wasn't the point. He felt guilty for being pleased with himself and hurried on, his head down.

Once he was into the forest, he paused again to look around. The trees were mostly oaks, with a few beeches, and the ground was covered with years' worth of fallen leaves, long since dry. He tried to think of some way to walk on them without leaving a trail, but he couldn't see anything. He started to pick his way across with a sigh, heading for a stream that he could follow back towards the road where he'd left Seregei.

Despite his attempts to step lightly, the leaves crunched faintly under his feet as he walked. He winced every time. When he looked back, he could clearly see the scuffs in the leaves, showing where he'd put his feet, and he stopped, wondering if there was anything he could do to hide them. He reached down and brushed the leaves about a bit to try to disguise the marks, but that just made it worse and he shook his head. He'd just have to keep stepping carefully.

Finally, he was out of the forest and faced with the path back up the reedy banks of the stream. Looking at it more closely, this was going to be harder than he'd originally thought. There wasn't another route that would keep him within a mile, though, unless he retraced his steps. He had to go up the stream.

By the time he'd made it back almost to the road, he was muddy, tired and convinced that he'd made an absolute hash of the whole exercise. Dispirited, he returned to where he had left Seregei. Hopefully he'd not be too disappointed.

Seregei was deep in conversation with a passing elf-woman when Lim arrived, and he hung back to wait until they were finished. He could catch words now and then and made out that she was asking him for some advice about an arrangement with elves outside Duamelti. He blinked. While he knew Seregei had influence with the Mixed-bloods outside the valley, it still felt odd to have it confirmed.

He couldn't help a moment's comparison to his father, who was so well-respected and influential in Silvren. The thought made him feel homesick again and he hugged himself, looking at the ground. What he had told Arani was true: he did like Seregei. Just as with his father, though, he knew he could never live up to his example. He was trying as hard as he could, but he knew it could never be enough.

There was one thing, though: Seregei wouldn't be angry with him. He'd shown that after the flood: no matter how stupidly Lim acted, Seregei hadn't been truly angry. He'd never done anything to punish him except with disappointment. That hadn't been enjoyable, but it wasn't so bad.

Up ahead, Seregei bade farewell to the woman and smiled at Lim, waving him over.

"You've finished?" he asked.

Lim nodded. "I hope it's all right."

Seregei gestured at Lim's muddy legs. "You look like you've given me an interesting trail to follow."

Lim's heart fell a little further as he remembered the muddy stream banks. "I'm sorry," he said quickly. "I didn't know where else to go that wouldn't be trampling on anything and wouldn't go too far…"

Seregei got up. "Don't worry, I'll do my best. If the worst comes to the worst, we'll just turn round and come back the way we came." He smiled. "Walk with me, and we'll discuss what you did as we go."

As they walked, Lim did his best not to give Seregei any hints about where he'd gone; the older elf didn't need the help. He hung back, watching as Seregei went down the path between the fields.

As they went, he couldn't help noticing that Seregei seemed to be paying more attention to the sides of the path than the path itself. "Seregei?"

"Hmm?" Seregei paused and turned.

Lim knitted his fingers together. "What are you doing?"

"Ah, yes" – Seregei ran a hand through his hair – "I should be explaining to you as I go." He pointed at the ground. "I'm not reliably going to be able to see your footprints on this ground, especially as I can't crouch to look closely. However, I would be able to see marks if you left the path, so I'm looking for that instead." He smiled. "It's a useful short cut, if you know what path someone started on."

Lim nodded, glad that taking the path didn't seem to have entirely been a cheat.

In the forest, Seregei was indeed able to follow the marks Lim had left on the leaves without too much trouble, and he paused when he came to the point where Lim had tried to disguise his tracks.

"It's best for you not to do this," he said. "You cause more disturbance that way. It's a fair mistake, though."

Lim nodded, despite his private disappointment.

Seregei tilted his head to the side, looking at him carefully. "There's no need to look so upset. You're only learning."

"I know, but..." Lim sighed. "I... wanted to do well."

Seregei smiled again. "That's a good thing, but there's no need to feel crushed if you don't do well the first time." He reached out and patted Lim on the shoulder. "I'm not disappointed."

That was a great relief to hear, but Lim just nodded and watched as Seregei set off again.

At the stream, Seregei stopped, frowning at the obvious path through the reeds and the two or three visible footprints in the mud. Lim felt like he was an inch tall as he looked from Seregei's face to the trail he'd left.

"Well, I'm not taking a crutch into that," Seregei said at last.

"I'm so sorry," blurted Lim. "I just couldn't think of a better way, and I didn't realise it would be so muddy..."

"If there are reeds like that growing, it's going to be muddy." Seregei shot Lim a curious look. "Don't you have fen in Silvren?"

Lim shook his head. He was pretty sure Seregei was disappointed now, but didn't say anything.

Seregei sighed and turned to go back the way they'd come without another word.

"I'm sorry," said Lim, going after him. He felt thoroughly embarrassed.

"If you don't have anything like that in Silvren, you weren't to know what it looks like," said Seregei, turning with a smile. "You'll know better next time, won't you?"

Lim nodded. "I'll try."

"That's all I ask." Seregei started to walk again with a sigh. "I will be *so* glad not to have to limp on this crutch any more."

Lim nodded, flexing his left hand absently.

"I think we'd better go back to the Guardhouse," Seregei continued thoughtfully. "I know I'm getting tired. How's your side?"

Lim blinked. "Better. It doesn't hurt as much unless… unless I move suddenly, or twist." Or use his bow.

"That's good." Seregei glanced sideways at him. "Something still bothering you?"

Lim nodded, resigned to the fact that Seregei seemed so able to read him. "It also hurts when I practice archery."

Seregei nodded. "There is a twist to the stance. I'm sure it'll pass as you heal. In the meantime, just go easy on yourself." He paused to pat Lim on the shoulder again, his movements slow and gentle. "No point straining it and stopping it healing."

Lim nodded. "Thanks."

Seregei grinned as he started to walk again. "Don't worry. Come on, let's get home."

Lim nodded and followed.

A couple of weeks later, the weather had turned very hot. A couple of months had passed since the flood and Seregei was finally off his crutches. He was going through drills on the grass outside the Guardhouse while Lim was away practicing his archery. Seregei knew he was out of condition, and he couldn't deny that he was getting uncomfortably hot. He sat down for a moment and took a drink of water, sighing. It was not good weather to wear a long-sleeved shirt, but he didn't really have a choice; he didn't want anyone to see his scars.

On the other hand, he wasn't expecting visitors, and Lim would probably be away practicing for a good while longer. He didn't like taking his shirt off outside, but… it would be considerably more comfortable. He'd finish his drills – they were shorter than usual in any case – and it would be fine.

Before he could change his mind, he pulled the shirt off and picked up his sword again, doing his best not to look at the scars. He went back to his practice, trying to concentrate on keeping good form, counting to himself as he moved his sword from one position to the next.

He was just starting to lose himself in his practice when he heard a half-stifled squeak from behind him. He swung round and saw Lim standing just at the entrance to the path that led down to the butts. He was staring at Seregei, one hand over his mouth, his eyes wide with shock.

For a moment, Seregei looked down at himself, seeing the scars as if with fresh eyes: some huge and jagged-edged, some carved into patterns, some more like brands than wounds. Without a word, he went over to the bench, picked up his shirt and put it back on. Then he turned to face Lim again.

Lim was still staring at him, chewing his finger.

"You're back early," said Seregei, more to break the silence than anything else.

"I'm sorry," said Lim, looking away. "My side was hurting, so I thought I should stop."

Seregei smiled. "That was sensible of you."

"But..." Lim's glance went back to Seregei.

"Really, it's fine." Seregei sheathed his sword with a sigh. "I should have..." Should have what? Warned Lim about the scars? Left his shirt on?

The awkward silence stretched as they both went indoors and put away their weapons, then went and sat in the common room on either side of a narrow table. Seregei started oiling his boots. Lim pretended to work on making a bowstring, but spent most of the time biting his nails. Seregei could tell he wanted to ask, but decided not to prompt him. If he was curious enough, he'd speak.

He'd finished the first boot when Lim finally broke the silence.

"How did it happen?"

Seregei glanced up. "The scars?"

Lim nodded.

Seregei sighed. In his head, he was at peace with the memory. At least, that part of it. There were other things he'd never come to terms with, but the thought of his scars no longer truly upset him. Despite that, he didn't want to tell the story. He didn't want to get himself upset in front of Lim, and he knew that if he tried to explain it would take him back...

Still, Lim needed to know sometime. Not only had the scars clearly upset him, but... Seregei remembered their conversation about Lim being less experienced and so more likely to die. Death under torture was something that any Swordmaster might face. At some point, Lim would have to know the truth. He needed and deserved that.

"S-Seregei?" Lim looked worried. "I'm sorry. It's not my business."

Seregei shook his head. "It is, but..." His eyes fell on Lim's broken hand and he remembered that he wasn't the only one with a painful secret. Though he'd never brought it up, that hand still unsettled him. He pointed to it. "I'll tell you the story when you tell me what really happened to your hand."

Lim instantly withdrew it, clutching it against his chest. "I shut it in a door," he said quickly, his expression guarded.

Seregei was sure that was a lie, and shook his head. "How did you get the scar, then? And why aren't the breaks in a straight line?"

Lim looked down at his hand. "It was an accident," he mumbled.

"What happened?"

Lim shook his head.

"Was it crushed under something?"

Lim glanced up, biting his lip, then looked down again. "It was an accident," he said again, a little more loudly. "He didn't mean to –" Then he fell silent, just glancing up for a moment.

"Someone crushed it?"

"He didn't mean to hurt me."

"So what happened?"

Lim pulled his broken hand a little closer against his chest, tears starting in his eyes. "I can't say."

Seregei's instinct was to stop pressing him, but he felt he was on the scent of something important. He wasn't sure what to ask, though. He sighed and reached across to pat Lim gently on the shoulder.

Lim licked his lips awkwardly. "It was my fault."

Seregei blinked. "I thought it was an accident?"

"He didn't mean to break my fingers."

"If someone crushed your hand... that doesn't sound like your fault."

"I shouldn't have..." Lim fell silent and shifted uncomfortably, looking down. "I shouldn't. You'd not understand and... I don't want anything bad to happen."

Seregei patted Lim on the shoulder again. "Listen," he said, keeping his voice gentle despite his worry. "If you're worried about someone tracking you down here, you don't need to be. I'll keep you safe."

Lim sniffed, wiping his eyes. "I suppose... it doesn't matter anyway. The wor-" He cut himself off again there, glancing furtively at Seregei again.

"The worst is over?"

"I'm grateful you took me in, I don't mean to –"

"No, no, don't worry about that. What's the worst? Having to leave home?"

Lim nodded, sniffling softly. "I shouldn't have run away," he said softly. "I shouldn't have done it. I just needed to try harder..."

Lim had been right about one thing: Seregei didn't understand. "If someone was hurting you, why was it wrong to escape?"

Lim shifted again. "Because it was my fault, and by running I hurt him."

Seregei was starting to get a nasty suspicion, but he didn't say anything.

"I just needed to try harder. He loved me. I didn't deserve it, but he loved me."

"And that's why he *broke your hand*?" asked Seregei before he could stop himself.

Lim nodded.

"Whoever this was" – Seregei didn't want to believe the growing suspicion – "he didn't love you. We don't do things like that to people we love."

"He did," said Lim stubbornly, despite the tears in his eyes. "I know he did."

Seregei just shook his head. He kept his hand on Lim's shoulder, considering giving him a hug. He resisted the temptation; he knew it wouldn't help.

Lim was crying in earnest now, hunched over and hugging his left hand to his chest. "I shouldn't have done it," he whispered, shaking his head. "It was wrong."

"What makes you think he loved you?"

Lim sniffed, wiped his eyes and said softly, "Fathers love their children."

Seregei stared, frozen for a moment. He'd suspected, but it was still a shock to have it confirmed. It took a while for him to shake it off and move around the table to give Lim a hug.

Lim tensed for a moment, holding his breath, and Seregei drew back. "You all right?"

Lim nodded, turning his shoulder. "Sorry."

"For what?"

"It's not something I should trouble you with."

"*You're* not the troubling one." Seregei frowned. "Your... your *father?*"

Lim looked pathetic. "I shouldn't have provoked him."

"Prov-" Seregei resisted the urge to throw his hands up. "How on *earth* did you provoke him to... potentially *cripple* you?"

Lim looked down at his hand. "I shouldn't have been late," he mumbled. "I know he didn't mean to break my fingers."

"Late?"

"I stayed late at archery practice." Lim looked up again. "He didn't –"

"What did he do?"

Lim shook his head.

Seregei had got over the shock, and managed to control the rising anger. 'Smooth like a river of fire,' he thought. 'Use it.'.

"Was that the first time he hurt you?"

"He was always sorry. He didn't mean it..."

Well, that was an obvious 'no'. Seregei shook his head, once again swallowing the anger.

"Why do you want to have anything more to do with him?"

Lim sniffed. "Why wouldn't I? He's my father."

Seregei just shook his head. He really didn't know how to deal with this. Lim had started to cry again, though, and Seregei hugged him. This time, he didn't pull away.

"You did the right thing by running," said Seregei softly.

"He loves me. I know he does."

"He hurt you."

"I deserved it."

"Not if you acted anything like you act here. Did you?"

Lim sniffed and nodded. "I tried, like I'm trying here, but I was never good enough."

Seregei sighed. "You're good enough for me. You make mistakes, but you're learning."

Lim sniffed again. "I really am trying."

"Good."

Neither of them spoke for a while. Lim kept crying softly despite his attempts to stifle it. Seregei held him, but kept staring at the opposite wall, trying to put the pieces together. He couldn't imagine that the person to hurt and frighten Lim so badly had been his father.

There was one thing he knew he ought to do, though.

"Do you still want to know about the scars?" he asked softly.

Lim sniffed. "You'd tell me?"

Seregei looked down at him. "Fair turnabout. If you still want to know, I'll tell you."

"I... if you don't want to tell me..."

"Lim, I admit that I don't like talking about it, but *if you want to know...*"

Lim shook his head.

"All right. If you change your mind, just ask me." Seregei didn't want to tell the story, but he also didn't want Lim to feel cheated, or as if he couldn't ask. He was glad not to have to explain it at once, though. He didn't want to think about it on top of what he'd just learned.

Lim pulled back. "But if you don't want to talk about it..."

Seregei shook his head. "No-one likes talking about where they got scars, but..." He sighed, looking away. "I should have warned you, and... the way I got them is something you need to know about."

Lim bit his lip, then sniffed and wiped his eyes. "I'll listen," he said softly.

Seregei shook his head. "It doesn't have to be now. You're upset." So was Seregei, however hard he tried to hide it.

Lim shook his head, then hiccupped softly and nodded. "I'm sorry."

"For being upset?"

Lim hiccupped again, and didn't pull away as Seregei hugged him once more.

CHAPTER FOUR

Lim trotted alongside Seregei, his eyes on the ground. He didn't feel happy, though he recognised and appreciated the fact that Seregei was trying to help him feel more comfortable. He still felt dirty inside, traitorous, even though it had been a couple of weeks since he'd told Seregei the truth.

He hugged his left hand against his chest, falling behind a few steps. Seregei glanced round and frowned a little.

"Are you all right?"

Lim nodded. "I just... don't feel well."

Seregei's frown deepened. "You don't have to come to this meeting. If you want, you can go back to the Guardhouse."

Lim was shaking his head before Seregei had finished speaking. "Sorry."

"Not at all." Seregei smiled a little, though it didn't quite reach his eyes. "I admit I'd rather you came; as I said before, I need to start teaching you about other sides of what we do."

Lim sped up again to walk beside him. "What are we doing today?"

"This is actually a fairly routine meeting. I go down often, as you've seen, but we actually plan to talk about the two-yearly ambassador exchanges with Silvren."

"I know of them," said Lim, remembering the Valley-elves that had come to visit Silvren when he had lived there. He'd never spoken to them, but he was aware of it when they were received at court.

Seregei smiled. "I suppose you *were* at Taffileti's court."

Lim nodded, but didn't elaborate. He didn't want to discuss his father any more than he had to. "Lord Taffileti is a good man," he said softly. "And a good king."

"Indeed he is." Seregei shot Lim a sidelong glance, then hesitantly asked, "I suppose it would be a good idea for you not to visit Silvren."

Lim felt slightly sick. He wanted to go back, but he was frightened of the possible consequences if he saw his father again. "Probably not," he whispered.

Seregei patted him gently on the shoulder and, almost to his own surprise, he didn't flinch.

"Seregei?" he asked after a moment's hesitation.

"Yes?"

"Were you... very angry?" Lim paused. He wasn't sure what he was trying to ask about. Seregei was staring curiously at him, though, so he continued, "About my father?"

Seregei sighed heavily, looking ahead. "Yes. Furious. Not with you, but with him."

"But..." Lim fell silent.

Seregei glanced at him. "There's no reason for me to be angry with you."

Lim still couldn't believe it, but he knew better than to argue. He wasn't going to be able to persuade Seregei of anything. After all, he really only had his own instinct to tell him his father loved him.

"Lim?"

Lim startled a little. He'd been lost in his thoughts and hadn't heard what Seregei had said.

"Sorry, I didn't hear you."

Seregei grinned a little. "Head in the sky. Don't worry, it wasn't important."

Lim looked at his feet, resisting the urge to scuff them on the ground. Seregei laughed softly and patted his shoulder again.

"Seregei?"

"Yes?"

"Why..." Lim bit his lip. He shouldn't question it, but he couldn't help wondering. "Why are you so kind to me?"

Seregei frowned at him. "Shouldn't I be?"

"Well... I..." Lim looked at the ground again. "I know I disappoint you."

"Do I have to go over this *again*?" Seregei shook his head a little. "You're learning. You make mistakes, but everyone does." He laughed. "When I was training it took me years to learn how to even make a stew over a fire. Celes used to..." Suddenly, his laughter faded. "Celes used to joke that if it took me much longer... he was going to send me out into the woods to learn or starve."

Lim bit his lip. "I'm sorry; I've upset you."

"No, it's not your fault. I've just... been thinking of them recently. The Swordmasters who taught me, you know."

Lim fidgeted, looking at the ground. He remembered Seregei telling him they'd been killed and didn't want to upset him by asking any more questions. "You really think I could follow you?" he asked at last.

"If I didn't, we'd not be having this conversation."

Though he was still confused, Lim couldn't help but feel pleased with that, and he smiled. Seregei's smile also reappeared.

"Come on," he said. "Or we'll be late."

Lim nodded and lengthened his stride a little to keep up with Seregei.

***

When they reached Caleb's study, he got up to greet them. Lim hung back and watched as the two older elves exchanged pleasantries. He felt out of place and painfully aware of how far below the king he was.

With a shock, he remembered that Seregei and Caleb were effectively the same rank, and Seregei thought him fit to be a Swordmaster. The thought gave him pause. It was difficult to even imagine himself standing there in Seregei's place. He shook his head, dismissing the idea as presumptuous.

"Lim?" Seregei gestured him forwards.

Caleb smiled and reached out a hand. "It's good to see you again, Lim. You look well."

"Thank you, my lord." Lim took the offered hand nervously. Caleb still seemed to tower over him. "As... as do you."

"How have you been getting on?"

"Seregei says I've been doing well."

Seregei nodded in confirmation and Caleb smiled. "Well, sit down. I'll be pleased to tell Taffilelti that."

Lim hesitantly took the seat Caleb pointed out.

"In fact" – Caleb also sat – "you may be able to tell him yourself soon."

Seregei shot Lim a look. "What do you mean?"

"He's planning to come and visit."

Lim felt like he'd been kicked. He startled forward in his seat, his heart suddenly beating in his throat.

Caleb fell silent and looked curiously at him. "Is something wrong?"

"I'm sorry." Lim wished he could sink into the floor. He looked down and fidgeted. "I just..." He barely noticed it when he started to bite his finger.

"Surely you'll be pleased to see Taffilelti?" Seregei didn't seem quite sure.

"Yes, yes of course, but... will he... who..." Lim gulped. "I assume he'll have members of his court with him... as an entourage?" He fought to stay calm and keep his voice casual, but it was a losing battle. If Lord Taffilelti brought his father... Lim didn't even want to consider what might be in store for him.

Seregei laid a hand on his shoulder, making him jump. "Lim, what's wrong?"

Caleb also seemed confused. "I assume he will. Seregei, what…?"

"I'm sorry." Lim had never felt so embarrassed, and he was almost ready to cry at the thought that he'd humiliated Seregei.

"Lim, what's wrong?" Seregei asked again.

Lim wrung his hands. "I'm so sorry, I shouldn't have said anything."

Caleb sounded confused as he said, "I'd have thought you'd be happy to see some familiar faces."

A familiar face was exactly what Lim was afraid to see. He swallowed hard against the tears that were threatening to spill over. He wouldn't tell the story to anyone else and he *certainly* wasn't going to embarrass Seregei any more than he had already.

"Lim." Seregei's tone was gentle. "Perhaps you'd better go outside and calm down a little."

Lim didn't argue, just got up and headed for the door, still fighting back tears. "I'm so sorry," he whispered, glancing over his shoulder.

Seregei was frowning, but he shook his head. "I'm sure there's a perfectly reasonable explanation. Come back in when you're ready."

Lim nodded and left. As he closed the door, he heard Caleb ask, "What in the –"

With those words ringing in his ears, he sat down on a bench in the antechamber and buried his face in his hands.

"Lim?" asked Ekehart, sounding startled. Lim looked up. He'd forgotten that Caleb's honour guard was waiting just outside the study.

"I'm fine," he said, swallowing hard. "Just… I'll be fine."

Ekehart frowned, but nodded and Lim hid his face again, trying to control himself as he waited.

"What in the world was that about?" Caleb asked as Lim left.

Seregei looked round; he'd been staring at the door. "I… don't know."

Caleb frowned a little. "You really have no idea?"

Seregei did have some idea, thinking back to what he'd learned about Lim's father. He'd not said anything to Caleb about it; it was Lim's business and he wasn't going to spread it around. Nonetheless, that little scene needed to be explained.

"Seregei?"

"You remember… I told you I thought someone had attacked Lim in Silvren?"

"Yes."

"It's true. And I think…" He glanced round again. "I think he's afraid that person will be with Taffilelti."

Caleb shrugged and shuffled through some papers, finally finding the one he wanted. "He's not bringing his whole court. Some guards and clerks, and his chief advisor."

Seregei sighed. "He clearly knew what was happening to Lim or he'd not have sent him here. I'd not have thought he would bring the person responsible for it with him."

Caleb was still frowning a little, looking down at the letter in his hand. "I've not told him much about Lim, or where he is."

Seregei shifted forwards in his seat, surprised at that. "I thought you were sending him news," he said softly, not angry yet, but aware that he soon might be. "I asked you to send him word of how Lim was doing... so he could pass it back to... his father."

Caleb nodded. "I know, and a couple of times I did, but he never said anything about Lim in his responses, so I stopped. I tried to make sure I knew about his progress, especially when visitors from Silvren came who might ask or if I was sending a messenger and Taffilelti might ask him, but..." He shrugged. "I've not told him much recently."

"So he might have no idea that someone in his entourage might meet Lim?"

"Perhaps. As far as I know, he never actually *has* asked for information."

Seregei sighed. "Well, I'd hope that he'd not bring them anyway. I'll talk to Lim, though; this is just speculation." Well-founded, but speculation nonetheless.

Caleb nodded. "I hope he feels better soon, but it's time we moved on to other matters."

Seregei ran a hand through his hair and nodded. "Yes, let's."

***

When Seregei left Caleb's study, Lim was sitting outside, his head in his hands. Seregei looked at him for a long moment, wondering what he was thinking. He certainly didn't seem to have noticed Seregei's presence. A noise beside him made him look round and he saw Ekehart. The Valley-elf gestured at Lim, raising an eyebrow.

"He's been like this the whole time?" asked Seregei softly.

"Aye. What happened? If you don't mind my asking, of course."

"Something upset him." Seregei took a step towards Lim and called his name.

Lim startled up, wide-eyed. "Sorry," he said, looking away. "I didn't realise you were there."

Seregei smiled, though his heart wasn't in it. "Head in the sky," he said softly.

Lim looked down and didn't say anything.

"Come on," said Seregei. "Let's get back."

Lim nodded and walked beside him in silence as they left the palace. Seregei nodded to a few people he knew on the way, but Lim didn't look up and Seregei was painfully aware of the curious glances he was attracting. He didn't want to question Lim in front of everyone, though.

At last, they were out of the city and Seregei purposefully took a less-used path. Lim stayed close beside him with only a moment's glance down the road they would normally have taken.

"Right," said Seregei, after a few minutes. "What was that about?"

"I'm so sorry, I didn't mean to embarrass you –" Lim started.

"I can tell you're sorry just from looking at you. I want an explanation, not an apology." Seregei knew his tone was harsh and regretted it when he saw Lim flinch, but that behaviour had been a shock.

Lim made as if to bite a finger, but said, "I'm... worried about who he'll be bringing."

Seregei frowned. "You think he might bring your father?"

Lim nodded.

"Why would he? He... knows what was happening, doesn't he? That's why he sent you away."

Lim nodded again. "But... Father is an important member of the court."

Seregei looked hard at him, but he didn't say anything else. "You're certain he'd come?"

"Yes..." Lim shuffled his feet. "I am sorry I reacted like that..."

"Don't worry about that. I'd rather you didn't do it again, but now I know why you were frightened." It wasn't as though any of them could have seen the news coming.

Lim smiled tentatively, then looked down at the floor. "I... I'm sorry, but... is there any way I could... avoid him?"

Seregei frowned, wondering. "I'm not sure."

"All right," said Lim quickly. "I don't mean to be difficult."

Seregei shook his head, thinking of the scene Lim had just made. "I don't want a repeat of what just happened in front of Taffileti and his court."

Lim bit his lip, looking down. "I won't do it again," he said, barely above a whisper.

Seregei didn't believe that. He'd seen enough of instant fear to know that Lim wouldn't be able to just hide a reaction like that one.

Lim shifted again. "He'll have been so upset I left. I..." He shook his head hard. "I ought to be there to greet him."

"You were sent away for a reason, Lim."

"He won't do it again." Lim looked up, teary-eyed. "He won't. He's always sorry."

"You don't believe that." If he did, he'd not have been so frightened. Seregei wondered how easy it would be to keep Lim out of the way during the visit.

Lim hadn't replied. He looked on the verge of crying again.

There wasn't much Seregei could say at this point, and he just started walking again. Lim followed silently. They were almost home before either of them spoke again.

"You're really not angry with me?" Lim asked softly.

Seregei sighed, wondering how to phrase what he was thinking. "I'm not angry, no," he said. "You didn't mean to cause trouble, you were just frightened. I wish it hadn't happened, though."

Lim sighed. "I'm sorry. I always disappoint you."

"I was... a little disappointed," Seregei admitted. "But I was mostly surprised. And somewhat embarrassed." Lim's steps faltered, and Seregei quickly said, "Don't apologise."

Lim faltered again and Seregei turned to look at him. He looked very uncomfortable, biting his lip miserably. Seregei sighed.

"Look, if you really don't think you can handle seeing Taffilelti or any member of his entourage, we'll think of something. You have to *tell* me, though."

Lim nodded. "I don't want to disappoint you," he said softly. "Not after all you've done for me."

Seregei nodded a little. "It'll be a few weeks, in any case. Late summer. Unless you tell me otherwise, I'm going to assume you'll be all right."

Lim forced a smile and Seregei sighed, reaching out to pat him on the shoulder.

"You can trust me, you know. Just tell me what you think you can manage, all right?"

"All right."

***

Seregei didn't think that Lim was at all comfortable, but he hadn't said anything in the intervening weeks. In fact, as they stood in the courtyard outside Caleb's palace, waiting to welcome Taffilelti and his entourage, Lim seemed to be putting a lot of effort into staying still and calm. Seregei had to admire his nerve, even as he inwardly shook his head. Still, if he could manage it, it would be for the best. Hopefully his father wouldn't be in the group.

They could hear hoofbeats on the road approaching the palace and Seregei felt Lim stiffen slightly. He shifted on his feet and put a hand on Lim's shoulder.

"There are other things I can send you to do," he whispered.

Lim shook his head. "I don't want to embarrass you," he said stubbornly.

Seregei nodded. "Only stay if you're sure you can keep your head."

There was no time to discuss the matter further, as at that point the first of Taffilelti's entourage rounded the corner: a pair of wood-elven guards. Taffilelti himself was a little way behind them, followed closely by an advisor and his honour guard, then more distantly by a dozen other elves:

guards, clerks and grooms.

Seregei still had his hand on Lim's shoulder, and as the group entered the courtyard he felt Lim start to tremble slightly. Taffilelti smiled a greeting at Caleb, then looked over at Seregei and his eyes widened as he saw Lim. His advisor rode up beside him and looked around with mild interest. Seregei noticed Lim's shaking getting worse as that elf looked at them and raised an eyebrow.

"Taffilelti," said Caleb warmly, stepping forward. "It's truly a pleasure to see you again."

"Likewise, Caleb," said Taffilelti. "And Seregei – it's good to see you well."

"And you." Seregei gestured to Lim. "This is Lim, my trainee."

Taffilelti and his advisor both looked at Lim, who bowed.

"No patronym, my Lord?" the advisor asked Taffilelti softly. Taffilelti glanced at him, but didn't otherwise respond. He just smiled at Lim.

"I'm pleased to meet you, Lim."

"And I you, my Lord," said Lim softly, his voice only trembling a little.

Taffilelti smiled again and gestured towards his advisor. "This is Ethiren, my chief advisor."

Ethiren bowed at the waist and Caleb and Seregei both inclined their heads to him in response.

"I'll have your horses taken to the stables," said Caleb. At once, several elves in Caleb's livery hurried out to take the reins of Taffilelti's and Ethiren's horses and position a mounting block for Taffilelti to step onto. He dismounted gracefully onto it and stepped away, patting his horse on the shoulder as he went.

"My own men will help take care of them," he said, gesturing behind him. Now that he had dismounted, there was a flurry of movement among his entourage.

Ethiren had also dismounted and went to stand by Taffilelti, a step or two behind his shoulder. The honour guard was behind them both.

"How is Kerin?" asked Taffilelti. "I would have expected to see him here."

"He takes his duties in the healing houses very seriously. Unfortunately, he couldn't be spared." Caleb half turned to lead the way into the palace. "Come in, Taffilelti, Seregei. I've ordered wine to my sitting room."

"Thank you. After our ride, I would appreciate something to drink."

"Ethiren is welcome to join us, of course," added Caleb.

Taffilelti nodded. "Thank you."

Ethiren just bowed his head.

"As is Lim." Caleb looked over at Seregei and Lim.

Seregei didn't think Lim could keep his composure much longer – he was still shivering – and shook his head a little. "Unfortunately, we have other business that I'd like Lim to handle." He glanced at Lim, who turned to look at him, a flash of almost pathetic gratitude crossing his face. "Would you go and check on those villages I was going to visit? Ask their pardon and say I'll come in person when I can. If you can, find out what exactly they need of me."

Lim nodded. "I will," he said aloud, then whispered, "Thank you," and ran off.

Seregei went over to join the others with a smile. "Sorry about that," he said, looking between them.

"Quite all right," said Caleb. "You two have your responsibilities, after all."

Taffilelti agreed with a slight inclination of his head. Ethiren just continued to watch Seregei measuringly.

Seregei watched him in return as they went through to Caleb's sitting room. He seemed to be aware of everything going on around him, his eyes moving restlessly with a calculating expression that Seregei didn't especially care for. Instinctively, he looked to see if Ethiren was armed and noticed the dagger at his belt, as well as a tell-tale bulge along the leg of one of his riding boots. Still, Taffilelti obviously trusted him; he stayed closer than the Wood-elven honour guard, though Seregei noticed that Ekehart was also keeping an eye on him as they went.

The four of them settled down in armchairs around a table in the sitting room – Ethiren sitting last, at Taffilelti's right hand – and Seregei looked around again.

Before he could speak, though, Caleb broke the silence. "I trust you had a pleasant journey, Taffilelti?"

"Indeed. Even the northern forest is a beautiful sight at this time of year." Taffilelti smiled a little.

"As beautiful as Silvren?" asked Seregei lightly, still watching Ethiren out of the corner of his eye. The Wood-elf ignored him.

"Of course not," said Taffilelti, his smile widening.

"Our season is really autumn," said Caleb, looking absently out of the window. "For all its better features, Silvren never has the same colour."

"I would never trade the birches," said Taffilelti with a small sigh. "You should visit yourself sometime soon."

"Perhaps I will, as a follow-up to this visit."

"The same goes for you, Seregei."

Seregei nodded. "It has been a while, and I should pay a visit to the North Silvren mixed-bloods."

"They've been doing well; our relationship with them has much improved, though there's still nothing to be done with the Wild Elves."

"Nothing to be done?" asked Seregei. He didn't think they needed anything but to be left alone.

"We tried reaching out to them in the same way as the other mixed-bloods, but..." Taffilelti grimaced. "They don't seem inclined to listen to diplomacy."

Seregei nodded. "Next time I'm in the area, I'll see if there's anything I can do."

"I'd appreciate it."

"I warn you, though, even my influence over them is limited."

A servant brought in some wine and Seregei accepted a goblet with thanks. He raised his eyebrows as he saw Ethiren take two and sip from one before handing it to Taffilelti.

Caleb frowned. "Taffilelti, you surely don't think you need your wine tasting in my halls."

Taffilelti smiled. "I'm sorry, Caleb; it's a habit we've developed."

"It was my idea, my lord," said Ethiren softly. "Forgive me if I've caused offence."

Caleb nodded. "As long as you're both aware that it's unnecessary."

"Of course," said Taffilelti, and took a sip of wine himself.

Caleb glanced at Ethiren. "I am curious, though: why would you taste Lord Taffilelti's wine, Ethiren? Surely that's more a job for Reiron?"

Ethiren said softly, "Perhaps, my Lord, but what use would a poisoned honour guard be if there were an attempt on my king's life? That is why I took this duty on myself."

"In any case, said Taffilelti, "Reiron is never present at meetings such as this." Like Ekehart, Reiron had stayed just outside the door of the sitting room.

Taffilelti glanced over to Seregei. "I was interested to see Lim with you."

Seregei smiled. "He's a good trainee; he works hard and is learning fast." He looked hard at Taffilelti as he asked, "Do you know him?"

"I know of him," said Taffilelti with a slight shake of the head. He didn't look at Caleb as he spoke. "He was once a member of my court."

Ethiren moved a little and Seregei glanced at him. He ignored the look and just took a sip of wine. His hand was trembling a little.

Caleb was frowning, but said, "We should leave that to another time."

Taffilelti nodded, and drank again. "This reminds me," he said, raising his goblet a little with a smile, "I brought some papers I'd like you to look over, Caleb."

Caleb laughed. "I think I can guess their subject."

"Not only wine, but that is what reminded me. I believe you also trade with the men of Falwar?"

"Yes – we have done for some years."

"They've been hoping to renegotiate the trading agreement with me, and I wanted to see how the terms compared, if you'd be willing to discuss it?"

Caleb nodded. "I can send for my own records, if you have yours with you?"

"I do." Taffilelti glanced at Ethiren, who set down his goblet.

"I'll go and fetch them, my lords," he said.

"I should go too," said Seregei, "since this doesn't concern me as closely." He glanced at Caleb. "Of course, if the subject changes…"

"I'll let you know," said Caleb with a smile.

Ethiren stepped aside to let Seregei leave first, but caught up to him as they walked down the corridor.

"Captain Seregei?"

Seregei glanced round. "Yes?"

"May I have a word with you about Lim?"

Seregei frowned, wondering what Ethiren might know on the subject. "Of course."

"I'm sorry to be the bearer of bad news – I can see you're fond of him – but…" Ethiren sighed. "He's not a… good boy."

Seregei's frown deepened. "What do you mean?"

"He likes attention and will lie to get it. Especially, I've many times known him claim that someone's hurt him or been cruel to him – other boys, you know – when no such thing has happened." Ethiren looked up at Seregei. "From what I know about the Swordmasters, I doubt you want a liar. I thought someone should tell you."

Lim had hardly been falling over himself to tell what had happened to him. "Well," said Seregei slowly, "thank you for telling me. That's not a habit he's kept up since he came to Duamelti, though. I still stand by what I said: he's been doing extremely well, and I'm proud of him."

Ethiren shook his head a little, but then said, "This is where I leave you. One of Lord Taffilelti's clerks had charge of those documents…" He looked around distractedly.

"Would they normally put them in your quarters?"

"Yes."

"The East wing, then, probably on the ground floor; that's where Taffilelti stayed the last few times he visited."

Ethiren smiled. "Thank you," he said, and started to walk away.

"Master Ethiren?" Seregei called after him.

He looked round.

"How do you know about Lim? I mean, I can see how you'd know him at all, but so well?"

Ethiren raised his eyebrows. "You mean you don't know? He didn't tell you?"

Seregei shook his head, though he had to admit he had a guess. "Tell me what?"

"Fancy that…" Ethiren smiled, flicking his braid back behind his shoulder. "You should ask him. Please excuse me – Lord Taffilelti will be waiting." He turned and left.

Seregei watched him for a moment, then shook his head and left the palace himself.

As he'd promised, Lim had gone to the three mixed-blood villages that Seregei had been intending to visit. It hadn't been easy to track down people in authority, especially in the first village, but at last he'd delivered the message that Seregei had been held up and sent his apologies. Unfortunately, he couldn't tell them when Seregei would come in person. He did manage to ask what it was they wanted to talk to Seregei about, though. Apparently one village wanted to talk about arranging for some disputes within the village to be heard. Of the other two, one was having a dispute with a nearby group of Valley-elves and wanted advice – they weren't willing to make any arrangements with Lim and he doubted that he had the authority anyway – and the third wanted help with charcoal-burning rights in the forest.

He jogged back to the Guardhouse, a little out of breath now. It wouldn't take long to get back, for all that he had a couple of miles yet to go. He enjoyed the run; it felt good to stretch his legs, to feel his own heartbeat and the breath in his lungs. Distances seemed meaningless as he ran, forest, fields and buildings racing by him.

It seemed only a few minutes before he jogged out of the forest onto the grassy area surrounding the Guardhouse. He sat down on the bench by the door for a moment to catch his breath, then got up to stretch.

At that moment, though, Seregei arrived.

"Back already?" he asked with a small smile.

Lim nodded, his good mood fading as he remembered who was down at the palace.

Seregei frowned a little. "Did you just arrive?"

"Yes. I was just starting to stretch."

"All right. I'd like a word with you, though. Come in when you've finished?"

"A- all right." Lim swallowed hard.

Seregei shook his head and smiled again, going to pat Lim on the shoulder. "No need to look so scared; you're not in any trouble. I just want to talk to you about something Master Ethiren said."

The name sent a chill down Lim's spine, but he nodded.

"Taffilelti asked after you, though."

That made Lim smile, touched that Lord Taffilelti remembered him. Seregei smiled back, patted him on the shoulder again, and went inside.

Lim finished his stretching quickly and followed him. He wasn't in the common room, but Lim could hear him searching for something from down the corridor. He eventually followed the noise to the other elf's bedroom.

Seregei was bending over a trunk that he'd pulled from under the bed, and was pulling papers out of it. Lim hesitated in the doorway. Seregei had wanted to speak to him, but he looked busy... in the end, he knocked tentatively on the door.

Seregei looked up. "Ah, there you are." He beckoned. "I trust everything was all right?"

"Yes. I asked them what they wanted to talk to you about, too."

"Ah, good. Thanks. I'll go round myself this afternoon. I just wanted to let them know." Seregei closed the trunk and sat down on the lid, gesturing Lim towards the chair on the other side of the room from the bed. "Sit down. I'm sure you're well aware of the other reason."

Lim nodded, feeling ashamed. He didn't look at Seregei as he sat down. It felt strange to be in here; he'd never come further than the door.

"You handled it better than I feared you might, but we do need to talk. I take it your father was with Taffilelti?"

"Y-yes." Lim kept his eyes on the floor, fidgeting despite himself.

"Will you tell me who?" asked Seregei gently.

Given all he'd already told Seregei, the name stuck in Lim's throat. Surely, while that element of truth remained untold, he'd not betrayed their secret. Surely. But he knew he couldn't stay silent forever. It wasn't fair. It wasn't right. Seregei needed to know.

Nonetheless, it took a few tries to say it. He took a deep breath, stammered, and finally forced out the words, "Master Ethiren." Then he looked up.

Seregei was nodding. "I thought so."

Lim blinked. "He's a good man, and a wise one," he said quickly. "Very loyal to Lord Taffilelti, why would you think..."

"First, the fact that you started to get frightened as soon as he rode through the gate. You didn't wait to see the rest of the entourage. Second, he went out of his way to tell me you were a liar, so he clearly had something to hide that you might tell me."

A sudden chill went through Lim at the accusation of lying. No-one would ever believe him. How many times had he been reminded of that? How many times had his father called him a liar and punished him for it? Reminded him that, even if he did think that the punishments were undeserved, nobody else would ever believe him?

Perhaps it had been true. He looked down, rubbing his broken hand, trying to choke back the tears. "I... I didn't lie," he whispered. "I'm not a liar."

"I know," said Seregei gently. "Once I had the true story out of you, I believed it."

Of course. He had lied to Seregei. He'd lied about how his hand was broken; he'd lied about his wounded side after the flood... "I'm sorry," said Lim.

"What for?"

"I *have* lied."

There was a pause, then Seregei reached over and tapped Lim on the shoulder. "Look at me, would you?"

Lim looked up. Seregei looked serious, but not angry.

"I know you lied about your hand because you wanted to protect your father. I know you lied about being hurt in the flood, though I'm still not sure I follow why you did that. Are there any other times I should know about?"

Lim swallowed hard. He wanted to say that his father hadn't really been the one to break his hand – his father would be furious if he found out – but he wasn't a liar.

He looked down. "I'm sorry," he mumbled.

"Should I take that as a yes?"

"No!" Lim looked up again, suddenly afraid that Seregei wouldn't believe him. "No, I've not lied about anything else. I'm not a liar." He wiped his eyes with the backs of his hands. "I'm telling the truth. Please believe me!"

Seregei took his hand. "I believe you."

Lim sniffed and wiped his eyes again, unsure what to say.

"I think he was just trying to discredit you. He said you liked the attention, which..." Seregei laughed a little bitterly. "I have to wonder what he was thinking; I've *met* you."

Lim swallowed hard. "Thank you."

Seregei looked quizzical.

"Thank you for believing me." Lim took a deep breath and let it out again. "I... was always afraid no-one would believe me."

Seregei nodded and squeezed Lim's hand. "I believe you," he repeated. "You've lied to me, but I know why, for the most part, and understand it wasn't from any ill will. I trust you, and I think you're telling the truth about what Ethiren's done to you."

Lim sniffed, feeling like a weight had been lifted from his shoulders. "He was sorry," he added hastily. "He didn't mean anything bad. I'm sure he wouldn't do it again."

Seregei shook his head. "Regardless, I don't want to give him the opportunity. I think it's best if you stay away from him."

Though Lim loved his father and didn't want to think that he might hurt him again, he knew that by running he deserved punishment, and was afraid to meet it. He just nodded.

"There are other errands you can run," said Seregei, "and in the meantime you can stay here, out of the way."

"Thank you," whispered Lim.

"All right. I don't want to put you in danger."

"Just…" Lim hesitated. He didn't want to ask any more, but there was something troubling him. "Please don't tell anyone?"

"What?"

"That Master Ethiren's my father and that…" Lim trailed off there, unwilling to put words to what his father had done. He wasn't sure how to express it, and somehow saying it aloud still felt like betrayal.

"I assume Taffilelti knows the truth."

"Yes." Lord Taffilelti had found him, after all, after that last night with his father. "But… I don't want anyone else to know. I don't want Father to get into trouble."

Seregei shook his head a little. After a moment, though, he said, "All right. I'll do what I can."

Lim sniffed. He wanted to thank Seregei again for all he'd done, but couldn't find the words to express his gratitude. All he could manage was "Thank you."

After Ethiren and Seregei had left, Taffilelti and Caleb sat in silence for a long moment. Taffilelti looked thoughtfully at his wine, wondering if Caleb was thinking of his long silence on the subject of Lim.

"I owe you an explanation," he said at last. He couldn't think of a better way to raise the subject.

"You do," said Caleb.

Taffilelti paused a moment, putting his thoughts in order and deciding what he needed to say. Upon consideration, he really should have foreseen this problem, but he'd been distracted by other things.

"Lim is Ethiren's son," he said simply. "That's why I was unwilling to discuss the fact that I'd sent him here before Ethiren left."

"And why you asked me to find a place for him, but never further acknowledged him?"

"Yes. I'm grateful that you found him somewhere, but after that I thought it better to let the matter rest."

"Why did you send him here?"

Taffilelti grimaced to himself, wondering how much of Lim's sordid story he wanted to tell. At last, he said slowly, "I tell you this in confidence and on the understanding that I couldn't prove it in open court: Ethiren used to mistreat Lim. I strongly suspected it for some years, but I knew I couldn't take a son from his father on empty suspicion, so I waited. I finally decided I couldn't wait any more when Lim ran away from home and came to me for help. After that I kept him away from Ethiren and sent him to you as soon as he was able to travel." He shook his head. "But I couldn't let Ethiren know where he was, as he would have every right to seek his return."

Caleb frowned. "Had I known that, I would have mentioned it to Seregei and Lim would not have been standing with us to welcome you today."

Taffilelti already knew he had only himself to blame for what had happened, and simply nodded.

Caleb sighed, sitting back in his chair. He sipped absently at his wine and looked out of the window. "Why is Ethiren still your most trusted advisor after a crime like that?" he asked.

Taffilelti couldn't help a rueful smile. "I've been called naïve, but I do know better than to turn away someone like Ethiren for a crime I can't even prove he's committed. He's always been loyal to me and he has the sense to see problems and solutions others – including myself – might flinch from. Now that Lim's out of his hands, I think he's harmless and see no reason to provoke trouble and lose a gifted member of my council."

Caleb smiled wryly for a moment, but then sobered. "This is a difficult situation," he said softly. "I'd rather not have any dispute with any member of your entourage."

Taffilelti nodded. "It's probably best if Lim stays out of the way for the rest of our visit."

"That's certainly true."

"I would like to speak to him myself, though."

"You'll have to ask Seregei about it. I'll mention this to him and see what he thinks."

"I'd appreciate it." Taffilelti knew better than to push matters, and while he did feel responsible for Lim and was interested to know how he was settling in Duamelti, he was unwilling to cause trouble over it, especially in the circumstances.

Caleb nodded. "I'll speak to him, and in any case he'll be present for other meetings." He took another sip of wine and sighed, then said briskly, "Shall we move on to lighter things?"

Taffilelti smiled, glad of the change of subject and that Caleb didn't seem overly offended. He drank some of his own wine and simply said, "Let's."

That afternoon, Seregei made his promised visit to the three mixed-blood villages, taking Lim with him. He went to the one that was having trouble with Valley-elves first; it was the closest.

They were welcomed and went to the village elder's house to speak to him. Several other elves crowded in as well. Seregei noticed that Lim was starting to look uncomfortable and put a hand on his shoulder.

"I'm fine," he said, blushing. "Sorry."

Seregei didn't really believe that, but nodded. "All right." He turned to the elder. "Lim tells me that you've been having trouble with Valley-elves."

The elder wrinkled his nose a little before replying.

"Do you prefer 'Irnianam'?" asked Seregei.

The other elf nodded. "I would. That's what I was always used to." He shrugged a little. "I know their name has changed, but that's still how I think of them."

"Very well, then. What have they been doing?"

"Encroaching on our farmland, and I'm sure I saw a group of them driving away some of our cattle."

"My cattle," said one of the other elves in the room angrily. "Two of them."

"And three of mine," said another.

"You graze them all together?" asked Seregei.

"Yes," said the elder, as Seregei had expected. "And it was on the day that those cows went missing that I saw Irnianam on the grazing grounds."

Seregei sighed. "All right. I'll see what I can do to find out about it. Were the cows marked?"

"Branded," said the elder. "We can give you their marks, if it'll help."

"It'll help prove it and identify the right cows." Seregei rubbed his eyes. "What else has been happening?"

"They broke a fence a few days back, and someone's been clearing brush in the woods around our village. Only we're supposed to be allowed to clear brush there."

Seregei nodded. "I'll see what I can do."

The elder nodded, looking relieved. "Those are the major things. For the rest… just minor annoyances." He scowled. "They have no respect for us."

Seregei nodded again with a small sigh. The two groups of elves in Duamelti had been living side-by-side for longer than he'd been alive, but they still didn't always get along. The other elf had summed it up well: lack of respect.

"I'll do what I can," he said, "And I'll let you know what happens."

"Thank you," said the elder. He looked genuinely relieved at having passed on the problem and Seregei smiled slightly as he left.

"The nearest Valley-elven village to them is just to the south," he told Lim as they went.

Lim nodded.

"I don't know when I'll be able to go and talk to them myself, but I'd like you to run and tell their village leader that I would like a word."

Lim swallowed hard and licked his lips, but nodded.

"You'll be fine," said Seregei, smiling. "You were this morning, after all."

Lim looked even more shaky, wringing his hands. "I'm sorry," he said, looking wide-eyed at Seregei. "I did make a fool of myself."

Seregei frowned, then realised what Lim meant. "I meant when I sent you round all these villages."

Lim did look a little happier at that assurance, but then he looked at his hands again.

"Lim," said Seregei.

"Sorry," said Lim, looking up again. "I'll go and take that message."

Seregei nodded slowly. "All right. By the time you catch up I may be finished with the next village, so look for me on the way to the third, all right?"

Lim nodded.

"And don't worry." Seregei forced a smile, patting Lim gently on the shoulder. "You do just fine when you don't worry so much."

"I'll try," mumbled Lim, looking at his hands again. "I'm sorry."

Seregei shook his head. "No need. Go on. I'll see you later."

Lim nodded and ran off. Seregei turned and continued on his way with a sigh.

"What am I going to do with him?" he muttered. Of course, in the short term that was obvious: keep him safe, busy and out of sight. He did hope that, once Ethiren was gone, Lim would calm down again. Perhaps finally getting the truth about his past off his chest would help, once the immediate cause for fear had left. Seregei just shook his head and carried on walking.

At the next village, he was once again enthusiastically welcomed. This time, though, there seemed to be no specific spokesman and he felt like everyone was trying to talk to him all at once.

"Quiet!" he shouted at last, raising a hand.

Silence fell at once.

"Now," he said, looking around. "One at a time."

There were quite a variety of problems. As he listened, Seregei resolved to have a word with the village elder; most of these didn't need to be brought to him, and seemed to have been left a while. In fact, one aggrieved elf had apparently been waiting a year for someone to tell her how her father's farm should be divided between her and her sister.

"Where is your elder?" asked Seregei, looking around. "He should have been dealing with these problems."

"Our elder died some months ago," said the woman, running a hand distractedly through her hair.

"Why didn't you select another one? Or tell me?"

"We... I don't know."

Seregei sighed. "All right. I'll do what I can for now, but if there are many things to hear, I can't deal with it all today. I'll hear the most urgent quarrels and come back in a couple of days to hear the rest and help you to select another elder." He sighed. Most villages had some sort of system in place for that, but apparently this one had broken down somehow.

He was able to settle a couple of the disputes then and there; they were urgent, but fairly straightforward and really just needed a disinterested judge with some common sense. However, the third village still needed his attention and he told them he had to leave.

"I will be back the day after tomorrow," he said. "You need a new village elder, though."

The elf he was speaking to – he seemed to have made himself something of a spokesman once everything had settled down – sighed and nodded. "I know," he said. "Usually it's a blood relative of the last one, but Fyodor was unmarried and had no siblings. We'll see what we can do."

"If you can't find one, I'll try to choose one from among you and you can start afresh. I know it's not as good, but it'll be better than what you have at the moment."

The elf nodded again. "We'll try to find someone."

Seregei smiled. "I'll see you in a couple of days, then," he said, and left.

The next village was some distance away, deep in the forest. That made sense, he reflected as he walked. After all, they were the ones who were interested in charcoal-burning. They were near another village and he suspected that that was the problem: who was allowed to burn where.

When he arrived, Lim was already there, talking nervously to a couple of other elves who were about his own age. Seregei smiled and waved, and Lim bade farewell to his companions and hurried over.

"Everything all right?" asked Seregei.

Lim nodded. "They said they'll see you in the next few days, whenever's most convenient."

"For me or them?" asked Seregei dryly.

Lim looked at the floor. "I didn't ask. I'm sorry."

Seregei smiled and patted him gently on the shoulder. "It's all right. I'll assume they meant for me and go the day after tomorrow; I plan to go back to that last village that day anyway."

Lim nodded and glanced round as someone called Seregei's name. He looked up and smiled a greeting as he saw an older elf coming over. Another was trailing a little way behind him.

"Good to see you, Captain," said the first elf. "I'm Jairi, the chief elder of this village." He gestured to the other elf. "This is Eoral."

"I'm a representative from another village just to the east of here," said Eoral, offering a hand.

Seregei shook hands with them. "Lim tells me there's been some question about charcoal-burning rights in the forest?"

Jairi nodded. "We think we can get things sorted out, but we'd like someone who isn't involved to have a look at the borders and make sure everything's fair."

Seregei smiled. "That sounds like a good idea."

"We'd have asked your trainee," said Eoral, nodding towards Lim, "But... we thought it would be best to ask an actual Swordmaster."

"Lim would be perfectly capable, but I'll do it, since I'm here," said Seregei. Out of the corner of his eye, he saw Lim's expression: a curious mix of gratitude and surprise. He smiled at him and followed the two elders out to where they had provisionally marked the border.

He was inclined to just agree with what they had decided unless there was an obvious problem, especially as they seemed to have agreed things happily between themselves. As they went, he beckoned to Lim to walk with him.

"Do they burn charcoal in Silvren?" he asked.

Lim nodded. "If anyone wants to burn, though, he has to get permission from Lord Taffilelti."

"All right. Here, as you can see, it's mostly worked out between villages. If there were a serious problem – too many burners, for example, or someone letting a fire get out of control – Caleb and I might get involved, but everyone tends to be responsible. Deciding the borders is mostly a question of common sense, which is why I think you could have done it."

Lim nodded, smiling.

As Seregei had suspected, the border that the villages had found for themselves was fine. It didn't seem to encroach on any other village's territory and it was roughly between the two, not cutting either off from any especially good areas or forcing them to go too far or set fires too close to their houses. For the most part, the inspection was just a pleasant walk.

"This looks good," he said to Eoral and Jairi. "For my part, I approve and wish you luck."

"Thank you," said Jairi, smiling. "I'm sorry we dragged you out here when your trainee would have been able to look it over."

"Not at all," said Seregei. "It's been a very pleasant visit."

"Can we come to you if there are any problems in future?" asked Eoral.

"Of course." Seregei smiled. "Is there anything else, while I'm here?"

They shook their heads.

"All right. If you do need me, you know where you can find me." Seregei shook hands with them again. "Good luck!"

"Thank you," said Eoral, grinning. "And to you."

Seregei nodded and turned to leave, Lim tagging along behind him.

As they walked, Seregei took a deep breath of the warm air and smiled. All around him, the air was full of the sounds of birds and insects. It smelled fresh and sweet, and under the trees everything had a wonderful golden and green glow where the light filtered through and between the leaves.

"It's a beautiful day," he said, glancing at Lim.

Lim nodded, also looking around. Seregei caught the ghost of a smile on his face and grinned. He thought he could feel something through empathy as well and that made his grin widen; the power only worked where there was mutual trust.

"Glad you came out with me?"

Lim looked round. "I hope I was helpful."

"I hope you learned from it." Seregei carefully reached over and put a hand on Lim's shoulder. "You've a home here, you know."

Lim blinked. "I... thank you."

Seregei nodded. "No matter what happens, that's the case."

Lim looked down. "I don't deserve this."

"It's not a question of deserving. Come to that, you certainly don't deserve anything else."

Lim looked up again. "I'm really grateful for all you've done."

Seregei smiled and squeezed Lim's shoulder. "You deserve a fighting chance."

Lim smiled faintly in response, but then looked forward with a sigh. "I... should speak to my father." He looked resigned and started to rub his left hand.

Seregei shook his head. "I saw how scared you were when he rode through that gate. I don't want you put in a position like that again."

Lim didn't reply, biting his lip.

"Lim?"

"I owe him that much," said Lim, looking at his hands. "I shouldn't have left him. It probably broke his heart..."

Seregei sighed. "Listen: talk to Taffilelti first. I'm sure he'll want to know how you're doing. He cared about you enough to see you safe, after all."

That got a startled look. "He cares about me? In particular?"

"There are a lot of people who do, you know." Seregei grinned at him and squeezed his shoulder again. "You're a good lad and we're fond of you, whether or not you think you deserve it. Trust me on that."

Lim nodded. "I... I'll try."

After finishing his afternoon meeting with his own advisor, Nairion, Caleb went to visit Seregei, intending to talk to him about a meeting between Taffilelti and Lim as he'd promised. He and Ekehart walked there, since it was a pleasant day, but they found the Guardhouse deserted. He guessed that Seregei and Lim had gone to visit those villages Seregei had sent Lim to that morning. He toyed with the idea of sitting on the bench outside and waiting, but he had better things to do, so he just left a note on the slate beside the door: 'Seregei, I want to see you – C'. Then he headed back towards the city.

On the way, though, he met Seregei and Lim coming in the opposite direction. He heard them before he saw them; Seregei's laugh tended to carry. He paused by the side of the road and waited for them to round the corner.

Seregei didn't notice him at first; he was looking at Lim. As usual, Lim was trailing a little behind, looking uncertain and worried. Caleb frowned a little, remembering what Taffilelti had told him that morning. Given that, he was surprised Lim always seemed so unhappy; why wasn't he glad to be away from home? It was understandable that he was worried now, but always?

His thoughts were interrupted, as at that moment Seregei looked round and saw him.

"Caleb?" he called, sounding startled and curious.

Caleb walked forward to meet him. "I was just looking for you at the Guardhouse."

"Something came up after I left this morning?"

Caleb nodded. "Something."

Seregei paused for a moment, then sighed a little. "Lim, why don't you head back on your own? I'll meet you there."

Lim nodded and bowed his head to Caleb, then sped off.

Caleb glanced at Ekehart. "You can go too, Ekehart," he said. "Meet me back at the palace."

Ekehart nodded, though he didn't look entirely happy. "As you will, my Lord."

"I'll walk him back," said Seregei.

Ekehart nodded again, then bowed to them both and left.

"So," said Seregei as they began walking slowly. "What did you want to talk to me so privately about?"

"Lim," said Caleb. "I was talking to Taffilelti about him after you left. Did you talk to him at all?"

"To Lim? A little," said Seregei guardedly.

"Master Ethiren's his father, and you were right: he did abuse him."

Seregei sighed. "That's what he told me too," he said softly.

"Taffilelti wants to keep this quiet, but he asked if he could speak to Lim, since he is interested in how he's doing."

Seregei nodded. "I'll talk to Lim about it, but I don't mind. I think it might do some good; Lim seems fond of him."

"All right. Let me know when you know."

"I will; I have to go into the city early tomorrow in any case. What else did I miss?"

"We talked about wine some more."

"Yes, I noticed you didn't serve mead."

"I don't get the impression he likes it much. He always chokes it down, but I thought this time I'd spare him the ordeal."

Seregei smiled a little. "You want something from him?"

"The fact that I want to be a good host has nothing to do with what I might want," said Caleb curtly.

Seregei's grin broadened. "Something he probably doesn't want to give."

Caleb scowled at him, but had to admit that he ought to discuss this with Seregei before he tried to push the matter with Taffilelti. "Bows," he said quietly. "Specifically, Silvren yew bows."

"Ah…" Seregei looked distantly at the sky. "Good luck."

"They've not been traded outside Silvren since…" Caleb frowned, thinking back to his history lessons. "Since the days of their wars with the Irnianam."

A slight twitch crossed Seregei's face. "And then I'd not be prepared to guarantee that it was the Wood-elves trading them."

That caught Caleb's attention. "You think it was one of the Silvren Mixed-blood tribes?"

"Things were a lot less solid then; the Wood-elves didn't have as many of the tribes under their control, and all it takes is expertise and access to the right wood."

"Might someone have that still?"

Seregei glanced at him. "It wouldn't surprise me, but don't try to stir up trouble. Many of the tribes have sworn oaths to Taffilelti now."

"Do you know which?" If anyone did, it would be Seregei, and Caleb was hoping that he could find a back way into that trade if Taffilelti wasn't willing to negotiate.

"Not off the top of my head, though I could probably find out," said Seregei slowly. "I'm not going to start trouble for them, though. If they've chosen to swear loyalty to him, they're not my concern, but they are still my people and I'm not going to put them in danger of any retaliation."

Caleb doubted that things were as serious as Seregei was suggesting. Before he could say so, he remembered that this wouldn't be an issue unless he suspected Taffilelti would object to this trade.

He sighed. "Well, we'll see how it goes."

Seregei nodded. After a moment, he forced a smile and said, "What else are you planning to get out of him?"

Caleb glared half-heartedly. "I'm sure you have your plans just the same as either of us."

Seregei shrugged a little. "I'd like to find out more about the tribes that have sworn to him, those he's talking to and what his actual terms with them are; that's no secret." He smiled. "As a matter of fact, while I'm in the city I might set up a meeting to talk about that with some of his entourage, before I meet with him myself."

Caleb laughed despite himself, wondering how it was that Seregei always seemed to find it easier to rule a people that was scattered across the whole world than Caleb found it to rule one valley.

"They're all fairly self-governing, aren't they?" he asked. "The tribes?"

"As a rule, yes. We sometimes have to step in, but..." Seregei glanced sidelong at Caleb. "Mostly these days we just have to stop interlopers from treading on the people of Duamelti: our primary care." He softened the words with a smile.

Caleb sighed. "Those days are past, Seregei."

Seregei shook his head. "Not for everyone, you know that." He glanced up. "We're almost there. I'll talk to Lim for you and see what we can arrange."

"Thank you. I'll let Taffilelti know."

CHAPTER FIVE

The next day, Taffilelti, Caleb and Ethiren had met for another meeting. Seregei wasn't there and Caleb was grateful. He didn't think he could have ignored the knowing look he knew the other elf would have given him when he once again sent for wine instead of mead. At least Nairion ignored it.

By an effort of will, Caleb didn't comment when Ethiren once again tasted Taffilelti's wine before handing it to him. Nairion glanced at him with a raised eyebrow, but didn't say anything. Taffilelti seemed to sense their discomfort all the same, however, for he shot Caleb an apologetic smile before taking a sip himself.

"I hope you had a peaceful night?" asked Caleb.

"Indeed we did. Your hospitality has not lessened with time," said Taffilelti.

"Indeed, it has increased," said Ethiren with a smile. "I don't recall being offered wine the last time we visited."

Taffilelti raised his goblet a little. "I will see about bringing in some mead for your next visit, Caleb."

Caleb had to laugh at that. "I look forward to it." He refrained from mentioning his low opinion of Silvren's mead.

"Is Seregei not joining us this morning?" asked Taffilelti. "I know he's already spoken to some of my clerks today."

"He had other business. I passed on your message from yesterday, though." Caleb knew better than to mention Lim by name. "When I saw him myself early this morning, he said he'd discuss it with you this afternoon, if you were available."

Taffilelti nodded. "Thank you."

"I suppose it would be inappropriate for him to send a trainee in his stead," said Ethiren softly.

"Indeed. Lim's not a Swordmaster yet, after all."

"I've nothing to talk to him about this morning in any case," said Taffilelti, glancing at Ethiren.

Ethiren nodded in confirmation.

Caleb didn't have anything for all three of them for that morning, but he also glanced at Nairion, just to make sure. Nairion frowned a moment, then shook his head.

"Very well, then," said Caleb. "Shall we begin?"

Taffilelti nodded, leaning forward in his chair. "Have you had time to look over those terms I showed you yesterday?"

Caleb nodded as Nairion began to rummage through the papers he was carrying.

"Here they are, my Lord," he said, holding out the paper Ethiren had fetched the day before.

"What do you think?" asked Taffilelti.

"They look fair to me – very similar to our own, with some exceptions. The price for portage is higher, I notice."

"We are further from their lands, so that seems fair," said Taffilelti.

Caleb hesitated a moment, then said, "I understand Ethiren went to speak to some of our merchants on the matter yesterday." He'd been wondering whether to bring it up, but felt he had to say something.

"Indeed he did. I hope you don't mind?"

Caleb would have minded far more had Ethiren been anyone else's advisor. "I'd rather you asked my permission in future."

"I apologise, Lord Caleb," said Ethiren, bowing his head a little. "I thought it would be best to speed discussions between yourself and Lord Taffilelti."

"Please don't do it again," said Caleb firmly.

Ethiren bowed his head again.

Taffilelti looked more uncomfortable, but simply said, "I'll see to it, Caleb. Since it's happened, shall we move on?"

Ethiren watched the people around the room carefully. Lords Caleb and Taffilelti were bent together over a map. Lord Caleb's advisor sat opposite Ethiren. When that elf glanced up, Ethiren smiled at him, as was appropriate, then looked back down at the map. He didn't especially care what was going on, but he faked interest and paid careful attention to what they were saying. That was what he was here to do, after all, however little inclined he was to sit idle and listen.

Lim was here.

He'd given the boy up for dead. He couldn't understand why he'd been lied to. He'd gone to Taffilelti, asked everyone he could for help, and they had found nothing. He'd thought his son eaten by spiders and all this time they had been *lying* to him. What had he done to provoke that?

He blinked and turned his thoughts back to the matter at hand. The boy could wait. He'd waited this long, after all.

Nonetheless, it wasn't as easy as usual for him to concentrate, or even feign interest. He had to consciously focus on what was happening. He told himself firmly that it would make others suspicious if he didn't do what he was supposed to, especially as Taffilelti had lied to him once already about the boy.

The thought made Ethiren all the angrier. That was his son. Nobody had the right to take his son from him.

Still, he pushed the anger aside. He had other things to think about that would be far more useful to him. Though he would not forgive Taffilelti, he wished to remain in his current position of power and for that he had to put such things aside. Besides, where would Silvren be without him, if the weak and soft-hearted king were allowed to rule alone?

Ethiren brushed a stray strand of hair out of his face and leaned forward, once again applying his attention to the discussion.

That afternoon, Taffilelti and Reiron, his honour guard, went up to the Guardhouse to meet with Lim and Seregei. Taffilelti had asked Ethiren to stay at the palace and work with Nairion on some new arrangements for Silvren to host Duamelti elves who were spying on Arket, a human realm to the south. Even had he not had this errand to run, he might have considered going for a walk. Though he'd never have admitted it to Caleb, Duamelti was beautiful, and the warm weather made it even better.

Still, it was difficult to enjoy the sunshine and the soft summer breeze; he was worried about the situation with Lim and Ethiren. He'd not expected them to run into one another like this, and he knew Ethiren was upset at the fact that Lim had been hidden from him. He was also worried about Lim; the lad had looked scared out of his wits the day before. Taffilelti had hoped that sending him away from Silvren would result in him getting over his nervousness. Apparently not. He sighed.

"My Lord?" asked Reiron from behind him. Taffilelti glanced over his shoulder with a smile.

"Nothing, Reiron. I was just thinking."

Reiron nodded and went back to his careful survey of the surrounding trees.

When they arrived at the Guardhouse, Seregei and Lim were sitting outside on a bench, engrossed in something Seregei was drawing on a slate. Nonetheless, Seregei looked up as Taffilelti approached.

"Lord Taffilelti," he said, nodding a greeting. Lim scrambled to his feet, starting to blush.

"I hope I don't interrupt," said Taffilelti, pointing to the slate. He noticed that it had a table drawn on it, but couldn't read the writing upside-down.

"I can come back to it," said Seregei. "I assume you're here to talk to Lim?"

Taffilelti nodded. Lim looked partway between horrified and delighted and started fidgeting with his left hand. Taffilelti winced internally as he saw that the bones were still out of line.

"Shall I leave you out here?" asked Seregei, glancing between them.

Taffilelti nodded. "It's a beautiful day." He glanced at Reiron. "Why don't you go with Captain Seregei? I'll stay nearby."

Reiron bowed. "Yes, my Lord."

"Come inside," said Seregei. "Do you play chequers?"

Taffilelti waited until they'd gone into the building before taking Seregei's place on the bench. He beckoned Lim to sit beside him and, after a moment's hesitation, the young elf did so. He kept biting the forefinger of his left hand and Taffilelti hid a frown. He'd forgotten that Lim did that when he was nervous.

"You look well," he said after a long moment.

Lim smiled. "As do you, my Lord." He sighed and shuffled his feet in the grass. "My father... is he very unhappy?"

Taffilelti looked away, across the open grass around the Guardhouse. "He... was, but mostly with me now that he knows you're here."

"I'm sorry; I know you told me not to let anyone in Silvren know where I am..."

"It's not your fault. You're a Swordmaster trainee now. If that means that one of your duties is to stand with Seregei when we visit, it can't be helped." He knew he should have paid more attention to where Lim was; had he done that, he'd have been able to anticipate this. He meant what he'd said, though: it couldn't be helped. "How are you getting on here?"

Lim actually smiled. "Seregei's very kind."

"That's good. You're learning a lot?"

"Yes." The smile broadened as Lim looked around. "He's taught me about history and some of how the Duamelti tribes and Mixed-bloods live and their history and traditions, and he's teaching me to track and wilderness survival and helping me practice dagger-fighting – I'm not very good; I'm having to relearn with my right hand – and my archery..."

Taffilelti grinned. "You're glad you did come here, then?"

Lim's smile faded and he looked at the ground with a sigh. "I... my father..."

"He's been doing fine. He was shocked when he found you gone, but he recovered." Taffilelti wondered if it would be better for Lim if he said that Ethiren didn't care about Lim's disappearance, but it would be a cruel lie and he didn't feel comfortable saying that.

Lim nodded. "That's good. I'm glad he wasn't unhappy." Nonetheless, he sounded wistful.

"You're better here. Especially as it sounds like you're much happier."

Lim sighed. "I... I'm sorry, I don't want to doubt you, I know you're doing what's best for me... but I feel... I shouldn't have left him."

"It was the right thing to do," said Taffilelti firmly. "Otherwise I'd not have told you to do it."

"I know," Lim said hastily, biting his fingertips.

Taffilelti took his left hand and frowned at it. Lim looked worriedly at his expression.

"I've taken good care of it, as best I could."

"I know. It was a bad break."

"I really appreciate what they did for it, and I can still use it."

"Yes, it is impressive that it's healed as well as it has." Taffilelti released Lim's hand again. "It doesn't hurt you?"

"No. It's stiff, especially in cold weather, but I can deal with that." Lim looked at his hand, carefully flexing his fingers. "Thank you."

"For what?"

"T-taking me to the healers and asking them to look after me."

"Would you have gone yourself, if I'd not found you?"

"I don't know." Lim fidgeted with his collar. "I just... I had to hide."

Taffilelti nodded. "All right. I'm glad you did, and that I found you."

Lim smiled fleetingly, but then looked away.

"Lim?"

"My... my father." Lim looked up again and Taffilelti was startled to see tears in his eyes. "He loves me, doesn't he? He's my father. How could he not?"

The question took Taffilelti by surprise. "Why do you ask?" he said, to stall for time.

Lim bit his lip. "Seregei said some things..." his voice shook and he looked down at his hand, but then shook his head. His voice sounded a little firmer as he said, "It's not true. It can't be. He loves me, I know it. He only did this because... because..." Tears welled in his eyes and his breath caught.

Taffilelti put an arm around his shoulders. "It's all right. We'll protect you: me and Seregei. He'll not hurt you again."

"I should speak to him. I need to apologise." Lim seemed to have got the sudden tears under control, but he still hiccupped once or twice.

"No, Lim," said Taffilelti gently. "You should not."

Lim just looked wretched. "He's my father," he whispered.

Taffilelti laid a hand on his shoulder. "Lim, look me in the eye."

Lim looked up and Taffilelti caught his gaze. At once, the younger elf began to look away, look down, but Taffilelti gently shook his shoulder and he looked up again.

"Trust me. You should never speak to him again."

Later that afternoon, Seregei was in the city to see about a stronger bow for Lim. He wasn't ready quite yet, but Seregei knew it might take some time to find him a bow, since he was still shorter than the average Valley-elf. The bowyer promised to see what he had if Seregei would return in an hour.

As he left the armoury, he was startled to almost run into Ethiren.

"Captain Seregei! Forgive me, I didn't see you there." Ethiren bowed.

Seregei nodded. "Quite all right. Are you going somewhere?"

"Just for a walk." Ethiren gestured towards the palace gardens. "Lord Taffilelti has no need of me at present. Would you care to walk with me? Only if you're not too busy, of course."

Seregei couldn't help wondering if there was more to that request, but nodded. "I need to go back to the armoury in about an hour, but I have nothing to do until then."

They headed for the garden side by side, in silence. Seregei didn't want to speak first. He was sure that Ethiren had something he wanted to talk about. Or, rather, someone.

"Have you spoken to Lim about how we know each other?" Ethiren asked, finally. He didn't look at Seregei and kept his voice low.

Seregei looked sidelong at him. "I think he'll tell me when he's ready. I take it you want me to know, though?"

Ethiren sighed heavily. "I'd rather it came from him."

Seregei nodded. "How long have you known him?"

Ethiren did look at him then, his gaze sharp. "All his life."

"You were friends with his parents, then?" Seregei kept his voice deliberately light.

The look sharpened, then Ethiren shook his head, looking away. "You... could say that. He hasn't mentioned... them at all?"

"He doesn't like talking about home. It's why I was surprised when you said he had a habit of trying to make people feel sorry for him and telling lies. He's never done that. In fact, he has more of a habit of hiding it when he really is hurt."

Ethiren was frowning. "That's quite unlike him," he said thoughtfully, looking away. He rubbed his eyes with a quick gesture. "He... really hasn't mentioned me at all?"

Seregei shook his head. "Would you have expected him to?"

Ethiren laughed bitterly. "I would. I'm his father."

Seregei tried to act as if that news surprised him. Fortunately, Ethiren didn't seem to notice anything amiss.

"As you can imagine," he said, "I had hoped he'd tell you." He paused.

"Both because it hurts to be disowned by my own son and because it would suggest he'd finally stopped *lying* to people."

"I'd not describe it as a lie. He just seems very uncomfortable with the subject of Silvren."

"I can't understand why. He was a difficult child, yes, but I tried so hard to raise him well and now I find that he not only left without so much as a *goodbye*, but he hasn't even told anyone whose child he is!" He looked sharply at Seregei again. "He's so young… didn't you wonder what he was doing so far from home, or consider contacting his parents?"

Seregei hesitated, unsure how to answer that. He didn't want to tell Ethiren what Lim had told him, after all, and without the context he couldn't very well say that Taffilelti had sent him. At last, though, he decided that the question had to be answered somehow. "I thought he was an orphan, actually."

Ethiren sighed. "Well, I suppose that does explain that." He shook his head, then suddenly said, "I'm sorry if I was rude; it's an upsetting subject."

"I can understand that. Do you have any idea why he would run away?"

"None at all." Ethiren rubbed his eyes again. "I always did my best with him."

"Out of interest, what happened to his hand?"

Ethiren startled, looking quickly at Seregei. "His hand?"

"His fingers have been broken. Do you know what happened there?"

"No, I suppose that happened after he left."

Seregei nodded slowly. "At least it seems to have been well-cared-for," he said, still watching Ethiren.

Ethiren also nodded. "I'm glad of that." He sighed. "Of course, I imagine you want to keep him here?"

"He's my trainee and I've grown fond of him," said Seregei, "but he's not a prisoner. If he truly wants to leave, I'll let him."

"He will once I've spoken to him," said Ethiren firmly. "I'd like to do that as soon as possible."

"We'll see." Seregei was sure that Ethiren shouldn't be allowed to speak to Lim, at least not alone. "You may be disappointed, though. He left, after all."

Ethiren frowned deeply, the frown slowly becoming savage as Seregei watched him. After a moment, though, the look vanished. "He will," he said simply. "I just need to talk to him and find out what he was thinking to leave."

"I'm not so sure. He's happy here. And, given that, do you really want to take him away when he's found a place for himself and is doing well?"

"He's *my* son." Ethiren's teeth flashed as he spoke. "You have no right to take him from me and he *will* come home with me."

Seregei had expected maybe some veiled scorn for the life of a

Swordmaster, ruler of Mixed-bloods. What Ethiren had actually said startled him into silence.

"So you'd happily uproot him again?" he asked after a moment.

Ethiren had looked away again and the trace of savagery had vanished from his face. "Do you have any children, Seregei?"

"No."

Ethiren shook his head a little. "I'd not expect you to understand, then. I'm sorry I lost my temper just there, but… losing him and not even knowing what had happened, or if he was alive or dead… it's been a torment to me all these years."

"You really don't know what would have caused him to leave?" Seregei ignored the fact that Lim had only been in Duamelti for a year.

"I'd like to speak to him about it. We quarrelled that evening, but I didn't expect a reaction as drastic as this." He shook his head. "I tried so hard to be a good father."

Seregei caught himself nodding understandingly.

"Would you mind if I spoke to him? This afternoon, perhaps?"

"I'm sorry – we both have things we need to do."

Ethiren sighed. "I understand," he said, a trace of bitterness in his tone. "At some point, though. You said yourself he's not a prisoner. Surely you don't mind me speaking to my son, who I've not seen in so long?"

Seregei felt caught in a cleft stick. After all, if he refused the request he'd need to give a reason. "I'll see."

Ethiren nodded and walked on.

The next morning, Taffilelti was reading over the hosting arrangements that Ethiren had prepared the day before. He wasn't expecting visitors and was surprised to hear a knock on the door of his sitting room.

Well, whoever they were, Reiron must have let them in; he was in the anteroom. So Taffilelti called, "Enter!"

It was Ethiren. He walked in at a measured pace, closing the door behind him, and his expression gave nothing away. That would have been unsettling on anyone else, but Taffilelti was used to Ethiren looking like that. The other elf stopped a few feet in front of Taffilelti and bowed.

"Good morning, Ethiren. I was just looking over these notes of yours." Taffilelti gestured Ethiren to a seat.

"Thank you, my Lord." Ethiren sat down. "I trust they're satisfactory?"

"Indeed. There are one or two matters I would like to discuss more with Lord Caleb – you did well to highlight them."

"Thank you. The question of protection in case of pursuit?"

"Yes. It needs thought; on the one hand I agree that we don't want to bring trouble on ourselves, but it does seem cold to close the gates on a Duamelti elf in that sort of danger."

"I think only of your safety and that of your people," said Ethiren smoothly.

"I know." Taffilelti smiled at him. "And I accept that it is a difficult question to answer." He sighed, but then tapped the clause in question. "I assume from this that you think we shouldn't let them back in?"

"I do, my Lord. Our relationship with Arket is already cold and we don't want them coming into the forest in hot pursuit of a Duamelti elf."

"But if he were merely a fugitive and not a spy who we had been harbouring, would we refuse him shelter?"

Ethiren frowned, looked as if he were about to say something, then shook his head.

"You think we should?"

"As I say, my Lord, I think only of the safety of Silvren."

Again, Taffilelti smiled. "I appreciate that." He noticed that Ethiren looked distracted and it took a moment for the other elf to smile back. "Is something wrong?"

Ethiren let out a breath in a sudden huff. "My Lord, may I speak freely?"

"Of course." When asked for his opinion, Ethiren didn't normally hesitate to give it and Taffilelti lowered the papers to listen.

"Did you know that Lim was here?"

Ah. He'd known that he would have to have this conversation at some point.

Ethiren was staring at him, frowning deeply. After a moment, he looked away. "I'm sure you have your reasons, my Lord, but I don't understand what I have done to make you hurt me so."

"Ethiren, I never had any intention of deliberately hurting you."

"Then why?" Suddenly the disinterested mask was gone. Ethiren's eyes widened. Taffilelti thought he caught the gleam of tears for a moment. "Why do this? Why take my son from me?"

Though the distraught look on his advisor's face wrung Taffilelti's heart, he couldn't help remembering Lim on that last evening he'd been with his father. "Ethiren, I think you know why."

Ethiren shook his head, now looking more confused than hurt. "I loved him with all my heart. I know I wasn't the best father, but he was all I had. I don't understand why you took him from me." He hunched his shoulders, looking at the floor. Again, he looked close to tears and Taffilelti pitied him, despite everything.

"Surely you realise that the way you treated him was unacceptable?" he asked softly.

Ethiren looked up, frowning. "Did he tell you something?"

"He didn't need to." The pity disappeared as Taffilelti once again remembered Lim's tearful face in the moonlight and the way he had cradled that broken hand. "How did you break his hand, exactly? Stamp on it?"

Ethiren was staring at him. "Did he tell you I broke his hand?"

"Who else would have done it?" This was where Taffilelti knew he was on shaky ground; he couldn't prove that Ethiren had hurt Lim. Not certainly; Lim would never speak against him, and he was the only witness.

Ethiren knew it too. "If you were so sure," he said hotly, "Why work in darkness?"

Taffilelti scowled. "Watch your tone, Ethiren," he said curtly.

"My apologies, my Lord," said Ethiren smoothly, though there was an edge there that Taffilelti didn't care for. "But I think it's a question I have a right to ask: if you were sure that I was treating Lim any worse than he deserved, why go behind my back and that of the court?"

"Because we both know that he was the only witness and would never speak against you."

"So you drew your own conclusions?" The edge was becoming more obvious and Taffilelti frowned, but Ethiren didn't seem to notice. "I never mistreated the boy. He's my son; don't I have a right to discipline him?"

"You do, but what I saw that night wasn't discipline."

"I never did anything he didn't deserve." Ethiren was sitting forward, his fists clenched. Taffilelti glanced at them, setting aside the papers, ready to spring from his chair.

"I don't believe that," he said. "And if you don't calm down, I'm going to call in Reiron."

Ethiren looked shocked. "Do you think *I'm* a threat to *you?*"

"You're acting very belligerently."

"I am?" Ethiren shook his head with a short laugh. "You stole my son and then accuse me when I grow angry about it!"

"Ethiren," said Taffilelti warningly. He moved to the edge of his own chair.

Ethiren moved back in his chair, hugging himself. "I'm sorry, my Lord. It just... surely you understand."

Taffilelti felt a little guilty for how he'd handled this, but he didn't think that excused Ethiren for anything. "I don't. As you say, he's your son. You're his father. How could you hurt him like that?"

"I didn't mean to. It was just... you know how I like everything to be in its place, for things to be on time, for... the world only works when it has order."

Taffilelti smiled despite himself and nodded. It was one of the things that made Ethiren good at his job.

"But he would *never* obey me and he stirred up trouble wherever he went. Sometimes I think he did it to provoke me, and he succeeded in that."

"That's not the Lim I remember."

"My Lord, I lived with him. Believe me, he was a troublemaker. I don't know how Captain Seregei copes."

"Maybe he's less determined to control everything around him," said Taffilelti, a little more sharply than he'd intended.

Ethiren shrugged. "Perhaps. But there's your answer, my Lord: he provoked me, he was disobedient, and I disciplined him, but I only did it because of how he behaved. I love him with all my heart and I only want him to come home, but Captain Seregei won't even let me speak to him." He looked up. "Would you intercede for me?"

Taffilelti winced inwardly, but he was still as determined as when he had spoken to Lim. "No. I don't think you should speak to him."

Ethiren's brows drew down in a deep frown. "Why not?"

"Because, whatever the reason, I think you've hurt him enough."

"With respect, my Lord, I don't think it's your decision to make," said Ethiren slowly.

Taffilelti stared at him, startled at such a direct denial of his authority. "I beg your pardon?"

"Though you are our king, you are still bound by the law. You don't have the right to take away my son without openly-debated cause any more than I have the right to take away anything that belongs to you."

"That analogy is imperfect, Ethiren," said Taffilelti coldly, "because Lim is not an item of property."

Ethiren waved a hand. "Nonetheless, do you see my point? You don't have the right to take away Lim without a proper hearing in which you actually try these accusations against me! Your crown does not give you that right, and neither does my loyalty!"

For a moment they locked gazes. Taffilelti was aware that Ethiren was right, but he still knew that he could not back down from this. Law or no law, he could *not* let Ethiren get at Lim now.

Ethiren looked away first and his tone was conciliatory as he said, "I'm sure you appreciate why I feel strongly about this, my Lord. Not only... does this touch me near, but I wouldn't have anyone call you a tyrant."

Hearing the word spoken aloud shook Taffilelti to the core. He swallowed hard. Of course, that was the word for a king who ignored the law.

Ethiren shook his head sadly. "So I'm sorry if I'm disrespectful, though I must confess that it saddens me that you would take it like this." He looked up. "In the past, I've always felt I could advise you even if you didn't like what I said."

Taffilelti looked away. "It's not that I don't like what you say, Ethiren. I trust you to give me good advice or you'd not be chief among my advisors and head of the council. However, nothing you've said convinces me that it would be safe for you and Lim to meet."

Ethiren looked plaintive. "You think I'd hurt him?"

"You have before."

Again, there were tears in Ethiren's eyes. He sat back in his chair and rubbed his eyes as if defeated. "Is there nothing I can say to change your mind?" He looked up. "I've only ever served you, my Lord. I don't understand how you can do this to me."

"I'm not trying to hurt you. I'm trying to protect Lim. As his father, surely that's something you understand?" Taffilelti felt deeply uncomfortable and the word 'tyrant' was still echoing in his ears. He moved back in his own chair, though he couldn't relax.

"I understand, though…" Ethiren shook his head. "I don't think you need take such drastic steps to defend him from *me*. I'm his father and I love him. Of course, if it's really what's best for him then I'll sacrifice my own feelings – I've always tried to do what's right by him, after all – but you must forgive me if it hurts me."

Taffilelti nodded. "I'm glad you understand," he said, though he was pretty sure that, even if Ethiren understood, he didn't accept.

That afternoon, Ethiren had some time to himself and he knew exactly how he intended to spend it. He would not stand for this any longer. He felt as if he was being laughed at and scorned, and he would *not* remain idle while he was mocked. He deserved better, and he intended to take it.

Before anything else, he would go and find that boy. Once that part of his life was back in order – or as much as it ever was where the boy was concerned – he would see to the rest.

He had eyes for nothing but the road in front of him as he walked. He'd asked directions to the Swordmaster Guardhouse before leaving the city and it was a straight road for most of the way. He knew that Seregei had other business this afternoon. Hopefully, he'd have left Lim behind. Ethiren had no intention of talking to anyone but his son. He knew they'd try to fob him off as they had done every time he'd tried to get to him so far, but he'd not let them do that today.

A moment's compulsion made him flex his ankle and he felt the comforting pressure of his boot knife against his leg. He'd been trained by some of the best teachers in Silvren, and he had often felt that they were holding him back. Perhaps today he could prove it.

Whatever happened, he was not going to leave without taking back what was his.

Lim had stayed behind when Seregei went to speak to one of the Mixed-blood villages again. The older elf had left in a resigned mood, muttering to himself about settlements that let things reach utter chaos before contacting him for help, and had warned Lim not to expect him back before evening.

Lim had decided to try to impress him by memorising a map that showed the main areas of Mixed-blood settlement in the world.

He wasn't so engrossed in his studies that he didn't hear someone approaching the door, though. He looked up and his heart seemed to stop as he saw his father. His expression was stormy. Lim felt himself starting to shake. He didn't think there was another way out.

Then he caught himself. Why was he considering running? His father loved him, he'd never...

He knew he couldn't fool himself. What he'd done was amply deserving of punishment. He couldn't expect anything else. So he didn't try to run. He froze in his chair, staring as his father entered the room.

Ethiren looked at him for a long moment. "Lim," he said at last, his voice shaking.

Lim stayed tense, wondering what that tone portended. "Fa-father?"

"I want a word with you." Ethiren stepped around the table and grabbed Lim's arm. "In private."

He was supposed to stay in the common room in case someone visited. He needed to be there in case someone wanted to know where Seregei was.

Nonetheless, he didn't argue. He just nodded and followed his father into one of the side rooms. His heart was hammering so hard he could barely hear. He licked his suddenly-dry lips and tried not to tremble. He couldn't look away from his father's face. It was so hard to read. It might turn to anger at any moment.

Again, he reminded himself that his father would never hurt him. He loved him. Unless he deserved to be punished. And he did. Lim bit his finger to try to distract himself. It didn't help.

In the empty bedroom, Lim drew as far away as he could against the wall furthest from the door. Ethiren slammed it behind him and drew the bolt. Then he turned to face Lim.

Lim could feel himself sweating. The shaking was getting worse. Still, he forced himself not to cower. "Father, I..."

"This had better be an excellent explanation," said Ethiren coldly.

Lim licked his lips again, but his voice seemed to have died. "I'm sorry," he croaked. He felt too scared to even move.

Ethiren shook his head, his gaze suddenly gentling. "Why did you do this to me?" he asked quietly.

Lim looked down, feeling like a speck of muck on the floor.

"Do you even begin to understand what you've done, my son?"

"I left you," whispered Lim. Death would have been a relief.

"You did. It broke my heart. I couldn't believe it when I found you gone."

Lim felt tears welling in his eyes and hugged himself, sniffing.

"You never wrote to me, never..." Ethiren's voice hitched. "I thought you were dead."

The tears were starting to spill over.

"Oh, by all that's holy!" exclaimed Ethiren. "Of course, now you'll start crying and make out that I'm being cruel."

"I'm sorry..." Lim wiped at the tears. "I'm not doing it on purpose, I'm so sorry, I don't mean to upset you, I just feel so guilty."

"Liar. You obviously didn't feel guilty enough to *do* anything. How long have I been here? A couple of days and not so much as a kind word from my own *son*!"

The words cut like a knife and, to Lim's shame, another sob shook him.

"Why do you do this? Every time I try to talk to you and make you see how you hurt the people around you, you just start *crying*. I hope I didn't raise you to act like an *infant*."

"I'm sorry..."

"If you were sorry, you'd not do it." Ethiren began to pace back and forth. "Every time I try to reach out to you, you just throw it back in my face. Do you really take such joy in hurting people, boy? I don't think I raised you to be like this." He sighed. "I tried so hard, but I suppose I must have done something to offend the Lord and Lady and they're set to punish me for it."

Lim couldn't stop crying. Every word fell like a blow and no matter how he tried he couldn't calm himself down. After all, didn't he deserve this? His father loved him. He'd not hurt him for no reason.

He remembered Seregei insisting that his father didn't love him, but he squashed the thought. It couldn't be true.

"Are you *listening*?" hissed Ethiren.

Lim flinched, looking up. "Y-yes, Father," he whispered. He wiped his eyes and willed the tears to stop.

Ethiren made a disgusted noise. "If I didn't love you so much, Lim, I'd break every bone in your body for doing this to me. I've given you so many chances, have poured everything I have into you and *this* is how you repay me: leaving without so much as a backward look, taking up with some Mixed-blood order as if you never were a Wood-elf, and finally trying to manipulate me with your snivelling when I finally find you to call you to account. What have you got to say for yourself?"

Lim swallowed hard and took a deep, hiccupping breath. "I... I didn't want to leave."

"Oh, *really*?"

"Lord Taffilelti... he told me I should go." Another swallow. Another deep breath. The look on Ethiren's face made Lim want to throw up, but he forced himself to continue, "He saw my hand and..."

"Did you tell him *I* did that?"

Lim instinctively threw up a hand to defend his face. "No, no, of course not!"

"Good, because we both know it would be a lie."

Lim vividly remembered his father crushing his hand under a booted foot. The memory shook him to the core and for a moment he stopped shaking, staring at the other elf in silence. Again, he wondered. Seregei had said that nobody hurt the people they loved.

"What are you looking at me like that for?" asked Ethiren. The anger had vanished as if it had never been. He looked as if Lim had just cut him to the quick. "Why would I ever have hurt you? You're my son. My only child. You mean the world to me, whatever you've done. Why would I hurt you like that?"

"I... I don't know." Lim looked at the floor, once again feeling small and dirty and guilty. He wondered if his father could read his doubts.

"Surely it's impossible. You must have imagined that. You know I wouldn't do something like that, don't you?"

Lim couldn't answer. He had done it. Lim would never forget.

"Did you catch it in something and crush it accidentally?"

No. Despite what he'd told everyone who asked, he hadn't. He couldn't bring himself to say so, though.

"Lim, that's what happened, isn't it?" Ethiren sighed. "Why do you always do this? Make out that I'm some sort of monster who would take pleasure in torturing his beloved child?"

"I didn't tell anyone you'd done it," whispered Lim.

"I've worked hard to gain a place on Lord Taffilelti's council, however little he appreciates what I bring to it. Do you like discrediting me and trying to make me lose that place?"

"No..." The whisper was almost a whimper.

"Why are you so scared of me?" Ethiren still sounded hurt and gentle. Lim looked at him warily, then caught himself.

"I... I don't want to be punished," he whispered.

"Why would I punish you?"

"For leaving you."

Ethiren nodded. "And that's not all you've done."

"It isn't?" Lim frantically searched his mind for more misdemeanours. If he could remember and confess them, maybe that would help and he'd be forgiven.

Ethiren's gaze hardened. "You mean to say you don't even know what I'm talking about?"

"I'm sorry!"

"Those words are *meaningless* coming from you."

Lim flinched, pressing himself closer to the wall. He started to apologise again – maybe if he said it enough it would change something – but stopped himself just in time.

Ethiren was looking at him with an expression midway between a snarl and a sneer. "Well?"

"I... I don't know," whispered Lim. "I'm s-" Again, he cut himself off.

Ethiren snorted. "I don't know why I expect better, but somehow I keep having hope." He sighed, shaking his head. "Well, to start with," – his expression turned angry again – "how *dare* you insult Lord Taffilelti by putting any blame on him?"

Lim flinched, feeling as if something had squeezed his heart. Of course, it had been wrong to immediately cite Lord Taffilelti. He'd not considered it as blaming him before, but given that leaving had been wrong...

"But... but he ordered me to go. I was obeying him," he said, his voice tilting towards a plea.

Ethiren's lips drew back from his teeth and Lim flinched.

"Don't blame Lord Taffilelti for *your* filthy actions, boy," he snapped. "Why don't you tell the truth? You decided to go, to leave the home I'd given you without a backward look, but you're trying to dodge responsibility for your actions – as usual – and pin the blame on our noble king! That's it, isn't it?"

Lim couldn't answer. That wasn't true, but he was too frightened to contradict his father.

"*Isn't it?*"

"Yes," Lim blurted.

"I thought as much. Well, before we leave you can damn well apologise to him and *mean it*, is that clear? None of your snivelling and sympathy-seeking." Ethiren looked him up and down with a look of disgust. "You know, I almost feel sorry for Captain Seregei. He's a good elf and obviously thinks he's doing the right thing by trying to make something worthwhile out of you, but there's really no point in his efforts. It took a lot of nerve for you to come to him and leech off him, however much of a come-down this is from the life I would dearly have loved to give you."

Lim swallowed hard, feeling as if he had just been crushed a little further into the floor. He thought back over all the times he'd failed, all the times he'd disappointed Seregei. There were so many of them... why had Seregei let him stay so long? Perhaps it was pity and hope that he could give him some sort of worth.

"He'll be happy to see the back of you," said Ethiren with a shrug. "He can find himself a proper trainee."

Lim bit his lip, still looking at the floor.

"He was glad to hear I was going to take you home, you know. He's a good elf, that one, but you've been a great disappointment to him, whatever he tells the rest of the world."

Lim could feel the tears gathering again as he thought of all the times Seregei had tried to reassure and encourage him.

Ethiren sighed. "I know it's a disappointment when you'd finally managed to delude yourself into thinking that someone like you could be useful to someone like him, but it's time someone told you the truth."

"He… he really said he'd be glad if I left?" Surely not. Lim had just been starting to believe that he was doing well, that Seregei was satisfied with him.

"Yes. He seemed quite relieved."

That was too much and Lim started to sob.

Seregei had not had an easy time of it in the village. However, at last he had managed to sort out the most complicated and long-standing cases, and had the names of a few elves who would be prepared – and able – to act as elders. He'd arranged for them to meet him at the Guardhouse later that afternoon so that he could speak to them privately.

First, though, he was making a quick trip into the city; one of the cases he had heard that day involved some local Valley-elves and he wanted to check the village borders with Caleb's Mapkeeper. He'd put off a decision in that case, and would send it back with the elder he chose.

When he arrived at the palace, he noticed a couple of Taffilelti's clerks standing together in a corner of the courtyard. One was holding an armful of documents and looking worried while the other gestured helplessly.

"Is everything all right?" asked Seregei, going over to them.

They looked up, both looking slightly apprehensive, then bowed as they recognised him. The one with the documents said, "It's Master Ethiren, Captain. I'm supposed to take these to him" – he shifted the documents – "but I can't seem to find him anywhere. Have you seen him?"

"Might he be with Lord Taffilelti?"

The other Wood-elf said, "Lord Taffilelti gave Master Ethiren the afternoon to himself."

Seregei frowned, looking around. He'd met Ethiren out for a walk that time; perhaps he'd done the same again: gone out into the gardens? When he asked the Wood-elves about that possibility, though, he learned that they'd already considered it and looked for him there, to no avail.

"Would anyone have seen him? He doesn't have a guard, but is it likely that someone would have been keeping an eye on him?"

The Wood-elves glanced at one another.

"It's possible," one said at last. He looked around and waved at someone behind Seregei. Seregei looked round to see a wood-elven guard approaching. He bowed to Seregei, then glanced curiously at the two clerks.

"We're trying to find Master Ethiren," the elf carrying the documents said.

"Oh" – the guard gestured towards the gate – "He went out for a walk a little while ago."

Seregei frowned. Ethiren hadn't exactly expressed any enthusiasm for exploring Duamelti. "Which road did he take?"

The guard might have read something in his tone, for he hesitated before replying. "I hope I didn't do ill, Captain. He went by the east road, heading out of the city."

Seregei's heart skipped a beat and he licked his lips, taking a deep breath. That was the road that led towards the Guardhouse. "He didn't give any indication of what he was doing?" He felt a growing sense of unease that went deeper than his suspicion, but he didn't have time to work out where it came from.

"Not to me, sir."

"Right." Seregei licked his lips again. "Well, that's my route home. I'll see if I can see him on the way. Meanwhile, one of you go immediately and tell Lord Taffilelti that I suspect Ethiren has gone to speak to my trainee."

They nodded, looking confused. Seregei waved a quick farewell as he turned and started through the gate, breaking into a jog as he went.

He wanted to hurry, to run with all the speed he could muster, but he kept his pace steady as he went through the city. Once clear of its gates and its people, he would speed up. His breathing came quick as he hoped he would not be too late. With the Lady's blessing, he would overtake Ethiren on the road – he should have asked the guard how long ago Ethiren set out – or find that his fear was unfounded and Ethiren really had simply gone for a walk. He doubted it, though. He was becoming increasingly sure that the feeling in the back of his mind was Empathy. Lim was in trouble.

It seemed to take forever for him to reach the Guardhouse, even at a full run, and he approached the door carefully, panting to catch his breath. The building looked empty. He knew that Lim wouldn't have abandoned his post without good reason and his heart sank as he went in. No sign of anyone.

Normally, he would have called Lim's name to let the young elf know he was home, but this time he kept quiet, listening.

His worst fears were realised as he heard a raised voice from one of the spare rooms. Ethiren.

There wasn't time to fetch his sword. The daggers he always carried would have to do, if fighting were necessary. He crept down the corridor, listening until he found the right room. He gritted his teeth in fury as he heard Lim's voice, raised in a plea. He tried the door handle. Locked.

It went against his nature to break into one of the Guardhouse bedrooms, but there was no time for niceties. Seregei backed up and ran at the door, shoulder-first. It burst open under his weight.

Twin cries of shock greeted his arrival. Ethiren had been standing behind the door and Seregei almost collided with him. Lim was huddled against the far wall. Seregei put himself between them, side-on so he could see them both. Ethiren looked utterly shocked, balanced uncertainly on his back foot. Lim stayed huddled, his expression a mixture of shock and misery. His eyes were bloodshot and his face streaked with tears, but he didn't look like he was hurt.

"What's going on?" demanded Seregei.

"That's none of your business," said Ethiren, planting his feet and raising his head. "Lim's coming home with me, that's all you need to know."

Seregei looked at Lim in shock. The expression on the younger elf's face told him all he needed to know.

"Not unless he *truly* wants to," he said, keeping his voice calm with an effort.

Ethiren looked at Lim, who looked at the floor.

"Lim," said Ethiren sharply.

Lim's lip wobbled as he fought back tears. "I… I tried so hard," he said to no-one in particular.

"I know," said Seregei gently. "Like I said, I'm proud of you. I don't want you to leave unless that's really what you want." He glanced at Ethiren. "But I want to hear you say it without your father here."

"You needn't coddle him, Captain," said Ethiren. "We both know the situation and I'll be glad to take him off your hands."

Seregei frowned. "Well, I'll not be glad to see him go," he said curtly. "I'll not stop him if that's really what he wants, but…" He looked over at Lim, who was staring at him. He wasn't crying any more, but he still looked awful as he bit one of his forefingers as if trying to draw blood.

"Ethiren, I think you should leave," said Seregei, looking back at Ethiren. He didn't know quite what had happened here, but it smelled rotten.

Ethiren frowned. "No, I won't. That's my son and you are *not* going to take him from me again."

Seregei set his teeth. "He'll go where he wants, however much I'd miss him."

"Then that settles it." Ethiren turned back to Lim. "Come on, we're going home."

Lim hesitated and Ethiren paused, balanced mid-turn. "Lim?" he said softly, his voice suddenly sad. "Don't you want to come home with me?"

Seregei glanced at Lim, who was still hesitating. At last, he said, "I… would like to go home."

Ethiren shot Seregei a triumphant look, but Lim hadn't finished.

"Especially if…" – he sniffed and rubbed his eyes before looking at Seregei – "you really don't want me here."

"Not want you here?" echoed Seregei. He fought the urge to throw up his hands. "Why *wouldn't* I?"

"We don't need to discuss this," said Ethiren coolly. "You said you wanted to know what he wanted, and he's said it: he wants to come home."

He extended a hand towards Lim. Seregei was moving even before he had registered that Lim had tensed at the gesture. He stepped between them and folded his arms.

Ethiren's neutral expression twisted into rage for a moment, but that was gone in a flash to be replaced by a look of heartbreak and betrayal.

"Why must you all act against me?" he asked softly. "What have I done to deserve this?"

Seregei didn't look round, but he thought bitterly of Lim's broken hand and the way he flinched when Seregei made a sudden movement.

"At least this is less painful than what I've already suffered today," said Ethiren bitterly.

"Leave the room and let me talk to Lim in private," said Seregei. "If he truly wants to go with you, you've lost nothing."

"Why should I go?"

"Because he's clearly frightened of you. It's no choice if it's made under threat!"

"Frightened?" echoed Ethiren. He looked past Seregei. "You're not frightened of me, are you?"

Seregei glanced over his shoulder as Lim said, "No," doing his best not to look it. "You're... you're my father."

"That doesn't mean you can't be frightened of him," said Seregei gently.

"Yes, it does. There's no reason. I know he wouldn't hurt me."

"Indeed I wouldn't," said Ethiren. "No matter how much I may be accused, I'd not do anything of the sort." He glared at Seregei for a moment, then looked back at Lim. "You love me, don't you?"

Lim nodded.

"And you know I love you?"

This time there was a long pause before Lim slowly nodded again. Seregei could feel his reluctance.

"So let's have no more of this silliness," said Ethiren. "Stop bothering the Captain." Again, he beckoned.

Lim took an unwilling step forward, but Seregei laid a hand on his shoulder. "Ethiren, leave," he said firmly. "I want to talk to Lim in private."

Lim shot Seregei a worried look, but Seregei kept his eyes on Ethiren, who was staring at him with his jaw set.

"You don't mean to let me have him, do you?" he asked softly.

"I don't mean to let you drag him away."

"You have no right to keep him from me; I'm his father." The sorrow was gone from Ethiren's face and voice. His tone was flat and his eyes blazed with anger.

Seregei shifted to put himself between Lim and Ethiren again, making sure he was balanced in case of a fight. Something in Ethiren's expression sent a shudder down his spine.

Ethiren must have seen that he was preparing for battle; he too shifted a little to get into stance. "I'll not let you take what's mine."

"Lim doesn't belong to anyone."

"But –" said Lim from behind Seregei.

"*Anyone*," Seregei repeated. "Not his Captain, not his father."

"Give him back," said Ethiren, as if he'd not heard, "Or I'll take him."

That was a fight Seregei was sure he could win, but he didn't want to try it, especially in front of Lim. The young elf was still hovering behind him, as if unsure what to do. At least he'd not tried to get by. That alone made Seregei certain that he didn't really want to leave.

"Seregei?" said Lim softly.

"Yes?"

"You don't have to... I'll leave."

Seregei glanced at him, forcing a smile. "You don't have to," he echoed.

Lim blinked, but as he started to speak again, Ethiren talked over him. "We both know he's a burden on you here, Captain. You needn't put up with him any more" – his voice tilted back towards longing for a moment – "I get my son back, and we're all happy."

"He's not a burden," said Seregei, wondering if he'd said something to give Ethiren that impression. "And if I thought that Lim going back to Silvren would make *everyone* happy, I'd not stop him."

"It will," said Ethiren, his eyes widening. "You'll not have to tolerate –"

"It's not a question of toleration," snapped Seregei. "But that wasn't my point."

Ethiren snorted. "You're worried about him being unhappy? Believe me, there's nowhere he'd rather be than at home with a father who loves him."

That was probably true, but Seregei stood his ground and Lim didn't step around him.

The savage edge returned to Ethiren's voice. "Captain, step aside."

Seregei tensed, watching Ethiren for the first move. "No."

"So be it." Ethiren suddenly bent and snatched the knife from his boot. He was lunging almost before Seregei realised he'd actually done it.

Seregei's instinct was to sidestep. He planted his feet; Lim was behind him. He grabbed Ethiren's arm and pulled him to the side. Ethiren yelled in protest, twisting free.

"Lim, run," snapped Seregei, drawing his own knives. He parried a wild blow aimed at his head. Sheathed one knife and grabbed Ethiren's arm again. "Ethiren, stop this!"

Ethiren's face was inches from Seregei's. His jaw was set, his eyes narrow. He tried to twist away again. Seregei didn't loosen his grip. When

Ethiren still didn't relax, Seregei twisted his wrist. It made him drop the knife.

Seregei breathed a sigh of relief and glanced over his shoulder to check on Lim. The younger elf was visibly shaking, leaning against the wall, but before Seregei could speak to him he felt Ethiren dive for the knife.

Seregei yelled, "Ethiren, no!" He tried to keep his grip, but Ethiren twisted away. Seregei drew his other knife again. He didn't want to kill, but Ethiren wasn't going to go down easily. Ethiren lunged at him. Missed and drew back, crouched. Seregei glanced back at Lim. He'd slid down to crouch against the wall.

Movement caught the corner of Seregei's eye. He dodged a wild slash. Parried another. As he tried to grab Ethiren again, the other elf stabbed at his hand. He drew back just in time.

"Ethiren, drop the knife," he snapped.

"You give me back my son!" Ethiren brought the knife down in an overarm slash. Seregei blocked it. Stabbed, aiming to the side. Ethiren stepped back.

Seregei took a couple of steps and parried another blow, twisting to deflect and hold it. This time Ethiren didn't draw back. For a moment Seregei could feel Ethiren's breath on his cheek.

Then the Wood-elf moved. His knife slid off Seregei's. Seregei took a moment to step back. A flash of light towards his chest. He dodged. Tried to get back in front of Lim.

He felt a sharp blow to his left side. Then a cold feeling.

He gasped. The injury turned hot. He could feel something running down his flank. Didn't dare look. Started to turn to attack left-handed, trying to ignore the tearing feeling, but Ethiren pulled the knife free.

Then the pain came. Seregei's left hand came open, releasing one knife. He fell headlong. Barely managed to keep his right hand closed around the second knife. He could feel the blood still running. Deliberate blow meant mortal danger. He tried to force himself up, to pull himself together, to continue the fight...

Just as he looked up, started to raise his right hand to parry a blow, he heard a yell. Ethiren was standing over him, half turned away, knife in hand. Seregei couldn't see what was happening, but at that moment Ethiren jerked. His breath rattled in his throat. He collapsed across Seregei's legs.

Lim had been standing behind him. The young elf's face was grey except where blood was splattered on his cheek and forehead. His right hand was still raised, also covered in blood. He was shaking, his breath coming in deep, fast gasps, his eyes wide. His very breathing looked fit to tear him apart.

Seregei instinctively looked down at Ethiren. He was face-down, Seregei's dropped knife buried in the back of his neck. By the angle, the knife was lodged in his spine.

"Lim?" asked Seregei softly, finally moving to press a hand to his wound. His own touch made him gasp, but he tried to ignore it.

Lim's breathing had got even faster. He looked as if he might faint. He still hadn't moved.

"Lim!" Seregei half shouted, then winced at a warning pang from his side.

It had had an effect, though; Lim's eyes focussed and he lowered his hand.

"S-Seregei?" he whispered, his voice very small and high-pitched. That seemed to break a spell; tears welled in his eyes and he buried his face in his hands, talking wildly, his voice still a hysterical whimper. Seregei couldn't make out what he was saying, but he had to make him stop.

"Lim, look at me!" he said firmly.

Lim looked up, his eyes wild. "I had to. He was going to kill you. But…"

"Calm down," said Seregei as soothingly as he could manage when his vision was starting to swim. He forced himself not to look at the wound. "It's all right."

"*I killed my father!*" wailed Lim.

"Lim!" Seregei's breath was starting to come short. "I need you to calm down."

Lim's gasping breaths were breaking into sobs now, but he bit his lip and hugged himself. His eyes were still wild and he was still shaking.

Seregei pushed himself up on one elbow. He had to close his eyes for a moment as his side protested and he felt another rush of blood over his hand, but he pushed that aside. He didn't want to ask anything of Lim, but he had to. For both their sakes.

"Lim, are you listening?"

Lim nodded jerkily, finally looking at Seregei.

"You need to go and find help."

"But…" Lim's eyes strayed back to Ethiren's body.

"I can't go anywhere like this. You need to run and find a healer."

Lim took a shaky breath, hugging himself again. "I killed him…"

"Lim, you need to *go now.*" Seregei put as much force into the words as he could muster. "Run!"

Lim took another breath, looked at Seregei – and at the pool of blood gathering under him – and nodded. Then he carefully stepped around him and left. As Seregei lay down, he could hear the faltering steps start to quicken to a run as Lim went through the common room and out of the door.

He took a deep breath and concentrated on the ceiling. He wished he'd been able to let Lim mourn – whatever else, he had loved his father – but there was no choice. He needed help, and Lim needed something to do. Handling what he'd just done would have to wait.

CHAPTER SIX

Lim couldn't believe it. He couldn't believe what he'd done. He'd killed his father. Killed the one who had loved him, raised him, cared for him no matter what. He'd killed him. Stabbed him in the back.

The thought made him sob. He felt like he was being stabbed himself. The shock made him trip over his own feet and he fell headlong. For a moment he couldn't get up, just lay and cried. Then he remembered Seregei lying in his blood. Remembered what he was supposed to be doing. Another guilt twisted at him, but he forced himself to get up. Ran on, trying to go as fast as he could.

His feet had never felt so heavy. His head felt as if it would float off his shoulders. He was dizzy and almost fell again. He glanced down at his hands. Saw the blood. Felt bile rise in his throat. He was a murderer. Maybe he deserved to be hanged.

He managed to swallow before he could be sick and stumbled on. He needed to get a healer. He couldn't let Seregei die. He'd already murdered his father. He wouldn't let Seregei die. He'd failed him enough.

The thought that Seregei had been so disappointed in him made him choke again, hugging himself as he tried to keep running. He didn't want to leave. He truly didn't. Even to go home. He'd been happy…

"Lim!"

The voice finally cut through his thoughts and he realised the other elf had shouted at him several times. He looked up, swallowing. He'd not meant to let someone see him snivelling like this.

It was a member of the Royal Guard. He put his hands on Lim's shoulders and looked hard at him.

"Lim, look at me," he said, not unkindly. "Is any of that blood yours?"

The question made Lim break down again. He couldn't answer. He couldn't explain. He sobbed helplessly into his hands until the Valley-elf

126

gave him a slight shake and called his name again.

"Look me in the eye, Lim. What happened?"

Lim shook his head hard. A healer for Seregei. He needed a healer for Seregei. He took a hiccupping breath and managed to blurt out, "Healer... Seregei..."

The memory of his father driving a knife into his friend's side once again made him feel like he was the one who had been stabbed. For a moment it dried his tears. He tried again.

"S-Seregei's... Seregei's hurt. He needs a healer." He swallowed hard against the lump in his throat and his breathing caught on a few more sobs.

He looked up as he heard hooves approaching and the Valley-elf looked round too. It was a group of horses, carrying guards in Silvren livery. It took a moment for Lim to realise that Lord Taffilelti was riding among them. The expression on his face made Lim shrink back, but the thunder was gone in a moment as Lord Taffilelti looked at him.

"Lim, what happened?" he asked gently.

The tone made Lim almost start to cry again. He didn't deserve that. He was a murderer. He'd killed his father.

"Lim?" Lord Taffilelti said again.

"My Lord, he's just told me that Captain Seregei is injured," said the Valley-elf. "Is there a healer in your company?"

Lord Taffilelti's eyes narrowed and Lim flinched. The Valley-elf looked at him in surprise. He bit his lip, looking at the floor. He raised a hand to bite his finger, but once more felt sick as he saw the blood on it.

Then Lord Taffilelti was giving orders for someone to ride back and fetch a healer. "Lim, ride with us," he said. "Have you seen Master Ethiren?"

Lim couldn't stay calm any more. For a moment he thought he really would be sick. He felt himself shaking. He couldn't speak.

"Lim," said Lord Taffilelti firmly, leaning down a little in the saddle. "What happened?"

Lim swallowed as hard as he could. "I... I had to," he whispered. "He was going to kill Seregei. I had to do it. I had to..." He couldn't hold the tears back any more and buried his face in his hands.

"Reiron," said Lord Taffilelti, "Take Lim on your horse. We'll go on ahead to the Guardhouse."

"Lim, take my hand and I'll pull you up."

Lim looked up, sniffling and wiping his nose on the back of his hand. Lord Taffilelti's honour guard was offering a hand and he helped Lim to clamber onto his horse, riding pillion. Lim buried his face in the other elf's back. He could still feel himself shaking.

"Are you all right, back there?" asked Reiron.

Lim could only manage a whimper. He felt a twinge of shame. He was acting like a child. His father had been right. And he'd killed him. No wonder Seregei wanted rid of him.

As Reiron spurred his horse on, Lim clung on around his waist. He could barely even cry any more. He felt wrung out. There was nothing left in him. He just held on, his eyes tight shut, wondering if there was anything left that he could do.

Seregei wasn't sure how long it had been since Lim had left. He kept his eyes on the ceiling, trying to count the grains in the wood and ignore the blood still running from his side. He didn't dare move his hand, even to slip a pad under it to absorb the blood, and he didn't dare look to see how much it was bleeding. At least it seemed to be less.

He took a deep breath and let it out again. He felt light-headed, sick and faint. He knew he needed to keep still and stay awake, but he was tired. He shook his head and took another deep breath. Lim would be back soon. He was a fast runner, after all, and Seregei was sure he'd understood the importance of haste.

He couldn't help a slight chuckle. It seemed it was his turn to take a side wound. Lim had taken one in the flood, after all.

He laughed until he was tired and his head lolled to the side. At once, he looked up again, going back to counting the grains of wood. How long had it been now? He couldn't tell; for all he knew, he'd lost consciousness. He sighed. By the sun, it hadn't been long, though. There was no need to try to get up and seek help for himself. Not yet.

He still felt dizzy, and his mouth was dry. He had no water with him. His legs felt cold and tingly, but he forced himself to lie still and not think about the fact that Ethiren was still lying across his legs. Trying to move him would disturb the wound, and Seregei thought the bleeding was finally stopping.

He wondered faintly if that was because he was running out of blood. He knew he'd already lost a lot. He sighed.

His eyes had fallen closed and he didn't remember closing them. He wondered if the noises he could hear were his own heartbeat, but there was no mistaking the sound of a voice swearing and then yelling, "Here he is!"

He forced his eyes open as someone knelt beside him. A Wood-elf: one of Taffilelti's guards.

"Captain Seregei?" he said clearly. "Can you hear me?"

Seregei nodded. "Yes, I can. Where's Lim?"

"Outside."

"He all right?"

"He..." The wood-elf's eyes strayed to Ethiren's body.

Seregei nodded. "I saw him when he left... I can guess." He wondered if Lim had told them who had killed Ethiren. If they thought it was Seregei, let them. He'd sort that out later.

"We've sent for a healer. He'll be here soon."

Seregei nodded again. "I... know I've lost a lot of blood."

"It'll be all right."

Seregei sighed, letting his eyes fall closed again. It was still hard to stay awake – even harder now that more time had passed – and he didn't have to. Help was on the way…

"Captain Seregei!" The Wood-elf gave his shoulder a slight shake. "You have to stay awake."

Seregei sighed. "I know. It's just hard." He felt someone lift Ethiren off his legs and sighed in relief. "He is dead?"

"Yes. What –" The Wood-elf cut himself off there.

"I'll explain later, probably to Lord Taffilelti. Does he know what's happened?"

"Yes. He's outside with Lim."

"Good." Seregei sighed again. If Taffilelti had had the sense to send Lim away from Silvren before, he'd probably be able to do something for him now. If nothing else, he at least knew the story and could understand why Lim had killed Ethiren.

Another pair of feet entered the room in a rush and Seregei looked up, smiling as he recognised Arani.

"I came as quickly as I could," said the healer breathlessly as he stepped around Seregei to see the wound. "How are you, Seregei?"

Seregei forced a smile, though he suspected it looked more like a grimace. "I've been better. I don't know how much blood I've lost."

"What happened?"

"Ethiren and I were fighting. He got under my guard and stabbed me."

Arani glanced off towards Ethiren. Seregei craned his neck to see for himself what had happened to the dead Wood-elf and sighed in relief as he saw that someone had covered him with a cloak.

Arani didn't comment, though, he just asked, "How long ago did it happen?"

"I'm not sure." Seregei looked at the Wood-elven guard.

"We met Lim about ten minutes ago and he'd run from the Guardhouse."

"About twenty minutes, then," muttered Arani, digging in his bag. "Are you strong enough to keep your hand where it is, Seregei?"

Seregei chuckled despite himself. "I think it's stuck."

"Well, keep it there and keep pressing on the wound until I tell you to move."

"I will." Seregei sighed, closing his eyes for a moment. "Are you sure Lim's all right?"

"He's very upset. I saw him on the way in. I was surprised he wasn't here with you, actually." Arani laid a hand on Seregei's forehead. "You're still awake?"

"Yes." Seregei opened his eyes again, though his eyelids were heavy. "It's probably for the best that he stays out there. I just wanted to be sure he was all right."

"He looked upset, but he'll be fine." Arani smiled a little. "You just worry about yourself for the time being."

Seregei smiled back. "I'll try."

Arani took out a roll of bandages and then started to cut Seregei's shirt away from the stab wound. "Do you know how deeply he stabbed you?"

"No." Seregei winced at the memory.

"All right. How about the knife? Do you know anything about it?"

"He dropped it..." Seregei looked around. The Wood-elf crouched beside him got up to search.

"There it is." He picked it up and showed it to Arani.

"Good," muttered Arani, going back to his work after a brief glance. "It's sharp. That means a clean wound."

Seregei chuckled. "I know it would have hurt even more if not, but... I'd still not say 'good'."

Arani absently patted him on the forehead. "All right. It's time to move your hand. Try to stay awake and keep talking to me."

Seregei gritted his teeth. "No promises."

Several hours later, everything was quiet again. Taffilelti was sitting in one of the chairs in the common room, keeping an eye on Lim. He had to admit, he felt worn out. His back and head ached from tension, but he did his best to keep it hidden, at least from Lim. He hadn't missed the concerned looks that Reiron kept shooting him.

Lim was curled up at the end of the couch on the other side of the room, hugging his knees to his chest and staring at the floor. He'd refused to go anywhere else once he'd been assured that Seregei would be all right. He didn't even want to go and sit with the older elf as he slept.

Taffilelti looked away with a slight sigh. At least the shaking and crying had stopped, though he suspected that was only because Lim was too exhausted to carry on like that any more.

"I'm sorry," Lim said suddenly. He hiccupped softly and hugged his knees a little tighter.

"What for?" Taffilelti asked, keeping his voice gentle. Lim had apologised over and over again that afternoon, apparently for everything he could think of.

"You're being" – Lim hiccupped again – "very kind. I shouldn't ignore you like this." He looked up wearily. "I'm sorry."

Taffilelti shook his head. "It's been a long day for all of us. I'm not surprised you're tired."

"I shouldn't, though." Lim looked back at the floor. "After all I've… all I've done…" His voice cracked, but he didn't shed a tear. Taffilelti wondered whether to ask him any more questions now that he seemed less hysterical.

Behind his chair, Reiron stirred and Taffilelti glanced at him. He smiled apologetically, but then nodded towards Lim with an enquiring look.

Taffilelti sighed, then nodded a little. "Don't ask too much, though," he whispered.

Reiron bowed his head, then addressed Lim. "Lim, why don't you want to be with Captain Seregei?"

Lim looked up, looking stricken, but didn't answer.

"He's your friend, isn't he?" asked Reiron.

Lim bit his lip. "I… he's been kind to me and…" He closed his eyes and buried his face in his knees. "I didn't want him to die," he said, his voice muffled.

"But don't you want to be there when he wakes up?"

"I shouldn't bother him." Lim sniffled, raising his head a little to rub his eyes. "He was so good to me and I disappointed him… I should have known I didn't deserve" – he gestured around at the Guardhouse – "all this."

Taffilelti frowned. "Did he tell you that?"

"My father said he'd told him." Lim let out a dry sob. "That he'd be glad to see the back of me and was… was happy Father was… here to take me away." He buried his face in his knees again. His voice was a barely-audible whimper, but Taffilelti could make out the words "killed him".

For a moment, he battled with words, unsure what to say. He didn't want Lim to hear the anger and slight fear. He'd known Ethiren was cold, of course. He'd known of his arrogance and his conviction that he was always the wisest person at council. He'd tolerated them; Ethiren was good at his job and it had seemed that he was harmless once Lim was out of his grip. He'd been enraged when he heard that his advisor had directly disobeyed him and gone to the Guardhouse. But a lie like that worried him. It was a cruel slander against the Swordmaster captain: an elf equal in rank and esteem to the king of Duamelti… or of Silvren.

He wondered with fear and anger what other lies Ethiren had told.

Fortunately, Reiron spoke while Taffilelti was still warring with himself. "Lord Taffilelti, may I speak freely?"

Taffilelti nodded. "Please do."

"I won't say much – it's not in my nature to speak ill of the dead – but when your father told you that, he was lying."

Lim looked at him for a moment, wide-eyed. "But… why?"

"Because he wanted you to leave here and never look back."

Lim hugged his knees. "He just wanted me to come home," he whispered, hunching his shoulders. "He loved me and..." He hung his head.

"I've spoken to Captain Seregei. I'm sure he'd have told someone else if he was really that upset with you and that something would have come of it if he had. Apart from anything else, even if he knew he couldn't send you back to Silvren, there are plenty of other jobs here in Duamelti. What possible reason would he have to keep you in the Guardhouse if he was really so disappointed in you that he'd actually be glad to see you go?"

Lim shook his head. "I don't know..." he whispered.

Taffilelti sighed. "Go and speak to Seregei, Lim. He's an honest elf. If he doesn't want you here, he'll say so."

Lim kept his eyes on the floor, wringing his hands.

"I intend to speak to him myself at some point. If you want, I'll ask him." Taffilelti smiled. "After all, there's no more danger for you in Silvren. You'd have a place at my court if you came back, but I won't force you. You've made a home here."

Encouraged by Lord Taffilelti, Lim went to Seregei's room to sit with him and wait for him to wake up. He hurried by the door of the empty room where... everything had happened. He couldn't face that again. He was glad the door was closed and barred.

Seregei's room was on the other side, a couple of doors down. The door was half open and Lim paused in the opening. He still didn't feel comfortable about the idea of going into Seregei's room, especially without his explicit permission.

From here, he could see Seregei, though. He was fast asleep, the blankets pulled up to his chin. He looked pale and his chest rose and fell unevenly. Lim was suddenly reminded of how he'd looked on the river bank after the flood. He wondered if that was one of the reasons Seregei had been disappointed in him: his lie about the wound he'd taken, and his foolish attempt to get home without any help. He knew Seregei had told him that he didn't want him to go, but what if that had just been an attempt to comfort him?

He leaned on the doorframe, his legs suddenly feeling wobbly as a wave of tiredness went through him. He wanted to lie down and sleep. For a sudden, childish moment he wanted to run to his room, lock the door and stay there. Perhaps all this would go away if he just hid.

He mentally slapped himself. He'd done enough today. He had to face it now. His father had so often told him he was a coward, that he acted like a child, that he was wicked and malevolent and disobedient. He'd always tried so hard to be better, and he wasn't going to give up on that now. His father had tried to teach him, and he would at least try to live by those lessons, even if he'd murdered the one who had taught him.

There was one thing he could no longer deny, though: Seregei had been right. His father should not have forced him to lie and then punished him for it. That was not a fair or loving action.

The thought made him feel faint again and he rubbed his eyes. He needed to sit down, if nothing else. He'd never felt so tired. Perhaps he should go back to the common room.

But Lord Taffilelti was there, and he'd told Lim to come and sit with Seregei. He looked for a moment at the chair pulled up beside Seregei's bed, then took a deep breath and stepped over the threshold.

Nothing happened. Seregei didn't even stir. Lim couldn't help a sigh of relief as he went to the chair and sat down. He still didn't feel like he should be here, though. Seregei had always respected his space and had never entered his room. It was one of the things that had made him happy here.

He hugged himself, biting his lip and staring at the floor. After all Seregei had done, this was how he repaid him.

As he sat there, he remembered something Taffilelti had said as he wept and confessed the murder and tried to beg for mercy, fully expecting all the rigors of the law. Taffilelti had said that it was no murder. That Lim had acted to save the life of another. Just as he would not have been a murderer had he been the one under Ethiren's knife, he was not a murderer when he had killed to save Seregei.

But then he shook his head. Seregei was a great fighter. He could have defended himself. Lim knew he shouldn't have panicked as he had. Besides, why would his father kill someone? He was a good man. He'd just been angry. That was Lim's fault anyway. This was all his fault. Seregei was hurt. His father was dead. It was all his fault.

"Lim?"

The voice cut through his thoughts and he looked up. Seregei's eyes were open and he was smiling.

"How are you?" he asked. His voice sounded hoarse and weak.

Lim swallowed hard. "I'm sorry," he said. "This was my fault. I shouldn't have…"

Seregei frowned. "Shouldn't have what?"

"I provoked him. If I hadn't done that he wouldn't have been so angry. He wouldn't have attacked you. He just wanted me back. I should have gone with him. I shouldn't have tried to stay when I'm just a burden to you…" The words tumbled out and Lim only fell silent when Seregei reached out and tapped his knee.

"You stop that," he said sternly, but then smiled. "Let me get a word in."

Lim bit his lip. "Sorry."

"Right. First of all, please stop saying you're a burden to me." Seregei rubbed his eyes. "You're not. I'd not have kept telling you I was pleased with you if you were."

"But Father said you'd told him you'd be glad —"

"Your father," Seregei interrupted, "was a *liar.*"

Lim was too startled to say anything to that.

"I never told him *anything* like that. He asked if I wanted you to stay and I told him the truth: you're my trainee and I'm fond of you. I said what I said to you: you're not a prisoner and if you want to leave I'll let you, but I certainly don't want you to go."

Lim wasn't sure what to say to that. He still didn't want to believe his father had lied to him, but he didn't want to contradict Seregei. And why would Seregei spare his feelings now, after all he'd done?

It must be true.

"I murdered him," he whispered. "Surely you don't want me now, after I k-killed my own father."

"Why did you do it?" Seregei asked softly, reaching out a hand.

Lim watched the movement carefully, but when Seregei just lowered his hand to the blanket again, he looked at the floor. "I had to," he whispered.

"Why?"

"I was scared... I thought he'd kill you. You were lying on the floor and he raised his knife and I was *scared.* I didn't want you to die; I knew I had to do something and... I didn't know what to do." Lim hugged himself. "I tried to grab his arm but he hit me... then I grabbed your knife and..." He couldn't go on.

"I didn't know he'd hit you," said Seregei softly.

"Not hard," said Lim quickly. "It didn't even bruise. He didn't mean to hurt me, he was just angry and it was my fault..."

"For trying to stop him?" asked Seregei dryly.

"For upsetting him. I should have just done as he said. Then you wouldn't be hurt and he..."

Seregei shook his head. "He had no right to try to drag you away when you didn't want to go."

"He's my father. I shouldn't have left him in the first place."

Seregei looked hard at him. He looked even paler than he had before, Lim noticed. "Lim, do you trust me?"

Lim nodded. For once, it was true. Seregei had never hurt him. Even to spare his feelings, he'd never lied to him.

"Then listen to me: he had no right to treat you as he did and you had every right to want to escape. You did the right thing when you listened to Taffilelti and ran away."

"It was my fault. I shouldn't have..."

"I know that" – Seregei pointed to Lim's left hand – "wasn't the only time. And I saw the state you were in when I arrived today. He had no right to do that to you. It was cruel. He especially had no right to tell you that you weren't wanted here."

"But I shouldn't have…" Lim hung his head. He was too tired to argue any more and couldn't think how to end that sentence.

Seregei patted his knee. "I'm sorry you had to fight him today," he said softly. "I *should* have been here. You never should have had to face him."

Lim blinked. "You don't have to… you had more important things to deal with."

"I have a duty to make sure you're safe, and I failed you. I'm sorry." Seregei smiled wanly. "I'm glad you're all right."

"It… it wasn't your fault."

There was a knock at the door and Lim looked round with a start. It was Reiron.

"Some of Lord Taffilelti's entourage has returned to escort us back to the palace," he said. "He asked if there were any messages to take back. Apparently one of Master Kerin's assistants will come in about an hour to make sure you're all right, Captain."

Seregei nodded. "I think we can manage until then. Thank you, Reiron, and please pass on my condolences to Lord Taffilelti."

Reiron nodded. "I will." He smiled at Lim, then left again.

"Thank you!" Lim called after him.

Seregei chuckled. "You'll see them both again, don't worry."

Lim nodded, licking his lips nervously. "Lord Taffilelti said I wasn't going to be punished," he said after a moment.

Seregei stared at him and started to say something, then caught himself. The slight smile died on his lips. "For what?" he asked. "Killing Ethiren?"

Lim looked at the floor, making himself take a deep breath. "Yes."

"I agree with him. It wasn't murder, Lim. You had a reason."

Lim sighed. "I just… I knew when I did it that I was at least risking killing him. I just… I panicked."

"I know." Seregei patted his knee. "And I'm actually pretty sure he would have killed me had you not acted."

"He wouldn't –" Lim started. "He didn't mean…"

"If he didn't mean to hurt me, he might have stabbed me by accident, but he'd have *reacted* to that." Seregei sighed. "I can't imagine he'd have kept hold of the knife. You let go of mine, for example."

Lim nodded.

"No, I do believe he meant to strike again, and you had every reason to think the same." Seregei smiled. "I mean it: you didn't murder him."

Lim couldn't agree with that, but he couldn't argue any more. He leaned forward, his head in his hands. "I'm so tired…"

"I know," said Seregei gently. "You should probably get some rest yourself, but thank you for sitting with me."

"Would you like me to leave?" asked Lim, sitting up.

Seregei chuckled. "No. I appreciate the company. Nonetheless, I know you're tired." He reached out again and Lim once more watched his hand. "There's no need to look at me like that. I'm not going to hurt you."

Lim immediately looked away. "I know."

Seregei took and held his hand. "This is all I wanted to do. Are you sure you're not hurt?"

Lim nodded. "I'm sure."

"Good. I was worried, you know."

Lim looked up. Seregei was smiling slightly and he couldn't help smiling back. "Thank you. And…" He looked at their clasped hands. "I would like to stay, if you'll let me."

"Of course." Seregei squeezed his hand. "But… I realise I still owe you a story."

Lim looked up. "What?"

Seregei reached across with a wince and pulled up his sleeve. Lim saw one of the scars coiling up his forearm and shuddered. In everything that had happened, he'd almost forgotten those.

"Do you want to know how I got them? After all, you told me the truth about your hand, I owe you the truth about my scars."

Lim swallowed hard. "I don't want to ask… I know it's a painful memory."

"It is, but you still need to know. Apart from anything else, I remember you thought I could never be killed." Seregei smiled wanly. "Though even then you'd had to save my life once."

Lim looked down.

"Lim? I'll tell you if you're interested in knowing."

He nodded. "All right," he whispered.

Seregei squeezed his hand again. "Well… I was brought up in the Guardhouse. My parents were Swordmasters before me and after they died the surviving Swordmasters raised me. I started training and became a Swordmaster as young as I could."

Lim nodded.

"After that, though…" Seregei looked away. "We were ambushed by a group of humans who had a grudge against us. The details don't matter right now. Just…" He sighed. "It was the worst attack against us in memory. They captured us all and…" He took a deep breath and let it out again.

"You don't have to tell me," said Lim quickly, feeling guilty for causing Seregei this much distress.

Seregei smiled wanly. "I owe you the truth," he said softly. "Even apart from anything else, you need to know what can happen." He pressed Lim's hand. "I'm afraid your father isn't the only one out there who likes to hurt."

"He didn't do it for pleasure," said Lim quickly. "He did it because I made him angry."

Seregei shook his head a little, but just continued, "You know what torture is?"

Lim nodded.

These humans... tortured the others to death. One after another, while the rest of us... listened to the screams." Seregei took another deep breath and let it out, closing his eyes tightly.

"Seregei..."

Seregei shook his head again. "I was the last one, and they gave me these scars." He gestured to his arm again. "Carved them on with a hot knife." He gritted his teeth and shook his head again. "So... that's how I got my scars, and how it is that I'm the only Swordmaster now." He sighed. "Maelli was still alive when they found us, but died soon afterwards from his injuries. He was Captain for... about three days, I think, since Seri died first." He swallowed hard. "Sorry, it... doesn't make that good a story."

Lim gulped. "I shouldn't have asked," he said, looking away. "I'm sorry."

"I meant it. You need to know and I owe you truth." Seregei forced a smile. "Neither of us is a liar, after all."

That made Lim smile despite himself. "Thank you."

Seregei nodded. "I should sleep some more," he said softly. "Do you want to stay here and sit with me, or...?"

"I'll stay, if you don't mind."

Seregei smiled again. "Keep an ear out for anyone coming to the door," he said. "Wake me if you have to. I'm expecting a few visitors, but if you tell them I'm injured, they should be able to come back when I've recovered a little."

Lim nodded and watched as Seregei fell asleep.

Two weeks after Ethiren's death, Taffilelti and his entourage were leaving. Seregei was well enough to go down and see them off now, though he was glad to have Lim with him as they walked down to the city for the first time since he had been wounded. He did his best to conceal the occasional fits of dizziness and stabs of pain that still plagued him as they went; Lim had spent most of the time since that day looking horribly worried and Seregei didn't want to make that worse if there was no need. He could tell when he needed rest, and would sit down for a while if he had to.

"You're sure you don't want to go with him?" he asked Lim.

Lim shook his head. "If you want me to stay, I... would prefer that."

Seregei smiled. "I do, and I'm glad. Is the Guardhouse beginning to feel a little more like home now?"

Lim looked away, his expression haunted. "I... I'm sorry. I don't know if... Silvren will ever not be my home. I can't go back, though. I'd always remember." He bit his lip. "Though I can't see that door without thinking of what I did, and... sometimes when I'm alone in my room I remember it as if it were happening all over again."

Seregei paused, frowning. "I didn't know that," he said seriously.

"I deserve it," whispered Lim. "It's like in stories when the murderer hears his victim's heartbeat wherever he goes."

"Except that it wasn't a murder." Seregei went to put a hand on Lim's shoulder, but hesitated before touching him. Now that he was a little more awake, he remembered that Lim didn't like being touched, and was determined not to do it without warning.

Lim, however, just glanced at his hand and looked away again. He didn't flinch when Seregei patted his shoulder, and Seregei smiled.

"At least you don't have to be frightened any more."

"I wasn't –" Lim cut himself off there and sighed. "All right, I was frightened, but only... I was afraid of being punished."

Seregei patted his shoulder again. "Nobody likes to be hurt," he said softly.

"But you're brave enough to face it."

"You're not leaving when you could," said Seregei with a smile. "I think you've some courage in you too."

Lim looked a little sceptical at that.

"I mean it: I've told you how I got these scars and you realise that something like that could happen to either one of us, but you still want to stay."

Lim smiled a little, but the smile faded as he said, "It's more that I don't want to leave."

***

When they reached the palace, Taffilelti's entourage was well on the way to being ready to leave. He himself was still inside, but there was a confusion of horses and elves in the courtyard as the Wood-elves prepared their baggage and got into order for his arrival. One came forward to greet Seregei, looking a little flustered. Seregei recognised him as Ridani, the clerk who had taken over assisting Taffilelti after Ethiren's death.

"Captain Seregei, Lim," he said, bowing. "My lord should be joining us soon, but he left orders that you were welcome to join him and Lord Caleb if you so wished."

"Thanks, Ridani," said Seregei. "Where are they?"

"In one of the receiving rooms, I believe."

Seregei nodded, thanked him again and led the way inside. It was easy to spot the right room; Reiron and Ekehart were sitting together outside.

"Seregei," said Ekehart warmly, getting up to greet them as Reiron slipped into the room to announce their arrival. "I'm glad to see you looking so much better."

Seregei smiled, taking Ekehart's hand. "I'm on my feet, at least. Have I missed much?"

"I couldn't say, but" – Ekehart glanced over his shoulder at the door as Reiron returned – "go on in." He smiled a little at Lim. "Both of you."

Lim looked a little surprised at that, but followed Seregei as they went in.

"They obviously still trust you," Seregei whispered to him.

Caleb was standing by a side table, pouring a couple more cups of mead, while Taffilelti sat on one of the couches. He smiled a welcome as Seregei and Lim entered. Lim hesitated, but Seregei paused and beckoned him forward.

"Take a seat, Seregei," said Caleb, offering one of the cups. He gave the other to Lim. "There you are."

"You look much better," said Taffilelti. "I trust everything is going well?"

Seregei nodded as he sat down. He had to shift about a little to ease the strain on his side, but then he could relax with a sigh. "It's healing," he said simply.

"Good." Taffilelti looked over at Lim, who had settled himself nervously on the edge of a chair. "And I hear you plan to stay and continue your training, Lim?"

"With your permission, my Lord," said Lim.

"I sent you here with a request that Caleb find you a place. It would hardly be gratitude to order you out of the place he found."

Caleb chuckled. "And I have no objection to him staying."

"I hope not," said Seregei, raising his cup a little to Caleb, "otherwise you and I would have a disagreement. I owe my life twice over to Lim, apart from anything else."

Taffilelti frowned into his cup. "And… I should have seen earlier what sort of elf Ethiren was," he said slowly. "I hold no grudge, Lim, and I meant what I said when I told you it was no murder."

Lim looked at the floor. "Thank you," he whispered.

Seregei smiled at him and raised his cup again before taking a drink. "Now," he said, "What did I miss while I was trapped in my bed?"

***

Seregei sat leaning against one of the trees surrounding the Guardhouse, watching Lim practice his archery amid the occasional whirl of autumn leaves. As ever, he looked like a different elf, though even when he was relaxed there were lines on his face that hadn't been there before and he looked thinner than when he'd arrived the previous year. Still, he was smiling faintly as he held the bow ready to loose, practicing keeping his aim steady. He had moved to the more powerful bow in the month since Ethiren's death and he was still improving as he grew stronger and even a little taller.

Seregei sighed, wondering if he had done the right thing by taking Lim to train. He was practically a child, after all, still growing in body and mind. The thought led to another, though: had he known that Lim wasn't an orphan, he might have sent him back to his father.

The thought made him shudder as he remembered the scene he'd stumbled on that day. He didn't think he'd ever forget the sight of Lim huddled against the wall in tears, Ethiren's words twisting a knife deeper and deeper.

The *thunk* of arrow hitting target distracted him and he smiled as he saw the shaft quivering in the centre of the target.

"Good shot!" he called to Lim, who glanced round with a smile. Seregei smiled back, any fleeting regrets vanishing like mist in the sun. Lim was young, he was shy, he was strange, but he was a good elf, and he really would make a fine Swordmaster one day.

Swift

Book 6

CHAPTER ONE

Though on the face of it Lim was hopelessly over-matched, he had one advantage over his opponent. Seregei was tall and strong, but Lim was *fast*.

He ducked a sweep aimed at his neck and darted a stab towards Seregei's midriff. The other elf jumped back with a curse and Lim followed up, feet moving fast. Seregei sidestepped and Lim had to shift quickly to avoid the stab aimed at his side. This time it was Seregei's turn to press the offensive, but Lim kept moving, dropping to the floor and rolling almost to Seregei's feet.

"Don't do that!" cried Seregei.

"Why, because it's a good way for me to beat you?" Lim grinned, starting to scramble up again as Seregei stepped back.

"No." Seregei put a foot on Lim's chest and pushed him back to the floor, putting the edge of one knife against his throat. "Because it's a good way for *me* to beat *you*."

Lim grimaced, suddenly feeling very small.

"Yield?" asked Seregei with a small smile.

"Yield," said Lim softly.

Seregei grinned, tossed the wooden practice knife aside and reached out a hand to help Lim up. Lim took it, briefly considered using it to pull Seregei over, and decided against it. Apart from anything else, he'd probably be expecting it.

Seregei pulled him up, laughing. "You were doing well up until that last bit," he said, bending to pick up his dropped knife. "I think I'm pretty much done with you."

"What do you mean?" asked Lim, though he was pretty sure he could guess.

Seregei's smile widened. "I think it might be time to find you a Task, brother mine."

1

Lim grinned back. He had thought that was what Seregei had been leading up to, but his smile slowly faded as he thought about what this meant. He'd be a Swordmaster. It was what he'd been working towards for years, but the reality was a little frightening. He still wasn't entirely sure he could cope with it.

"What is it?" asked Seregei.

"Are you sure I'm ready?" Lim asked, as they headed back into the Guardhouse. "That I'd make a good Swordmaster?"

Seregei rolled his eyes. "Not this again. Honestly, Lim, you have to believe in yourself at some stage. Trust me, I'd not tell you that you were ready if you weren't, and I'd not have wasted my time training you if I didn't think you'd make a good Swordmaster." He smiled a little and clapped Lim on the shoulder. "You might not trust yourself and your own judgement, but grant me some credit: you can trust mine."

Lim smiled, feeling better, but as he sat down in one of the chairs in the Guardhouse common room he couldn't resist saying, "Says the elf that was so convinced those caves were safe."

Seregei winced at the memory. "Well, I think I paid for that. I'm still impressed that I don't limp; that rock almost cut my leg off."

"We did get out." After a moment, Lim added, "I think it had more to do with my digging than your judgement, though."

Seregei stuck his tongue out, but also sat down, kicking off his boots and leaning back comfortably. "Your muscles will stiffen if you don't stretch."

"Hypocrite." Nonetheless, Lim started to stretch his arm muscles with a slight wince.

"Don't change the subject." Seregei grinned. "We were discussing the fact that you're ready to be a Swordmaster. I mean, it's been ten years. I've taught you everything I know and you're the best archer I've ever seen. I'll admit that you didn't learn that from me."

Lim smiled a little. "You're no archer."

Seregei waved a hand in acknowledgement of the truth of that. His bow was unusually long and reinforced to take advantage of his great height and strength, but he wasn't very good with it.

"But you've even mastered lockpicking," he said. "I never thought you'd get that."

Lim blushed, rubbing absently at his damaged left hand. He was left-hand-dominant, as much as any elf was dominant with one hand, but since his hand had been broken it had been difficult for him to do anything with it that required delicacy or strength. It had taken him months just to learn how to write again, and his handwriting was still barely legible.

Seregei was looking sympathetically at him. "You all right?" he asked.

Lim chuckled, trying to sound normal. "Of course," he said. "I'm fine."

Seregei looked sceptical, but nodded and got up. "Come on," he said. "We should either stretch and change our clothes, or spar again."

Lim thought about it. He was starting to feel a bruise on his shoulder now that the adrenaline was wearing off and he didn't really feel like another match, but he knew it would be good for him.

"You pick," he said.

Seregei grinned, leaning over to one side to stretch. "Whenever you say that, my friend, I know that you don't want to carry on, but are worried that I'll think less of you if you tell me as much."

Lim grimaced, embarrassed. "Are you using empathy, or do you actually know me that well?" he asked.

Seregei laughed. "A little of both," he replied, leaning to the other side. Lim hitched his shoulders, but couldn't help a small smile. Seregei's empathy only worked on those he knew and trusted, and Lim could never take for granted the fact that he was in that group.

A yawn surprised him and Seregei laughed.

"When did you get to sleep last night?" he asked.

"Too late. It's your fault, keeping me out tracking until even the moon was abed." Lim caught himself as he spoke, looking quickly at Seregei. It didn't seem that he'd overstepped; Seregei laughed.

"She was not. It was cloudy, that's all."

Encouraged, Lim waved a hand. "You admit it: that's why I could not find those tracks that you seemed to think were there!"

Seregei rolled his eyes. "They were clear as day," he said.

"Perhaps, but the night was *not*."

Seregei looked about to retort when there was a knock on the open door and an elf stepped into the room.

"Captain Seregei?" he said. "Lord Caleb wishes to speak to you."

Seregei sighed a little. He didn't like it when the king of Duamelti sent for him; he felt that it showed that the other elf was getting ideas above his station.

"Is it important?" he asked after a moment.

The messenger looked uncomfortable. "He... he didn't say, sir."

"Do you know anything about what he wants to talk to me about? I'd like to rest a while and change my clothes. Is that possible?"

"He looked worried."

Seregei sighed again. "Very well, I'll come straight away." He glanced over at Lim and said, "Remember to stretch and take a nap." He gestured down the corridor that led from the common room to the bedrooms. "You do look tired."

Lim nodded and began unlacing his boots as Seregei followed the messenger across the grassy courtyard around the Guardhouse, into the forest.

Seregei strode down the path, ducking around stray branches that hung over the road. He wondered whether to see about getting some of these branches cut back. The path up towards the Guardhouse from the city of Duamelti was well-maintained and frequently-used and the higher branches provided shade, but the lower ones were a nuisance to someone as tall as Seregei. He even towered over most Valley-elves, for all that they were the tallest of the elven races.

He and the guard crested a ridge as they came out of the trees and the valley of Duamelti was spread out before them, all green with the forest turning to purple heather near the tops of the hills that formed its border. The city nestled in a bend of the main river directly in front of him, protected from floods by a huge dam that formed a pool and sent the river around the city. There were a few boats out on the pool and Seregei smiled, wondering if there would be a chance for him to go swimming this afternoon.

He shook his head to banish the thought, though, and turned his attention back to the city. He would see what Caleb wanted, and then make plans.

He parted from the guard at the palace gate, after an enquiry about Caleb's whereabouts, and went straight to the king's study. As he went, he ignored the startled stare of a small group of humans – from the forest around Duamelti, by the look of them – who clearly had not expected to see an elf that was seven feet tall and broad across the shoulder to go with it.

He entered the study without knocking and leant on Caleb's desk, looking down at him. Caleb did not get up to greet him; he simply raised an eyebrow.

"You sent for me," said Seregei. "You know how I feel about that."

Caleb rolled his eyes. "Just sit down, Seregei; I've not got time for power plays."

Apparently this was serious, but Seregei remained standing. "What's the matter?"

"Sit down and I'll tell you. You don't like being sent for and I don't like craning my neck to talk to someone."

Seregei smiled despite himself and sat down. "Right. I'm sitting, so what's the matter?"

Caleb sighed. "Have you heard of Esgal?"

Seregei shook his head.

"He's our spy in Arket."

Seregei did his best to hide his ignorance, but Caleb apparently noticed and added, "A few days' ride south-east of here, a little way from Silvren. It's a kingdom of humans. They don't like elves."

Seregei nodded. "But how does an elf remain hidden there?"

Caleb looked pained. "At the moment, he doesn't. Esgal has been captured."

Seregei bit his lip, feeling a small stab of pity for Esgal, even though he'd never met him. He didn't doubt that the simple phrase 'they don't like elves' meant that there was a great deal of suffering in store for him.

"I see that you appreciate the problem," said Caleb.

"I do indeed, but why did you summon me to tell me this?"

"Esgal is a Mixed-blood, and therefore one of your people. He also has access to a great deal of secret information. It would be very dangerous for the men of Arket to learn some of the things he knows, and..." He trailed off, shifting in his chair and looking away.

"They'll torture him," Seregei finished bluntly. Seeing Caleb's expression, he added, "Yes, I said 'torture' and I'll say if again if I want, so calm down."

Caleb glared at him. "Yes," he said calmly, "They'll torture him, and I'm sure I don't need to tell you that given time they'll break him and he'll tell them all they want to know."

Seregei winced. "But what can I do about it?" he asked again.

"I was hoping you could rescue him," said Caleb.

Seregei nodded slowly. This was potentially a Task. It had to be something that could be done by one person working entirely alone, though, and he'd need more details before he could commit Lim to it, as well as speaking to Lim himself. Still, even if it wasn't a suitable Task, he and Lim might do it together.

"Can you tell me anything else?" he asked.

Caleb smiled a little, probably guessing that Seregei had all but decided. "We got a message this morning from his partner to say that he'd not returned from a visit to a particular small town on the border." Caleb pulled out a map, frowned over it for a moment, then pointed to a dot on the border of a shaded area labelled 'Arket'. "That was where he normally met his human contacts. His partner suspects that one of them betrayed him."

"How long was he overdue when his partner wrote to you?"

"Two days. He was only supposed to be gone one day and was gone three."

Seregei winced. In that time, anything could have happened.

"We know that they tend to keep captured elves when they have them in the king's city, several days' journey through the mountains. There's no reason to suspect that they'd not take Esgal back there, but we don't know how they'll transport him."

"What's the chance that they'd kill him out of hand?"

"Not very high. If their previous behaviour is any indication, they'll want to interrogate him before they kill him."

Seregei nodded. "So we don't know how he's being held or what state he'll be in, but they'll probably be taking him from this town back through the mountains and he'll probably still be alive?"

"Indeed."

"Could he have simply met with an accident?"

"I doubt it. The road to this town is easy and, in any case, someone would have found his body."

"Will we be able to meet up with his partner?"

"He's probably already on his way back. We usually think it safest that way, in case… Esgal betrays him in turn."

Seregei nodded again; that was a worry. "Very well, I'll consider it."

"Thank you," said Caleb sincerely. "I owe you a favour."

Seregei laughed. "You owe me many favours, Caleb, but I've not yet said I'll do it. I'll let you know before this evening."

Caleb nodded and Seregei got up to leave.

"See you this evening," said Caleb. Seregei nodded absently and left.

All the way back to the Guardhouse, he was thinking. It might not be a good idea to set this as Lim's Task; they had no idea what sort of thing he might be up against. Perhaps this would be ideal for a fully-trained Swordmaster: a few guards that might be overcome without too much difficulty and an able-bodied captive who wouldn't need too much help on the way back. On the other hand, Lim might be faced with a dozen heavily-armed men and Esgal might be half dead and unable to help himself. In that situation it was a job for half a dozen elves, not one, and he might be sending Lim to his death by assigning him that mission.

At last, he sighed and shook his head. Worrying about it wouldn't change anything. Lim was an adult and normally fairly responsible. Seregei would tell him the situation and let him decide, offering the choice that he himself would come and help.

There was another thing to worry about: despite their best efforts, it might not be possible to rescue Esgal. He might be too severely injured, so that he couldn't be moved. He might be too heavily guarded so that even the two of them together couldn't reach his side, and even if they could they couldn't get out again and would end up being captured as well. What then? Seregei wasn't prepared to take that sort of risk, not when he was the only remaining Swordmaster. The name had to be passed from mentor to trainee and he couldn't take stupid risks with his life. If he died, it would be the end of the tradition. The Mixed-bloods would lose their nominal leader and the Irnianam – the Valley-elves, as they now called themselves – would finally take over Duamelti entirely.

He chuckled humourlessly. Apart from anything else, Caleb would never let him hear the end of it. So what was to be done if Lim, or Lim and himself, couldn't rescue Esgal?

Well, Seregei would never forgive himself if he had to leave Esgal alive.

He tensed a little as he heard a rustle in the tree above him. He kept walking as though he'd not noticed, but his hand crept to the hilt of one of his daggers. Now that he was paying full attention to his surroundings, he was aware that someone was following him, sneaking through the trees as silently as a squirrel.

He only knew of one people that could manage to be as stealthy as that: Wood-elves.

He reached out with his empathy, looking for the person trailing him, and confirmed his suspicions in a moment, though the other elf immediately shielded his mind.

"I know you're there, Lim," said Seregei, grinning.

Lim swung down from the tree to land lightly on the ground beside him, falling neatly into step with him. Seregei pulled Lim's braid and laughed as he was swatted lightly on the shoulder in return.

"Whatever were you thinking about?" asked Lim. "I've been on your tail half the way back and you only just noticed."

"I'll tell you when we get inside."

Lim nodded, his smile fading. "*Is* it serious?" he asked.

"Potentially." Seregei pushed the door open and went in, flopping into his favourite chair.

"I thought Swordmasters didn't flop," said Lim, closing the door behind him and going to sit in a nearby window seat. Seregei ignored the remark.

"All right," he said. "There's a mixed-blood elven spy in a mortal kingdom to the south of here. Apparently they…" He decided to use the same phrase as Caleb; Lim would know exactly what he meant. "They don't like elves. And they've captured him."

"He'll break under torture?"

Seregei nodded, impressed. "Yes. Caleb wants him rescued."

Lim shifted to the edge of his seat. "When do we set off?"

Seregei raised an eyebrow at him. "Did I say we were going?"

"Well… you'd not be telling me this if we weren't."

"I still have to decide whether it'll be too dangerous for the two of us, or straightforward enough that it would only require the one, or somewhere in the middle."

Lim's face fell. "You'd not go without me?"

"No. No, if I decided that it would be safe for one, then the one going would be you."

"You mean…?"

"I'd have this mission as your Task, yes."

Lim's face split in a broad grin and he shifted still further forwards. "So what are the problems?" he asked. "Tell me: why are you worried?"

Seregei raised an eyebrow. "I'll tell you, and I want you to tell me if you're not certain you can do this, is that clear? I'll come with you and won't think any less of you if you need me, and another Task will come along soon enough."

Lim nodded.

"We don't know how they'll be guarding or transporting him or where exactly he'll be by the time we get there, or what sort of state he'll be in. If they follow their habits he'll be somewhere in between where he was last seen and the main city of the kingdom, and they'll have kept him alive, but they may already have started to torture him, so he may be severely wounded, or they may have rushed taking him back and by the time we get there they'll already be in the city."

Lim nodded.

"I told Caleb I would let him know tonight, and if you go or we go together it'll be tomorrow or the next day at the very latest."

"What kingdom was it?"

"Arket."

"I know the place." Lim pulled on the end of his braid, looking thoughtful. "Hmm... I honestly don't know. I'd like to try it, and I think that unless there's something... unless he's under heavy guard or too badly hurt to move I could do it alone. What do you think? I'd certainly be prepared to try."

Seregei smiled proudly. "I agree: you could probably manage barring any serious complications. Caleb probably has more details than he was prepared to share with me, though. Why don't you go down to talk to him and then come back and we'll decide whether it'll be you alone or both of us together."

Lim nodded, looking half nervous, half excited. "Shall I go now?" he asked, "Or think it over a little longer?"

Seregei thought about it, feeling a moment's temptation to let Caleb stew, but then he mentally slapped himself. What was wrong with him? He and Caleb were not the only people in this. If they could get the details finalised today, he and Lim, or Lim alone, might be able to set off tomorrow, and that was a day less that Esgal was in the hands of elf-haters. Not only would he suffer less, but there was less chance that when they arrived he would already be ensconced in some dark, secure prison, less chance that he'd be seriously hurt or dying, less chance that they'd already have broken him.

"Go now," he said.

Lim nodded, got up and left with a farewell wave of his hand.

Lim ran all the way to Caleb's palace, the trees on either side blurring with his speed, exulting in the feeling of the wind on his face and the possibility that, so quickly, he might have a Task and be on the way to being initiated as a full Swordmaster. He ran through the courtyard and up to the main door, pausing to reassure a worried-looking guard that nothing was wrong and to ask him where Caleb was. Learning that the king was in his study, he parted from the guard with a last assurance that he was just in a hurry and there was no urgent news that needed to be shared throughout the court.

He paused a moment to catch his breath and gather his courage, then knocked on the door of Caleb's study.

"Enter!"

Caleb was at his desk and got up, looking surprised, as he recognised Lim.

"Lim? What brings you here?" he asked. "Did Seregei send you?"

Lim nodded. "He told me about this rescue."

Caleb nodded and pushed aside the letter he'd been working on, gesturing to a chair. "Sit down. Has he decided already?"

"I might go on my own," said Lim, sitting down, "but it depends on the details."

Caleb smiled a little. "How much has he told you? It can't have been much, he only just left."

"I ran all the way here."

"I see." His ability to run quickly had been the first thing that Lim had told Caleb about himself. "Well, you know the basic situation, I assume?"

Lim nodded. "Seregei summarised what you told him."

Caleb sighed. "Well, I don't know too much more myself. You're really planning to go alone?"

Lim nodded, trying to hide his own sudden nervousness at the idea.

"Well..." Caleb bit his lip. "I suppose it might be, but I really don't know. As I say, I told Seregei everything I know about it. We'll only be able to find out more if we wait for his partner to return."

That would take some time and Lim was fairly sure he'd be able to do it alone, provided nothing unexpected happened and his luck was good. That bit of uncertainty made him doubtful, though. His luck had never been particularly good.

"If he's still relatively unhurt," he said slowly, "How likely is it that he'll be able to attempt to escape?"

Caleb shrugged a little. "Assuming that he's not severely injured or bound too tightly to move, he'll do his best, but since we don't know how he's being held or treated..."

Lim nodded. "But he's not likely to freeze if I can release him and he's able to run."

"No. If he can run, he will."

Lim smiled a little. So all he had to do was find Esgal, see how seriously hurt or weak he was, and hopefully create a situation in which he could escape. He suppressed a nervous chuckle. Well, *that* wouldn't be too hard, would it?

"Do you intend to do it?" asked Caleb.

"As far as I'm concerned, and Seregei's said that he'll think about it and may come with me."

Caleb grinned and relaxed a little. "That's good news." He took out a piece of paper and pushed it across the desk. It was a sketched portrait of an elf with short hair, a sharp jaw, large eyes – the artist had done an excellent job of capturing their lively sparkle – and a broad smile.

"Esgal?" Lim asked.

"Yes; you'll need to know what he looks like, I assume. That was drawn by his wife."

Lim nodded, trying to ignore the fact that he now had a face to put to the name, and the knowledge that Esgal was married to a talented artist. That brought this closer to home.

"All right," he said. "I'll head back to Seregei. I'm pretty sure that one or both of us will leave in the next couple of days, though."

Caleb nodded. "Thanks," he said. "Take the drawing with you. I'll tell Alydra that you're going and she may come down later this evening."

Lim paused in the act of getting up. "Alydra is his wife?"

"Yes."

Lim left feeling like tomorrow wasn't soon enough.

Seregei was sitting in one of the trees that surrounded the Guardhouse, playing his flute, when he saw Lim coming. He wasn't running, as he had been when he set off, and as he walked he was apparently lost in his thoughts. Seregei raised the flute to his lips again and carried on playing.

"Hello," said Lim as he walked under the tree.

Seregei jumped down. "So you weren't so distracted it sounded like birdsong."

Lim smiled. "I'm a Wood-elf. I'd have to be deaf to mistake the sound of a flute for the sound of a bird."

"So what say you, having spoken to Caleb?"

Lim showed him a drawing of an elf. "This is a picture of Esgal. I'm going to do it."

"Did you learn anything else about the situation?" asked Seregei, deliberately not looking too closely at the smiling face drawn on the paper.

"No, Caleb said he'd told you all that he knew. Apparently if he can he'll try to escape on his own, though."

"I see. Well, that'll make it a little easier. It does still rely on him being in a fit state to try."

"I know."

Lim seemed depressed and Seregei gave his shoulder a small shake.

"Lim, do you need my help?"

He frowned. "I... I don't think I do."

"You want to take it as your Task, then?"

He nodded, smiling a little.

Seregei patted him on the shoulder, feeling strangely proud. "Well, you're ready to go," he said. Is there anything you still think you need to practice for the rest of today?"

Lim bit his lip for a moment. "Could you help me choose things I'll need to take?"

Seregei nodded and led the way inside.

An hour or so later, they were halfway through a discussion of whether or not Lim would need spikes for his boots, since he'd doubtless be spending some time in the mountains. Suddenly, there was a knock on the main door. Seregei left Lim in his room, worrying over his pack, and went to see who it was.

It turned out to be an elven woman, holding a bundle under one arm. Her eyes were bloodshot and her face flushed, as though she'd been crying.

"Hello?" said Seregei uncertainly.

"My name's Alydra," she said. "Lord Caleb told me that you were going to go and search for my husband."

Seregei nodded. "Your husband's name is Esgal?"

"Esgal son of Eldaron, yes."

Seregei beckoned her to come in. "Lim!" he called, then gestured to her to take a seat. "I'm not going myself," he explained. "Lim will go on his own."

"Isn't he only a trainee?" Alydra asked, looking sceptical.

"He's had all the training of a Swordmaster. Just because he's not been initiated, that doesn't make him unable to do this."

"I... I suppose. But are you sure he's capable?"

Seregei was aware that Lim had arrived in time to hear her say that, and it was for his benefit as well as hers that he said, "I have absolute confidence in him. If I could do it, so can he. You can rest assured that if he doesn't bring Esgal back, it was because it was impossible."

"Couldn't you go with him?"

"If possible, someone should stay to look after things here." He smiled a little and made the guess that she was a Duamelti Mixed-blood. "You know that, surely?"

She nodded, then seemed to notice Lim.

"You're Lim?" she said.

He nodded. "Are you Alydra? Lord Caleb gave me your portrait of Esgal."

She nodded, smiling a little. "I drew it just before he went on this latest mission, but he's only been away a year. He may have grown or cut his hair, but he shouldn't look too different."

Lim nodded, still looking a little haunted, and Seregei realised why he'd been looking so depressed before.

Alydra sighed. "I mainly came round to bring you this," she said, holding out her bundle. Lim took it, looking at it curiously. Alydra continued, "It's some of his own clothes; I don't know if he'll have anything to wear when you rescue him. If you can't take them with you, I understand, but I thought it might be a nice thing to send."

Seregei agreed with her; if nothing else, it would be good for Esgal to have a clean outfit to change into.

Lim nodded and said, "I'll do all I can to fit it in."

She smiled and got up, dusting down her skirt. "I'll leave now," she said, and turned to Lim. "Please let me know as soon as you get back? And... let me know even if... you couldn't bring him back. I want to know what happened to him."

Lim nodded. "I promise," he said.

She smiled again and left, rubbing her hands up and down her upper arms as she walked.

Lim was chewing his lip, still looking at the bundle of clothes.

"I guess I definitely don't have room for those spikes," he said quietly.

Seregei put an arm around his shoulders and hugged him lightly. "It's summer," he said. "You shouldn't have too much trouble with mud or snow. Just be very careful about where you're going."

Lim nodded.

"Lim?"

"Yes?"

"Don't let this get to you. You already knew you were dealing with a living elf, who presumably had a family and certainly had a spirit that could feel pain and fear."

"I... I know. But meeting her and having her give me these for him... it just brings it home. Makes it more real."

Seregei nodded. "So do your best, but don't let this sort of worrying distract you." He led the way back down the corridor to Lim's room, deciding with a sigh that at some point he'd have to tell Lim about the extra decision he'd made: the one about what to do if Esgal couldn't be rescued.

"Did you mean what you said?"

"What?"

Lim smiled a little. "That you had absolute confidence in me."

Seregei poked his shoulder. "Don't fish for compliments. You've rotten self-trust and a ruined left hand, but you've learned well enough and I think you'll be fine."

He grabbed the contentious spikes and put them back in their cupboard. As he did so, he couldn't help a rueful look around; Lim's little room was normally so neat and tidy that it barely looked like anyone lived there. Now the two cupboards stood open, one of the drawers under his bed was pulled out and there were things scattered all over the bed and the floor.

"Put that bundle in the bottom of your pack; you'll likely need everything else before you need that. Where's the healing kit you plan to take?"

Lim had been staring at nothing, fidgeting with a strap on his pack, but he looked glad of a distraction as he picked up a small, well-fastened bag. "Here it is."

"Has it got everything you'll need?"

Lim began to rummage through it as Seregei folded an extra blanket and laid it in the pack on top of Esgal's clothes.

"Where are your saddlebags?"

"I'll be taking Winnowil?"

It hadn't occurred to Seregei that Lim wasn't planning to ride. "Why wouldn't you?" he asked.

Lim bit his lip. "I hadn't thought about it."

Seregei ruffled his hair. "You should have done."

Lim grimaced, smoothing his braid. "She'll not do well in real mountains, and it'll mean I'll have to stick to roads."

"She's a sensible horse; if you cache some of your gear you can turn her loose and she'll wait for you. Besides, unlike me, you'll be able to *tell* her to wait." Like all Wood-elves, Lim was able to communicate with animals. He'd tried to explain it once, but Seregei still didn't understand how it was possible.

Lim nodded thoughtfully and then laughed a little. "And I don't know how I was planning to bring him back if he wasn't able to walk."

Seregei felt a moment's worry. How much had Lim actually thought about this mission?

"Are you sure you don't want me to come with you?" he asked, dropping the light-hearted tone. "You could do most of it, but are you sure you don't need my help and we'll wait for the next possible Task?"

Lim shook his head. "No, no, I'm sure."

"You just don't seem to have thought too hard, that's all."

Lim shook his head again. "I know... I just didn't expect that it would be appropriate to bring Winnowil, so none of the rest of it was an issue..."

"Transporting Esgal if he's unable to walk is an issue either way. How do you plan to get him through the mountains if it comes to it?"

Lim bit his lip, looking even more uncertain. "He should still be able to hold on to my back. If he's so weak or seriously hurt that he can't even do that... I... it depends how far into the mountains I am, I suppose. I might be able to get him to the nearest place I could bring Winnowil, since I'm bringing her, and hide him while I fetch her. It's not ideal, but if I'm on my own I don't see what else I could do. Sweet Lady, I don't even know how tall he is."

Seregei nodded, feeling a little guilty for making Lim so worried, but not very. He needed to make sure the younger elf had actually thought about the difficulties this posed and didn't just go rushing off without a thought for what he would do if something went wrong.

"That's pretty close to what I'd be able to do as well. As for his height, I'm sure that Caleb or Alydra would have mentioned it if he were abnormally tall or short, so you can probably safely assume that he's around your height, maybe a little taller. I doubt he's as tall as a Valley-elf. It might not be easy, but you should be able to carry him a short distance if you have to."

Lim nodded, looking a little happier, and went back to looking in his healing bag.

"Given what I'm doing, I'll probably need some more bandages," he said. "Shall I get them from the healing room?"

"Yes, you do that. I'll replace them while you're gone."

Lim nodded and hurried off, disappearing down the corridor to the healing room at the far end from the common room. Seregei frowned a little. When he got back, he was going to have to give him that last instruction.

It didn't take long for him to return with an extra fistful of bandages and a small pot of salve for blisters.

"What's that for?" asked Seregei, gesturing to the salve as Lim packed it.

"If they've been making him walk far, his feet'll be blistered. I can think ahead when I try." He smiled a little.

Seregei nodded. It wasn't something he'd thought of. "Just remember to keep it off anything bleeding."

"I know."

Seregei smiled, but then quickly sobered. "Have you thought about what you'll do if you can't rescue him?"

Lim blinked. "No," he said slowly. "But I can tell you have. Is it likely?"

"I'm thinking about if he's too badly hurt to be moved, or so heavily guarded that you can't reach him without putting yourself in mortal danger."

Lim began to make up a bedroll. "I honestly don't know what I'd do," he said slowly. "Maybe..." He turned worried eyes on Seregei. "Maybe you're right and you should come with me."

Seregei sighed. He'd not meant to make Lim doubt himself. "You understand what they'll do to him if you leave him alive in their hands?" he said. He knew he had to make Lim see the logic for himself, not just tell him.

Lim nodded, his left hand twitching a little. "And I know what that would mean for us," he said quietly. "Is... is it true that anyone will break in the end?"

Seregei nodded. "It depends on the skill of the torturer; sometimes the victim dies before he breaks, but anyone can be broken, given time and skill." With a shiver, he thought of the Swordmasters who had trained him. Fortunately, they had all been killed before they could reach that point.

Lim nodded, going back to his bedroll. "I... but if I couldn't rescue him... what else could I do?" He suddenly looked up. "You're not suggesting that I..."

For a long moment they stared at one another. Seregei deeply regretted asking Lim to make this sort of decision, but it had to be done.

"Seregei," said Lim coldly, "If this is because you've already seen me kill another elf..."

"This has nothing to do with Ethiren," said Seregei quickly. "This is because it would be much crueller to leave Esgal alive."

Lim scowled, tying off the bedroll and stuffing it into his pack as though he had a personal grudge against them both.

"Well, what do you suggest instead?" Seregei asked, half trying to make Lim understand why he'd suggested such an act, half genuinely curious to see if another mind could come up with an alternative.

Lim paused for a moment, then sighed deeply. "I don't know," he said. "I... I can't think of anything. But..." He looked up and there were tears in his eyes. "I killed Ethiren in hot blood a-after everything he'd done..." His breath hitched for a moment. "I don't think I could do it again, not to someone who'd never done anything to me, not to someone already hurt or bound and defenceless."

Seregei hugged him, gently smoothing his hair and smiling as Lim hugged him back.

"I pray you don't have to make the decision," he said quietly, "But I wanted you to know that it might become necessary to kill him."

Lim broke away and wiped his eyes on the back of his hand. "It'll be a very, *very* last resort."

"Of course! I'd not expect killing another elf to be anything else."

Lim nodded, wiping his eyes again.

"Where's my cooking set?" he asked after a long moment, with false briskness, "Should I take it?"

"Yes. You might not want to cart it when you're on foot, though that's a decision you'll have to make when you get there, but you should have it."

Lim nodded, smiling wanly. "I know that a nice hot cup of tea has often helped when we've been out overnight."

Seregei grinned, glad that Lim seemed to be recovering, the shadow passing. "Yes, what food do you plan to take?"

Lim frowned. "How long will I be away?"

"That I don't know, or what sort of terrain you'll be facing. You may be able to find food on the way."

"But it'll take time," said Lim. "I should take at least enough to get me there. How far away was Esgal captured?"

"A few days' ride, according to Caleb."

"So I should take enough for at least a week," said Lim thoughtfully.

Seregei nodded. "See, you can think about these things when you try," he said. "Take tea, especially since *you* like it when you camp. Small comforts make all the difference."

Lim nodded. "Have we any of those broth cubes?"

Seregei didn't remember seeing any in the store cupboard, and said so. "Go look," he suggested. "I'd also suggest biscuit."

"Obviously."

"And..." Seregei frowned. "Actually, crushed apple doesn't travel well."

"Not in a pack or saddlebag," agreed Lim, scooping his tinderbox from the shelf by his bed and packing it. "I'll put most of the food I'll take in a saddlebag; the other one can take extra food for Winnowil."

"She'll be able to graze some of the way, so take advantage of that."

"But mountain grass isn't good for supporting a horse."

Seregei nodded. "Nonetheless, it'll be something. Can you navigate by the stars? Do you want to run over that again tonight?"

"Provided it isn't cloudy, I think I'll be fine."

"You *think*? Well, *I* think you need to run over that again tonight."

Lim nodded. "I'll go and see what food I should pack," he said. "Then we're almost done."

Seregei laughed. "That was the most frenzied packing I've ever seen. Check the stores cupboard and get biscuit and broth cubes if they're there. If not, there should be a small box with compartments containing salt and some herbs. You can take that." He waved a finger. "But I want it back!"

The box in question had been a gift from Swordmaster Celes, Seregei's own mentor, but he didn't tell Lim that. While he was gone, Seregei slipped into his own room and took another box from a drawer. It was full of honey fudge: a delicacy that he and Lim both enjoyed, though Lim still preferred candied fruit. He wrapped several pieces in a handkerchief, returned the box to its place and went back to Lim's room to slip the fudge into his bag. He hid it near the bottom, where Lim would be pleasantly surprised to find it later.

When Lim returned, he had a wrapped packet of biscuit – uninspiring stuff, but it would keep him going – and had managed to find a small box of the broth cubes. They packed the broth cubes in with his cooking gear.

"You can take some fresh stuff for the first few days, but eat that first. If you can find fresh food on the way, do so, but don't let it slow you down."

Lim nodded. "I'll find some fishing line, but I won't try too hard to forage until we're on the way back."

"Provided you're not being followed."

"Grant me some credit!" protested Lim. Seregei had to smile. It still felt good to hear Lim express any confidence.

"Do you think you're ready to leave tomorrow morning?" he asked as they went and sat back down in the main room.

Lim nodded. "As soon as I can catch Winnowil and get her ready. I can have the saddlebags packed tonight, so I'll be able to leave soon after first light."

Seregei nodded. "You know how to travel across country, so I won't insult your intelligence by telling you."

Lim smiled.

"You may have to make inquiries and try to get some rumours before you go too far; someone's bound to have seen or heard of an elven prisoner being moved back to the king's city. The town where he was arrested is right on the border, probably at the beginning of a pass on a trade route, so you should be able to find it."

Lim nodded. "I can take the road towards Silvren and then turn towards it. I can travel faster by road and I'm less likely to get lost if I go that way."

"It's less direct and you'll have to be more discreet as you approach, but…" Seregei frowned. "I do agree that you should take a route you know."

Lim nodded again. "I can probably gauge at what point it's getting dangerous to ride openly."

"Just don't leave it too late."

"I can put my hood up and make myself less obvious."

"That will make you look more suspicious. Just be careful."

Lim had slept surprisingly well on the night before he was to set off, despite his nerves. Though Seregei thought he was ready and he did trust his mentor implicitly, he could never entirely shake the feeling that he couldn't cope with what was being asked of him. As he dressed he toyed briefly with the idea of asking Seregei to come with him, but then discarded it. After all, Seregei thought he could do this. He didn't want to disappoint him. In any case, he had always known that he could trust Seregei's judgement.

An hour after first light they had eaten and Seregei helped Lim to prepare Winnowil for the journey. Lim checked the saddlebags again before strapping them behind his saddle, but he thought he had everything. If not, he'd have to go without. At last, he strapped on his own pack, checked that he had spare bowstrings and his utility knife, and let Seregei give him a boost onto Winnowil's back. She snorted at the extra weight and shook her head, but settled down again as he gave her neck a gentle stroke. Silently, he closed his eyes and imagined them arriving back safely in Duamelti and himself giving her a mint-rubbed carrot: her favourite treat. He communicated that image to her and received a feeling of agreement and contentment in response. He smiled, stroked her neck again and opened his eyes.

"Ready?" asked Seregei.

Lim nodded.

"Are you sure you've got everything?" Seregei folded his arms.

Lim smiled down at him, relishing the feeling of being the taller one for once. "I'm sure."

"It's still not too late for me to come with you."

"I know" – Lim took a deep breath – "and I don't want you to."

"All right." Seregei patted Winnowil as she nudged him. "You know what you're doing and where you're going. You have to go and get Esgal and bring him back without help from Duamelti. You can accept assistance from others along the way, but if I have to go and find you later, the Task is void."

Lim nodded, feeling suddenly a little sick. This was it.

Seeing his expression, Seregei smiled. "You'll be fine," he said. Then he stepped back and waved. "I'll see you in a couple of weeks!"

Lim nodded, waved in farewell and urged Winnowil on.

He trotted through Duamelti, waving to people he knew as he went, and out of the south gate. At the next fork, he'd head south-east.

CHAPTER TWO

As Lim drew closer and left the road to Silvren, he could sense that people were growing curious. Up until this point, most people had been ignoring him. Humans around Duamelti tended to be indifferent to elves and he was on the road to the Wood-elven kingdom of Silvren, so they assumed he was heading home. The thought had made him wince and he turned away from it at once.

Now, however, he was riding away from his homeland. On the evening of the third day out of Duamelti, he halted a little way off the road, overlooking a small group of wooden houses, gathered around an open square. The town was nestled in a hollow beneath steep foothills while the road ran on into the mountains. As he looked along it, he could see what looked like two passes, one either side of a particularly sizeable mountain. He took his saddlebags and tack off Winnowil and hid them, then told her to wait for him and headed down towards the town.

The men on the gate didn't seem too worried about a stray traveller and didn't ask him to lower his hood. He was very glad about that, since he guessed that this was the town where Esgal had been arrested and he didn't want his identity to be revealed so soon, before he'd even managed to pick up any news about him. After all, this was the only place he had any real chance of that. He could run if he had to, even with his pack still on his back, but he didn't know what he would do then.

The town's main street wasn't crowded, but Lim had to sidestep several times to get past people. Fortunately, none of them looked too hard at him. He caught sight of a bush on a pole raised high above the street – the usual sign in human towns for an inn – and smiled to himself. That would hopefully be a good place to get news. As he walked, one of a couple of running children collided with him, gasped an apology and ran on. However, he had felt the small hand reaching into his pocket and grabbed her before she was even out of arm's reach. She looked him in the eye for a moment, eyes wide and innocent, but apparently realised that she wasn't fooling him; she shamefacedly handed back his purse.

"Thank you," he said, keeping her at arm's length as he took it. "Now off with you."

She shot another look at him, then scurried away and he headed on, reaching the inn without further incident. Seen close, he noticed that it had a stone foundation and looked larger than the other buildings. The door opened directly into a large room crowded with several long tables, with a counter at one end. It looked clean, at least, with fresh rushes on the floor. A glance around showed that there were maybe a dozen mortals, both men and women, scattered around the room. He bought a mug of ale and went to sit at the end of a settle in the corner, out of the way and almost out of sight: a weary traveller who didn't know anyone here and just wanted to rest for a while.

Soon, what little attention he had drawn faded and everyone went back to their conversations. A man was complaining about his employer, who had docked his pay for what he considered a very spurious reason. Two women exchanged stories about their husbands, laughing uproariously enough to almost drown out the words of a young woman sitting at a table near Lim, talking to a couple of friends.

"Yesterday, I tell you," she said, "My brother's in the Watch, he was one of the ones on patrol when they arrested him."

"They waited so long to get an elf out of the town?"

Lim pretended to take a sip of his drink. Any thoughts he'd had of actually drinking the cloudy, foul-smelling brew had quickly vanished, but he didn't want people wondering why he wasn't drinking.

The woman continued, "Darin said that they were waiting for some men to come up from the city to get him. Apparently he's dangerous; he's been going in and out for ages and they want to know where he's been hiding and who he's been talking to."

"So they took him straight back? They can't have waited for any time at all, I didn't see them."

"You don't see anything past the bottom of your tankard, Lenry," said the second man, elbowing his friend in the side and making him cough on his ale.

"They went back by the low pass to get back faster," said the woman, a hint of pride in her voice at having information her friends apparently lacked.

Lim was distracted from his eavesdropping as a small group of men came in and headed straight to the bar. As he pretended to drink, he watched them talking quietly to the landlord and decided that they weren't ordering a round of drinks. His suspicion was confirmed as the landlord, looking worried, pointed in his direction.

Suddenly, sitting in the corner didn't seem such a good idea.

He put down the mug and started to get up to head for the door, pretending he hadn't noticed their interest. Hopefully, he could at least get to somewhere where he could make a run for it if he had to. Then one of the men went to step in his way and tried to grab his shoulder. He dodged, but the reaching hand caught his hood. It slid back just enough to reveal his face and his unmistakably pointed ear.

The man swore. Several people gasped and moved away. The other men moved to surround Lim and cut him off from the door. There was no more point in keeping his hood up and Lim pushed it back so that he could see better.

"Elf," said the man, "you are hereby bound by law. Lay your weapons on the ground."

Lim couldn't see a way to get out of this. Perhaps he might be able to climb over a table and fight his way past the men between him and the door, but he doubted it. Looking around, he caught the eye of the young woman, still sitting near him, and an idea struck him.

In a quick movement he grabbed her by the arm, pulled her out of her seat and drew his knife.

"Let me leave or I'll kill her!" he said, adding a worried edge to his voice. If they had any sense at all, they'd know that he was much more dangerous if he was nervous.

Apparently they had sense. They backed off a little and tried to look less threatening, but still didn't move away from the door.

Lim mentally kicked himself for getting into this situation. If they called his bluff he didn't have very many choices and they were all bad.

One of the woman's companions got up, pulling out a short and very notched eating knife.

"Unhand her, vile beast!" he said, waving it.

There was a small gasp around the room as everyone waited to see what Lim would do. Fortunately, he didn't have to decide, as the woman said, her voice trembling, "Sit down, Tane, and do as he says!"

Lim looked as fearsome as he could and one of the guards cursed, stepping away from the door.

"Let him go," he said to the others.

Lim made his way carefully to the door, taking the woman with him. As soon as he was safely outside, he released her with a sigh of relief, pulled up his hood and began to walk quickly away. He turned, however, startled, as she called after him.

"Hey," she said. "Aren't you going to ravish me or something?"

Surprise as much as anything else made Lim start to laugh. "Why would I do a horrible thing like that?" he asked, his voice shaking a little.

However, as he looked at her expression – she seemed hurt rather than frightened – he had to add, "I'm sure your young man in there – Tane, was it? – would be happy to oblige, though." Then he stepped back towards her, took her hand and kissed the knuckles. "Thank you," he said, smiling as he noticed that her face was a picture of utter shock. Then he turned and hurried away, not looking back as she went back inside, presumably to tell the story of her escape from the terrifying, lascivious elf that had taken her hostage. It would probably earn her a few drinks, at least. With that thought, he put her from his mind. He had to worry about getting away before those men came after him.

He went through the gate, taking care not to look as if he was hurrying. His heart skipped a beat as one of the guards called after him.

"Planning on going much further tonight?" the man asked in a friendly tone.

Lim turned to look back, taking care to keep his face mostly shadowed. "Not much," he said. "But there's another hour of daylight yet."

"Your errand must be urgent."

Lim smiled. "Indeed. I only came looking for directions, but all the town is in uproar, so I decided to hurry on and hope I can guess it for myself."

"Perhaps I can help?"

"I'm hoping to go over the low pass to the king's city."

"Ah, well, you'll want to go back up to the ridge and head along it for a few hours, through the forest, then go right at the main fork: the last one before you reach the edge of the forest. There's a lightning-struck tree in the fork, you can't miss it. As a warning: a party of royal soldiers has already gone that way – yesterday afternoon – and if you catch up to them I'd stay away."

Lim inclined his head a little, inwardly exulting. "Thank you."

"Best wishes!"

At that, Lim hurried on, hoping that he'd be well clear before the news reached the men at the gate that an elf had been in the town and had headed in this direction. Hopefully his luck would hold and they'd not make the connection before he was past the point where they might ambush him.

He got to Winnowil and saddled her, then mounted and set off at a brisk trot along the road that the man at the gate had indicated. As he looked back, he couldn't see anyone on his tail, but he soon lost sight of the town as he continued along the ridge and it disappeared into its hollow.

He kept trotting until it was almost dark, just light enough to find a hollow of his own off the road to camp. There, he rubbed Winnowil down and gave her a small measure of the grain he'd brought along. Finally, he settled between two rocks, a blanket around his shoulders, munching on a piece of biscuit. He probably couldn't take her much further; he didn't know what the terrain would be like from here into the pass and he'd be better able to evade pursuit on his own.

On the other hand, the guards in the town probably expected to be chasing a traveller on foot. The extra speed might stand him in good stead, and if Esgal had only been moved the day before, he would be better able to catch up. He wished he knew how they'd been transporting him – on foot? By horse? In a cart? He didn't know, though he recalled that the gatekeeper hadn't mentioned anything about the soldiers having a cart. That might mean nothing, but it was worth remembering.

Still... He looked up at where the mountain was shrouded in darkness above him, then down at his once-broken left hand. He wasn't much of a climber, and short cuts made for long delays, but he might be able to cut corners that a large group travelling by road could not. He certainly couldn't do that with a horse.

Winnowil blew at him and he chuckled, patting her on the nose. He looked into her eyes and envisioned her staying in this forest, wandering about and eating grass here and there as she found it. In the image, the sun rose and set five times and then she left. Then he pictured the same scene, but this time he added the sound of a whistle and himself returning. That meant that she was to stay and wait for five days or until he returned and whistled for her.

She nuzzled his ear and blew in his face and he smiled. That meant that she was contented, and therefore that she didn't mind being left alone.

In the morning he would pick out the things that he needed to take with him into the mountains and cache the rest, then head off on foot. If he wasn't able to rescue Esgal in the mountains, then he could return, retrieve Winnowil and his gear, and head through the pass with her. Hopefully, though, it wouldn't come to that. Decided, he laid out his bedroll, curled up and went to sleep.

***

Lim woke with the dawn; it was cold and misty and he scowled. Not good weather for trying to find his way over an unfamiliar mountain. He would rather have waited for the mist to burn off, but he had no time to waste. He ate breakfast, put some necessities in his pack, and hid the rest under a cairn of rocks. There was nothing there to attract scavengers and the cairn looked fairly natural, so it shouldn't attract too much attention. Then he gave Winnowil a goodbye pat and kissed her on the nose.

"I'll be back in a couple of days," he promised. "Don't go too far, all right?"

She nuzzled him, then turned and trotted off into the mist. Feeling rather lonely, Lim hitched up his pack, tightened the straps, and started up the path towards the mountain. On either side of him, increasingly sparse pine forest loomed out of the mist, the branches of the trees dripping with the damp. Some were festooned with bejewelled spider webs, reminding him with a small shudder of the spiders of Silvren, which were large enough to eat elves. He shook his head, once more dismissing thoughts of the forest that had been his home.

As his directions said, he soon came to a fork in the road marked with a huge lightning-struck dead tree, taller than any of the other trees in this forest. He celebrated with a sip of water from his bottle and a few minutes' rest, then took the right fork and walked on. By now he'd been walking for a couple of hours and the mist was burning off. He could see the mountain more clearly. Now that he was closer, it looked larger. It was bare above the forest's edge apart from a few patches of green that he could only guess were clumps of bushes. He couldn't see any way over it apart from the road.

He noticed as he went that a fair-sized group had passed along here not too long before, and paused to inspect the tracks when he reached a fairly damp patch of ground that had taken them well. Yes, it looked like a large group of booted mortals – maybe half a dozen? A few more? It was hard to be certain. He also couldn't tell if they'd had a captive with them, but there were no horses. At least, there were no recent horses. A cart had passed, but those tracks were considerably older than those he was looking at. He smiled a little. Maybe this was the group he was looking for, and they were indeed on foot. That would make it much easier to catch them. A little heartened, he stood up and went on.

After a couple more hours, he was out of the trees, though, as he had thought, there was still some stunted vegetation clinging to the thin soil. He felt very glad that he had chosen to leave Winnowil where he had; the path looked rough and rocky even where it had been cleared. He wondered if the high pass was smoother, even if it were longer.

In front of him, there was another fork. The main road clearly bent around to the right, but there was another path, narrow and twisty, heading straight up the spur of the mountain in front of him. He looked about, hunting on the increasingly stony ground for tracks, and found that the large group undoubtedly took the main path. Should he take the smaller trail? He bit his lip, trying to decide. After a moment, he walked a little way back and squinted up at the mountain, trying to guess its shape. He thought that the road was just going around an outcropping and would curve back, so this small path would rejoin it. That would make it a short cut and he might be able to overtake them. On the other hand, there might be a very good reason why the main path bent around, such as a sheer cliff. Then it would just be lost time.

Rather like the time he was spending standing here and debating, really.

It looked like it was a real trail, albeit one that was rarely used. That meant it had to lead somewhere, even if it could only be taken by walkers. He'd at least give it a try; they had a day's start on him and he needed a short cut. If nothing else, from the top he'd be able to get a better idea of the chance that the two roads joined back up. Decided, he began to climb.

The path was rocky and steep. A few times he was almost on hands and knees, and by the time he stopped to rest, every muscle in his body was aching. He knew that if he sat still for long they'd stiffen, so he forced himself to go on until he'd reached the top of the spur and stood still for a moment, panting, a little frustrated with himself. Clearly, he needed more practice with climbing real mountains, rather than the hills around Duamelti. He shook his head a little and looked about. Things didn't look so much different from here, but he could tell he was standing on a rock spur jutting out from the main body of the mountain. The air was chill and a steady wind whistled by, making him shiver despite the warm sun. He could still see the path stretching out ahead, straight on while the road obviously went in a massive loop to his right. Encouraged, he forced his aching, burning muscles to move again and walked on.

He crossed the spur in about an hour and continued along a narrow trail that was little more than a goat track. Though it was narrow, it was wide enough for him to walk along and the sheen of water left by the mist on the surface of the rock had now dried in the sun, so he wasn't too worried.

At last, it widened out again and he paused for another rest, sitting down on a rock to eat a piece of biscuit for his lunch.

He was making good progress – this short cut had worked so far – but he couldn't rest long; they had a day's head start on him, and it would be that much harder to rescue Esgal once they were out of this wilderness.

He ate the last mouthful and began strapping his pack back on, groaning as his muscles complained, but then suddenly heard voices.

"I'm telling you, if he falls down once more, I'm not going to be responsible for my actions."

"You were the one that suggested giving him that stuff, it's *your* fault he's groggy."

Lim almost dropped his pack and hurried to the edge of the path. How hadn't he heard them coming? Either he'd not been paying attention – he kicked himself – or they'd been travelling in silence. He braced himself against a rock and peered down at the road as a group of men – he counted nine – came around the corner.

"Well, it's stopped him making so much trouble, hasn't it?" said one man, waving a hand back towards the rest of the group. "We'd be miles further along if he'd not kept trying to fight when we first set out. Besides, that was a close call him getting his hands in front. Tell me with a straight face you don't think it's a good thing we've not had a repeat of that."

One of the nine was stumbling at the end of a rope that was knotted around his neck, the other end held by a man walking in front of him. There was a sack over his head, so Lim couldn't see his face, and his hands were manacled behind his back. Lim wasn't surprised when he tripped and fell headlong, unable to see where he was going or use his hands to balance. He grimaced in sympathy as two of the guards pulled the prisoner – presumably Esgal – back to his feet, pulling on his arms and twisting them almost enough to pull them out of their sockets. There was now a dirty, bloody scrape down the right side of his bare chest and Lim was surprised that despite everything he'd not cried out once in pain. Perhaps he was gagged under the sack.

Lim pulled away from the edge, deciding that this wasn't a good place to try mounting a rescue. He needed to be at least a little prepared, and not in a place where the opposite side of the road was a precipice. Here, if Esgal staggered or was pushed or pulled just a few steps to the right, he would fall.

But Lim smiled as he picked up his pack, strapped it on and hurried with renewed vigour along his path. He was now ahead of them, and looking ahead he could see that there was another rock spur. That would slow them still more. His muscles still ached and his pack was heavy, he still wasn't certain what he was actually going to do – eight men were a lot for one elf – but his goal was finally in sight.

***

As the day was drawing to a close, Lim looked down at the road with approval. It had turned into a long defile leading up to the pass and, while he didn't relish the thought of waiting here – it was cold now that he was approaching the top of the mountain – the long, narrow valley was made for an ambush. He thought that was the best way to approach a rescue; if that gatekeeper had warned him against joining the guards when he thought he was a human, it was clearly too big a risk to go near them however he did it.

He began picking his way among the boulders littered on either side of his goat-trail, looking for a place to camp. He needed somewhere out of the way, fairly sheltered from the weather and also where he might lay hidden. He also had to be able to hide Esgal and take care of him if he needed it. He'd not got another look at the group since that first glimpse, so he had no idea whether Esgal had been more seriously hurt since then. The first man's words about what he'd do if Esgal fell again hadn't boded well for his treatment, but Lim thought that he'd only been staggering because he was blind on rough ground and probably exhausted, not because he was hurt. That was encouraging; it meant that, given time to rest, he would recover and wouldn't need too much help getting back to where Lim had left Winnowil.

Lim paused to look at one of the lengthening shadows. It definitely looked darker than the rest, and he picked his way over to investigate. His luck was in: it was a small cave, apparently unoccupied, large enough to lay out his bedroll with some space over and to sit up. It went back far enough into the mountain that his camp would be sheltered and faced down the slight slope, so it wouldn't fill with rain. He gratefully set his pack in it and went to have another look at the road while there was still some light, hitching his shoulders to relieve the ache.

He had to squint to see in the fading light. Even in this narrow slot, he couldn't jump down and fight eight men on his own. He fingered his bow and wondered if he would be able to shoot surely enough to kill them from up here, then go and retrieve Esgal. He frowned. Even if he could be that certain of his marksmanship, with aching shoulders and having to aim downwards – something he'd never tried with a longbow – it would take time. He still didn't know if they'd kill Esgal if it came to it.

Kill Esgal...

For the first time since he'd set off from Duamelti, Seregei's suggestion came back to him. He absently fingered his bow again. Such a step wouldn't be necessary here, not unless something very bad had happened, but what about if he couldn't think of a plan? What if he did have to follow them, unable to do anything, until it became truly impossible to rescue Esgal? Would a quick arrow to the throat really be the only way?

He shook his head. No, he couldn't think of such things. For now, he had to come up with a plan to rescue Esgal here. Then it would never have to become an issue.

He looked again at the narrow path and the rocks piled all around him. At least he was pretty confident that his enemy would also camp at night; they'd have to be stupid to travel through the mountains in the dark. But as they were travelling down that path in the morning... he wasn't sure he could hit them with arrows quickly enough, but could he roll some of these rocks down to at least cause confusion? Then it would take them longer to realise what was happening and to decide to slit Esgal's throat rather than let him be rescued.

They'd likely be running around more and therefore harder to hit, he reminded himself.

Could he use the rocks to kill them? It was a very dangerous plan. Once he started a boulder rolling he had no control over where it landed, and if he accidentally killed Esgal he didn't think he could live with it on his own conscience even if he never had to face Alydra.

But he couldn't really think of another plan.

He sat down with a sigh. There had to be another way. Just rolling boulders down and hoping was a huge risk, especially as the person he was trying to spare was the least able to dodge. With another sigh, he got up and walked up and down the edge a few more times, frowning down at the road. He noticed that the sides of the valley pinched in near the entrance. Maybe if he could get most of them to run back that way, he could block that bottleneck? Then he'd have fewer to deal with. Esgal would be in the group that remained trapped; he couldn't run fast enough to keep up. Then Lim could climb down and get him out.

He fetched his rope and let it down the cliff to test its length: easily long enough to reach the road, with several feet of slack. Well, there was his way up and down once he'd overcome the problem of the guards. He hoped that Esgal would be well and strong enough to climb or at least to cope with being hauled up with the rope tied around his body; he had no idea where he might find an easy way up here from the road.

It was getting too dark to see the road down below and he coiled the rope again with a sigh, then went back to his cave. He'd just have to camp down for the night and hope that he was able to come up with a more solid plan in the morning, when he could see better.

The stone felt hard and cold through his bedroll, but he shifted about until he found a halfway comfortable position, then closed his eyes with a sigh, trying not to worry too much. He was sure there was no way they could have left the road and although they were a long way behind him – enough to give him several hours in the morning – they couldn't be so far behind that it would be another day. With any luck he'd manage some sort of successful plan, and then he and Esgal would be on their way back home.

***

When he woke up in the morning it was with a groan of pain; it seemed that every muscle in his body was lining up to protest everything he'd been doing the day before, compounded by the further offence of spending the night with nothing between him and bare stone but a bedroll designed more for portability than comfort. For a fleeting moment, he wondered why he had agreed to train as a Swordmaster rather than taking another job in the kennels or the stables. Those would have been good work for an exiled Wood-elf.

He shook his head and berated himself. It would take a lot for him to be the most unfortunate elf on this mountain and until that happened he should do something constructive. He dragged himself upright with a few more groans, then limped over to have another look at the road as he ate his breakfast. He still couldn't come up with a better plan than the one he'd had last night. He sighed, swallowing the last bite of food, and began to stretch his sore muscles; it wouldn't do to be this stiff. Maybe the best thing to do would be to just wait and see how they arranged themselves as they walked. It was a very narrow road, maybe they'd be almost in single file. If nothing else, he could follow them for the day until they stopped to camp, then try to sneak in and spirit Esgal away when most of them were asleep and off their guard.

He didn't want to rely on that plan; his high path might run out at any time, so he got ready, rolling boulders to the edge where he could tip them over at a moment's notice, and tying the end of his rope firmly around a large one that wouldn't move even when he threw his entire weight against it. Hopefully it would remain just as firm when he was dangling from the rope. Finally, he laid a folded blanket along the edge of the cliff, so that the rope wouldn't fray against it

He remembered that Esgal had been manacled and went to get his lockpicks from his pack, then suddenly heard voices. They had arrived.

He hurried to the end of the valley and peered over the edge, ignoring a persistent ache in his right thigh, and smiled as they came around the corner. He was relieved to see them; it was already noon and he'd been starting to wonder if they had travelled by night.

They seemed alert, but the narrowness of the road had them all in single file. Esgal still stumbled uneasily at the end of his leash, weaving drunkenly from side to side and staggering as his guard tugged on the rope to make him keep up. Lim watched him with pity and no small amount of worry. Surely this wasn't just exhaustion. He couldn't be this tired so early in the day unless they'd not let him sleep, and he looked much too giddy for it to be something so simple. It was as if he'd lost a lot of blood, but Lim couldn't see any serious wounds. Maybe he was weak with hunger or thirst?

Well, he'd find out when he got down there. He took a deep breath to brace himself, then started the first rock rolling.

As he'd expected, they thought a rockslide was starting and began to run back the way they'd come. Esgal lagged behind. He stumbled and fell as the man holding his leash yanked on it. Lim grimaced; that must have hurt, though once again Esgal didn't cry out. No time to dwell on it as he sprinted along the path. He could easily outrun the men down below even though his was a rougher path. He reached the boulders he'd prepared over the chokepoint and waited until most of the men were through. Esgal's guard had remained behind and another had stopped to help him. Lim knew that he couldn't wait; those two would only be leaving with Esgal. He gave the first boulder a shove that sent it bouncing down the slope, starting off a small genuine rockfall as it went. A few more followed it and a slab of rock slid from the far side of the road, blocking it utterly. He paused to catch his breath, trying not to cough on the clouds of gritty dust. Then he hurried back to his rope. He had to get down there while he still had cover and they were distracted by the rockfall.

As quickly as he could, he took hold of the rope and lowered himself down the cliff, bracing his feet against the rock. As soon as he reached the bottom, he dropped the rope, wincing. His hands were rope-burned and painful, but he ignored them and hurried over to where Esgal still lay motionless, abandoned by his guards as they went to see if they were trapped. Lim could hear voices shouting back and forth across the new rock wall as he dropped to his knees beside Esgal, pulling his bow from his back in case he needed it. The other elf was breathing, and Lim sighed in relief. So far, his plan had worked perfectly.

"Hello?" he said softly, shaking Esgal's shoulder a little, being very careful not to hurt him. He glanced up with a gasp as he heard a shout and the sound of more sliding rock, but it didn't seem to have anything to do with him. He noted a man's voice shouting that someone was trapped, but at that moment Esgal shifted and moaned softly. He was conscious. Probably just conserving his strength and waiting to be picked up. That was all the reassurance Lim needed and he drew his knife to cut the cord that was tied around Esgal's neck, holding the sacking in place. He was just starting to saw through it when he heard a shout and looked up.

One of the men had returned and was now running towards him, grabbing at the sword at his belt.

"What do you think you're doing?" he yelled.

Lim moved with the speed of long practice. He scrambled up as he nocked an arrow, drew and loosed in a single movement. The arrow hit the man in the throat and he clutched at it for a moment, his eyes wide. Then his knees buckled and he collapsed without a sound. Lim took a couple of deep breaths, fumbling for another arrow in case the other man also returned.

At last, he was convinced that the other man must have made it over the rocks or been buried by the second slide he'd heard – perhaps that was the person who had been trapped – and he set down the bow and arrow. Finally, he could cut the rope around Esgal's neck. With that gone, he was able to pull away the sack and get his first look at Esgal.

He was still recognisable from Alydra's drawing, though his face was badly bruised. His nose was bloody and looked broken, and his lips were swollen and cut. Most worrying, though, was the fact that his large, bright eyes were dull. He'd not reacted to the sudden light as Lim pulled the sack from over his head and he didn't even seem aware that he was looking at an elf. There was no relief, or even surprise. He just stared blankly ahead.

"Is your name Esgal, son of Eldaron?" asked Lim, trying to keep the near-panic out of his voice. Was he already too late? Should he have taken the risk and attacked earlier?

Esgal blinked and nodded a little. "E-Esgal," he said hoarsely, then his head lolled sideways and his eyes fell closed.

"Esgal!" called Lim, gently slipping a hand under his cheek and making him look up again. "Esgal, can you hear me?"

Esgal opened his eyes again, looking confused and a little frightened.

"My name's Lim. I'm a Swordmaster trainee. I'm here to rescue you. Are you hurt?"

Esgal stared at him uncomprehendingly, his brow creased in a small frown.

"Do you understand?" asked Lim, beginning to wonder if something had addled Esgal's wits. Maybe a blow to the head...?

Then, with a shock, he remembered one of Esgal's guards saying that he'd been given something, and the implication that that was why he kept falling over. So this was what he'd meant.

"Esgal, you've been drugged, haven't you?"

Esgal frowned at him again, then slurred, "You're an elf?"

"Yes."

"You're real?"

"Yes, I'm real. You're not dreaming." Lim looked round, biting his lip in worry. "Esgal," he said, speaking as clearly as he could. "Can you tell me if you're injured?"

"I... I don't know." Esgal also spoke slowly, trying to enunciate. "I'm numb."

"Can you get up?" Lim put an arm around Esgal's torso, almost carrying him, and led him over to a spot under the cliff face where there was some shade and they could wait until dark. Now that the dust had settled, they'd be clearly visible climbing back up, especially as getting Esgal up there would be a slow job with him in this state. Lim couldn't feel any injuries across Esgal's back or ribs, so it should be safe to pull him back up. Not easy for either of them, but not outright dangerous. Still, with his hands still bound and as weak and groggy as he was, he'd not be able to keep himself from simply slipping out of a loop. Lim frowned over at the rope as he helped Esgal to lie down. There was probably enough slack in it to tie a sling, when the time came. In the meantime, he'd let Esgal rest and hope that no-one would come to investigate that guard's disappearance.

Esgal fell asleep very quickly, now that everything was quiet and no-one was forcing him to stay awake. Lim gently ran a hand over his head, looking out across the road and wondering what to do.

His eyes went to the heavy manacles around Esgal's wrists. Well, he could try to get those off for a start. He took out his lockpicks and frowned at them. He'd never had to do this for real, only in training, and he really hoped that he didn't screw it up or jam the locks. He had done on numerous occasions in practice, after all.

Still, if he could at least get one open, Esgal would be almost able to use his hands freely, even if one was still weighed down until they got home and found someone who knew what they were doing. With that in mind, Lim took the picks and inserted them carefully into the keyhole of the right manacle. As he fumbled, he comforted himself with the fact that the lock didn't look too well made. The manacles were designed to stop the prisoner pulling them open or slipping his hands out of the shackles, not to be secure against someone with lockpicks and plenty of time. And he did have plenty of time, he reminded himself. The daylight would hold for hours, and they were safely sealed off from the surviving guards. He could tell that from the fact that, despite a few shouts and the sound of moving rocks, no-one had made it past that rockslide.

He was almost there when his left hand slipped and he dropped the two he was holding.

He swore, cursing his hand and his own clumsiness. At least he'd not slipped enough for the pick to leave the keyhole and jab Esgal's wrist. He sighed, took a deep breath and tried again. This time, when he was almost finished, Esgal sighed and twitched in his sleep.

Lim froze. "Please keep still," he whispered. If Esgal tried to move his arm, he'd drop all the pins he'd managed to get. Fortunately, Esgal just sighed again and fell still. Lim also sighed in relief and went back to fishing for the next pin.

This one was the last and once he'd found it and pushed it up, the wrench turned as though it were a key and the lock clicked open. He grinned in private triumph and gently pulled it away from Esgal's wrist, shifting the now-free arm to lie in a more comfortable position. Esgal slept on.

Lim stretched his aching arms and hands and leaned over Esgal again to work on his other wrist. This one was still more awkwardly placed and he wondered if he dared move Esgal to give himself a better angle. He couldn't really reach the lock from here; Esgal's arm wouldn't twist that way without hurting him and Lim couldn't get around him because he was lying so close to the cliff.

"Esgal?" he said softly. Esgal didn't even twitch. "Esgal?" he said a little louder. Still nothing. Apparently he was very deeply asleep. It was probably tiredness combined with the drug he'd been given. His breathing and heartbeat were a little slow, but no more than Lim would have expected from an elf in a deep, dreamless sleep.

"All right. I'm going to roll you over so I can get at your other arm more easily. You'll probably then be more comfortable as well. Don't worry," he said as he moved Esgal's still-chained arm out of the way and prepared to roll him onto his back and then his other side. "I don't mean you any harm."

Esgal didn't react as Lim rolled him over, apart from a slight hitch in his breathing that quickly evened out again.

Now it was easier to get at the lock and Lim managed to get it in one try. Finally, he pulled away the manacles and laid them aside, arranged Esgal's arms so that he would be more comfortable and stroked his hair again.

"There you go," he said, unable to suppress a grin. "You'll be all right."

He hid the manacles under some loose pieces of rock and sat down with his back against the wall, closing his eyes for a moment. It would be a couple of hours until it was dark enough to conceal their climb. He could get up and down by feel well enough with the rope to help him, so he didn't need to wait for the moon to rise. He stifled a chuckle. If he was lucky, they needn't even know that Esgal had been rescued.

There was, however, one obstacle to that.

Lim got up and went over to the corpse of the man he'd shot. He sighed a little, looking at him, but shook his head. He'd had to do it to protect himself and Esgal. No use brooding on it. Besides... he looked back over at Esgal, who was still deep in his drugged sleep in their patch of shade, bloodied and bruised. This was one of the people who had done that to him, to someone bound and unable to defend himself.

Lim shook his head. Brooding again. Wasting time. He crouched down beside the body with another sigh. Well, he couldn't leave his arrow in the wound or they'd know at once that another elf had been here. He pulled it out, grimacing as it came free with a nasty sucking noise, and set it to one side. Now, he was trying to make them think Esgal had escaped rather than being rescued. How might he have done that? A short knife that he saw strapped to the man's leg would have been within easy reach from the floor and Esgal had already managed to get his hands in front once. If he'd grabbed at the man's leg, perhaps to trip him, he could have taken the knife. Lim drew it and frowned. No-one would believe that Esgal had simply managed to stab his guard in the throat, especially blindfolded. He didn't want to desecrate a corpse, but he glanced back at Esgal. They needed all the start they could get once the humans had made it past the rockslide...

Before he could change his mind, he carefully put several shallow slices in the man's hands and forearms, as if he'd been trying to fend off wild blows. Then he added some shallow stab wounds to his torso, such as might have been left by a panicking captive just trying to land a serious wound. Finally, he pushed the knife into the arrow wound to change its shape and pulled it back out, feeling slightly sick. Esgal would have used it to cut himself free if he was still blindfolded, so Lim wiped some blood onto the cut ends of the rope that had been around Esgal's neck and wiped the blood from his hands onto the sack. Then he dropped both items and the knife beside the man's corpse and stepped back.

He nodded to himself. Perhaps they'd spot the attempt to cover up a rescue, but it was less likely and he didn't think there was any more he could do. Would Esgal have taken the knife? He picked it up and considered it. He himself would take the sword that had fallen from the man's hand, but Esgal... he shook his head and dropped the knife.

He didn't think he could do any more here, so he picked up his arrow, which had dried in the meantime, and put it back in his quiver. Then he went back and sat beside Esgal. He toyed with the idea of trying to set his nose while he was unconscious and unable to feel the pain, but decided against it. He didn't know how deeply unconscious Esgal actually was and didn't want to wake him by hurting him; he was already scared, there was no need to give him actual reason to think he was in danger. Lim just sat back against the cliff, glancing up at the rapidly-sinking sun, and closed his eyes to doze.

He mentally kept track of the passage of time and opened his eyes again when it was almost completely dark. He was sharp-eyed and had grown up in Silvren, so he had good night vision and was just about able to pick out his surroundings. There was the rope, not far off. He wondered if he could carry Esgal over to it, but decided that pulling him up would be much less dangerous if he was at least partially conscious. Besides, it was only fair to try to explain to him what was happening.

"Esgal?" he said softly, crouching down and gently shaking Esgal's shoulder. "Esgal, wake up, it's time we got moving."

Esgal whimpered and flinched away. "I... I'm so tired," he moaned. "Please, just a little longer."

"You have to wake up, Esgal. It's just for a little while, then you can sleep again."

Esgal twitched again and gasped.

"My... my hands... I can move..."

"I got the chains off while you were asleep."

"But... why?"

Apparently he didn't really remember that he'd been rescued. Maybe the darkness was confusing him. "Do you remember the last time you were awake?"

Esgal paused for a moment, then said, "You. You're an elf."

"Yes. I rescued you. But we need to move; my camp's at the top of the cliff."

"I can't climb."

"I know. Just come over here; there's a rope I'm going to use to pull you up."

Lim put an arm around Esgal and helped him to stand, then led him over to the rope. He made him sit down and tied one loop under his arms and another around his knees, making sure the knots were fairly snug so that even if he lost consciousness he shouldn't slip out of it. He made sure he explained every step and Esgal didn't seem too bothered until he tried to straighten one leg and felt the constrictions around his knees and body. Then he went pale and shook his head a little, closing his eyes as if to shut out his surroundings, too weak to try to struggle.

"Esgal?" Lim put a hand on his shoulder. "It's all right. You're safe."

"Still here?" asked Esgal, opening his eyes again.

"Yes, I'm here. I'm going to climb back up to the top of the cliff and pull you up. Try to keep your feet towards the cliff so you can fend yourself off. Do you understand?"

Esgal nodded. Lim gave him a last pat on the shoulder and, as quickly as he could, climbed back up the rope. Once there, he untied it from the boulder and passed the end across his back to help him take the strain. He could brace it safely this way in case his left hand slipped. He forced his feet against the boulder and took a deep breath, then he took one end of the rope in each hand, one either side, and began to pull.

It took him about ten minutes to haul Esgal up to the top and over the edge, then he finally untied the sling, pulled him a little further from the edge and all but collapsed beside him to catch his breath. His hands burned from the friction and he looked at them, grimacing though he couldn't see their state in the dim light. He wasn't sure how much more he'd be able to do, but he had to try. First, he had to get Esgal back to the cave to rest more comfortably.

He picked himself up, helped Esgal to his feet and led him back to the cave. He seemed even less conscious than before, just going where he was led, dragging his feet and tripping even when there was nothing there to trip on. Lim was used to the idea that elves were always sure-footed and this made him cringe. At last, though, they reached the cave and Lim helped Esgal to lie down on his own bedroll.

"There," he said, patting him on the shoulder again. "You get some more sleep. I'll look after you."

Esgal sighed softly. "All right," he said, then sighed again and relaxed as he fell asleep. He snored softly as he breathed through his mouth, his nose blocked with blood and swelling.

Lim gently laid a blanket over him, then slipped outside to retrieve his rope and the spare blanket that he'd used to pad it from the edge. While he was there, he'd quietly celebrate his achievement in picking those locks.

He retrieved the blanket, which looked rather worn where the rope had rubbed it, and held it up to look at the damage. He'd be able to darn it as soon as he had the time. Only then did he look down and see that the men were working to get over the rock fall. A few lay some distance off, apparently injured, while another tended them. That left two or three carefully shifting rocks. One shouted out a name, presumably that of the dead guard. He didn't sound optimistic.

Lim couldn't help a moment's relief. By the time they had got through, discovered Esgal's escape and even thought of looking all the way up here for him, both elves would hopefully be long gone.

With that thought, he carried the rope and blanket back to his cave and sat down on his pack to rest, the blanket around his shoulders. He couldn't in good conscience sleep so close to his enemy, but he might at least doze.

***

He was rudely awoken by a cry of pain, and he startled awake to find that the moon was rising and he could see Esgal. He'd moved, and his breathing was now fast and jagged.

"Esgal?"

"The... the drug... is wearing off..." panted Esgal, and he laughed bitterly. "The numbness... is going... with it."

Lim laid a hand on his shoulder. "How bad is it?"

"Not too bad." Esgal's breathing was slowing now. "Just a shock. I think... my muscles are sore, and I tried to move and... suddenly felt the aches."

Lim smiled, patting his shoulder. "Well, welcome back to the land of the living."

Esgal chuckled, shifting with a small wince to look up at Lim more easily. "Thanks," he said.

At this new angle Lim noticed that Esgal's eyes were still unfocussed, though he otherwise looked much livelier now that he'd slept off the drug. His worry suddenly returned.

"Are you sure you're all right?" he asked.

Esgal bit his lip, turning his head slightly. "All except the fact that... I still can't *see*."

Lim's own eyes widened. "What? But... how?"

"I don't know." Esgal also sounded more worried now. "I thought my sight would return when the drug wore off... but, now that I think about it..." Worry was now growing almost to panic. "I don't know when it happened." His words began to speed up. "The... the cell they locked me in was dark, and I was struck on the head a couple of times, what if... oh, *Spirits*, no..."

Lim also felt panicky, but he laid his hands on Esgal's shoulders. "All right, calm down," he said, keeping his voice as steady as he could. "You're going to be fine. Give it a little longer, maybe with time it'll return."

Esgal nodded. "All right," he said, shaking his head and slowing his breathing apparently by sheer will. "All right, I'm fine. Can I have a drink?"

Lim passed him the water bottle. It took him a moment to remember that he had to put it into Esgal's hand, not just offer it. Esgal pushed himself upright, wincing, and drank a couple of mouthfuls.

"How much do we have?" he asked.

"I'll be able to refill it, don't worry. You drink as much as you need."

"Thank you." Esgal took a longer drink and put the bottle down with a sigh, absently fumbling for the lid and closing it. "That's good. It seems forever since I last had clean water."

"What did they give you to drink?"

"That was how they got the drug into me." Esgal shuddered. "They knew that, even with the best will in the world, I needed water."

Lim grimaced in sympathy and helped Esgal to pull the blanket from the bedroll around his shoulders.

"How's the pain now?" he asked, to change the subject a little.

"Better." Esgal tipped his head back against the wall and closed his eyes, hugging the blanket a little closer. "I just ache from walking so hard for so long." He fingered the scrape on his chest, brushing off flakes of dried blood. "I fell over several times too."

Lim nodded. "I saw you fall once. Do you want me to clean that up? And straighten your nose?"

Esgal touched his nose and hissed. "Yes to the former," he said. "The last thing I want is an infection. My nose... will that make me able to breathe more freely?"

"It might, though it'll still be swollen. It'll make it heal straighter, though."

Esgal nodded, smiling wanly. "All right," he said, hitching the blanket up his shoulders. "Where are we? It's cold."

"We're still on the mountain, in a cave," said Lim as he took out his healing kit. At least he had his night vision and could see well enough to treat the most obvious injuries. As he plunged his hand into his pack, he touched the bundle of clothes at the bottom and smiled. "I've some of your clothes here. Do you want to change into them? That'll be warmer."

Esgal smiled. "I'd like that. It should probably wait until after this, though." He touched the scrape again. "It was thoughtful of you. Thank you."

"Your wife's idea," said Lim as he trickled some water onto a rag and started to clean off Esgal's scrape.

Esgal's hiss of pain turned into a joyful laugh at the thought of his wife. "Ai, Alydra! It sounds like her. How is she? Not terribly unhappy, I hope?"

"As much as can be expected," said Lim, also smiling at Esgal's reaction.

"I suppose so." Esgal sighed and leaned back against the wall, relaxing as Lim continued to clean his wound. After a moment, he said, "I'm sorry – I know you told me, but my thoughts were full of resin. What's your name?"

"Lim."

There was a moment's pause as Esgal waited for the patronym, but Lim never used his, and as Esgal realised that it wasn't forthcoming he coughed awkwardly and took another sip of water.

"When did you last have something to eat?" asked Lim as he finished cleaning the wound. He could feel Esgal's ribs and it was clear that he'd lost weight recently; the bones weren't jutting yet, but they were definitely close under the skin.

"Last night, and the night before, but nothing between that and my capture, and very little at those times." Esgal shuddered again. "I only ate when they forced me to."

"Why?" asked Lim, without thinking.

Esgal opened his eyes and stared past Lim. "Because I didn't want to reach their city alive," he said simply. "I've seen what they do to elves that they capture."

Lim didn't want to hear about what Esgal had seen if that was the case, so he simply patted him on the shoulder and went back to cleaning the scrape.

"Do you know anything about my partner?"

"Lord Caleb mentioned him. I think he's all right."

Esgal nodded, relaxing a little. "I'm glad he had the sense to go."

Most of the dirt was gone now. Esgal had scraped off a lot of skin, but it wasn't deep.

"Is this the worst?" asked Lim.

Esgal raised a hand absently to his chest. "I think so. Apart from that and my nose I think it's just bruising." He reached up to touch his shoulder. It was badly bruised where he'd fallen during the rockslide, but the skin wasn't broken.

"This hurts," he said. "Am I right? Is it serious?"

"It's bruised. How deep does the pain go? Can you still move it?"

Esgal raised his arm and nodded. "It's all right," he said. "It does hurt, but I'm sure it'll be fine."

"All right. I'll bandage the one on your chest to keep it clean, then I'll sort out your nose."

"Thank you."

This time, Esgal definitely wasn't only referring to the offer to set his broken nose, but Lim pretended he'd not heard the undertones; to acknowledge it would be to prompt a display of gratitude that would be embarrassing for them both.

"Thank me after I've done it," he said, grinning. "I warn you: I'm not a healer and I've never set a broken nose before."

Esgal nodded. "I doubt you could make it worse unless you tried," he said.

"Don't say that," said Lim, giving the scrape a final wipe and reaching for a bandage. Esgal shifted to let him wrap it around his torso, wincing again. "Does that hurt?" asked Lim, tying it off.

"It's not the bandage. It just hurts to move."

Lim nodded, glancing at the doorway to the cave. He was hungry and knew that Esgal was probably famished. They'd not be able to move on again tonight. He sighed a little. There was no way to have a camp fire up here and it would have been a bad idea anyway; the light would have made their whereabouts very clear.

"What's wrong?"

"We'll not be able to leave tonight."

Esgal nodded a little. "Sorry," he said, "But... I know I could do with resting a little longer."

Lim smiled and patted him on the shoulder. "It's all right. I was also sighing because we can't have a camp fire up here, so I can't make anything hot to eat or drink."

Esgal licked his lips. "Honestly, I'd eat a dragon without too much preamble or many seasonings."

Lim laughed. "Well, I've not got a dragon, I'm afraid, just biscuit and dried meat."

Esgal also chuckled, tipping his head back against the wall again.

Lim stretched, eyeing him with some trepidation. "Do you want me to try your nose now?"

Esgal groaned, wincing. "It'll hurt, won't it?" He shook his head a little. "Ah, well, it has to be done. Go on."

Lim hesitated a moment, then laid a hand on Esgal's shoulder to brace him and took hold of his nose, grimacing at his half-stifled cry of pain. Then, as quickly as he could without messing it up, he pulled it straight.

He felt bile rise in his throat as it crackled under his fingers. Esgal's hand flew to his mouth to muffle his own cry and he tried to flinch, but his back was already to the wall. Blood trickled from one of his nostrils and he sneezed. Another sneeze made him groan and instinctively wrap an arm around his ribs as he futilely tried to wipe away the blood. Tears of pain and shock ran down his cheeks.

Lim handed him the rag he'd been using to clean his wounds and he held it carefully to his nostrils to soak up the blood.

"Sorry," said Lim. "I said I'd never done it before."

Esgal shook his head. "I know," he said, his voice a little muffled. "I don't blame you; I knew it would hurt..." He pulled the rag away with a disgusted noise and coughed. "It's all getting down the back of my throat."

Lim was getting very worried now. What if he had just made things worse?

Esgal seemed to sense it and smiled as reassuringly as he could, given that his face was covered in blood.

"I'll be fine," he said. "I've had nosebleeds before."

Lim still wasn't sure, but he nodded. "All right," he said, as he remembered that Esgal couldn't see him. "Sorry I hurt you, though."

Esgal chuckled, carefully wiping his eyes with the back of his free hand. "You were setting a broken bone; of course it was going to hurt."

Lim forced a smile and reached into his bag to fetch out Esgal's clothes. "When the bleeding's stopped, do you want to get changed?" he asked.

Esgal nodded, his eyes lighting up. "I've been wearing these since I was captured," he said, pulling at his dirty, torn breeches, "and I could do with something warm."

Lim pulled out the bundle and blinked as a small cloth packet also came out. Curious, he set the clothes to one side and picked it up. When he unwrapped it, he couldn't suppress his cry of surprise and joy as he saw what it contained. Honey fudge! He made a mental note to thank Seregei for this surprise gift.

"What is it?" asked Esgal.

"My friend Seregei must have slipped this in for me. It's a packet of honey fudge. Want some?"

Esgal instinctively reached out, but then hesitated. "Give me a minute for the bleeding to stop," – he smiled – "then I'd love to try a piece."

Lim put the clothes where he could reach them and told him where they were, then got out the remaining supply of food and looked at it. There was enough for both of them for the next three days, four if they were careful. It had taken him a day to get here, going as hard as he could. Esgal wouldn't stand being rushed like that, and in any case he couldn't hurry over rough ground, blind as he was. They'd be slower getting back, but hopefully not so slow that they wouldn't make it into the trees before running out of food. Once there, Lim would have a better chance of finding something for them to eat, and in any case he had left just over a day's supply for two cached with the rest of his gear. They'd not starve. He put the food away again and looked up at the stars. It would be a cold night, but they were sheltered from any wind here. A fire would have been nice, for its warmth and light, but they'd live.

Esgal had apparently also noticed the growing chill, for he shivered and pulled the blanket around his shoulders a little closer.

"It's getting cold," he said softly.

"It's a clear night, so I'm afraid it'll be cold."

Esgal sighed. "I wanted to see the stars again," he said mournfully, "but this is already more than I hoped for, so I can't complain."

Lim patted him comfortingly on the shoulder. "I'm sure your sight will return," he said, "and you've got years to enjoy the stars."

When Esgal was convinced that his nose had completely stopped bleeding, he changed into the clothes Lim had brought for him, relishing the feel of the warm, clean cloth against his skin. Lim smiled as he looked at him. Oddly, the clean clothes seemed to bring him more obvious pleasure than anything else that had happened so far. Lim reminded himself that that might be because Alydra had thought to send them: a practical and loving gesture that Esgal had clearly taken to heart.

Looking much warmer and more comfortable, Esgal accepted a piece of biscuit and a strip of dried meat and ate, chewing thoughtfully in between small sips of water. Lim also ate his dinner in silence, planning for the next day. They'd have to set off as soon as they could; it wouldn't do to meet a search party coming the other way. There was also the problem of water. Despite his words to Esgal, he wasn't sure there was a supply near their cave. He saw that Esgal had finished his biscuit and passed him a piece of fudge.

"Your friend's name is Seregei?" asked Esgal, before taking a small bite of fudge.

"Yes."

"It's not that common a name… the Swordmaster captain?"

"Yes, actually. I'm his trainee."

"I see…" Esgal ate a bit more fudge. "This is your Task, then?"

Lim nodded, then hastily added, "Yes, it is."

Esgal was starting to look sleepy again and Lim advised him to rest.

"We'll be leaving first thing tomorrow morning and you'll need your strength. I'm afraid it's an even rougher path back the way I came than the road they used to bring you here."

Esgal groaned in anticipated pain. "All right," he said, lying down and rolling himself up in the blanket. "I'll sleep. How far do we have to travel tomorrow?"

Lim frowned, trying to do the sums in his head. "I think it's about twenty miles to where I left my horse. I did it all in one day on the way up here, but we don't have to do it all in one day on the way back, don't worry."

"Good." Esgal sighed. "I'm not sure I could walk quite that far."

"Will you be able to travel tomorrow?"

"If you forced me to do so, I could probably travel tonight. Th-they managed to keep me going even when I was so exhausted…"

Lim once again put a hand on his shoulder. "We'll take it easy tomorrow," he said. "I'll not force you to go longer than you think you can."

"Thanks." Esgal sighed again. "Did you speak to Alydra?" he asked sleepily. "I know she sent these clothes, but…"

"Yes, I spoke to her. I also saw a portrait she'd drawn of you. That's how I knew what you look like."

Esgal smiled. "She's so good at drawing faces," he murmured.

"She didn't say much. I think she just wanted to make sure she could trust whoever was coming to look for you."

Esgal chuckled. "Yes… yes, I can imagine that. Mmm… I've missed her. It's the hardest thing, being away from her for years at a time, and it's not easy to write to her or send messages. It'll be good to see her again." With that, his eyes slid closed and he drifted off to sleep.

Lim sighed a little and got up, going to the door of the cave to look out. The moon was well up and he decided to slip out and see if he could find a spring or some other source of water; the water bottle was almost empty.

He began picking his way away from the cave, leaving little cairns of five small rocks at a time so that he'd be able to find his way back.

He hoped that he'd be able to find something. It wasn't the season for meltwater, even from the mountain's highest slopes above where he was standing. This mountain wasn't so high that there might be snow on it even in the summer. Still, he was sure that there'd be water somewhere.

He walked for about half an hour, hunting in small gulleys and frequently backtracking. The moon was full tonight so there was enough light to see, even though he'd not like to be travelling far with so little light. He stood still for a long moment, his eyes closed, listening for the tell-tale trickle of water among the rocks. He couldn't hear anything and scrambled a little further along his rough path before stopping to listen again. This time he did hear it: a small tinkling sound, though he couldn't quite pinpoint where it came from. A little further along and it was definitely getting louder; he was on the right track. At last, he tracked it down to a small gully, almost invisible among the rocks. A shallow stream ran down it and Lim scooped a little up in his hand to smell and taste it. It was very cold, but seemed pure and he filled his bottle. They'd have water for the morning now and could both drink their fill; he'd been holding back, uncertain if there really was water available. He suspected that Esgal had disbelieved his assurances and had been doing the same.

Encouraged, he picked his way back down the slope to his cave. Esgal was still peacefully asleep, unaware that he'd been left alone for even a moment. Lim curled up in the spare, now rather worn, blanket beside him. It was even more difficult to get comfortable now with only a blanket between him and the bare rock and he wished he'd thought to bring a second bedroll. He dismissed the thought; there probably wouldn't have been room for it anyway. He'd live. But it was with a wistful thought for his own bed at home that he finally fell asleep.

CHAPTER THREE

Lim woke up first in the morning. His throat was dry and he took a grateful sip from the water bottle. The day was fairly warm, despite the chill that lingered in his bones. His arms ached, but at least his legs didn't seem to hurt as much as they had the day before. He put this down to the fact that his entire body had reached a uniform state of ache and stretched, wincing. A glance at his hands elicited another wince. There were a couple of noticeable blisters on his fingers and where his thumb met his hand, and the palms were still reddened and scored with rope burns. He made a mental note that if he ever volunteered for something like this again he would bring gloves.

He glanced over at Esgal and grimaced sympathetically. The swelling around his nose seemed to have gone down a little, though he was still snoring, but bruising had darkened quite spectacularly around his eyes. There wasn't much Lim could be do about it, though, not here; there was nothing to make a compress that might bring the bruising and swelling down. Lim wondered whether he should have known to bring something that he could use and decided that, though it would have been a good idea, such things tended not to keep well. He didn't reliably know how to make them either, so it wasn't even worth bringing the dry ingredients.

The thought did, however, remind him about the little pot of salve that he'd slipped into his healing kit, for blisters. He fished it out and smeared some on his hands. At once, it began to soothe the burns and blisters and he sighed in relief. Then he got up with another groan and went to look outside. It was about an hour after sunrise, he judged. He'd let Esgal sleep for a little longer, then he'd need to wake him so they could eat and set off.

He didn't have to wake Esgal, though, as at that moment the other elf uttered a soft moan and stirred.

Lim went to kneel beside him. "Esgal?"

Esgal twitched, groaning again, then opened his eyes, as best he could against the swelling.

"Lim?" he asked.

"I'm here. How did you sleep?" Lim didn't like to ask if Esgal could see any better, in case the answer was no.

Esgal smiled a little. "Like a log." He tried to push himself up on his elbows and gasped in pain. Lim instinctively slipped an arm around his shoulders and helped him to sit up. "Thanks," he said. "I'm still very stiff."

"I imagine sleeping on the rock didn't help much." Lim smiled. "I could hardly move after my first night camping here, after climbing all the way up the mountain."

"How long were you waiting?"

"Oh, only overnight. Do you still think you'll be able to walk today?"

"Hmm... I'm stiff and my feet hurt, but I'll manage." Esgal sighed, closing his eyes for a moment, but then looked up with a small smile. "I've some strength yet."

"I've some salve for blisters if you want to put it on your feet," said Lim, offering it. "I've already tried it; my hands were rope burned something terrible from skidding up and down the cliff yesterday."

Esgal grimaced as he groped for the salve; apparently his sight had not yet returned. "And pulling me up, I imagine. Sorry."

Lim shook his head. "Not at all. It was my plan, after all."

Esgal found the salve and took it, fumbling the top off. Then he took off one of his shoes. Lim grimaced in sympathy; there was a magnificent blister on the side of Esgal's foot and another on the knuckle of one of his toes.

"I think I got something in my shoe at one point," said Esgal as he smeared salve on the blisters. "It was rubbing for ages. After a while I couldn't feel it any more, but I don't know if that was because it had slipped to somewhere where it didn't rub or because I'd just lost feeling due to the drug."

Lim took his shoe and had a look inside, then held it upside down and shook it. A couple of small stones fell out.

"I think it's gone now," he said. "I'm not surprised you've got blisters, though."

Esgal was now dealing with the heel of his other foot. "Spirits, how big is this one?" he asked, poking it.

Lim angled his head to look. The skin of Esgal's sole was thicker and he'd had his weight on it so the blister was flat, but enormous.

"A little bigger than the pad of your thumb, I'd judge," he said. That was going to be difficult and painful to walk on.

Esgal cursed, but put salve on it and pulled his shoes back on.

"Thanks," he said, holding out the salve. Lim took it and he continued,

"I think I'll be able to walk on them. That helped a lot, but I admit that I've not tried to walk without something numbing the pain."

Lim nodded. "Well, have some breakfast," he said, holding out a piece of biscuit. "And I've refilled the water bottle, so drink all you want and I'll fill it again before we leave."

Esgal chuckled. "So there is a water source nearby. I confess I thought you were only saying that to comfort me." He took a long drink and began nibbling on his breakfast.

Lim ate quickly and began putting everything back into his pack. Esgal apparently heard him, for he shifted off the bedroll, feeling for a rock to sit on instead. Eventually, he settled for sitting awkwardly cross-legged on the floor.

At last, they'd both eaten and Lim finished fastening his pack.

"I'm going to refill the water bottle," he said, reaching for it. "I'll be back in a moment."

Esgal nodded. "I may need help getting up," he confessed, and took a last swig of water before holding it out.

"All right. Just stay put until I get back."

When he returned with the water, Esgal had shifted to the entrance of the cave and was sitting on a small stone, smelling the air and apparently basking in the sunlight.

"Lim?" he asked uncertainly as he heard footsteps approaching.

"Yes, it's me," said Lim. "Stay there a moment longer while I get my pack on, then I'll help you up."

Esgal nodded and took another long breath. "It's warmer out here," he said.

"I know, out in the sun." Lim hauled the pack back onto his back with a groan and began fastening the straps.

"What's wrong?" asked Esgal. "You groaned."

"I'm stiff too, that's all," said Lim.

Esgal nodded and shifted to accommodate the arm Lim wrapped around his torso to help him up, careful to handle him more gently than his captors had after his fall the day before.

"All right?" he asked, steadying him while he awkwardly found his feet.

"All right," said Esgal, fumbling for Lim's pack and laying a hand on it. "I'm afraid you'll have to tell me if the ground is rough, though."

"We'll go fairly slowly. I'll take the smoothest path, and you just follow me. Feel with your feet as you go and you should be all right."

Esgal nodded, looking a little happier as he heard the encouraging tone in Lim's voice. "I'll do my best."

Despite that, they still moved infuriatingly slowly, picking their way along. A couple of times Lim had to grab and steady Esgal as he almost tripped; the strain was clearly exhausting him, but they both knew that there was no other way to move. Lim couldn't carry him and he couldn't walk any faster or with any less care or he'd do nothing but trip and fall. That would slow them just as much as well as giving him more injuries.

At noon, they'd just reached a point halfway back to where Lim had first seen Esgal and he decided that they should stop to rest for a while. Esgal gratefully sank to the ground, leaning against the cliff beside the trail, his eyes falling closed.

Lim shook his shoulder to rouse him and handed him another piece of biscuit.

"Here," he said. "The water bottle's beside you."

"How long can we rest?" Esgal asked, his voice faint and weak.

"Maybe as much as an hour, but no longer."

Esgal nodded, nibbling listlessly at the food for a moment before letting his hand fall into his lap.

"I'm hungry," he said softly, "But I'm too tired to eat."

Lim bit his lip in worry. "You need to eat it, Esgal," he said.

"I know, but it feels like it's almost too much effort to swallow." Esgal took a few more small bites and sighed. "I'll just rest for a bit and catch my breath."

Lim didn't want to force him to eat, but knew that he needed food or he'd never have the energy to go on. Still, he patted him on the shoulder and said, "So long as you've finished it before we move on, you'll probably be all right. But you have to eat it."

Esgal chuckled faintly. "Yes, Mother," he said sleepily. "I'll eat my greens."

Lim also laughed, and went back to his own lunch.

By the time almost an hour had passed, Esgal had eaten his biscuit and seemed rested enough to go on again. Whenever the path was wide enough, Lim now walked beside him, an arm around his shoulders to support him as he weaved on his feet. He gasped a little every time his right foot hit the ground. After a little while he took to only walking on the toe of that foot, but the limping got worse as that in turn began to take a toll on the muscles of his leg. After a couple of hours, Lim declared another rest and helped Esgal to sit down on a rock.

"Here," he said, taking out the salve again. "Put some more of this on that blister of yours."

Esgal took it with thanks and pulled off his shoe to smear the salve onto his heel. He sighed in relief as it soothed the pain. "Can I put some on the other foot as well?"

Lim nodded. "That's why I brought it."

Esgal pulled off his other shoe and Lim gasped a little. The blister on the side of Esgal's foot had burst and the other one looked close. His foot was bloody from the continued rubbing on the tender skin under the blister and it looked terribly painful.

Esgal frowned as he carefully touched it. "What's happened?"

"The blister's burst," said Lim. "Don't put any salve on it; it'll sting. The other one's near to bursting and it'll bleed too if we just let it, so hang on a moment." He took out his healing kit and threaded a needle. It wasn't sterile, but it was clean, and that was the best that could be done up here.

"What are you going to do?" asked Esgal as Lim took his foot on his knee.

"Burst it in a controlled manner," said Lim. "I'm going to put a needle through it with a piece of thread. The thread will soak up the fluid, making it flatten out. It'll hurt, but not as much as having it burst on its own. Then I'll bandage your foot."

Esgal nodded, and only let out a hiss as Lim pushed the needle through the blister. It took a little while for it to deflate, then he pulled out the thread and threw it aside, wiping off the needle on his handkerchief. He'd sterilise it when they reached the bottom and had a camp fire. Then he washed the worst of the blood and fluid off Esgal's foot and bandaged it.

"There," he said. "That should keep it clean and pad it a little. Just let me have another look at your shoe."

The inside of his shoe was also bloody and unpleasant, but Lim found what was causing the problem: another small stone had lodged in the inside of his shoe, right where the side of the ball of his foot rested. No wonder he'd been having so much trouble. Lim removed the stone, and they forced the shoe on over the bandaging.

"Thank you," said Esgal fervently as Lim helped him to stand up again. "That's much less painful."

Lim smiled sympathetically. "I've had blisters. I'm impressed you're walking at all with one that size on your heel."

Esgal sighed. "I wouldn't be if I had any other way of getting down."

They went on again, still moving slowly, Esgal doing his best despite his blindness to keep up with Lim and not fall. He did trip once, landing on his knees, but he wasn't badly hurt and Lim helped him up again.

They eventually stopped under an overhang that formed a shallow cave, a little further on from where Lim had first seen him.

"We've made good progress today," said Lim, handing Esgal some food. "If we do that again we'll be down into the forest tomorrow, and then it'll be much easier."

Esgal sighed. "I'll be glad to never have to walk another mountain trail as long as I live," he said wearily, biting into the biscuit Lim had given him.

Lim thought uneasily of the steep slope at the beginning of this side trail. It had not been easy to walk up; what would it be like to climb down? And to climb down it with Esgal?

"There's one bit tomorrow that's harder. It's quite steep and rough, but it's the last bit of trail. After that we're on road."

Esgal groaned in anticipation, letting his head fall back against the wall.

"Is there any other way out?" he asked.

"No, not that I know of."

"All right." He sighed heavily. "I'll do my best." Another sigh and he ate another couple of mouthfuls of food, though he didn't look very interested in it. "I'm sorry. After all you've done for me I seem to do nothing but complain."

Lim blinked in surprise. He'd not really thought that Esgal was complaining unduly, and said so. "It would be far more annoying if you were obviously cold, or tired, or in pain and didn't admit it," he said. "I said I'd take care of you; I don't mind."

Esgal smiled for a moment and finished his food, then stretched, wincing.

"Here." Lim unpacked the bedroll and laid it out. "You get some sleep."

"Thank you." Esgal lay down, feeling for the blanket and pulling it over himself. After a moment, he said sleepily, "Lim? Why did you rescue me?"

Lim was surprised again. "What else was I to do?" he asked. "I'm originally from Silvren. I've heard some of the stories. I couldn't leave you here."

"But you've never even met me before."

"Doesn't matter. I'd not have been able to live with myself if I'd left an elf to suffer like that when I had the chance to at least try to help him."

Esgal seemed satisfied with that, for he sighed a little, then said, "Thank you. I... I owe you more than I can ever repay."

Lim had been right about how embarrassing this was and he looked at the ground. "You don't owe me anything. Anyway, we still have to get back to Duamelti."

Esgal chuckled. "That's... true..." he said, and sighed as he fell asleep.

Lim sighed a little, looking out across the path into the distance. They'd not made bad progress – they were about halfway back – but he couldn't deny that he was very worried about how Esgal would cope with that rough stretch right at the end. He knew that he couldn't carry him down, even if he did something like going down first, leaving his pack at the bottom and coming back. There was no way he could keep his balance going down that slope carrying another elf. They'd just have to do their best. It didn't help that that was also the beginning of the area where they were most likely to be spotted by anyone searching for them; anyone coming up after him would pass through there, as would Esgal's former captors if they'd chosen to go back to the town for help.

Once down, he and Esgal would have to go along the road for a way, though once they hit the trees they'd be able to keep off it a little better. Unfortunately, it was a pine forest and didn't provide much cover on the ground, but it was fairly dark and he thought there was enough shelter due to rocky outcrops and the undulating ground that they'd be able to keep fairly out of sight, at least from anyone casually looking for them.

He sighed again. There was no point in worrying like this; it wouldn't help and was just tiring him. He should try and get some rest himself. The cover here wasn't ideal, so he couldn't let himself fall deeply asleep, but he might doze.

***

Again, he woke first, but when he glanced at Esgal he saw that his companion was not sleeping peacefully; he kept twitching and whimpering.

"Esgal?" Lim said softly, shaking his shoulder. "Esgal, wake up, you're safe."

Esgal jerked awake and lay still for a moment, catching his breath.

"Are you all right now?" asked Lim, leaning down a little to look at his face.

"I... I think so." Esgal rubbed his eyes and blinked a couple of times. "Is... is it bright here?"

Lim blinked in surprise and considered the question. While the sun wasn't hitting them directly, it was a fairly bright morning, he supposed.

"Relatively," he said. "Why?"

Esgal smiled a little. "Because I think I can see your outline." He reached out and, with only a moment's fumbling and hesitation, laid a hand on Lim's shoulder. "It's just the faintest silhouette, but I think I'm seeing you against the sky."

Lim had been surprised, but once he'd got over that he laughed out loud in joy. "That's wonderful!" he said. "Why, that means your sight's returning."

Esgal also grinned. "Very slowly, but it might come back."

Lim patted him on the shoulder and got out some food. "Here's some breakfast. We'll have to set off as soon as we can."

Esgal nodded, beginning to eat as Lim ate his own breakfast.

"Lim?" Esgal said suddenly.

Lim had just started to pack up their makeshift camp. "Here I am."

Esgal looked round at him, looking worried. "How do I know I'm not dreaming?"

Lim raised an eyebrow. "That's a very philosophical question."

"I'm serious," said Esgal, his voice low. "I went to sleep last night and dreamed that I was just waking up still a prisoner, and I'd just had a wonderful dream in which I'd been rescued, but that's all it was: a dream. And then at the end of that, I lost consciousness there and woke up here. How... how do I know which one's the dream?"

Lim frowned. Honestly, he didn't know. He'd never had any reason to give such questions very much thought. Eventually, he said, "Well, if you were still a prisoner, dreaming of being free, do you think your dreams would include blistered, bloody feet, rough paths, cold, hunger and exhaustion and the loss of your sight?"

Esgal blinked and took another couple of bites of food.

"I don't think so," he said at last. "I know once, before you rescued me, when... when I was in a cell back in the town... it was the last time I wasn't too exhausted to dream, and I dreamed that I was waking up safe back home." His breath hitched. "Alydra was by my side, and all this was over."

Lim laid a comforting hand on his shoulder. "So, you see, I think you can know that this is real if only because if your heart was seeking an escape into your dreams, I doubt it would bring everything that you're still enduring with it."

Esgal smiled wanly and laid a hand on Lim's. "I think you're right. Thank you."

Lim squeezed his shoulder and went back to packing.

"How are your feet this morning?" he asked, taking out the pot of salve and placing it within Esgal's reach. "The salve's beside you."

"Thanks." Esgal pulled off his right shoe and began to smear salve on the blister on his heel. "This one doesn't feel too bad, but I'll reserve full judgement for when I've tried to walk on it for a while. The others do hurt. Will you take a look at them?"

Lim nodded. "Let's see," he said, and Esgal pulled his right shoe back on and extended his left foot. Lim took his shoe off and unwrapped the bandage. It was stained with blood and fluid, but the one he'd popped was still closed, and the other didn't seem to be any worse.

"They look all right," he said. "As soon as we can, you'll want to clean them off and let them air for a while, but that'll have to wait until we're off the mountain."

Esgal nodded and Lim re-wrapped the bandage and pulled his shoe back on.

"All right." He stood up and strapped on his pack. "Are you ready to go?"

"As ready as I'll ever be," said Esgal with a smile.

Lim helped him up and they went on.

They managed to reach the steep slope in one run, taking only a few hours, but Esgal's head was hanging, his eyes half closed in exhaustion. He kept stumbling as he walked and Lim helped him sit down and told him to rest. He himself would look about to make sure they wouldn't be seen climbing down and try to find the smoothest path.

He picked his way down, moving rocks that looked light enough to be moved where it would help to straighten and smooth the path. It was steep, but he thought that if they took it very slowly and carefully Esgal should just about be able to manage. He also found a nook behind a large boulder, fringed with bushes, where they could lie hidden and rest afterwards with less chance of being seen by a passer-by. Encouraged by that discovery in particular, he scrambled back up the slope and sat down beside Esgal.

"Do you want to eat lunch now or wait until we get to the bottom?" he asked, rubbing his already-aching legs.

Esgal thought about it. "How long would you say it'll take?" he asked.

"Maybe an hour?"

"Hmm... I can wait, I think." He smiled a little. "I'd not say no to another bit of that fudge, though."

Lim laughed. "I'll tell you what: we'll have some biscuit now, and a bite of that dried meat, and then we'll each have some fudge at the bottom. That'll be something to look forward to."

Esgal smiled. "All right then." He accepted the food Lim handed him. "What's the supply situation like?" he asked after a couple of bites. "Tell me honestly."

Lim also ate a little before replying. "We probably couldn't go on just what we have for another full day," he said, "But we'll be into the forest before we run out completely. I cached some more trail rations and I'll be able to find fresh food there, given a little time."

Encouraged, Esgal nodded and continued to eat.

When they were both finished and felt ready to go on, Lim helped Esgal to stand and they started down the slope. Lim walked almost sideways, reaching back with one hand to help Esgal, coaching him through almost every step. Esgal held onto Lim's outstretched arm with one hand, his other arm stretched out to balance himself, fumbling with each foot as he searched for the ground and paused to make sure that he wouldn't slip or stumble before he put his weight on it. Their progress was torturously slow and Lim kept looking around to make sure no-one was coming.

They were almost at the bottom when Lim heard hoofbeats.

Esgal had heard them too, for he looked round with an expression of utter terror.

"Get down," whispered Lim, pushing him down behind a rock. Esgal gasped as he hit the ground, but curled up to make himself as small as possible and remain hidden. Lim threw himself behind another rock, further away. Just then, the group came around the corner.

"Another path going up there," said one voice, and he heard the horses slow and stop. He bit his lip, looking across at Esgal. The other elf stayed curled up tightly.

"Do we know how he was travelling?" asked another voice.

"He set off from town on foot, he could have climbed that. Should we check?"

A sharp rock was jabbing into Lim's side, but he didn't dare move to avoid it with them so close.

"No, not if you're sure that camp we found was his. There were signs that he had a horse, and a horse couldn't climb a slope that rough."

"Those of us who are even convinced that was a camp."

"We've been over this: there was definite disturbance, and most of our trackers agree that someone spent the night there. No more argument on that."

"Could he have abandoned the horse?"

"We'd have found it by now. Come on, let's keep going. Apart from anything else, that path leads through the pass, same as the road. We'll catch him either way."

With that agreement, they headed off again.

Lim let out the breath he'd been holding. Still, he waited until his heart rate had slowed. When he was sure they were all gone and well out of hearing, he slipped out from behind his rock and went over to Esgal. The other elf was still curled up, apparently unaware of Lim's approach. Lim laid a hand on his shoulder to attract his attention.

Instantly, Esgal uncurled and leapt at him like a striking snake. The sudden blow knocked him down. Off balance, they both rolled down the slope amid yelps and curses. Lim's knees and elbows banged against rocks as they went. Small bushes cracked as they rolled over them. Finally, they landed hard. Esgal looked winded, but he still struggled. He kicked out, scratched at Lim's face, twisted away. At last, Lim managed to grab his wrists and hold them.

"Esgal, it's me!"

"No," gasped Esgal, ignoring Lim's attempts to calm him. "Oh, Spirits no, please, just kill me now..."

Lim pinned his hands to the ground. "Esgal! It's all right, it's me, Lim! You're safe!"

That time, it got through. Esgal squinted, trying to make out Lim's silhouette against the sky, then he relaxed.

"Spirits, Lim, I thought..." He sighed, letting his head fall back against the ground, still gasping. "Don't scare me like that... I take it they've gone?"

"Yes, they left before I came over to rejoin you. Didn't you hear them?"

"I wasn't listening." His breathing was starting to even out and Lim let go of him. After a moment, he pushed himself up and rubbed his eyes with the back of his hand. "By Valnen, I was so sure they'd found me."

"Come on," said Lim. "I've found somewhere to hide, and we can rest a while."

He helped Esgal up and led him over to the nook he'd found. There, they huddled side-by-side, catching their breath and letting their hearts slow.

"I was pretty scared too," said Lim, breaking the silence.

Esgal chuckled, hugging his knees. "I could hardly breathe until you actually touched me." He rubbed his eyes again. "I'm sorry I attacked you. I knew I couldn't get away, I just hoped that if I made enough trouble..."

Lim laid a comforting hand on his shoulder. "You all right?" he asked.

"Still getting over that," said Esgal with a wan smile.

Lim squeezed his shoulder, then reached into his pack. "Would that piece of fudge I promised you help?"

Esgal's soft laugh sounded rather forced, but he said, "There are very few problems that fudge can't help," and accepted a piece.

At last, Esgal seemed to have recovered. He put a little more salve on his blistered heel and Lim made sure that there was no-one coming, then they got up again and headed on. Now that the ground was smoother and softer, Esgal didn't need as much guiding and walked behind Lim, one hand resting on his pack so that he knew where he was going. Lim noticed with a small smile that it already felt warmer as they went down. Esgal seemed to have noticed it too; every time Lim glanced round, he was looking around and breathing deeply.

"It smells more like home," he said once.

Lim also sniffed the air and smiled. "My home, at least," he said wistfully. "There are fewer pines in Duamelti." He sighed, once again thinking of Silvren.

Esgal nodded. "I suppose it would smell more like Silvren. We lived in a settlement near it, but never actually visited. Are we into the forest yet?"

"Not yet." The forest was spread out before them, a carpet of dark pine trees. They'd be there soon. "Very nearly, though."

Esgal nodded again. "All right," he said. "What do we do when we get there?"

Lim glanced at the lengthening shadows. They'd taken a long time getting down that slope and resting afterwards. "We'll go a little way into the forest and find somewhere sheltered to stop, then we'll camp down for the night," he said. "At some point I need to go back to the camp I made on the way up here. It seems they found it, but didn't discover the things I cached there, which is fortunate; I left my tack. I'll also need to find my horse. Then we can head off for home."

"So you did have a horse? I wondered how you'd made it here so quickly from Duamelti."

"Yes, and you'll be riding her once I've retrieved her. I assume you can ride?"

"Yes, well enough if you lead her. I don't need eyes to stay in the saddle, at least."

"No, and I'll lead her, don't worry. We won't be going faster than I can walk unless they catch up with us, and then we'll ride double and try to lose them."

Esgal nodded. "All right," he said a little uncertainly.

"What's wrong?" asked Lim, looking round.

"If they catch up with us."

"They may catch up with us, but they won't catch us, don't worry."

A small smile. "I'll do my best not to."

Lim reached back and patted Esgal's hand where it rested on his pack, and they walked on.

It wasn't long before they were past the fork and into the forest. Lim led the way off the road and they picked their way carefully between the trees. It was darker here and there were plenty of things for Esgal to trip on, so they went much more slowly until, at last, they found a tumbled pile of rocks that formed a decent shelter. It would even block a small fire from sight of the road and the trees overhead meant that, provided it stayed small, it wouldn't be seen from the mountainside either. Even the smoke would be lost among the branches. Esgal took the job of clearing the ground; he piled pine needles by the rock to form a thicker cushion under their beds and twigs in the middle of the cleared space for the fire. Lim clambered up the rocks to get a better view around and decided that he'd be able to make it to his previous camp and back in an hour or so. He climbed down and told Esgal his plan.

"I'll go and fetch the rest of my gear and come back," he said, emptying out his pack so that he'd be able to carry things in it. "That'll mean that we'll have something to cook in and can at least have some hot tea."

Esgal looked pleased at that idea, but sounded a little nervous as he asked, "What shall I do while I wait for you to come back?"

"Stay on this side of the rocks. When I come back I'll whistle. If you hear anyone else coming, find a cranny and hide in it."

Esgal nodded. "I can do that," he said.

"All right." Lim patted him on the shoulder, put on his empty pack and headed off. Hopefully, he was right: it wouldn't take long to return to his camp and no-one would be guarding it in the hope that he would return.

As he went through the forest he made a deliberate effort to keep low in folds in the land, keeping a careful ear out for the sound of approaching feet. It was relatively easy even for a human to walk quietly on pine needles, but he didn't hear anything. He saw a single horseman trotting down the road and lay flat until the man had passed, hoping that Esgal was safely hidden behind his pile of rocks.

At last, he was drawing near to his old campsite. Approaching it from the forest, it looked quite different, but he was sure that the little stand of rocks was indeed his camp. He crept up on it very slowly, an arrow nocked to his bow in case he did need to fight. He couldn't see a campfire, but he'd camped there himself without one. At last, he climbed over the rocks and looked down into the campsite.

He let out a sigh of relief and chuckled softly as he saw that it was empty. Even at that small release from tension, he felt drained. He jumped down and went over to the rocks were he had cached his gear. The ground was trampled about by mortals, but, as he'd thought, his cache was undisturbed. He quickly put his tack, saddlebags and excess equipment into his pack, then swung it back onto his shoulders. He'd leave by the road, he decided, rather than wasting time and wearing himself out by climbing back over the rocks. He listened before stepping out into the road, but couldn't hear anything. Apparently all searching had been called off for the night. He slipped around the rocks and back into the forest, keeping his bow strung part in case he should run into some stray searcher who wanted to make trouble for him, part in case he spotted anything that he could shoot for dinner. It wasn't likely; most game went to bed with the sun, like civilised creatures, and it was very nearly dark. He whistled as he approached the rocks where he had left Esgal and was relieved when Esgal called a greeting back.

"Hello," he said, rounding the corner. "I got my things."

Esgal nodded. "I thought so," he said. "As for me, I've discovered that there's a spring under these rocks."

"Really?" Lim squinted at the rocks in the dying light. "But there's no stream running away." Now that he thought about it, though, he could hear a slight trickling noise.

"It's there nonetheless," said Esgal, feeling his way over to a hole. He stuck his hand in almost to the elbow. "Here. My hand's in water; feel for yourself."

Everything Lim had ever been taught spoke against sticking his hand into a random hole in a rock. Apparently Esgal had not had the benefits of wilderness survival training. Still, he reasoned as he went over, there was little reason for him to have had such training, and he was probably far better at other skills that were useful for a spy. Besides, if there was a snake in there and it was disposed to attack it probably would have bitten Esgal by this time. Esgal moved out of the way and Lim stuck his hand down into the hole. He was surprised as it plunged into a small pool.

"By the Lady, you're right!" he said. "Just let me see if this stone can be moved so I can dip into that pool..." He felt around the edges of the stone and the ones above it. They seemed secure and he thought he could move one stone without bringing the entire thing down on them both.

Esgal had been listening to what he was doing and leaned in again to help. With Lim's direction and some fumbling, he braced his hands against the edge and together they pried it from its resting place, sending insects scuttling everywhere. Lim carefully laid the rock aside and they looked down at the pool, which shimmered a little in the dim light that filtered between the trees as the moon rose. Lim could also see where it ran through a channel it had carved itself from somewhere else in the heap. Presumably it then just sank into the ground.

Esgal went to dip some up and drink, but Lim stopped him. "Not from the pool," he said. "It's not running water; goodness knows what's living in it or has been swimming in it. I'll check what's running into the pool to see if it's pure, and then we can drink that."

Esgal nodded and moved back. Lim dipped up a little of the water and smelt it. It smelt a little peaty, but nothing to be worried about. The taste was similar.

"All right," he said. "It's probably better boiled, but it won't kill us."

Esgal nodded. He didn't seem as eager to drink now, though, and waited patiently for Lim to set and light a small fire.

It took a while for the fire to catch and get to a stage where they could use it for cooking rather than only light, but the warm, dancing glow made Lim feel a lot better just by being there, and as he held his needle in the flame he noticed Esgal staring straight at it with a peculiar expression. It took a long moment for him to realise a possible reason.

"Can you see it?" he asked as he put the needle away. "The fire, I mean."

Esgal nodded. "Just," he said. "I can see dancing light."

Lim grinned and patted him on the back before going to catch some water in the smallest cooking pot to make tea.

It took a while for the water to heat and the tea to brew. Lim kept an eye on both while Esgal just stretched his hands towards the flames and basked in their warmth. Even if he'd been totally unable to see the flames, he could feel the heat, so Lim knew he wouldn't burn himself.

He'd brought two cups and as soon as the tea was ready he poured it out and handed one cup to Esgal. He took a careful sip and sighed. Seregei had been right that it would do wonderful things for his own morale to have tea. He drank a little more and sighed again as it warmed a path right down to his stomach. Esgal also looked much happier as he drank. The flickering light made it difficult to tell, but Lim thought a little colour had returned to his face under the bruising.

"How's your nose?" he asked.

Esgal touched it carefully. "A little better," he said. "I can almost breathe through it again. I'm a little surprised that fall down the slope didn't knock it again."

"Probably because you were facing me, so your face never hit the ground."

Esgal nodded. "I suppose." He took another sip of tea, then added, "I am sorry I attacked you like that. I just panicked."

"I can't say I blame you," said Lim softly. "I might well have done the same in your place."

Esgal smiled a little and drank a little more, then suddenly asked, "What would you have done if you couldn't rescue me? Or if they had found us?"

Lim blinked and drank some more of his own tea, wondering how to answer that.

At last, he said slowly, "What I was told before setting off was that..." He hesitated, still unsure how to continue.

"Go on," said Esgal at last, his voice very quiet. "I have to know."

"I was told that in that case I should kill you."

Esgal sighed softly and took another drink. Then he asked, "And would you have done it?"

Esgal didn't seem as upset as Lim had anticipated, so he hesitated before answering, "No, I don't think I could. Not like that: in cold blood, when you were helpless."

Esgal put his head on one side, looking hard at Lim across the fire. He looked very serious and a little sad. "Do you know what they'd have done to me?"

Lim bit his lip. "Yes," he said at last, since the question didn't seem to be rhetorical.

Esgal looked at him again. "Would you really have left me alive?"

Lim was getting very uncomfortable. "Esgal, I really don't know. I've never been in that situation before. If our positions were reversed, could you have killed me?"

"Yes," said Esgal, without hesitation.

That wasn't what Lim had been expecting and he choked on his tea. "Honestly?" he asked, coughing slightly.

Esgal hugged his knees against his chest with his free arm. "Yes," he said again. "And you'd not be the first. I've killed three of their prisoners already; I was unable to help them any other way."

"Elves?"

"Yes. Wood-elves, I think. I poisoned them so that their guards would think they'd died naturally in their sleep. I... I learned the names of two first, but the third was too far gone to tell me his." Esgal's voice was growing worryingly distant. "It would have been a slow death, but a peaceful one: just a sleep from which they will never wake. Better that than... what they were doing to them."

"Esgal," said Lim, setting down his mug and starting to shift towards the other elf.

"Th-they'd broken every bone in Thanyel's arm, over s-several days, I think..." Esgal's breathing was beginning to hitch with the beginning of tears.

"Esgal!" Lim moved to kneel beside him.

Esgal didn't acknowledge him, still staring blankly into the flames. "And... and Nelya, poor little Nelya... they'd flayed off strips of his skin a-

and salted the wounds... and..."

"Esgal!" Lim shook his shoulder. He started, turning to look at Lim, wide-eyed. A couple of tears spilled over, but as he looked at Lim he seemed to come back to himself and remember where he was. Lim held onto him a moment longer, then asked, "Are you all right now?"

Esgal looked back at the fire, nodding slowly. After a moment, he said, "So... to answer your question..." He looked back at Lim with a small smile. "Yes. Had I seen you in captivity, and if I knew there was no way I could rescue you... I would kill you and be glad of that one more stain on my soul."

Lim found that disturbing, but he realised what Esgal meant, so he didn't say anything, but just squeezed Esgal's shoulder again and sat down beside him.

"Will you promise me something?" Esgal asked.

"What?"

"If we're cornered and there's no way for you to escape with me, I don't ask you to stay and try to help me." He took a deep breath. "But don't leave me alive."

"Esgal, I..."

"Please promise me: if we're cornered, do your best to escape, but first cut my throat. I don't want them to take me alive."

Lim sighed. He didn't think it would ever become necessary to keep the promise, though, and was it so very different to the original decision to kill Esgal if he couldn't rescue him?

"Very well," he said. "But I won't do it until the very utmost end of need."

"Thank you." Esgal smiled a little. "I know it's a lot to ask, now that you do know me, to kill me."

Lim forced a chuckle. "I think we should stop talking about death."

Esgal nodded and looked back at the fire, taking another drink of tea. "It's been on my mind recently, that's all."

Lim put an arm around his shoulders and hugged him for a moment. He tensed, but then relaxed as he remembered that he wasn't under threat.

"I'm sorry to hear that," said Lim.

Esgal chuckled and shrugged him off. "It's all right," he said, with forced brightness. "It's over now."

Lim nodded, even though he was still worried.

"Want some supper?" he asked. "I can boil some more water and try to do something to make that dried meat a little bit more interesting." Perhaps he could use a broth cube and make soup.

Esgal grinned and drained his cup. "Yes, *please*. I'll fetch the water. Let's have the pan?"

Lim passed it to him. "Remember to take it from the stream, not the pool."

Esgal nodded and felt his way back over to the spring.

It seemed to take forever for the broth to boil and the meat to soften, and the pleasant-smelling steam that rose from the pot just made Lim feel more hungry. At last, though, it was done. Lim took it off the fire and shared it between their mugs. After a moment for it to cool, he handed Esgal his with a piece of biscuit. After several days of hard going on meagre rations, the soup and biscuit felt like a feast and they sat in silence to eat. At last, Lim tipped his mug to get the dregs and wiped around it with the last scrap of biscuit as Esgal licked the crumbs from the corners of his lips and sighed in pleasure, leaning back against the rock, his eyes falling closed sleepily.

"I'll never take hot meals for granted again."

Lim smiled as he took Esgal's mug and went to rinse them both, and the pot. He'd have to find some food tomorrow so they could keep the remaining trail rations in case they needed them on the way home. "Is Alydra a good cook?" he asked absently.

Esgal laughed. "Not really. I'm actually better."

"Another reason for her to miss you when you're away," said Lim with a grin.

"Well, she *can* cook, but everyone agrees that I'm better at it."

"And the more modest?"

Esgal pretended to throw a handful of pine needles in Lim's general direction, then sighed and leaned back again, closing his eyes.

"Tired?" asked Lim.

"Yes," said Esgal, "But..." He chuckled. "I feel more alive now than I have for days."

Lim smiled and nodded a little. "Here," he said, digging out the bedroll. "You get some sleep." He laid it on the heap of pine needles and small detritus that Esgal had made

"When are we setting off tomorrow?" asked Esgal, lying down and pulling the blanket over himself.

"I'm not sure. I'll have to forage for some food and retrieve my horse, as I said."

Esgal nodded. "How much chance is there that they'll find us here?"

"It looked like they were searching further up the mountain first. Then they might scour around more down here, but I think we'll be all right for a couple of days. We'll leave as soon as we can, though." Lim smiled a little. "I think we could both do with a rest."

Esgal nodded. "I know I could," he said, stifling a yawn. "Thanks."

Lim squeezed his shoulder. "Go to sleep," he said. "I'll see to the fire."

Esgal smiled and closed his eyes, apparently asleep in moments.

Lim sat by the fire a while longer, letting it die down. He sighed a little and closed his eyes, listening to the sounds of the forest all around their little camp and enjoying the smell of wood smoke and the sharp scent of the pines. It made him a little homesick now that he was paying attention, but he enjoyed the familiar smell nonetheless. Now that everything was quiet, he could hear an owl in the distance: a little mountain owl, judging by the double call. If so, it was out late. He sighed again as he heard the calls retreat into the distance until he could no longer hear them. Now the forest was completely silent.

Perhaps that was fortunate; it meant that no-one was out beating the bushes for them. However, it also meant that there was no sound to block out the memory of Esgal's words. There was nothing else for Lim to dwell on.

It wasn't the request that he kill Esgal that he found so disturbing; it was the low, dead voice in which Esgal had told the stories of those elves he'd seen in captivity, and had killed.

Again, he wondered whether he could do that. Faced with an elf who'd been in prison for who-knows-how-long and had had every bone in his arm deliberately smashed – he reflexively rubbed his left hand – and had nothing else to look forward to, could Lim slip a dose of some poison into his next meal and walk away, knowing that he would soon die?

He shivered. While he wouldn't want to leave that elf alive, he didn't want to think that he might be able to murder someone helpless, whatever the alternative might be.

He shook his head hard and got up to walk up and down, trying to hum something. He also needed to get some sleep. While not as worn out as Esgal, he was tired, and he'd be walking on the way back. He just wasn't sure he could sleep with those words running around his head. *They'd flayed off strips of his skin... they'd broken every bone in his arm... the third was too far gone...*

He shook his head hard. No use getting all worked up. There was nothing he could do for those three elves. He should just feel glad that he'd saved a fourth from meeting the same fate.

The fourth elf was the one who had murdered the first three.

Again, he shook his head. Who was he to judge? He was a murderer just as Esgal was, after all, and had he not been lucky and found a plan to rescue Esgal, he might have been a murderer twice over. He still felt it wasn't the same as his own killing, though. Ethiren had been about to stab Seregei. Had Lim not intervened... he shook his head a little. Best not to think about what might have happened. But the elves that Esgal had killed had been no threat to him. They'd not even been able to defend themselves. Surely that made it different. But what else had there been to do? Leave them to die slowly? Surely that would be murder just the same...

"Lim?"

He spun round as he heard a voice call his name. Esgal was awake, propped up on one elbow, looking towards Lim with a confused expression.

"What's wrong?" he asked. "You're kicking the ground; you sound worried."

Lim shook his head. "It's nothing, Esgal," he said, going to sit back down by the fire. "Go back to sleep."

Esgal frowned and sat up fully. "It doesn't sound like nothing," he said softly. "You've listened to me; is there something you want to talk about?"

Lim sighed, wondering what Esgal would think if he were to tell him what was worrying him. The fact that those frightening words were going around in his head seemed very juvenile next to the fact that Esgal doubtless had images to go with them and the fact that he had to live with the three ghosts.

"Lim? Perhaps I can't see you, but I know something's wrong."

Lim sighed. "What you said about those three: Thanyel, Nelya and the other one."

Esgal shivered a little and nodded. "Did I disturb you?" he asked, his voice giving nothing away about what he thought of that possibility.

"A little. Not so much by what you said you'd seen, though that was part of it, but by what you said you'd *done*."

Esgal let out a small, slightly hysterical laugh. "The fact that I killed them?"

Lim shook his head. "I don't know any other way of explaining what's bothering me," he said.

Esgal sighed. "I'm sorry," he said, "I shouldn't have burdened you with it. You didn't deserve that."

"Esgal, please don't..." Lim sighed and went over to sit beside Esgal, who simply hugged his knees, resting his chin on them. After a moment's silence, Lim said, "I know there was no real choice."

Esgal nodded. "I knew that," he said, his voice very small. "I didn't make any of those decisions lightly. And... I..." – a small choking sound, like the beginning of a sob – "I did speak to them. Thanyel and Nelya knew what I was planning. Knew or guessed; I never told them in as many words, but I said I'd help them and I'm sure they understood. The third... I don't think he really knew I was there. He... he just lay there... and cried."

Esgal himself was definitely crying now, though he tried to hide it from Lim. Lim gulped, unsure what to say or do. Eventually, he put an arm around Esgal's shaking shoulders.

"I'm sorry," he said, after a moment. "I never should have made you relive it."

Esgal shook his head. "I brought it up in the first place," he said softly. "It's just... it's been on my mind ever since I was captured. Mostly just hoping and wishing there was someone who'd do the same to me. And you rescued me rather than killing me..." He shot Lim a small sideways smile. "It's still haunting me. With your help, I escaped alive. Maybe if I'd thought a little harder I might have found a way to get them out too."

Lim sighed. "I'm afraid I don't know the answer to that," he said. "But what would you have done? Looking back, you remember the situation in each case, as clear as day, I'll warrant. What could you have done otherwise?"

It was something that Seregei had tried to get him to do when he thought back to the day that he had killed Ethiren: if even with hindsight he couldn't come up with an alternative, then he could believe that none had existed and live with the decision.

Esgal thought for a moment, then looked at Lim. "What do you know of it?" he asked. His tone was curious, rather than accusatory. "When have you killed someone before? I thought you said that..."

"I've never killed someone in cold blood," Lim corrected.

Esgal nodded a little, but still looked hard towards Lim, his unfocussed eyes surprisingly sharp. "Will you tell me? Is that the thing that makes this so..." He waved a hand vaguely. "Makes this cut you deep as well?"

Lim wondered how much to tell of what he had done. He still dreamed about it sometimes, though he knew that he had no reason to feel guilty.

At last, he said, "An elf gone amok. He was on the verge of murdering my dearest friend. I... stabbed him in the back."

Esgal nodded and put his own arm around Lim's shoulders. "Someone you knew?"

Lim wondered again how to describe his relationship with Ethiren. Some might have said father and son. Lim didn't agree any more, though as a child he'd loved him and thought himself loved in return. After years, he'd persuaded himself that the fact that Ethiren had sired him didn't make him a father. Not when – as he now appreciated – that elf had made his life a living hell for almost as long as he could remember.

"Yes," was all he said. "I knew him."

Esgal started to say something else, but then fell silent.

"I'm sorry," he said, at length.

"No," said Lim. "I am. I shouldn't have started this conversation again."

Esgal nodded. "Was I right to be worried?" he asked. "Worried that something was bothering you?"

Lim shrugged, but smiled at him. "I suppose," he said.

Esgal sighed and looked at the dying embers of the fire. "I can see it," he murmured. "The fire. It's just bright enough, and the night is just dark enough. I can see the difference."

Lim squeezed his shoulders. "I'm going to bank it in a moment, so we can both get to sleep," he said. "Is that all right?"

"Would you be able to sleep with it burning?"

"We mustn't risk it getting out of control."

"All right." Esgal stretched. "All right. Go on."

Lim looked at him with some worry and he smiled.

"I'll be fine. It just preys on my mind. I need to get back and..." he shook his head a little. "Tell someone. That's why I wanted to know their names before... So I could go to Silvren when I can and tell their families what happened to them. Not the whole truth. Not my part in it. Just that I know they died in prison." He sighed and a small smile touched his lips as he tipped his head back. "Before they could suffer too much."

Lim squeezed his shoulder again and went to bank up the fire so that it wouldn't blaze or catch anything else while they were asleep. When he was done, he noticed that Esgal was still sitting up.

"Esgal, you need to sleep," he said.

Esgal started, then nodded and lay down, pulling the blanket over himself again. Lim took his own blanket and joined him on the pile of pine needles, rolling himself up in it and closing his eyes with a sigh. He wasn't sure how much sleep either of them was actually going to get, but at least this bed was softer than bare rock, and warmer too with a little insulation from the chill of the ground. He heard Esgal sigh behind him and reached over to pat his shoulder.

"You all right?" he asked.

"Tired, shaken," replied Esgal.

Lim nodded and patted his shoulder again. "I know," he said. "Just try to get some sleep. I wish you pleasant dreams."

Esgal laughed softly. "You too, my friend," he said. "You too."

Lim smiled, closed his eyes and quickly dozed off.

***

He was halfway through a confusing dream involving horses with writing in the markings in their fur when Esgal twitched in his sleep and kicked him. It was morning, though, so he didn't bother trying to get back to sleep, but got up as carefully as he could and stretched. His muscles twinged, but it wasn't nearly as bad as it had been over the last few days. Their little camp was as isolated as before and he blew the sullen embers of last night's fire back into life, then set some wood on it to keep it going and glanced over at Esgal, who was twitching in his sleep again. Concerned, he went over and called the other elf's name softly, putting a hand on his shoulder.

Esgal jolted awake with a gasp and lay still for a moment as he caught his breath.

"Bad dream?" asked Lim.

Esgal nodded a little. "I woke up a prisoner again," he said softly.

Lim grimaced. "Well, I assure you that it was only a dream," he said, squeezing Esgal's shoulder again. "How's your nose?"

Esgal instinctively touched it. "A little better," he said. "I think the swelling's going down a bit."

"The bruising around your eyes is starting to fade."

Esgal grinned shakily, pushing himself upright. "Ugh, I'm still stiff," he said, stretching and flexing his fingers.

Lim nodded. "So am I," he said, "But it'll pass. We'll be able to rest a little while today, so that'll help."

Esgal nodded. "Is there anything I can do?" he asked. "I still can't see..." He sounded resigned to that and Lim bit his lip.

"Is it getting any better?" he asked.

"It's hard to tell; there isn't a lot of contrast down here, and that's the thing I seem to manage."

Lim nodded. "All right. We'll see when we get out of the forest."

"Pun intended?" asked Esgal with a grin.

Lim buried his face in his hands. "No," he said, thinking about how nice it would be to be able to make it so that the last few seconds had never happened, but Esgal started to laugh.

"All right," he said. "I'll wait *and see*."

Lim felt so small that an ant could probably step on him and crush him without even noticing it.

"I'm going to go and see if I can find something to eat," he said, keeping his face hidden in his hands. "Remember what I told you yesterday?"

"That if I hear someone coming, I should find a crack in the rocks and hide in it?" asked Esgal. "Yes, I remember."

Lim nodded and headed off into the forest, stringing his bow. It was more likely that he'd be able to find some sort of game, now that it was daylight. Being a Wood-elf, he was light-footed and his feet made barely any sound as he walked lightly over the needles – something he couldn't manage among the oaks and other leaf-dropping trees of Duamelti – so he didn't even need to try too hard to stalk anything. Some fresh meat would be delicious and he licked his lips in anticipation. Even mushrooms or something of the sort would be a change from dried meat and trail biscuit.

He found some mushrooms growing on the underside of a rotting log and a few early blackberries on a bramble bush nearby, but he was about to give up and head back when he spotted a rabbit. In a moment, he'd nocked an arrow, aimed and loosed. The arrow struck the rabbit behind the shoulder, going straight to its heart and killing it in its tracks. Lim collected it with a small smile. That was enough to feed them for today, and maybe he'd be able to shoot another or find something else to take with them. He weighed it in his hand at the thought and wondered if he'd even need to; it was a large rabbit. Perhaps the people in the town fed and trapped them. If so, he and Esgal would need to be careful to avoid any hunters coming to check their snares.

When he returned to the camp Esgal was doing his best to tend the fire, gauging the heat with his hand as he fed it from a small pile of twigs beside him.

"You stand a better-than-even chance of burning yourself, you know," said Lim, setting down the rabbit and taking the pouch that held the berries off his belt. He also dug out the mushrooms and set it all down on the ground beside the fire.

Esgal looked up with a small smile. "I know," he said, "but I wanted to do something to help and I'm being careful."

Lim smiled back. "Thanks," he said. "But I'll take over now. Why don't you fetch some water in here" – he handed him the pan – "and we'll make some tea."

Esgal nodded and accepted the pan, sniffing at the air. "I smell blood," he said. "I take it your hunting trip was a success?"

"I shot a rabbit," said Lim with a nod. "It's got a fair amount of meat on it; there must be some good eating around here. We'll eat some now and cook the rest so it'll store better and we can take it with us. I'll set that going and then go and call for Winnowil."

"Winnowil?" asked Esgal, returning with the water.

"My horse."

"All right. So we leave...?"

"As soon as we can, if that's all right. We should travel fairly quickly until we're out of striking distance of the town, and possibly after that to cover as much ground as possible before any pursuit can begin."

Esgal nodded. After a moment, he asked, "How long until breakfast?"

Lim chuckled. "Here," he said, picking up the berries and handing them to Esgal. "You can eat these now. They're only just ripe, so they may be a little sour, but they're the only things that won't need any preparation."

Esgal took them with thanks and tried one.

"Mm, this one's a little sour, but not too bad." He grinned. "Thanks."

Lim nodded. "That's all right," he said, and set about preparing the rabbit. They'd not have time to do anything with the skin, which was unfortunate; Lim didn't like to needlessly waste any part of anything he'd killed and skins were almost always useful. It couldn't be helped, though; he didn't really want to delay an extra day just so that he could preserve the skin. He moved a little way away from their camp to gut the rabbit, shaking its innards out into a hole that he dug in the soft, peaty ground with a stick and his hands so he could bury them straight away. Then he skinned it and, with a last moment's regret for the necessity, put the skin in the hole as well. Finally, he scraped the earth back into place, disguised it with pine needles and twigs and went back to the camp to finish the butchering process.

Esgal had been looking after the water and as Lim returned he said that it was boiling. Lim set the rabbit down in his second pan and took the hot water with thanks, pouring it into their mugs and adding a little tea to each mug.

"Wait a bit for it to cool," he said, handing Esgal his, and set his own down on the ground beside him so that he could prepare the meat for cooking. When he was sure he'd got everything he could, he laid a few strips in one pan with the sliced mushroom and put it on the edge of the fire so it could all cook together.

"I'm sure I don't need to tell you how to deal with it," he said to Esgal, guiding his hand to the handle of the pan and handing him the cooking fork, "since you're such a good cook."

Esgal smiled at him. "I'll call when it's done," he said. "I should be able to tell by the smell."

"Probably better not call out," said Lim. "I'll stay within sight. Just wave at me."

Esgal nodded and carefully moved the pan over the fire. "Is it over it properly?" he asked. "I can't quite tell."

"Yes," said Lim. "Thanks for doing this."

Esgal nodded again with a grin.

Lim went and buried the bones just as he had the rest of the inedible parts of the rabbit, and then climbed up to the top of their rock to look around. He could see the road, but it was deserted. Looking up, he could see that the small amount of smoke from their fire was indeed quickly lost among the branches and needles of the trees, so he was fairly confident that it wouldn't act be too handy as a signpost to anyone who might be looking for a camp, especially if they were still looking further over the mountain.

He also looked for any sign of Winnowil. He couldn't see her, so, with a last look around, he pursed his lips and whistled.

Down in the camp, Esgal startled. "Lim?" he called softly.

"That was me, sorry," said Lim, and Esgal nodded, visibly relaxing.

Again, he whistled as in his earlier message to Winnowil, a little louder, carefully pitching it so that to any but an animal's or a wood-elf's ear it sounded like the shriek of a bird.

After another moment's wait, his sharp ears caught the sound of hooves, trotting uncertainly towards him between the trees. He whistled a third time and they picked up in speed, and after a moment he grinned to see Winnowil trotting towards him. He jumped down from his perch to meet her and she snorted a greeting, lipping at his ear.

"Esgal, this is Winnowil," he said. "Winnowil, Esgal."

Esgal bowed his head a little, not seeming overly fazed by being introduced to a horse. Lim brushed a hand across Winnowil's back, dislodging needles, and decided that she'd need brushing before they set off. He sent her an image of her lying down and resting until dusk began to fall, then Esgal riding her. When she nuzzled him in response, he added an image of her in her own paddock, cropping grass. She nudged him and he laughed, patting her neck. "You lie down here and keep out of sight," he added, partly for Esgal's benefit.

She pawed at the ground, then folded her legs and lay down, shifting to scratch her belly on the ground. Lim patted her again and fetched a double handful of grain from his saddlebag, feeding it to her from his hands. She ate, licked his palms to get the last specks of dust and nudged him again.

"You'll get some more when we set off," he told her, sending her an image. "Now you lie quiet. We need to stay hidden."

Esgal had pulled the pan away from the fire and was sniffing its contents speculatively. Lim could smell it from where he stood and the scent made his mouth water.

"I think this is done," said Esgal.

"Let me see?" Lim cut open a piece of meat and a piece of mushroom. Both seemed cooked down to the middle. "Yes, that'll do."

He set the pan to one side and burrowed the second pan with the raw meat into the embers of the fire, then put the third pan of the set upside down over it.

"What in the world are you doing?" asked Esgal, his head on one side.

"Making an oven," said Lim, grinning. "We needn't pay as much attention to the meat that's cooking in there if it's got a lid."

"Did you put any water in there?"

Adding a double handful of water was a delicate operation and Lim still accidentally singed his fingertips, but then they settled down to eat their meal. Esgal used the cooking fork to spear bites of meat and mushroom, while Lim used his knife. He hadn't really noticed how very hungry he was until he got the first bite. It was a little tough, but that wasn't as important as the fact that it was delicious, and the tastes of the mushroom and rabbit had mingled as they were cooked together. He wasn't certain he'd had many meals as good as this one, and there wasn't nearly as much of it as he'd have liked.

Judging by the way Esgal kept hunting about in the pan with his fork, even after Lim had assured him that here was none left, he agreed. Eventually, Lim took the fork and pan away and went to rinse both items and his knife in the little stream and pack them away.

"I'll get everything packed up," he said, "Then I'll brush off Winnowil, saddle her and we can be off."

Esgal nodded. "Shall I just stay here?"

"Yes, I'm afraid I can't think of anything you might be able to do."

Esgal nodded and shuffled back from the fire to sit against the rocks. "In any case, I'm sleepy after that meal. If I do doze off, wake me."

Lim chuckled. "How else would I get you onto Winnowil?"

Esgal smiled a little and nodded, then sighed again and closed his eyes.

Fortunately, he wasn't sitting on the bedroll and Lim was able to roll and pack it without disturbing him. After all, he'd need to be rested, even though he wouldn't be walking. Lim kept the blanket out for the time being; Esgal might want it while they were travelling, so he'd put it on top.

When he carefully checked the meat it still wasn't quite done. He sighed impatiently, but then shook his head at himself. So far, they still seemed to be safe. It was worth spending a little more time in a safe, sheltered campsite while they had it. Nonetheless, he wanted to be moving; it would be even safer to be well away from here. He occupied himself by brushing the mud and needles from Winnowil's coat. She'd been rolling, but fortunately was fairly dry and he was at least able to clean spaces for her tack and the saddlebags. She wasn't terribly presentable, but at least she wouldn't suffer from saddle sores. He picked out her feet, smiling despite himself as she flicked him with her tail as she always did, and patted her on the shoulder.

"Don't go rolling again," he said aloud, rubbing her ears. She snorted and shook her head and he patted her again before going back to check the meat a second time.

This time it was cooked through and he carefully took the pans out of the fire so it could cool enough to pack. While he waited, he washed the top pan and used it to carefully pour water on the fire. It had left a black, burned mess, but he stamped and kicked it about as best he could to make sure it was completely out and wouldn't spread. Then he put back the sods he'd cut to make the fireplace and frowned. A scattering of needles would disguise it, but even so he suspected that a tracker would identify it at a glance. It couldn't really be helped, though; he'd just have to hope he'd hidden it well enough that it wasn't obvious.

He consolidated the remaining trail food into one packet and used the other for the meat, then cleaned and packed up the remaining pan. Then he stuffed the blanket into his pack and went to tack up Winnowil.

At last, they were ready to leave. He refilled their water bottle and replaced the rock over the spring, and it was time to wake Esgal and leave.

Esgal had apparently been very deeply asleep and it took a while to wake him. Lim felt sorry that it was necessary, but there was still a lot of daylight left and the earlier they set off, the better.

At last, Esgal was awake enough for Lim to boost him onto Winnowil's back and hand him the reins.

"I'm just going to kick that pile of pine needles about and make it less obvious that someone camped here," he said, "Then we'll set off."

Esgal nodded, shifting on Winnowil's back and instinctively looking around. Lim scattered the needles all over the campsite, spreading them as uniformly as he could manage. It still wasn't perfect, but it was the best he could really do. Then he laid a hand on Winnowil's neck and looked up at Esgal.

"Ready?" he asked.

Esgal nodded and Lim walked forwards, leading Winnowil with a hand on her shoulder. He walked at his normal pace, heading north-west as best he could reckon, and she kept pace with him. At least he'd end up on the right side of the forest, then he could navigate normally, and they were heading away from the road. He listened carefully as they went for the sound of any searchers making their way through the woods, but there was nothing but the sound of wild animals scurrying away from the sound of Winnowil's hooves. He took a deep breath and let it out again in a sigh.

"What is it?" asked Esgal.

"It feels good to be going home," said Lim.

He could hear the smile in Esgal's voice, though he didn't turn around to see it, as he replied, "It does indeed."

CHAPTER FOUR

They kept going until it began to get dark. For the first few hours they kept to the forest, but at last Lim decided they were far enough from the town that it was safe to strike out along the edge of the trees and make for the road. They'd travel faster that way. It was the road to Silvren, and while the people here didn't necessarily like elves, he knew that they were not outright hostile to them.

Esgal didn't seem so sure.

"Are you certain we're safe?" he asked, looking down towards Lim as he heard Winnowil's hooves beating on packed earth, rather than grass.

"Not entirely," Lim confessed, "But we're not going to be entirely safe until we get home, unless we stop a while in Silvren."

"I know that as a rule people are less likely to attack us on their own account out here, but news could have reached them that I, at least, am wanted." Esgal looked around nervously.

"We're not too distinctive, especially not as they could reasonably assume that you're a wood-elf just as I am." He made for a rather slim Wood-elf, but his build was close enough.

"I don't have a braid." Esgal absently touched his shoulder-length hair.

"You look like you've got into trouble of some sort. You wouldn't be the first wood-elf to have had his hair cut off by bandits."

Esgal nodded and sighed. "How much further?"

"Are you tired?"

"A little. I'm more hungry than anything else, though."

Lim nodded. "Just a little further, then we'll find somewhere to rest a while."

They went on for another hour, then Lim found a sheltered place near a stream where they could camp for a couple of hours while they waited for the moon to fully rise. It was waning now and wouldn't provide as much light, but it was only a couple of days from the full and they were on a road that wouldn't be too hard to follow. He helped Esgal dismount and sit down, then removed Winnowil's tack and let her stray on the grass while he and Esgal rested and ate some of the meat he'd cooked that morning. It wasn't as filling a meal as he'd have liked, but it was something, and it would keep them going another few hours. He was also getting sleepy now that he was sitting down. It had been a long way to walk, even if the terrain wasn't as rough as it had been in the mountains.

"Lim?" said Esgal softly.

"Yes?"

"I said: how long do you think it'll take to get back?"

Lim shook his head. Now that he thought about it, Esgal had spoken, but he'd not really registered it.

"Sorry, I must have dozed off. It took me a few days, but I was going at more than a walking pace, so I'm not sure how long it'll take at this speed. Maybe four days if we don't stop for too long at a time."

Esgal put his head on one side. "Do you want to doze for a while?" he asked. "I know you won't actually sleep, but you sound very tired. I'll stay awake and listen; I can doze when I'm riding, but you have to stay alert when walking."

Lim was about to refuse, but thought about it for a moment. He was tired, and he knew it would do neither of them any good for him to push himself too hard. An hour's doze would mean that it would be longer before he, at least, had to rest again. He took a drink of water – it still tasted peaty and he decided that he would refill it before they left – and sighed.

"All right," he said. "How good are you at judging time?"

Esgal pointed towards the moon, and the silhouettes of the mountains against it.

"I can just see the moon," he said. "I'll judge an hour by that."

"All right," said Lim again. "I'll doze for an hour, then. Wake me if you hear anything coming."

Esgal nodded. Lim quickly got the blanket out of his pack, wondering as he did so how much of its contents could probably be reorganised into his saddlebags; if he didn't have so much to carry, he could keep going longer, and Winnowil wasn't very heavily burdened now. He decided to put off the decision and rolled himself in the blanket to sleep.

***

It seemed like no time at all before Esgal was shaking him awake.

"It's a shame to wake you," he said as Lim sat up, rubbing the sleep from his eyes, "But I'm pretty sure it's been an hour."

Lim nodded. "Thanks," he said, shaking his head. He felt muzzy with sleep, but knew that he'd feel better given time. "Are you rested enough to go on?"

Esgal nodded. "Are we going to keep going all night?"

"We'll go until the moon starts to set, then we'll stop for a few more hours. I'll try to find somewhere sheltered enough for us all to sleep," said Lim, getting up and walking over to Winnowil to pat her. "Do you want to stay there until we're ready to go?"

"All right," said Esgal, "But is there anything useful I could do?"

Lim thought about it as he retrieved Winnowil's tack and began to put it on her. "Do you know where the stream is?" he asked.

Esgal put his head on one side to listen. "I can find it," he said. "That way?" he pointed in the direction of the stream.

"Yes," said Lim. "It's within sight, so I'll keep an eye on you. Empty this out" – he picked up the water bottle and gave it to Esgal – "it tastes peaty and I think what's coming down the stream is actually purer."

Esgal nodded. "I'll refill it," he said and got up to start picking his way towards the stream, feeling with each foot before he committed to a step. Lim watched him out of the corner of his eye as he strapped his saddlebags to Winnowil's back and gave her some grain. The bag of grain was now depleted enough that he could pack the spare blanket with it. He thought he might have been able to fit the bedroll – almost all that was left in his pack – in there too if he dismantled it, but didn't really want to do that at the moment.

Esgal returned and gave Lim the water bottle. He added it to the half empty pack, then spent some time adjusting the straps until it was comfortable again. At last, he helped Esgal to mount and they set off again.

They walked on through the night, occasionally stopping to let Winnowil drink at streams and graze while Esgal dismounted to stretch his legs. In the dark, Lim couldn't see any landmarks, but luckily it was fairly clear and he was able to see the northern stars. He could guess distance and the stars kept them going in the right direction.

They each ate another scrap of meat when they started to get hungry, but didn't stop to do it. As the moon sank, Lim started to look for a spot where they could lie hidden and sleep, as he'd promised. At last, he found a birch thicket in a sheltered hollow on the side of a hill. The nearest stream wasn't close, but it was within striking distance for Winnowil and this would do for a few hours' sleep.

"Esgal?"

"Hmm?" Esgal looked up. He'd apparently been dozing off.

"We'll stop here and camp for a few hours."

"All right." Esgal slipped off Winnowil's back and Lim steadied him as he landed. "What is 'here'?" he asked, looking around.

"It's a thicket on the sheltered side of a hill," said Lim. He set Winnowil's saddle on the ground next to the saddlebags and went to remove her bridle. "Hold on a minute and I'll get some food and the bedroll out, and find you somewhere to sleep. The trees are pretty close together."

Esgal reached out tentatively and felt a tree trunk. "All right."

Lim patted Winnowil and she went off to drink at the stream. "She'll come back when she's had some water," he said to himself, and turned to Esgal. "Come on," he said, and took his hand to carefully lead him to a spot in the middle of the thicket where there was space for them to lie down. "Here we go. We're sheltered here and we can get a few hours' sleep."

Esgal crouched down and felt the ground, clearing away sticks and stones that he found as Lim unpacked their bedding from the saddlebags. When the ground was clear, he laid the bedroll out and put his blanket beside it.

"I'll tell you this," he said, "I'll not be sorry to go back to sleeping on a real bed."

Esgal glanced at him. "Do you want to sleep on the bedroll?" he asked. "I can sleep straight on the ground for tonight – you need rest more than I do."

Lim quickly shook his head. He'd not intended to make Esgal feel guilty. "It's fine, really; you've got more bruises that need to be kept off the floor than me."

Esgal laughed, but then sobered. "Are you sure?" he asked.

"I'm sure."

Esgal accepted that and lay down on the bedroll, pulling the blanket up to his chin and closing his eyes with a sigh.

"Do you want me to stay awake and keep an ear out?" he asked sleepily.

Lim laughed softly as he also lay down. "Even if I'd been intending to ask, you look so peaceful that I wouldn't have the heart," he replied. "But I think we're enough out of sight and out of the way here that it won't be necessary."

Esgal nodded and sighed, relaxing a little. Lim also closed his eyes, repeating to himself that he could only sleep for a few hours, and allowed himself to doze off.

***

When he woke, it was to find that the sun was already high and filtering down through the leaves and branches above him. Judging by the noise, there was a bird's nest in the trees, and the birds were not happy to see the two interlopers that had arrived in their thicket during the night. Lim rubbed his eyes as he tried to identify them. Blackbirds, he realised, recognising the alarmed triple call. Talking to birds – especially birds he didn't know – was different from talking to furred animals; it actually required whistling and chirping in the correct patterns. His Blackbird was somewhat less than fluent, but he managed to chirp a rough message in the bird lingua franca, indicating that he and his friend were not a threat and would soon leave. It seemed to help a little, at least enough that it would no longer be obvious to a passer-by that those birds were agitated about something out of the ordinary.

Lim stretched and glanced over at Esgal, who was still asleep. He looked peaceful, which was a relief; apparently he was not suffering one of those dreams that made him think he was still a captive dreaming of freedom. Winnowil was standing a little way off, her head down, apparently dozing as well. She had been rolling and her coat was dirty, but it helped her to blend in with her surroundings; her dapple-grey coat, now blotched with brown dirt, looked rather like the mazed trunks of the trees and the sun peeking between their leaves.

Lim got up, stretching again, and took a drink of water. They'd go over to that stream and refill the bottle before going much further. He also took stock of the supply situation. He thought they could each have some biscuit for breakfast, with a slip of meat, but they'd have to either find some more food today or start being very careful; there hadn't been *that* much meat on the rabbit. He sighed, wondering how long it would take to get home, or at least reach a place where they could realistically stop and hunt, gather or fish. On the road today, he'd at least look out for any more ripe fruit that they could eat as they went.

Beside him, Esgal stirred and groaned softly. "Lim?" he said, rolling onto his back and looking around. "Oh, trees!"

Lim wondered if that was just an exclamation, or if Esgal could see the interlacing branches above him.

"I'm here," he said. "How're you feeling?"

Esgal tore his gaze away from the trees and pushed himself upright. "My legs are stiff," he said, "and I'm hungry, but much better apart from that. I can see the trees silhouetted against the sky."

Lim smiled. "I wondered if you could," He got out some biscuit from his pack and handed it to Esgal with some meat. "Here. We'll have to be a bit careful how much we eat, and keep an eye out for anything we could use to stretch out our supplies a little more, but I think we'll make it back."

Esgal nodded and began to eat. "How much longer, do you think?" he asked.

Lim shrugged. "At this pace, maybe three days, but we'll be into friendlier territory soon. I cut a bit of a corner with our route yesterday, so we don't pass as close to Silvren as I did on the way out, but we should get back faster than we would have done had we taken that road."

"Why didn't you take the shorter route on the way out?"

Lim winced. Esgal didn't sound accusatory, but he couldn't help a flash of guilt. "I wasn't quite certain of my destination, so I thought it better to stick to the main roads. I know exactly where Duamelti is, and the land all around it, so I can come in from almost any direction and take a more direct route. I also couldn't travel as far at night. I can navigate by the stars, but –"

"I thought you must be doing that last night."

"Yes, but it was a similar problem: I wasn't certain where I was going, especially as the moon wasn't full."

Esgal nodded, licking the last crumbs from his fingers.

"So when do we set off?" he asked.

"First, I should probably have a look at those injuries of yours," said Lim, "The scrape and the blisters: see how they're getting on."

Esgal nodded and began to pull his shirt off so that Lim could unwind the bandage wrapped around his chest. The scrape was healing fairly nicely and showed no sign of infection. Evidently Esgal had been lucky and Lim had managed to clean it properly despite the less-than-ideal situation up on the mountain.

His left foot, on the other hand, was still in a pretty bad state. Another blister had begun to form where the bandage rubbed under Esgal's shoe, and the one that had burst looked seepy. The other had hardened into an ugly but harmless, for the moment, flap of dry skin that would tear off if provoked. Lim washed them and sighed, wondering what to do.

"What is it?" asked Esgal.

"I'm in two minds whether to leave them open, since you're riding and there won't be anything to rub them, or bandage them to keep them clean."

"Could you bandage them but leave my shoe off?" asked Esgal. "That way some air will get to them, but not too much dirt."

Lim frowned. It wasn't ideal, but bar emergencies Esgal would be staying on Winnowil for most of the day and it was probably the best option available to him.

"I think that's what I'll have to do," he said, and took a clean length of bandage, wrapping it around Esgal's foot. As he worked, he asked, "How's the other blister?"

"Much better now that I'm not trying to walk on it."

"Good," said Lim, tying off the bandage. "I'll leave it alone, then." He glanced up. "Stay there while I pack and then I'll help you mount Winnowil."

Esgal nodded, but sighed a little as Lim rolled up the bedroll and put it into his pack.

"What is it?" asked Lim.

"I wish there was more I could do to help. I feel like I just sit here idly while you do everything to help me."

"Esgal, you're the one more in need of help. I can cope." Lim was almost startled to hear those words from his own lips, but pushed the thought aside.

Esgal nodded, but still looked unhappy until he looked up at the sky.

Then, he smiled.

"I can see the trees," he said softly. Lim smiled and left him looking at the silhouettes as he fetched and groomed Winnowil, gave her some grain, tacked her up and made sure that he'd packed as much as he could into the saddlebags. Then he went back and helped Esgal to stand and hop over to her. It wasn't easy for him to mount and Lim half lifted him into the saddle.

"Have you got your other shoe?" he asked, glancing at Esgal's bandaged foot.

Esgal nodded and pointed to his belt. The shoe was attached by the laces. Lim nodded and, with a small sigh, led Winnowil on.

For about an hour, there was no sign of trouble. Lim was glad; he was still sleepy He guessed that Esgal felt the same way; he sat quietly in the saddle, his head down. Lim kept glancing back at him to make sure he was all right, but was increasingly preoccupied with worry that he'd missed the turning onto the west road in the night. If Esgal realised something was wrong, he didn't say so.

Finally, Lim spotted the gap in the distant mountains and sighed in relief. That meant they hadn't come as far as he'd hoped, but also that they wouldn't have to backtrack.

"I can see the next landmark: where the road goes through the mountains," he told Esgal when the other elf asked what was happening. "We can probably take another short cut here and go straight through the gap."

Esgal smiled. "I'm happy with anything that gets us home faster," he said softly. "Lead on."

Lim patted Winnowil's neck and turned off the road. The terrain was rough, full of steady humps and hollows covered with short grass, but easy enough to cross as long as they kept to a walk. Once Winnowil stumbled over a sudden drop and Esgal almost fell, but he kept his seat and the only sign that it had alarmed him was the way that he clung to the saddle after that.

After about another hour they found a pool hidden in a small dell and Lim helped Esgal dismount for a rest. "Are you all right?" he asked as he helped the other elf to sit down.

Esgal nodded, rubbing his eyes carefully. "Just tired," he said with a wan smile. "I have to admit, this ground is difficult to ride on when I can't see what's coming."

Lim winced. "Sorry about that. I think it's only about another hour or so before we get back onto the road through the gap."

Esgal nodded again. "I'll be fine."

Lim passed him the water bottle and went to take a look around. The gap in the mountains was indeed much closer and he thought they'd cut several hours off their journey. He smiled as he turned to look back the way they'd come, but he smile faded as he saw a cloud of dust on the road. It didn't look like it was caused by a gust of wind and he squinted, leaning forward a little. He gritted his teeth as he saw movement a little ahead of the cloud.

"Esgal, we've been followed," he said, stepping back down into their dell.

Esgal went white, his hands tightening on the water bottle.

"They're on the road, but we need to hide." Lim laid a hand on Winnowil's head and sent her an image of herself lying down in the dell. She lay down and he patted her, then crouched down himself. "Lie down and keep low," he told Esgal. "We're probably all right as long as they don't see movement; we're some distance from the road."

Esgal lay flat, looking a little more confident, though he was still pale. Lim patted his shoulder and peered over the edge of the dell. Hopefully Winnowil was lying low enough. She was probably easiest of the three of them to see; Esgal was dressed in drab colours and Lim was all in green.

Lim glanced over his shoulder at Winnowil, then quickly took out the spare blanket and pulled it over her body. It was dark brown, which would be better than light grey.

Another glance at the road proved that the men didn't seem to have noticed anything; they rode on.

Lim sighed in relief. "They're not turning," he told Esgal. "We'll stay here until they're out of sight, but then I think we can move on."

Esgal nodded, relaxing a little. "Tell me if they do change course, will you?" he whispered.

"I will."

Lim's heart skipped a beat as the horsemen suddenly drew to a halt. He bit his lip as they stood still for several minutes. He couldn't see what was happening. They were well past the place where he and Esgal had left the road, so they couldn't have seen their tracks, but he couldn't help a nervous glance around. Winnowil was still lying down, her head down as she ate a semicircle in the grass. He didn't think she was visible, but it was possible...

He looked up again as movement caught his eye and he saw that the horsemen were riding back down the road. He bit his lip.

"Lim? What's happening?" whispered Esgal.

"They stopped for a while, and now they're going back the way they came."

"Then we're safe?" Esgal raised his head a little.

Lim hesitated, then said, "Not quite yet."

Esgal nodded and lay flat again, closing his eyes. Lim continued to watch as the riders moved back down the road. He prayed they'd not leave it. On this ground, their horses couldn't go at much more than a walk, but nor could Winnowil and if he and Esgal tried to flee they'd be seen.

He sighed in relief as the horsemen went straight on into the distance with no sign of stopping, until they were once more nothing but a dust cloud on the road.

"They're gone," he told Esgal, sitting up.

Esgal visibly relaxed with a sigh, then opened his eyes again.

"How close did they come?"

"Not very, but I could see them quite clearly." Lim pulled the blanket off Winnowil. "We had better move on as quickly as we can."

Esgal sighed again and nodded. "You'll have to help me up."

"Of course." Lim patted Winnowil as she scrambled up, then went and half lifted Esgal to his feet. On the sloping ground, it was difficult for him to hop and he almost fell, but at last Lim boosted him back into the saddle and they went on.

For the rest of the day, they stopped as little as possible and never for longer than it took to let Winnowil drink and to take a mouthful or two of water themselves. They passed quickly through the gap and then could make straight for Duamelti without using the roads. The terrain here was friendlier and Lim thought it was getting warmer as they made their way back into the forest. He kept watch for any ripe fruit he could pick for them to eat as they went, but there was nothing promising. He tightened his belt and kept looking.

At last, he decided they had to stop for the night. His legs felt like lead, Esgal was drooping where he sat, and even Winnowil looked genuinely tired. They couldn't keep going without at least a few hours' rest.

He found a sheltered spot with a small stream, more out in the open than anywhere they'd camped so far, but Lim was confident that they were now into territory where people would just ignore two camping elves. After all, they were only a couple of days' walk from Duamelti now and the humans here were fairly friendly. There was still a danger of pursuit, but as long as they kept moving at a good pace tomorrow, Lim thought they'd be all right. He untacked Winnowil as Esgal once again cleared sticks and stones from the ground where they planned to sleep.

While Winnowil went to drink at the stream, Lim checked Esgal's foot. While the air hadn't had the chance to do it any good, it wasn't getting any worse and he bandaged it up again. Then he looked into the saddlebags to see what food they had left. After the long walk on not much food, he was very hungry. Unfortunately, their supplies were low. He sighed. He wanted something filling to eat, but he knew that they had to preserve their dwindling store of biscuit.

"Esgal?" he said.

Esgal looked up from where he was fumbling with the knot of the bedroll. "Yes?"

"I'm going to scout about for something to eat." He hesitated, unwilling to ask something of Esgal that he felt he should do himself, but remembered that it might actually make the other elf feel better. "Will you collect as many sticks as you can find without going too far?"

Esgal nodded. "What shall I do if I hear someone coming?" he asked.

"Don't draw attention to yourself. If they attack you, yell and I'll come back as fast as I can."

Esgal nodded, looking uncertain, but when Lim asked if he was sure he was all right he nodded a little more confidently.

"I'll be fine," he said, going back to the bedroll.

Lim wasn't entirely sure, but he turned and headed off, looking for anything that would be filling: roots, perhaps.

He did have to admit that there was a much better chance of finding food here than in the darker forests that grew near Silvren. However, he didn't have much luck at first. He wondered fleetingly if there was a settlement nearby, or if he had unwittingly stumbled into the gathering grounds of a nomadic group; no matter where he looked, he couldn't find anything edible.

He did find a stick that would be suitable for digging and continued to search, swinging it in his hand as he went. He mostly concentrated on the ground; he'd given up on finding fruit. Bracken roots would do, or dandelion, though it would take some time to gather enough of those.

He sighed in relief as he came upon a damp ditch with some familiar purple flowers growing in the bottom, but upon closer inspection they proved to be foxglove and he moved on, biting his lip. He was starting to get genuinely worried that he wasn't going to be able to find anything and he didn't want to let Esgal down; he knew the other elf was just as hungry as him.

On the other side, though, he rounded a bush to find an open space with a cluster of mature bracken fronds. He grinned and reached up to brush his hair back from his face. The leaves themselves were inedible, but the roots would make a good meal and he set about digging up a couple of the plants. That wouldn't be too much of a loss.

Digging up the roots needed care to make sure he got them up completely, but they were a good size and he cut the fronds away with a small smile, then gathered up the roots and returned to camp.

Esgal washed them in the stream and filled a pan with water while Lim dug a fire pit and set a fire.

Esgal yawned, raising a grubby hand to his mouth.

"I'm tired," he said. "How much longer before we can sleep?"

"Depends if you want any supper," said Lim, putting a few more sticks on the fire.

Esgal pulled a face at him. "All right," he said, "Allow me to rephrase that: how long until dinner is ready?"

"I'm not sure," said Lim. "I think it might now be hot enough to boil that water. Let's have it? And the roots?"

Esgal handed him both and he set the water to boil while he cut the bracken roots into small pieces. Then he put them in the water and added a stock cube so that it would have a little flavour. He knew he probably should have skinned them first, but he remembered hearing that there was a lot of goodness in edible skins and he was disinclined to waste that.

After about another half hour, the roots were cooked soft and Lim cut them into smaller and smaller pieces so that they'd absorb as much flavour as possible. Then he drained the broth off into their mugs to serve as soup and they sipped that while they waited for the roots to cool enough to eat with their fingers. The soup was hot and delicious, if weak, but it awakened Lim's hunger to raging levels and he could hardly wait for the roots to be cool. It wasn't until he was half done with his soup that he was able to touch the food, but then he told Esgal that it was ready and they scooped lumps up with their fingers, rolling it into balls to eat. It was still wonderfully hot and felt satisfyingly solid as Lim ate, though an occasional bit of skin got stuck in his teeth. Still, it had absorbed the flavour of the broth and he could taste the herbs in it as if he'd never tasted them before. When he'd finished, he leaned back with a sigh, finally feeling that his hunger was satisfied.

"That'll be good for tomorrow," he said with a smile and drained the last of his considerably cooled soup.

Esgal grinned too, sipping at his own soup. "Thank you."

Lim patted him on the shoulder. "I'm going to bank the fire now," he said. "It's probably best if we go straight to bed and sleep a few hours, and then head on again by moonlight."

Esgal nodded, finishing off his soup and stretching a wistful hand towards the fire.

"It's so warm," he said quietly. Lim bit his lip.

"All right," he said after a moment, "I'll wash the cups and the pot out first and pack them away, then I'll bank it."

Esgal nodded. "Thanks," he said.

Lim washed out the pot and cups – it took some scrubbing with a handful of rough grass to remove the cooked-on residue – then banked down the fire. They'd use it to make tea in the morning, so he didn't put it out completely.

Esgal yawned widely. "I'm not sure why I'm so tired," he said, "given that you were walking all day while I rode."

Lim shrugged a little, stifling a yawn of his own. "You're injured and not as strong as I am to start off with. I think you're burning all your energy keeping going even though you're not walking. That's why we'd be going much more slowly if you were on foot."

Esgal nodded and went to lie down on the bedroll and pull the blanket over himself.

"Should either of us keep watch tonight?" he asked, yawning again.

Lim chuckled. "Even if I thought it was necessary, it wouldn't be you after that," he said. "Go to sleep, I'm sure it'll be fine."

Esgal yawned again and curled up to sleep. Lim went to the stream for another drink, looking around as he did so. The entire area seemed to be deserted, so he went back to his blanket and lay down, falling asleep almost before he'd laid down his head.

***

He woke up to find that it was daylight and birds were singing merrily in the trees around their camp. He swore, scrambling up. So much for travelling by night; it was almost noon and they needed to get moving.

"Esgal!" he called, shaking Esgal's shoulder. Esgal startled awake with a gasp, his breathing slowing once more as he recognised Lim's voice. "Sorry to startle you, but it's late. We need to get going."

Esgal shook his head, also scrambling up. "How late?" he asked, rubbing his eyes. "Are we skipping breakfast?"

"I'm afraid so. We'll each take a bite of something on the road, but we need to go."

Esgal nodded. "Shall I put out the fire?" he asked.

"Probably better not," said Lim, rolling up the bedroll and stuffing it into his pack. "I'll do it."

Esgal nodded and carefully sat down where he was, hugging his knees, while Lim once again poured water on the remains of the fire and stomped it out, finally laying the turves he'd cut out back over it. It took time, but would make it harder to track them. Then he tacked up Winnowil – she'd not rolled in mud today, fortunately – gave her some grain, picked out her hooves and helped Esgal to mount.

"Here," he said, handing him a piece of biscuit. "I'm afraid this'll have to be breakfast."

Esgal nodded, taking it. "What's the rush?" he asked as Lim started walking, leading Winnowil and nibbling on his own biscuit. "I thought you said we were safe here?"

"I don't want to stay in one place for too long," said Lim. "I am sure that no-one around here would do us any harm, but that doesn't mean that no-one from Arket would be able to catch up."

"All right," said Esgal with a sigh, rubbing his eyes again. He didn't sound happy, but when Lim asked, he simply said, "I'm still tired, woken suddenly from sleep."

"I'm sorry about that." Now that he'd calmed down a little, Lim knew he could have woken Esgal more gently.

"It's all right. I understand. I..." Esgal shot a fearful look over his shoulder. "I don't want to give them a chance to catch up either."

Lim just wordlessly patted his hand.

They kept hurrying along for about an hour, then at the crest of a hill they paused for a moment to catch their breath. Winnowil blew at Lim and he turned to pat her, then saw something coming along the road behind them. Biting back the rising feeling of alarm, he squinted and tried to make out what it was.

"What's wrong?" asked Esgal, also twisting to look around.

Now Lim was sure: it was a small troop of horsemen, similar to the group that had almost caught them as they came down the mountain. They didn't look much like just some ordinary group of riders, out enjoying the fine weather. He swore. The hilly terrain made it difficult to judge distances, but they were worryingly close, especially going at that speed.

"Lim?" asked Esgal, his voice rising a little in alarm.

"Sit tight," said Lim. He braced his hands on Winnowil's back and vaulted up behind Esgal. "Let's have the reins."

Esgal handed them over and Lim took them in one hand, wrapping the other arm around Esgal's waist to hold him steady.

"Lim, what's *happening*?" asked Esgal, instinctively grabbing at Winnowil's mane as Lim nudged her on and she surged forwards.

"We've been followed," said Lim.

Esgal stiffened and made a little whimpering noise. Lim could feel his quick breathing and urged Winnowil on.

They galloped on for a little while, keeping to the road as that was the straightest and fastest route. Fortunately, there was not too much dust. Lim had the fleeting idea that he could turn off the beaten track into the forest; unlike his pursuers, he would probably still be able to find his way to the nearest gate. He shook his head. To go through the forest would be slower and would make them easier to track. It would be easy to hide an elf's footprints, but not to disguise the place where a fast-moving horse had pushed between the trees. Besides, it would simply be difficult to hide Winnowil. For all he knew they had a full description of the trio they were following. No, the best thing to do was to stay on the road and keep moving fast.

He could hear that Winnowil's breathing was getting laboured. This wild flight had probably gained them a small start, but she hadn't had much good grazing. She probably couldn't stand it much longer. He knew he couldn't keep driving her. Perhaps he could slow down. He glanced back, but couldn't see their pursuers.

"Lim." Esgal's voice was steady. "Remember what you promised?"

That was a promise Lim never intended to keep. He couldn't risk Esgal being caught, not so close. "I remember."

They were at the end of a long, straight stretch and he saw flashes of the horsemen about to turn onto it. Teeth gritted, he urged Winnowil on. Esgal took a deep breath and let it out again.

Another few minutes. Lim got a flash from Winnowil of herself collapsing mid-gallop. She couldn't go on like this. He sent an image of Esgal riding her through the gate alone. The answering impression was positive. That decided him.

He halted her and dismounted, laying a hand on Esgal's arm to tell him to stay. This was Esgal's best chance of staying ahead all the way home.

"What's going on?" asked Esgal. He sounded frightened now. Lim didn't blame him and felt sorry for what he was about to do, but there was no real choice. Judging by the earlier glimpse, they had mere moments.

"You're going to have to ride on without me," he said, taking a rope from his pack. "I'll tie you on so you won't fall and Winnowil knows the way home. Hold on and she'll get you back."

"But what will you do?" asked Esgal, shuddering a little as Lim passed a loop of rope around his waist and began to tie him into the saddle, fastening the rope to the baggage rings at the front and back.

"I'll run and hide in the forest," he said as he worked. "Promise me that you won't try to come back."

"I can't just leave you!" protested Esgal, with more passion than he'd put into any sentence so far. "Lim, I've seen what they'll do to you if they catch you, I can't leave you!"

Lim put a hand on his arm, aware of pursuit getting closer. "She can't take us both. I'll be fine, but if you don't swear to me that you won't come back, I'll remove the reins and tie your hands. Don't make me do that. Swear."

Esgal scowled at him. "Very well," he said, "But it's under protest."

"Protest noted." Lim took Esgal's hand and put the reins into it. "She'll get you home. Tell them I'm on my way and I'm not yielding yet."

Esgal nodded. "I understand."

"Right." Lim sent Winnowil an image of her paddock and slapped her on the rump. With a snort, she doubled her legs under her and sprang forwards. Esgal cried out and almost dropped the reins, but Lim had tied him securely and he was in no danger of falling.

Lim stood and watched them go for a moment. Then he darted into the trees, shoving an obvious path through the undergrowth as he went. Let them think Winnowil had left the road. He'd lose them himself later.

Esgal clung on for dear life as Winnowil thundered down the road. He could vaguely see light above him – he assumed it was coming from the sky – but nothing else. He had no idea how long he'd been riding. He ached, and his throat was sore and dry from drawing fast, deep breaths through his mouth; his nose was still painful and blocked. He could feel the leather of the reins in one hand, where Lim had put them, and the fingers of his other hand were tangled in Winnowil's mane.

The saddle beneath him; the hair and leather in his hands; the rope around his waist and legs were all that kept him anchored in an increasingly insane world. He wondered how far they were from home, and whether Winnowil really knew the way or if she was just galloping ahead out into the wilds. He was terrified of the idea of being lost out in the middle of nowhere, unable to find food and shelter, let alone find his own way home without his sight. The fear made him feel sick, and the feeling was only intensified as he thought of Lim, his friend, left behind to face their pursuers.

With a practised twist of thought, he put aside the images that threatened to surface and simply redoubled his grip on reins and mane, leaning forwards a little to help himself balance. Fortunately, the road seemed fairly smooth, with nothing for Winnowil to jump. That told him that they were indeed still on the road and had not veered off into the forest. Despite that comfort, the tension and the sudden exertion of moving with her as she galloped were exhausting, especially as he'd had very little to eat that morning. He suspected that Lim had given him most of the morning's food supply, but he was still hungry and he hurt all over, every bruise and every aching muscle coming back to haunt him.

He desperately hoped that they'd arrive soon.

He wasn't sure how long it was, but it couldn't have been less than an hour. He felt like he was going to pass out at any moment and he could feel Winnowil flagging again. Even her new uncomfortable, bouncing gait was beginning to slow, but at least he couldn't hear hooves running up behind them above the thundering of his heartbeat in his ears.

He could, however, hear shouts from up ahead.

For a moment, his heart seemed to stop. Could they have somehow got ahead of him and he was galloping straight into their grip? He snatched at Winnowil's reins, trying to slow her at least enough to figure out what was happening. Even dying of hunger in the wild would be better than recapture.

Then he realised that the voices were calling out in elven, shouting challenges and commands to stop. He pulled on Winnowil's reins and she began to slow, then shied. He'd have fallen had he not been tied to the saddle, but he dropped the reins and cried out as he was thrown forwards, hitting his nose on her neck. He could smell blood and raised a hand to mop at it, gasping in pain as he touched the break.

Someone was calling out to him and he realised they'd been speaking for a little while.

"Wha-what?" he asked. Winnowil started to walk forwards and he grabbed her mane with one hand, hunting for the reins with the other, aware that he was probably getting blood all over her.

"It's all right," said the same voice. "Someone's leading her. We just want to get you inside the gate. Is that nose your only injury?"

Esgal nodded, feeling his heart rate dropping as he realised that he was safe and someone was here to guide him again.

"I'm stiff all over," he said, aware that his voice was trembling but not especially caring. "And I can't see. Where am I? Is this Duamelti?"

There'd been a flurry of whispers and orders as he told them about his blindness, but he ignored everyone else as the same voice assured him, "Yes, this is the southern gate of Duamelti."

Esgal sighed in relief, his head spinning for a moment as he finally relaxed.

"What's your name?" the person asked.

"Esgal."

That prompted another round of whispers, but Esgal was too tired to care. The panic-strength was draining out of him and he felt dizzy and sick.

He assumed they were inside the gate as at that point someone untied him and helped him dismount. His knees collapsed under him as he tried to stand, but the person helping him caught him under the arms and supported him while he found his feet. He couldn't seem to stop shaking, though, and swayed as he tried to stand alone. He felt like the ground was spinning under his feet and staggered, almost falling again.

"Esgal!" He was caught and held. "Are you all right?"

"I think I'm going to faint," he whispered. At once, they helped him to lie down, right there on the ground, on his side with his head a little supported so that the blood from his still-bleeding nose didn't choke him. Someone kept hold of his hand and he could hear voices chattering all around him. He wanted to fall asleep, but the person holding his hand kept talking to him, keeping him awake.

Suddenly, he heard someone walking purposefully towards him, their feet unusually heavy for an elf. Someone else was talking to the newcomer, but they fell silent as they drew close.

"Can I have a word with him?" asked a strange voice.

The person holding his hand drew away, letting go of him. Alarmed, he groped about for them, but found someone else. This hand was huge and calloused: a swordsman's hand.

"Esgal?" said the stranger.

"Yes?"

"My name's Seregei."

Captain Seregei of the Swordmasters, presumably, but Esgal mostly cared that this was Lim's friend, who had given them the fudge. "H-hello," he said. "You're Lim's friend."

There was a small, relieved sigh, then Seregei said, "Yes, I am. I sent him to fetch you. Can..." – a small hitch in the words – "can you tell me where he is?"

Esgal bit his lip, unsure how to explain, the worry for Lim's safety all flooding back.

"If something's happened to him, I don't blame you for it," said Seregei softly, only a slight tremble in his voice. "But I need to know."

"He stayed behind," said Esgal. "He said that Winnowil couldn't carry us both, and we... we were being chased."

Seregei gulped softly. "By men from Arket?"

"Yes."

"Where did this happen?"

Esgal had no idea where exactly they'd been when Lim had made him ride on alone and no way to work it out.

"I... I don't know. I couldn't see where we were, and I don't know how long I rode to get here after he made me leave him. We'd galloped double from where he saw that they were after us, then after... I'm not sure, maybe... half an hour? An hour? He got off and told me to ride on alone."

Seregei pressed his hand a little. "Thank you, Esgal. He was alive and well when you left him?"

"Yes, as far as I could tell."

"Did he say if he wanted us to come and look for him?"

"He told me that he wasn't yielding and earlier that this is his Task."

"Yes, it is. Very well, then, I'll wait for him to return alone. Thank you." Seregei pressed his hand again, then released him and walked away. A couple of other people approached him and one asked if he could move onto a litter that they'd laid beside him. He thought he had the strength for that and pushed himself up to his hands and knees, then they helped him find the litter and lie down on it, covering him with a warm blanket. His nose had stopped bleeding at last, and someone helped him half sit up and handed him a drink. He sipped thankfully, enjoying the soothing coolness of the water against his dry throat. He was distracted from that, though, as he heard someone else coming.

"Esgal!"

He'd dreamed of hearing that voice again. The thought of never again hearing her say his name had been the only thing to make him cry his heart out during those long, dark days, chained in a prison cell or lying bound and drugged. That drug had almost sent him to oblivion, but not close enough that he was spared loneliness and fear.

"Alydra," he breathed, trying to guess which direction she was coming from.

Then she was there. Her arms were around his shoulders, her hair tickling his face as she hugged him. He was afraid to hug her back, afraid that despite all his hopes and all Lim's words of comfort, this was just another dream, and that if he touched her, it would vanish. But slowly he wrapped his arms around her waist and, tentatively at first, but then fiercely, he hugged her close to his chest. His muscles spasmed, he hugged her so hard. He felt his bruised ribcage creak as she hugged him back, but no-one kicked him awake. No-one jeered and laughed.

He heard a voice telling Alydra to let go of him; he needed to be taken to the healing wing. But though she started to release him, he couldn't let go of her. He felt tears welling in his eyes. Maybe it would be when he let go that the dream would end. He was so happy to be back with her...

"Esgal?" she asked softly, gently stroking his hair. "What's wrong? They need to take you to a healer, then you can sleep in a real bed." She laughed lightly. "I'll stay with you; I'll hold your hand, I'm not letting you go ever again, love. What's wrong?"

He took a deep breath, feeling it hitch on the lump in his throat that meant he was going to cry. "I'm scared," he said softly.

"Of what? You're home. No-one here's going to hurt you."

"I know that. I'm scared that this is all a dream and at any moment I'm going to wake up and find that I'm... I'm still back there." He couldn't say any more, the lump in his throat growing so large it almost choked him.

"Oh, Esgal," she breathed, and he could tell that she too was trying not to cry. "Esgal, this is real." She hugged him again. "If you can trust anyone, trust me. This is real."

He took another deep breath, blinking back the tears. It was all right. He was finally home. He let go of her and lay down on the litter, let her tuck the blanket back over him, and took her hand. He kept holding onto her as he was lifted and carried towards safety, a real bed, sufficient food, a long sleep.

"Are we nearly there?" he asked, shaking his head a little to rouse himself.

"Almost," she said, squeezing his hand. "And then they'll have a look at your nose and try to find out why you can't see, and then you can sleep."

"Can I have something to eat?" he asked, smiling at where he thought she was.

"If I have anything to do with it," she promised.

He nodded, sighing as he entwined his fingers a little more securely in hers. He was home. He was safe. Beyond all hope, he was safe.

He just hoped that Lim made it home safely as well.

CHAPTER FIVE

Lim continued to push his way through the forest, purposefully going against everything he'd ever been taught. Every instinct told him to be careful and leave as few tracks as possible. But now he wanted them to follow. If he could lead them out into the woods and get them lost, they'd not follow Esgal.

He crossed a muddy, marshy patch next to a stream and paused to listen. He'd hear them following; they had horses.

There was a shout: "Tracks here!" and the sound of a branch swinging back to hit someone, followed by a curse. He grinned; this was working. How much further he should he go before he started hiding his tracks? No time to think about it now; he could hear them getting closer and pressed on, leaving clear marks as he went.

He trampled through long grass, then dragged his feet through a drift of fallen leaves, kicking them up in a cloud, then splashed through another stream and made a mess as he climbed the bank. Finally, he scrambled up into a tree to get a look at the lie of the land. While there, he strung his bow, just in case.

He was a good distance from the road and not too far from Duamelti: there were just a few relatively low hills. It was evening now, but he'd make it by dark. There was no sign of how far Esgal had gone, but that was for the best; there was nothing for their pursuers to see either. He could see them, though: a group of horses gathered together in a clearing. There were no riders. The men were following on foot.

He frowned. That would make them faster across this terrain. Still, it meant they certainly weren't following Esgal. Even if they tried, they wouldn't catch him. He grinned and started to climb down.

When he was halfway, his grip with his left hand slipped. He fell with a startled cry into a bush. Worryingly close, he heard a shout.

Twigs poked and scraped him as he scrambled out of the bush. No time to be glad it had been there to break his fall; they'd heard him. He had to get away from here. He cursed his injured hand as he finally pulled free. At least he wasn't hurt.

They were coming now. He snatched up his dropped bow. Duamelti wasn't far if he ran and he thought he'd led them far enough. They'd not catch up with Esgal. He started to run as straight as he could towards a small, wooded pass.

He went faster now; he wasn't stopping to leave tracks. This was more in line with what he knew: quick and quiet, avoiding mud and deep leaves, taking to the trees when he had to. He could climb between branches with barely a rustle to mark his passing. That was easier than scrambling up the hill on foot like them.

He grinned. They'd not catch him, and he felt a rush of triumph as he crested the final hill. Now there was just a long downward climb home. He'd never been more glad to see the valley of Duamelti.

They wouldn't respect the border, though, if they even knew it was there. He was a long way from other elves and had to keep going. Still, he couldn't deny the feeling of safety and stopped to rest a while in the branches of a tree. For a moment he wondered with sudden worry whether they could have split their forces and some gone after Esgal. He shook his head, though; Esgal was the one they were after, wasn't he? If they knew he'd followed the road, why bother chasing Lim at all?

Nonetheless, he did have his doubts about that. It had been dangerous, and he knew he was supposed to bring Esgal back himself. He didn't think there had been any other option, but he had still abandoned the other elf to make his own way home. He shook his head. That decision might mean he'd failed his Task. Still, he was confident that it had got Esgal home safely.

He sighed and tilted his head back against the trunk of the tree. Now that he had stopped and no longer had to concentrate on flight, he felt the aches and pains in his muscles, the sharp stinging of the scratches on his arms and face, the burn of thirst in his throat. It was worth it to know that he'd won safety for Esgal, but he couldn't help licking his lips and wishing he'd brought his water bottle. It would have been heavy, but he very much wanted a drink. He'd have to find a stream. At least that wouldn't be too hard; Duamelti was full of streams and little rivers.

He climbed down from his tree, careful of his left hand this time, and set off in search of water. As he went, he absently pulled his hair back out of his face. It was straggling out of his braid, but there was nothing to be done about that. He'd just have to deal with it.

He grinned as he saw the glint of water ahead of him and hurried over to the small stream to dip up water and drink. It tasted cool and sweet and he savoured it, but as he scooped up another double handful he heard a shout from behind him.

"Tracks! He came this way!"

For a moment he froze. He'd known they could follow him, but it was different to find they had. He let the water drain through his fingers for a moment, then a shock of fear went through him. He had to run. *He had to run!*

He leaped up. Hurdled the stream. Fled, running for his life. The shout had sounded close. They might be right on his heels. Still, he was a fast runner. This was his element.

He was flagging, though. Hair clung to his face, sweat dripped into his eyes. He was gasping, the good of the drink gone.

They must have taken a short cut. He could hear them keeping pace. Perhaps they'd found a path. No time to wonder. He couldn't sprint; he had to keep dodging obstacles. Still, his stride lengthened as he went down the hill. If he could reach a settlement...

No. He couldn't do that. The realisation hit him like a blow. These were armed men who hated elves. He couldn't bring them down on unarmed innocents. He turned in his tracks and ran along the hillside.

He crossed a path and heard a shout. Kept running, his head down.

A flash of exultation. They'd not expected him to turn. If he could keep ahead, he could get round them. He could find the way to a gate. There'd be armed guards there. Perhaps then –

He ran out of the trees and onto bare rock, just skidding to a halt before he ran straight over a cliff into a deep ravine. For a moment he stared down twenty, maybe thirty feet into deep, dark water, then he turned, still gasping. They poured out of the forest. Maybe a dozen, all out of breath, their clothes torn, but armed. Too many for him to fight. Seeing him turned at bay on the edge of the cliff, they fanned out to stop him running back into the forest.

He nocked an arrow to his bow, even though he knew that his aim wouldn't be worth the trouble. He was gasping. His vision blurred with exhaustion and breathlessness. Sweat dripped into his eyes. He had to push loose hair back from his face with one arm. There was no way he could be sure enough of his aim.

Still, he had to try.

"You've led us on a merry hunt since you stole that other elf away, lad," said one of the mortals. "You've had a good run. Now put the bow down and come quietly. Don't try to be a hero; that's how you end up dead."

Lim remembered Esgal's words, the haunted look in his eyes, his request that Lim slit his throat rather than let him be captured, the few words of description about the suffering of those three elves that he had killed quickly rather than leave them to die slowly.

He took a small step back and gasped as he felt a rock roll over the edge behind his heel. Instinctively, he glanced over his shoulder. The fall was still long, and the water at the bottom was still deep.

"See?" said the mortal. "You can't run any further. Put down the bow and surrender. You have my word that we won't kill you."

"Aye," murmured Lim. "I've heard enough to know you'll keep *that* oath."

He glanced back again, lowering his bow a little to let them think he was considering it. The water was probably deep *enough*...

"This is getting tiresome, elf," the man said, an edge entering his voice. "Just put down your bow and step towards us."

With a snap, Lim decided. He loosed the arrow he had nocked at the man who had been speaking. Twisted, crying out as wrenching pain shot up his leg. Leaped, arms stretched out towards the water, his bow still in his hand.

He plunged into the water with a cold shock. It was lucky he'd not landed head-first. At once, he began thrashing about with all four limbs to break his plunge and make it back to the surface before he ran out of air.

It took forever. His lungs were bursting before his head finally broke the surface. He gasped for breath, working to keep himself afloat. An arrow plunged into the water next to him, followed by another, but he was being swept along by the river too fast to have to worry about their aim being true. Still, to be on the safe side, he took a deep breath and went under again, intending to swim as far as he could underwater.

When he tried to kick, though, another sudden pain seared his leg. He let out the breath in a cry and had to surface to take another. For a moment he thought he'd been hit, but when he ran his other foot up that leg, he couldn't feel a shaft or a wound.

He looked ahead and swore as he saw that the canyon narrowed up ahead and there were rocks in the river. A glance up, though, showed that they weren't following right along the edge and there was a slight overhang. He could probably get out onto a rock and be sheltered. With that aim in mind, he started swimming towards the bank.

It hurt. His leg was killing him, but he bit his lip and kept going. If he could make it out of the water and let them think he'd been swept into the rapids and probably killed, he'd be all right. That would buy him time to see what was wrong with his leg.

At last he grabbed at a ledge just out of the water, putting his bow on it and lodging his fingers into a crack. He grimaced as he was swept along a little way, ripping the skin. At last, though, he managed to get a grip on the damp stone and pull himself out of the water. He slumped down on the rock to catch his breath.

They'd stopped shooting at him and he thought he could rest a while.

He bowed his head and continued to gasp, hoping that he could still make it to safety.

After meeting Esgal at the gate, Seregei had taken charge of Winnowil. She seemed glad to have someone familiar take her head and lead her off to her paddock, and he occupied himself with rubbing her down and washing the blood out of her mane. He wished he could speak to her; she might have some idea what had happened to Lim.

He shook his head. The last Esgal knew, Lim had been alive. He couldn't go out and look for him without invalidating his Task, and he'd sent the message back that he wasn't giving up. He evidently thought he could make it home on his own.

The thought made Seregei smile as he wrung the water out of Winnowil's mane. She shook her head and he spluttered as drops of water splattered across his face, but the weather was warm enough that he could just turn her into the field without having to dry her any more. She'd be able to rest there and walk about so that she wouldn't stiffen and go lame.

He leaned on the gate for a while, watching her and still trying not to worry. Still, as he turned and made his way back up the path to the Guardhouse, he couldn't help it. This was a lot to ask of a lone elf, especially one who wasn't that experienced. He stood by what he'd said to Alydra – Lim was perfectly capable – but he had never had to deal with something like this, especially on his own.

He shook his head hard, trying to banish the thought. That was the point of the Task, after all, and he *knew* Lim could manage. He fetched some papers from his room and sat down at a table in the common room. He'd promised Caleb that he'd go over these notes from a meeting with some human merchants, and now was as good a time as any.

At least the worst hadn't happened. When one of the gate guards had run up to the door with the news that Winnowil was approaching the gate with only one rider, Seregei had assumed that Lim had indeed had to make the decision to kill Esgal, and he'd expected to find an emotionally distraught but physically well new Swordmaster waiting for him. Instead, he'd found a riderless horse, fresh blood smeared on her mane and neck, and elves crowding around an ominously still form on the floor.

Then he'd decided that Lim had been driven off and had returned home unsuccessful and severely wounded: almost the worst of all worlds, the worst being that he'd been captured and now lay in prison next to Esgal. Upon drawing nearer, though, he'd seen that the elf was a stranger: Esgal himself, he now knew.

He sighed. It was almost evening now, though it would remain light for some time. He wondered if Lim would be back before dark or would decide to camp somewhere.

He was distracted from his thoughts as he once again heard hurried feet approaching the door. He sprang up and went to meet the messenger. With any luck...

The elf was a mixed-blood: a farmer, by the look of him. He staggered to a halt and Seregei caught him as he almost fell.

"What's wrong?" he asked.

"H-humans..." the elf panted. "Don't know... where from... came suddenly... have to help us!"

Seregei nodded and helped him inside. "Sit down while I get my sword."

The elf half-collapsed on the couch, gasping.

Seregei reached his room in a couple of quick strides and pulled his sword from under the bed. It was the work of a moment to buckle it to his back. He reached over his shoulder to check it was in place, then hurried back to the common room.

The elf was still panting, but he looked better. "My village... I'll show you," he said.

Seregei nodded. "I'm ready." As they left, he asked, "Have you alerted the army?"

"Someone... ran to the nearest gate."

"Good."

They jogged most of the way, but the messenger soon flagged. He gasped out, "half a mile on... west road... straight on" and Seregei rushed ahead. He wished there'd been time to get details, but speed was more important. At least he'd not be the only one there. Some of the gate guard would have come.

He was right. When he arrived, he could see elves in Duamelti livery already in the village. They were fighting humans in the main street, between the wooden houses. He drew his sword over his shoulder as he dashed down the street towards the battle. Counted. Half a dozen humans, five elves, best guess. They'd not seen him yet. If he could get around one of the buildings, perhaps an ambush...

A Valley-elf screamed. His sword dropped from his hand as he clutched a wound. The human facing him made as if to stab.

"Get away from him!" roared Seregei.

The human startled, looking up. The elf reeled back. Another stepped in to defend him as he retreated into the shelter of a building.

Seregei changed course as he passed the first house. Locked blades for a moment with a human who was trying to break down a door. Bore him down with weight and speed. Felt a stinging slash across his arm. Dodged another blow. The man in front of him cried out as Seregei's attacker accidentally stabbed him. Another elf killed that one. Seregei nodded thanks.

"The villagers?" he asked.

"In their houses," the elf replied, "or fled."

Seregei nodded and blocked another attack. The blow jarred his hands. He couldn't move his sword fast enough. Let go with one hand. Drew a knife and stabbed, then pulled back with a twist and a rush of blood. The man fell against him.

A cry from a little way off. He looked to see another elf killing the final human. He winced, looking around.

"We should have kept one alive," he muttered.

An elf with an armband denoting rank came over. "Captain Seregei," he said with a small smile. "I'm Captain Tiabre."

Seregei nodded at him. "I came as soon as I could. Do you know why they attacked?"

The elf shook his head. "The messenger who came for help said they were looking for someone. Do you know anything about that?"

Seregei frowned, looking around. The door of one of the houses opened and an elf nervously peered out. Seeing the battle over, he came over to them.

"Thank you," he said fervently.

Seregei smiled at him, but the smile faded as he said, "I hope they didn't cause too much damage. Is anyone hurt?"

The elf looked around distractedly. Other elves were also emerging from their houses, gathering in worried groups. A few of them were talking to the soldiers, gesturing to the buildings, the surrounding fields and the dead humans. The elf looked back and said, "I... they were questioning Atakir. That's when we sent for you." He glanced between them.

"Is he all right?" asked Seregei.

The elf glanced over his shoulder again, then pointed. "There's his brother. Atilya!" he called, and waved.

The elf looked up, then hurried over, weaving between the soldiers who were now dragging away the bodies.

Seregei nodded a greeting. "I hear these humans were questioning your brother: Atakir. We just wanted to ask if he was hurt."

Atilya winced. "He'll be all right, sir, though I don't think he'll want visitors," he said. "He'll carry bruises for a while, but we managed to get him away before they could hurt him badly." He clenched and unclenched his fists, looking over his shoulder. "I'm glad you came," he said, looking back. "I don't think we could have defended ourselves."

Seregei smiled, glancing sideways at Tiabre. "It's lucky you sent for us. Do you happen to know what it was that these humans wanted?"

Atilya shook his head. "Not really. Atakir said they were asking him about an elf they'd chased to somewhere near here. They thought we might be sheltering him."

Seregei frowned. Lim? Esgal? "Did they give any details?"

Atilya shook his head again. "Sorry, sir."

"Someone you know, perhaps?" asked Tiabre, tilting his head to look at Seregei.

"Perhaps. My trainee should be arriving back from his Task soon, and he may not be coming back by the road." Seregei sighed.

"Once we've finished here, my men and I can help you search, at least for a little while."

"We'll have to keep it this side of the border, but that would be a great help," said Seregei. "Thanks."

They carried the humans' bodies out of the village and, with the help of the villagers, dug a pit in the woods to bury them. Seregei wanted to go and start the search for Lim, but he did his best to help; though the attack on the village had been unjustified and he didn't regret the fact that he and the soldiers had killed these humans, it would be wrong to deny them a proper burial, and the more people helped, the faster it would be done.

At last, though, he stood back from the raw heap of earth over the grave and wiped his brow with the back of one hand as he looked up at the sky to judge the time. He sighed. It had been a couple of hours now and it was getting dark.

Tiabre also shot a look at the sky, then at Seregei. "We'll not be able to do much tracking in this," he said, "Especially if you're looking for a Swordmaster who didn't want to be found."

Seregei grimaced, looking around. He had to admit that that was true. "Does anyone know what direction they came from?" he asked, looking around at the gathered villagers. He couldn't see Atilya; he'd presumably returned to care for his brother.

One elf volunteered that they'd come down from the hills, across the fields. "I'd expect they came through the wooded pass, but there isn't a road through there," he said.

Seregei nodded. "I suppose that means they could have taken any route through the forest?" he asked.

The elf who had spoken nodded.

"I don't think there's much chance of finding anything tonight," said Tiabre seriously. "I'll tell my commander and we'll help you search tomorrow, but I don't think it's worth it tonight."

Seregei sighed, looking up towards the hills. They loomed black against the dark-blue sky. He knew Tiabre was right; if Lim didn't want to be found, it would be almost impossible to track him in the dark with no clue as to where exactly he was. The very fact that the humans had come here to search indicated that following their tracks would be no help, and for all he knew, Lim had managed to lose them before they ever entered the valley. He might not yet have crossed the border himself.

He sighed again and nodded. "All right. I'll give him overnight."

Tiabre reached up to pat him on the shoulder. "We have torches; we'll escort you back home, if you want. It'll be even darker under the trees."

Seregei nodded. "Thanks."

For a moment, Lim lay still, catching his breath and shivering as the cooling air cut right through his wet clothes. On top of everything else, it was starting to get dark and the wind whistled chillingly through the narrow canyon. He was pretty sure, though, that he'd lost his pursuers. He sighed and pushed himself upright, moving to inspect his hurt leg.

He couldn't see anything wrong, but when he rolled up the leg of his breeches he noticed that his calf was a little swollen compared to the other leg. It was a little warm to the touch, as if bruised, though he couldn't see a mark and he didn't think he'd hit it on anything in the fall. He swore softly. Evidently he'd damaged the muscle. That would take a while to heal, but he'd have to get back home before he could worry too much, and that wouldn't happen if he stayed here. He looked around, but didn't think he could climb up even if he was sure that the mortals weren't waiting for him at the top. When he tried to envision a map of where he was, he decided that the best way to get home might be to swim.

That was if he could swim with this leg.

He could make it easier, though: he unstrung his bow and put the string in his pocket, aware that it would almost certainly be useless even when it had dried. His bow would probably be all right as long as he was careful about drying it so that it didn't warp, and he strapped it to his back along with his quiver. Then he took the one bandage that he always carried in the survival pouch at his belt and wrapped it as tightly as he could around his injured leg. Hopefully that would support the muscle enough that he'd be able to swim, and now that he had both hands free it would be easier.

With those things done, he looked downstream. The rapids went on for a little way, but he thought that with care he'd actually be able to clamber along the rocks on the edge. That would be hard on his leg, but he couldn't see a reasonable alternative.

He was starting to feel really cold, and he knew that if he stayed here much longer not only would he start to get dangerously chilled but his leg would stiffen to the point where he could no longer use it. So he took a deep breath and started moving, creeping along the rocks as carefully as he could. He almost slipped and fell a couple of times and more than once had to curl up for a little while and hold his leg until the pain faded. At last, though, he'd reached the end of the rapids and paused for another rest. With a chuckle, he thought that at least here he didn't need to worry about thirst.

Carefully, he slipped into the water. It felt surprisingly warm now that he was wet and cold, and he started to swim, allowing himself to be swept along to conserve his energy as best he could. At this rate, so long as he didn't meet with any more rapids or – Lady forbid – a waterfall, he'd be back home in a few hours.

It was getting darker, though.

He swam over to the side of the river and pulled himself out on a ledge once more to think. He didn't dare try to swim in the dark in case he did run into those rapids or that waterfall. He wasn't entirely sure what river this was and didn't want to stake his life on the assumption that it would stay calm. He needed to be able to see danger coming.

On the other hand, he was cold and it would only get colder. He had no intention of escaping and surviving the dive into the river only to die of the cold. The ledge went a little distance and he got up and tried to walk, only to fall against the wall as his leg collapsed under him. He swore creatively and rubbed at it. No, he couldn't walk, but he pulled himself upright against the wall and managed to limp a few steps before pausing with a sigh. After a moment's rest he carried on, relying on the movement to keep him warm. It didn't really help that he'd not eaten anything since that morning, and not much before that. He felt hollow inside and was starting to get a little light-headed.

At the end of the ledge he paused to think for a moment, trying to decide what to do next and waiting for the giddiness to pass. There was still enough light to swim on, he decided, and he thought that the gorge opened up ahead. If so, he might be able to get enough light from the moon or stars to swim into the night. So with a sigh, he slipped back into the water and swam on.

The gorge did indeed open up, the river pouring down something that looked rather like a combination of rapid and waterfall. He glared at it, but at least here he could climb out of the river and limp alongside it, stopping to take frequent rests. He also had the comfort that he recognised this place, though that meant that he knew the river would not be easy to follow. Nonetheless, the land on either side would be worse, especially with his injured leg. It would hardly support his weight and walking was very tiring, but he forced himself to keep going until the land around had flattened enough for him to be able to look down the hill. He let out a sigh of relief, half collapsing to sit on a rock, when he saw lights being lit in the city of Duamelti not too far below him. A glance up at the sky showed that it would once more be a fairly bright night, but he'd been right: the river was rough and started to delve back down into a canyon as he looked down it.

He sighed. He'd have to stick to the river if he didn't want to deal with a very steep slope or a cliff before he reached home, and he really didn't think he could climb. At least it did look like he'd have enough light, so with another sigh he climbed back into the river and set off down it once more.

The next several hours passed in a blur. He was hungry, cold, exhausted and in pain, but he managed to swim from rock to rock, fending himself off them, clinging to them from time to time to rest. The moon was already beginning to set, and there was nobody about, but he paddled as best he could on along the river towards civilisation.

At last, he was within the city. On either side rose silent houses, the occupants still fast asleep. No use getting out here; he wasn't sure how far he could walk without help. He swam through the great pool, blessing the fact that it was clear of obstructions, and finally managed to pull himself out of the river at the small dock near Caleb's palace. He was just trying to stand, leaning on the wall, when he heard a challenge and someone running towards him.

"Halt!" shouted one of the guards. "Stand still and state your name and business!"

"It's... it's all right," said Lim, extending his hands in a sign of peace and trying not to wobble. He was shivering and the world was spinning around him, but he managed to continue, "I'm Lim. Lim the Swordmaster trainee. I... I made it back."

His vision was starting to tunnel and there was a ringing in his ears.

"T-tell me Esgal got..." He couldn't managed to say any more and didn't know how they were reacting to either of the things that he'd said, for at that moment the world finally winked out and he felt himself falling. At least the darkness into which he plummeted was warm.

CHAPTER SIX

Seregei had just drifted into an uneasy slumber when he was woken by someone beating on the door of the Guardhouse. He pulled on a shirt and hurried to see what was the matter, hoping that this time he was being summoned because Lim was home; that hadn't been the case the last few times.

The guard at the door was grinning and said, "Lim just arrived by river."

Seregei sighed with relief, leaning against the door frame. "How is he?" he asked.

"Exhausted, but not badly hurt. He must have been swimming for some distance, though."

Seregei nodded. "Where is he now?"

"Down by the palace, though they may have moved him to the healing house."

Another nod. Seregei hunted for his boots for a moment and pulled them on. As he started to lace the first one, he glanced up at the guard again. "You said not *badly* hurt."

"When he climbed out of the river there appeared to be something wrong with his leg; it was bandaged. I don't know anything more; I came to get you straight away."

Seregei nodded and finished lacing up the second boot. "All right," he said. "Let's go."

Together, they hurried back down to the palace, heading for the healing house. There was enough of a commotion going on to convince Seregei that Lim had indeed been brought there already, so he simply asked where he was and was directed to one of the small side rooms.

Lim was still lying on a litter, soaking wet. Evidently they'd not yet had time to get him onto the bed. As Seregei went in, he stirred a little and moaned.

"Lim?" Seregei said softly, joining the healer and her assistant.

Lim opened his eyes and squinted vaguely at Seregei. "'gei?" he mumbled.

"Yes. Well done, Lim." Seregei crouched down and took Lim's hand. "What have you *done* to yourself?"

"Leg..." Lim shook his head. "I've hurt my leg. Did Esgal... did he get back?"

"Yes, and he's fine. He's just down the corridor, actually, probably asleep, so don't go making too much noise, all right?"

Lim chuckled. "So I did it?" he asked.

"Did what? Rescued him and got him and yourself back? What do *you* think?" As he spoke, Seregei took a towel that the healer's assistant passed him and carefully began to help remove Lim's wet tunic and shirt.

Lim sighed as he moved to pull his arm free of one sleeve of his shirt. "Good," he said. "Look..." He held up his hand and Seregei saw that it was rope burned and blistered. "Next time I'm taking gloves. And a few more supplies."

Seregei laughed, though he looked with pity at Lim's hand. "How's his leg?" he asked the healer as he handed the towel on to Lim.

"I think he's just pulled a muscle," she said, "But it's hard to tell when he's still cold; it's all in a knot. We'll need to get a better look to be sure"

Seregei nodded. "All right, brother mine," he said, patting Lim on the head. "Looks like we need to get you warmed up. Apart from the leg, how do you feel?"

"Hungry, cold, tired." Lim smiled a little. "Glad to be home."

Seregei had to smile; it wasn't often that he heard a complaint from Lim. He patted him on the head again and took the nightshirt that he was handed.

"There were humans chasing me," said Lim as Seregei pulled the nightshirt over his head. "I don't know what happened after I lost them."

"They attacked a village, but don't worry: the villagers summoned me and some members of the army."

"Everything's all right?"

"Yes." Seregei patted Lim's head again, then turned to the healer and asked, "Can he have something to eat?"

The healer nodded. "We've sent for some soup," she said. "Will you help us get him onto the bed?"

Seregei gently slipped his arms under Lim and lifted him onto the bed, then tucked him in. Lim sighed and let his eyes fall closed, quickly falling asleep again. Seregei smiled a little and stroked his wet hair as the other two elves slipped out to leave the friends alone, the healer telling him to call them back or ring the bell above Lim's bed if he needed help.

"I'm going to have to think of an epithet for you, aren't I?" he said softly. He smiled. He probably should have occupied himself with that rather than worrying himself sick that he had thrown Lim into a situation that was far over his head. He shuddered a little, then shook his head. No use dwelling on the terror he'd felt in that split second when he saw Esgal, or how hard it had been to keep his voice steady as he spoke to the injured, exhausted elf. He'd been convinced that Esgal was alone because Lim was captured or dead.

But no. Here he was, safe and triumphant. Seregei smiled, once again feeling strangely proud of the progress Lim had made.

He laughed softly. "I remember when you arrived in Duamelti, you silly elf," he murmured. "Shyest elfling I've ever met. And now look at you!"

There was a knock on the door and Seregei got up to answer it. Outside was the healer's helper, holding a tray with a bowl of soup. Seregei mentally searched for his name as he came in, but couldn't remember it. He knew they'd been introduced at some point in the past and cursed his own memory.

He put it from his mind, though, and went to shake Lim awake. He was very deeply asleep and woke slowly and groggily, but peacefully, which relieved Seregei. They exchanged a few words – Lim barely seemed awake – and then Seregei took responsibility for feeding him the soup, spoonful by spoonful, while the healer's assistant supported him. He didn't look entirely happy with being spoon-fed like a child, but didn't make too much of a fuss. He just finished the bowl and dozed off again.

Seregei gave it back to the assistant and leaned back in his chair with a sigh.

"We can set up a pallet in here or the outer room if you want to sleep," said the assistant, looking hard at him. "I don't believe you've slept a wink all night."

Seregei started to say that he was fine, but decided against it. By the look of him, Lim wasn't going to wake up any time soon, and he didn't need Seregei to keep a vigil at his side.

"All right," he said, stretching. "I'll get some sleep. Thanks."

They laid down a mattress and some blankets in the outer room and he went to go to sleep, squeezing Lim's hand a little in farewell.

"Wake me if he wakes up, will you?" he asked as he removed his boots.

The assistant nodded and Seregei lay down on the mattress, closing his eyes and relaxing. At last, he no longer had to drive himself mad with worry and lie awake for hours. With that comforting thought, he fell asleep.

***

When he woke naturally, he assumed that Lim was still fast asleep. In fact, he'd hardly moved since the night before, though someone had removed one of the blankets as he started to warm up. Seregei went over to him and ran a hand gently across his brow. It was much warmer than it had been the night before, without actually being hot due to fever. He heard someone come in behind him and turned, then smiled as he saw that it was a healer: Arani, a friend of his. He inclined his head a little in greeting.

"Good morning," said Arani, coming over. "How's he doing?"

"Better than last night," said Seregei.

Arani laughed. "Yes, I did know he'd improved at all." He also felt Lim's temperature and smiled. "I also had a look at his leg."

"What's happened to it?"

"Nothing too serious, don't worry: he's pulled the muscle. Painful and he'll limp for a while, but it'll heal fairly fast. We are planning to put him on crutches for a couple of weeks to make sure, but he'll be fine."

Seregei nodded. "And how's Esgal?" he asked.

Arani smiled. "Doing very well. I personally think Alydra could be trusted to look after him, but a couple of my colleagues really want to keep an eye on him, part to make sure his sight really does begin to return as we expect, part to make sure that muck the humans gave him didn't have any other side effects."

Seregei nodded. "What are they doing about his sight?" he asked.

"Just trying to stop him using it too much; they think that if too much light gets to his eyes that *will* cause permanent damage."

Seregei frowned, wondering how the healers were planning to stop Esgal from trying to look at things. Noticing the confused expression on his face, Arani smiled.

"I can guess what you're wondering," he said. "They've bandaged his eyes."

"Blindfolded him? How did that go down?"

"Surprisingly well." Arani grimaced a little.

"What does that mean?"

Arani shook his head at Seregei's suspicious tone. "Really, he took it very well. Obviously, we had explained what we were doing, so he didn't just wake up this morning to find himself blindfolded, and Alydra was with him. I think he felt that if she agreed with what we were doing it must be all right." He sighed a little, sadly.

"Do *you* think he's going to regain his sight?"

Arani sighed again. "It's not..." He shook his head. "I don't know. I don't like the fact that it's lasted as long as it has. I agree that trying to see will not have helped, and he's done nothing else for several days now."

Seregei grimaced.

"I shouldn't really discuss this, especially in front of Lim." Arani brushed his hand over Lim's head once more. "Even if he is so deeply asleep I'd be worried if I couldn't see that he *is* breathing."

Seregei smiled a little, but sobered as he asked, "He *will* be all right, won't he? Lim, I mean."

"I think so," said Arani. "I don't believe there's anything really wrong with him apart from the pulled muscle. This is just a natural sleep brought on by some days of walking and worrying with only a few hours' doze to sustain him." He laughed a little. "I've had this problem with your people before: you *do* need sleep."

Seregei smiled. "By 'your people' do you mean Swordmasters or Mixed-bloods?"

"Swordmasters. You know that perfectly well."

Seregei laughed. Of course, Lim was a Swordmaster now, or very nearly. He'd not yet taken the oath, but after that he was in for the rest of his life, and Seregei had no doubt that he'd do it.

"I've been trying to think of an epithet for him," he said, sitting down on the chair by Lim's bed. "Something to do with this Task would seem appropriate, but I suppose that I'll have to wait for him to wake up and tell me about it."

Arani shrugged. "Well, Esgal's awake if you want to go and ask him what he remembers. He's probably recovered enough to tell you the full story now."

Seregei nodded and watched Arani go.

For a moment more he watched Lim sleep, wondering if he would show any sign of wakefulness, but in the end he made the same decision as he had the night before: Lim just needed to be left alone to sleep in peace. He wasn't gravely wounded, and if he woke and wanted something he was perfectly capable of ringing the bell himself. That, after all, was why it was mounted above the bed. So Seregei squeezed Lim's hand in farewell, got up, and went down the corridor to Esgal's room.

He knocked on the door and Esgal called to him to come in. He was surprised to find the other elf alone, but despite the fact that Arani had told him about the treatment they were trying on him, he was more surprised by the bandages wound over Esgal's eyes.

"Who's there?" asked Esgal, suddenly sounding a little nervous.

"It's me: Seregei. Sorry, I wasn't expecting to find you all on your own."

Esgal smiled. "I persuaded Alydra to go and get some rest," he said, "but I'd appreciate some company."

Seregei accepted the invitation and sat down on the chair by Esgal's bed.

"How's Lim?" asked Esgal. "They told me that he arrived last night."

"He's fine. He swam down the river, if you'll believe it, and pulled himself out on the dock by Caleb's palace."

Esgal laughed. "That can't possibly be the first place he was able to get out!"

"No, but given that it was the small hours of the morning, it was the only place that he could reasonably expect people to see him and help him," said Seregei seriously.

Esgal's laughter died on his lips. "'Help him'? Is he hurt?"

"Not badly, but he was very tired."

Esgal nodded. "So where is he now? I'd like to talk to him... to thank him."

"He's asleep just down the corridor. I daresay that as soon as he wakes up he'll be wanting to look in on you."

Esgal smiled a little. "He's welcome at any time."

Seregei nodded. Esgal reached out with one hand, groping about in air for a moment, before Seregei took it and pressed it gently.

"You sound very proud of him," said Esgal. "He told me you were friends, but... are you related in any way? Brothers?"

Seregei laughed a little. "That's probably the easiest way to think of it," he said, "But Lim's family is a complicated thing and I don't think I have the right to explain it to you."

Esgal nodded. "I noticed that he doesn't use a patronym," he said casually.

"I'm not telling you," said Seregei, equally casually, "So there's no point in trying to wheedle it out of me. It's his business, and if he wants to keep it to himself then that's his prerogative." Now that he was no longer in danger, at least.

Esgal accepted that with a small smile.

After a moment, Seregei asked, "How much do you remember of the last few days?"

Esgal put his head on one side, the smile gradually fading. "Since Lim rescued me? Most of it. Before that..." He hesitated. "They'd drugged me because I kept trying to fight back, so some of it's fuzzy, and... I'd honestly rather not talk about it, but if it would be useful in helping others..."

Seregei held up his free hand. "No, I'm not asking about anything before Lim rescued you, for the moment. I'm curious about how he did it, and how he got you back. I'll also ask him the same questions, but I'd like to know your perspective."

Esgal nodded, looking a little happier at that.

"Well..." He leaned his head back a little, thinking. At last, he said, "I don't remember much of the actual rescue. Just a lot of noise and shouting. Someone pulled me over at one point and I hadn't the strength to get up. I assume that was my guard; he was leading me by a rope around my neck." Esgal touched a red, chafed line across the back of his neck and Seregei winced in sympathy. "Then someone was shaking my shoulder and shouting at me. I suppose it was Lim, though as I say" – he shook his head – "it's difficult to remember anything. He knew my name, though, and cut off the sack that they'd tied over my head. I knew he'd done it because I could breathe much more easily." Again, he shook his head a little. "I don't really remember anything else between then and when I woke fully. I'm sorry."

Seregei nodded. "That's all right," he said. "I suppose this all happened while you were still drugged?"

"Yes." Esgal ran an absent hand over his own hair. "Yes, it did." He sighed. "Well, I woke up when I tried to roll over in my sleep. One of the effects of the drug was to numb all the pain I was in, so when it had worn off..." He chuckled. "There were quite a lot of muscles that were aware that I'd not been receiving visitors and still wished to complain."

Seregei also laughed.

"We rested for the rest of the day. Lim gave me food and water and did his best to set my nose." Esgal's hand went to his broken nose. It looked better than it had, but was still misshapen and badly swollen. The blow it had got the day before – presumably from Winnowil's neck – had done it no favours. "Then he helped me walk." He smiled a little. "He kept watch and helped me on every step all the way down the mountain. I was slow, and..." He shrugged a little, looking down. "I complained a lot, but he said it was all right."

Seregei nodded again. "I think I agree with him."

Esgal chuckled. "Ah, you didn't hear how much I complained! But I admit it: I was cold and hungry and tired and not a little scared." He sighed. "We... we did once run into some searchers. He managed to hide us both and we remained hidden, though... I was sure they'd found me when he came over to tell me they were gone. But then we were off the mountain and travelling was much easier from there on."

Seregei made a mental note to ask Lim about that incident.

"We made a proper camp that night, and I was able to help. I found water while he was retrieving some things he'd hidden on the way up, and when he found food and lit a fire I could cook. We set off the next morning and were travelling almost solidly all the way back. I'm not sure how much he ate, and I know that he didn't sleep much, given that he was walking and I was riding."

"So that continued until he told you to ride on alone?"

"Yes. I persuaded him to sleep a couple of times while I did my best to keep watch, and he relaxed much more as we came closer to home, but I could still tell how exhausted he was." Esgal bit his thumbnail. "And then he spotted that we had been tracked and jumped up on Winnowil behind me. We rode for some time, but he stopped and said that Winnowil couldn't stand that pace doubly loaded and I'd have to go on alone." He looked down and fiddled with the blanket, one finger absently running along the stitching on the hem. "I... I didn't want to leave him like that. I... knew what... they'd do to him if..."

Seregei pressed Esgal's hand. "It's all right," he said, "You don't have to think about that."

Esgal chuckled bitterly. "As if I can ever stop thinking about it," he said softly. "But I already feel guilty enough for burdening Lim with those memories; I won't do the same to you. He tied me to the saddle and told me to ride on alone. I just hung on to Winnowil until I arrived at the gate, and you know the rest."

Seregei nodded. "Thanks, Esgal. I don't suppose you know how they managed to track you so far without either of you noticing it?"

Esgal shook his head. "Maybe they just headed for the nearest... but no, Silvren is much closer. No, I don't know, I'm afraid."

Seregei nodded again. "All right," he said. "Do you know when Alydra will return? Would you like me to stay with you until then?"

Esgal smiled a little. "I don't rightly know how long she's been away, but I'd like to have someone to talk to." The smile broadened. "The healers keep telling me to rest, but I've had enough sleep, I can't just lie here much longer or I'll run mad. Does sitting here talking to you count as rest?"

Seregei smiled and settled himself more comfortably in his chair. "I think so, as long as I don't say anything to get you upset. What do you want to talk about?"

They sat together for about two hours, Esgal asking questions about everything that had happened while he'd been away, down to the doings of the smallest elfling in his home village. Seregei answered everything he could, enjoying seeing Esgal's face light up and hearing the delight in his voice.

At last, Alydra arrived, and though she scolded Esgal for still being awake rather than getting more sleep, she didn't seem truly angry with either of them.

"Thanks for sitting with him, Captain," she said, as Seregei stood up to let her take his place.

"Not a problem," said Seregei. "I was meaning to talk to him in any case, and it was no trouble to stay."

With a last wave and word of farewell, he left the room and headed back to check on Lim.

He was still apparently asleep, but when Seregei said his name he opened his eyes a little groggily, blinked a couple of times, and smiled.

"Hey," he said.

"Hey," said Seregei, sitting down beside him. "How do you feel?"

Lim smiled. "Still a little tired, and hungry, but otherwise much better."

"That's good. You've slept for..." – Seregei glanced at the window to check the position of the sun – "about half the day, so I'm not surprised that you're hungry again. Want me to go and see about getting you some food?"

Lim nodded. "Not soup again, though, if there's any alternative?"

Seregei laughed. "I'll go and see."

He fetched some bread and cheese for himself and Lim from the main hall, where lunch was being served for Caleb's household; the Swordmasters had a standing invitation to eat there. One of the cooks asked after Lim and gave him some candied plums that were actually supposed to go to the royal family's dining room. Seregei thanked her fervently as he wrapped them in a napkin and promised not to tell. Those would be a treat, he thought with a smile as he headed back to the healing house.

Lim was dozing quietly, but looked up when he heard Seregei come in and eagerly pushed himself upright.

"Any luck?" he said hopefully.

Seregei tried to look contrite, but laughed and handed over Lim's share of lunch. Lim happily took a couple of bites of bread as Seregei sat down beside him again.

"When did you last have a decent meal?" he asked.

"Define 'decent'," said Lim, and nibbled on the cheese, closing his eyes a moment as he savoured it.

"'Not trail food'."

"Well..." Lim swallowed. "To be fair, those mashed bracken roots were all right, and Esgal is indeed just as good a cook as he claimed, so that rabbit and mushroom stew thing he did was really good. Apart from those two nights, I've not had a decent meal since I left. And I had to pretend to drink mortal ale."

Seregei stared at him. "*Why?*" he asked.

"Long story." Lim took another bite of his food and smiled sheepishly. "It involves me trying to overhear rumours about Esgal."

Seregei raised his eyebrows. "You know you're going to have to tell me the whole thing at some stage," he said.

Lim nodded. "But not right now?" he asked softly. "I need a moment to get it all straight in my head before it's fit to be told."

"What do you possibly need to do to it? This isn't a singing of ballads in the great hall."

"I know." Another bite. "But... I just need to think some of it over a little." He kept his eyes on his blanket, his shoulders hunched.

Seregei put a hand on his shoulder and he looked up, swallowing. After looking him in the eye for a moment, Seregei said softly, "Well, get it straight quickly, because I need to think about an epithet for you."

Lim probably would have choked if he'd had anything in his mouth. "An epithet?" he asked, staring at Seregei.

"Of course. All Swordmasters need epithets."

"So I..."

Seregei only just remembered to move slowly as he ran a hand through his hair. "Sweet Lady's bountiful mercies, Lim, you went all the way to

Arket, rescued Esgal and brought him back here safe and well. Of *course* you succeeded."

"Even though I made him ride back alone?"

"Yes. What would have happened had you not done that?"

Lim shuddered. "They'd have caught us both," he said softly.

"Exactly, and *that* would have been a failure."

Lim's lips quirked a little in the beginning of a smile.

"Look, you made a judgement call that Winnowil and Esgal could get back safely on their own. I'm not going to tell you it was a great idea or a stupid one. It worked out. I've had great ideas that *still seem like great ideas in hindsight* that haven't worked out."

Lim chuckled. "Like yelling at Caleb in public that one time?"

"I didn't know he had guests, and no, that was not one of those ideas. That was a terrible idea that looks like a *worse* idea in hindsight."

Lim was actually laughing now and Seregei smiled. It felt very good to hear that laugh. He stretched out his legs and leaned back in his chair to relax as Lim finished off his lunch.

"Anyway," he said, "to get back to the point, your judgement call worked out and you did what you set out to do: got Esgal out of Arket and back to Duamelti and also got back yourself without anyone having to go and fish you out of that river."

Lim chuckled, looking down again. "It was probably a bad idea to jump into it. I mean... maybe I could have taken them on, but there were a dozen of them and only one of me, and I wasn't sure of my aim."

Seregei held up his hands. "Lim, you're going to have to backtrack a little, I'm afraid. What exactly are you talking about?"

Lim looked up and smiled sheepishly. "Why I jumped into the river. Off a rather tall cliff." He looked down again. "It was probably a stupid idea, but..."

Seregei put a hand on his shoulder. "And why was it? To escape from the men I fought?"

Lim played with the blanket. "Yes. I ran, but I was tired and I think they just came right down the hill in a straight line. They cornered me against a cliff and it was either jump, surrender and be taken prisoner or be killed, so I jumped." He shrugged. Then he looked up. "My bow, is it..."

"It's at the armoury, being very carefully dried," said Seregei. He'd asked about it while on his trip to get lunch, and the elf to whom he'd spoken had seemed pretty confident that it would dry without warping.

Lim nodded, sighing with relief. "That's good," he said. "I was worried when I jumped, but I didn't know what else to do."

Seregei patted him on the shoulder. "It was a very dangerous, stupid thing to do," he agreed, "but not as stupid as surrendering so that they could bind you and take you back to do whatever horrible thing to you, or trying to take on a dozen men, all well-armed, in a hand-to-hand fight. They were able to give a good showing against six of us, after all."

"Was there anything else I could have done?"

"How would I know? I wasn't even there. If you can't think of anything, there probably wasn't anything."

Lim nodded, looking considerably happier. "It's not the only stupid decision I've made, either," he said, toying with his braid. It looked distinctly the worse for wear.

"Let me get a comb, and I'll fix that for you," said Seregei. "While I'm doing that, you can tell me about the other stupid decisions."

He borrowed a comb from Arani, and began unbraiding and combing out Lim's long hair, trying to straighten out the tight kinks to make it easier to braid it. It needed washing, but that could wait.

"Right," he said, "Off you go."

"You want them in the order I did them, or in order of stupidity?"

"Surprise me," said Seregei with a grin, looking up from the unruly mess of Lim's hair.

"All right." Lim shifted, gasping a little as Seregei inadvertently pulled on a tangle. "Well, the first one in the order I did them was probably going into that inn, and sitting in the corner away from the door."

Seregei grimaced. "Was this an inn in Arket?"

"Yes."

"I suppose you ended up cornered."

"Yes. A group of men came in and the barman pointed me out."

"You weren't openly in there as an elf, were you?"

Lim shook his head. "I had my hood up, and tried to use words that would mask my accent, but I suppose they were just looking for someone suspicious. But when I tried to run one of them knocked my hood back and that was that."

Seregei grimaced again. "How in the world did you get out of that?"

Lim blushed. "I pretended to take a woman hostage and told them I'd kill her if they didn't let me leave."

"Damn it, Lim!" Seregei immediately started to modulate his voice as Lim flinched, but the younger elf continued before he could say anything else.

"I know! I know I shouldn't throw death threats around, and I shouldn't have treated an innocent that way, but..." – Lim brushed a strand of loose hair back from his face – "I didn't know what else to do. Again, there were a dozen of them and only one of me, and I didn't want to start a big fight in there anyway."

Seregei sighed, imagining the setting. There probably had been ways out of there that hadn't involved anything so stupid and dangerous, but he couldn't say for certain; he'd not seen it. Perhaps there had been enough of them that the numbers were just too uneven, or they'd managed to place themselves just so that there was no way to get by without starting a serious fight.

"Can you think of an alternative now? Honestly?"

Lim closed his eyes and sat very still, probably reliving what had happened. At last, he opened his eyes again and said, "No."

"All right, then. I suppose there wasn't really one."

Lim nodded, relaxing a little, apparently relieved. "I might have been able to climb on a table, or perhaps I could have…" He shook his head. "I considered other things at the time, but I still don't think they would have worked."

Seregei nodded. "So what was the next one?"

"How I decided to rescue Esgal."

Seregei raised his eyebrows. This was probably going to be interesting.

"I'd managed to overtake them, and I decided that this particular spot where the road passed through a gulley would make a very good site for an ambush, but again, I was outnumbered."

"I'm starting to think I should have gone not because you couldn't cope with the rescue alone but because you were always outnumbered," said Seregei seriously.

Lim nodded. "So I decided that I'd wait until they came along, see how they were arranged along the road and then, if they were separated out enough, I'd roll boulders down the cliff to separate Esgal from his guards and climb down myself to retrieve him."

Seregei buried his face in his free hand. That was such an incredibly dangerous plan that he didn't even know where to begin.

"Is that the last of them?" he asked evenly.

"There's nothing else that trumps those two," said Lim sadly.

"Right. Well, those were indeed pretty stupid things to do, and I'm guessing you did go through with that ambush scheme?"

Lim nodded.

"Well, we'll never know what would have happened if you'd tried to rescue him earlier or later, so I'm going to chalk that up to another judgement call that might not have worked." He patted Lim on the shoulder. "You were pretty lucky."

"I know," said Lim, smiling.

Seregei started to braid his hair. "So I'm not sure anyone would have done better in your place. I possibly should have gone with you just to even the numbers a bit, but that makes me all the more impressed that you managed it alone, even if you did have to take some incredible risks to do it."

Lim smiled again. "So you still think I'm fit to be a Swordmaster."

"Yes," said Seregei. "Which brings me back to the question of an epithet." He tied off the braid and flicked it back over Lim's shoulder. "What do you think of 'Lucky', given how much luck you had on that Task?"

Lim started to laugh, but shook his head. "Seregei, I think that's the most luck I've had in my entire life."

Seregei had to agree with him there. It was certainly the most *spectacular* run of luck he'd ever had. "All right then," he mused, and smiled. "I'll think of something else."

Lim shot him a look over his shoulder. "That's the only thing you could come up with?"

"I'm still waiting to hear the full story."

Lim sighed. "Well... all right. I've told you about the inn..."

"I guess the journey down there was uneventful?"

"Yes."

"All right. Tell me from when you left the inn. You let the girl go, obviously."

Lim nodded and told him about leaving the town and climbing the mountain until he had caught up with Esgal and his escort.

"How were they transporting him?" asked Seregei, "And how bad did he look? He mentioned to me that he'd been drugged en route, but..."

"You spoke to him already?"

"While I was waiting for you to wake up."

Lim nodded. "They were all on foot. They'd manacled and blindfolded him, but he wasn't bound apart from that, though he did look very weak and groggy. I didn't realise what was wrong until I spoke to him, though." Then he continued the story, telling how he had hurried ahead and prepared the ambush, finally managing to separate Esgal from his guards and get him to a sheltered spot to wait until dark.

"You said that he was chained?" Seregei prompted, wondering how Lim had managed to get Esgal free and back up the cliff.

"I picked the locks on the manacles," said Lim, a note of real pride entering his voice for the first time since he'd started telling the story. "Picked them on the second try for one and the first for the other."

The grin that had been spreading across Seregei's face turned to laughter and he patted Lim on the back. "Well done!" he cried. "I must admit, I didn't know how you'd manage in a real situation if you had to pick locks. I was wondering if you'd stolen the key from one of his guards."

Lim blushed. "I honestly didn't even think of that. It was probably for the best. I didn't want them to know he'd been rescued and I think it worked; the ones we ran into on the way down didn't think I could have used the high trail I was on, so they probably still haven't checked, and we'd have been sunk if they'd even tried, but I don't think they even made the connection between us until much later. I'm getting out of order again, aren't I?"

"Don't worry, it's relevant. That choice was for the best if that was how it worked out; things probably wouldn't have ended well if you'd been cornered with Esgal to look after."

Lim shuddered. "No," he said quietly.

Seregei's smile also faded as he looked at him. "Lim, what is it? What's wrong?"

Lim shook his head. "Just something Esgal said, at our camp once we got off the mountain. It was the first time we had a moment to do something other than walk, eat or sleep. I... I think he was also pretty badly spooked by our nearly being caught once."

Seregei frowned. "What did he say?" he asked.

Lim sighed. "That... that he'd killed three elves that they were holding prisoner, and if we were cornered I... should do the same for him." Once he'd started, the words tumbled out. "He told me what a bad state they were in: the elves he killed. I... I think I agree that it was a mercy, and he also wanted to know what I'd have done if I'd not been able to rescue him for some reason. I told him that... that I was supposed to kill him – that was what set this discussion off – but I don't think I could have done it. That's why, I think, he wanted me to promise that if it came to it I wouldn't let him be taken alive."

Seregei shifted to put his arm around Lim's shoulders. He was shivering, but not actually crying. "You all right?" Seregei asked after a moment.

"Yes... yes, I think so," said Lim. "It just... I don't know whether I actually would have been able to do it. Not in cold blood, to a friend that I was supposed to keep safe, not even knowing how they'd hurt him if I failed."

Seregei hugged him. "I've got no problem with you not wanting to kill someone," he said softly. He knew that killing Ethiren had affected Lim, and he was glad that he showed absolutely no sign of treating killing other elves as a way to solve his problems.

"But what if I had to and I couldn't?"

Seregei sighed. "I think what happened to Ethiren counts as 'had to', don't you?" Seregei's hand went to his side. The wound had healed, but he still remembered how Ethiren had stabbed him.

"But that was different. That was in hot blood, someone... who'd *hurt* me. Even so, I was *panicking*. I couldn't see another way. I couldn't do it to someone helpless."

Seregei nodded. "I don't know how you'd react in that situation," he said softly. "Honestly, I don't know how *I'd* react in that situation. But you've made a few judgement calls in this Task so far. Some good, some bad, some stupid. What would be your call if you were cornered and you could run but Esgal couldn't, and you knew that if you stayed you'd both be taken captive and tortured until you broke?"

Lim shook his head. "Sitting here, it's easier to say that I'd keep my promise and kill him, but I don't know that if I was standing there with a knife in my hand I could actually look into his eyes and... do it."

Seregei sighed. "I don't know either," he said, "And I don't know how we could ever find out how either of us would react in that situation without actually facing it. And I don't know if I *want* to know."

Lim chuckled. "I'd rather not have further confirmation that I'd be capable of murder." He sat in silence for a moment, then looked up. "What do you mean, 'this Task so far'?"

"So far in the story," said Seregei, smiling and hoping to change the subject a little.

Lim took the gesture as it was intended and said, "All right. Where was I?"

"You'd just succeeded in picking the locks on Esgal's chains and freeing him."

Lim grinned. Not even the depressing nature of their previous discussion could entirely dim that triumph, and he was still smiling as he continued the story: how he'd pulled Esgal up to his cave and let him recover, then given him the clothes Alydra had sent and a meal, including some of the fudge Seregei had slipped into his bag. Seregei deflected his thanks with a laugh and patted him on the shoulder – he'd been starting to wonder if Lim had even found the little bundle. At last, the story meandered its way down to their close encounter with the search party.

"They were riding, so I heard them coming and hid Esgal behind the nearest rock, and just had time to hide as well before they came around the corner. Fortunately, as I said, they didn't think to look up that trail. They'd have seen us both if they'd even started up the slope."

Seregei nodded.

"I went over to tell Esgal that they were gone, but he was curled up so tight that he couldn't hear what was happening, and I didn't call his name as I approached, so when I touched him..." Lim shook his head. "I should have expected it. He panicked. He leapt at me and we rolled down the hill. I'm probably lucky that we landed with *me* pinning *him* or there's no telling what he'd have done. Probably punched me and run for it."

"He didn't recognise you?"

Lim stared for a moment, then said, "He couldn't see."

Seregei shook his head. "That wasn't what I meant!" Honestly, he wasn't *stupid*. "I mean, during this whole fight you didn't make a single sound that would let him recognise your voice?"

Lim shook his head a little. "We were both swearing a blue streak all the way down the hill. It wasn't far, but it was rough. Then when we got to the bottom I kept trying to call his name and calm him down, but he was too scared to listen." Lim shuddered. "It did eventually get through, and he settled down, but the whole thing really spooked him. We had to rest for a good while before we could go on again."

Seregei grimaced. "So what then?"

Lim told him about their camp in the woods and his attempts to find food, then the journey back, including the time he'd seen some of their pursuers.

"I thought we'd lost them after that, though; they showed no sign of knowing we were there."

"When did you realise for sure that you had been followed?"

"That morning. I have no idea how they tracked us so far. They must have done it by word of mouth, but I don't think *that* many people saw us." Lim shook his head. "I don't know. Maybe they just realised that we weren't going to Silvren and then decided that since I probably wasn't taking him out into the wild, we must be heading for Duamelti." He grimaced. "I probably could have been more careful, but we were hardly difficult to spot, and Esgal had no hood." He shook his head again. "I don't know."

Seregei nodded. That was a fair theory and it was hardly Lim's fault. It sounded like they really couldn't have run any harder, especially from what Esgal had said about how little rest Lim had been getting.

"Do you know why they followed you so far?"

Lim shook his head. "I got the impression when I was in the town that Esgal was valuable because they wanted to know how he'd stayed hidden for so long and who he'd been talking to."

Seregei nodded. Lim had probably reinforced Esgal's value by rescuing him, as well as making himself a target. All he said, though, was "All right. I'm not sure you could have avoided being followed, under the circumstances."

"I just noticed them that morning and rode double with Esgal for about half an hour, but Winnowil told me she couldn't go on with both of us, so I made him ride on alone and headed into the forest myself to leave tracks and make them think we'd left the road." He smiled fleetingly. "It worked and I kept ahead of them a good way, but then they managed to find me and I tried to outrun them. I'd been running for some time and..." He sighed. "I was tired. I was pulling ahead, though, when they ran me out of the forest and onto the cliff. That was when they offered a chance to surrender and I jumped."

Seregei nodded. "When did you hurt your leg?"

"As I jumped, I think. I remember it hurting as I twisted to dive and it hurt while I was swimming; I thought they'd shot me, but I couldn't feel a shaft in my leg and I was sure their aim wouldn't be that good. I found somewhere to climb out and have a look, and I could see that it was swollen, but couldn't tell what the matter was. I did my best to swim and climb down the river and finally got out at Caleb's palace." Lim grimaced. "Then I fainted."

Seregei smiled, patting him on the head. "I can't say that I'm too surprised."

Lim grinned. "You see what a terrible story it made?"

Seregei laughed. "I've done worse," he said. "If you want to make a song of it at your initiation, you've a few weeks to get it straight."

"Why a few weeks?"

"You need time to heal." Seregei grinned. "When you're such a fast runner, it's no fun to limp into your own initiation." He sobered as he added, "You also need time for second thoughts. It's a big decision."

Lim looked like he was about to retort, but then he simply smiled. "I'd not have" – he hesitated – "put up with you for so many years if I wasn't sure," he said, half jokingly.

"Listen, there's a reason that the Task and the oath are taken separately," said Seregei. "If anything about the Task gave you second thoughts, *tell me.*"

Lim nodded. "I never seriously had second thoughts. About being a Swordmaster, I mean. I had plenty about this specific trip and the choices I was making, but..." He smiled. "I was helping someone. Like you helped me."

Seregei had to look away, smiling bitterly. "You know I didn't just help you because it was my duty as a Swordmaster."

"Yes, I know. But... because you were, it put you in a better position to do it."

Seregei grinned. "So is that why you want to join me?"

Lim laughed softly. "It's..." he grinned at Seregei. "I think it's going to be... I don't really know how to put it. But yes. I helped someone. He was in trouble, and I was able to go and help him and stop other people from hurting him." He grinned again, a slight sparkle of tears gathering at the corners of his eyes.

Seregei took his hands and looked very seriously at him. "What if next time you failed?" he asked. "Would you be prepared to try again?"

Lim's own smile faded. "I'd have to," he said at last. "Or I'd not be able to live with myself."

"Because it would mean breaking an oath?"

"Because it would be my fault and it would be wrong to let someone else suffer for that." Lim's eyes were dry now. "I've been in pain, Seregei, the same as you. I'd not wish it on someone else."

Seregei bit his lip, feeling his own tears gathering. He wondered if Celes had been this proud when he'd made a similar declaration.

"You know it's not all heroic rescues and leaping off cliffs?"

Lim laughed. "I know, and I'm glad! But... at those times when it is... I can do something."

"And just like that," Seregei said softly to himself, "In that moment, a trainee became a Swordmaster."

Lim looked at him, but seemed aware that the words had not been meant for him; he just smiled a little. "So I'll do?" he asked.

Seregei grinned at him and ran a hand down his braid. "You'll do. Oh – here." He took out the candied plums and passed them to Lim. "A gift from the kitchens, but don't tell anyone where you got them."

As soon as he'd unwrapped the sweets, Lim's eyes lit up. "Thank you!" he exclaimed, looking up with a grin.

Seregei smiled and patted his shoulder. "Enjoy them. And get some more rest, or Arani will have my hide."

Lim nodded and lay down, while Seregei went outside.

He walked on for a while, straight along the road back to the Guardhouse, but then past it and on into the woods, along more and more untamed paths. Very few people came this way; there were other, smoother roads leaving the valley in this direction. He ducked under a branch with a small smile and made a mental note to bring a hatchet the next time he came. As he walked, he thought of epithets. Loyal, perhaps?

He heard a sudden rustle in the trees and grinned as he saw a pine marten scurrying out of sight. That really was a sign that few people came here. He sighed and walked on, listening to the sudden cries of birds and breathing deeply as he went. He always thought the air tasted cleaner up here.

Brave? No, that was too close to his own...

At last, he reached some seats carved in the stone, overlooking a beautiful view of the valley. His father had once taught him that the very first Swordmasters had carved these seats, to watch the sun rise, and he believed it. Now he sat in one and looked out over his home. He sighed and closed his eyes, letting the warm sun hit his face as he thought.

Once Lim had recovered a little more, he would take him to the palace to officially present him to Caleb. Since the Valley-elves had arrived, that had become tradition. In return, the king or queen would present each new prince or princess to the Captain of the Swordmasters. Neither ritual was any more than a simple gesture of respect, but Seregei liked them both.

After that, he would have to organise the ceremony itself. Again, he looked out over the valley with a sigh, searching for the great trysting-tree where· the initiation and accompanying celebration would be held. This valley had been his home all his life, and his mother's before him, and his father's, though he had arrived here as a baby. He knew this view so well: the houses clustered in little villages, the mountainsides fading to purple heather near the tops and green down below: light green for grassy fields dotted with sheep high on the hillsides; darker green for the deep forests, the deciduous trees still bearing their leaves at this time of year and the stands of pine and other such conifers showing up still darker among them.

For a moment, he heard the ghosts of the many other Swordmasters who had sat here before him. He knew all their names – he had grown up with the legacy of the Swordmasters, after all – but he only knew a few faces: his parents: Weyrn and Alatani, who had been the first female Swordmaster in generations; his 'uncle', Neithan, his father's trainee and closest friend; the Swordmasters that had raised him after his parents' death and Neithan's before them: Seri, Maelli, Derdhel, and Celes, his mentor. Finally, Seregei the Bold, until now the last Swordmaster, the fate of their long tradition riding entirely on his shoulders.

But now there was someone to follow him. Since – no, he wouldn't dwell on the details of that, not now – since he had been left alone, it had been very lonely in the Guardhouse. Now Lim was to join him. He'd come back very quickly; he'd been away about a week and a half, maybe a little more, and Seregei had expected him to take two weeks at the inside. But there, he'd been introduced as a fast runner. Seregei laughed. In fact, that was how Lim had apparently introduced himself to Caleb, back in those first, shy days: as someone who could outrun the West Wind. It had been one of the few things about himself that he was actually proud of.

Seregei smiled again. It was true. As well as having the makings of an exceptional archer, for all that he was still young, Lim was very fast.

Lord and Lady, he was young. That fact gave Seregei a moment's pause. What had he been thinking? Lim was *so young*; he'd not even been of age when he arrived and now he was only in his fifties. Still, that just proved what he'd been thinking: Lim had trained quickly and keenly, he was quick and clever in every way, he'd even aged fast. That last thought gave Seregei a twinge of regret, but it couldn't really be helped given what Lim's childhood had been like.

And just like that, Seregei had his epithet.

"Swift," he said softly, and then a little louder, "Our new Swordmaster's name is Lim the Swift."

Lim was back on his feet a couple of days after arriving home. He was convinced that he could limp about as he wished, but the healers insisted that for at least the first week he should use a crutch to keep as much weight as possible off his injured leg. Apart from that, he was free to leave and continue preparing for his initiation.

He stretched, wincing as his leg complained, and pulled himself up to stand, leaning on his new crutch. His muscles ached slightly, but he ignored the pain. He was going to visit Esgal first, and would then return to the Guardhouse; he'd not seen his new friend since he came home, but he knew he was still here and would be until the healers were satisfied that his eyesight really was returning.

After a moment longer to get his balance, Lim started off through the door of his room and out into the hall, towards Esgal's room. He could hear Esgal and Alydra talking as he approached and he smiled, pausing for a moment outside the door to listen. He would never eavesdrop on what exactly they were saying; he just wanted to revel for a moment in the fact that he, Lim of Silvren – Lim the Swift, as Seregei had told him he would soon be – had made this possible. He smiled in a moment's conceit. Had it not been for him, these two elves would never have seen one another again. He slipped into the anteroom and went to knock on the inner door, but they'd apparently heard him coming – it was difficult to walk silently with a crutch tapping on every other step – and Alydra opened the door.

For a moment she stared at him, then she let out a small cry of joy and threw her arms around him. He wobbled uneasily, but then caught his balance and hugged her back.

"I hope I'm not interrupting," he said.

"You're welcome at any time," she replied, still grinning.

"Lim?" called Esgal from inside. "Is that you?"

Alydra went back in and Lim followed her, smiling as he saw Esgal sitting on the bed, dangling his feet over the side.

"Yes," he said, and took the hand that Esgal stretched out in greeting. "Yes, it's me. How are you doing?"

"Better," said Esgal. He didn't seem bothered by the bandages over his eyes. "And you?" he asked. "Seregei mentioned that you'd hurt your leg."

Lim nodded. "Hence the crutch," he said. "I daresay that's how you heard me coming."

Esgal and Alydra both nodded.

"There are some things I need to do," said Alydra. She bent and kissed Esgal on the cheek. "I'll leave you two to talk and be back in a little while."

Esgal waved and Lim smiled at her. She smiled back and slipped out. Lim settled down on the chair beside Esgal's bed.

"She doesn't like hearing about the trip back," said Esgal softly.

Lim nodded and reached out to pat him on the shoulder, making him laugh. "You look much better."

"I feel better. I suppose it's just enough rest and food, as well as..." He smiled a little, looking away.

"Having Alydra with you?"

"Aye. I just couldn't think of a way to describe what I meant without being... sappy." He grinned. "But you're right: having her there makes a big difference." He smiled a little, that same bitter smile that Lim had seen several times on the road. "Though I still wonder if this actually was all a very long, very vivid dream."

Lim patted him on the shoulder. "I hope that the Lord and Lady wouldn't be that cruel."

Esgal laughed. "I'm not so sure about them, but I suppose that Valelei would be kinder."

Lim smiled. He'd forgotten that Esgal followed the Spirits, like so many Mixed-bloods. "Either way," he said, "I'm sure that no dream would have lasted this long. Do you still dream that you're back with them?"

"From time to time, but I always know that they were nightmares when I wake." Esgal looked away with a haunted expression. "I'd no longer be on the road."

Lim sighed. "Esgal..." he began.

"I'm all right," said Esgal, looking up again with a small smile. "I'm all right now. I'm home." He reached out, looking for Lim's shoulder, and Lim shifted to let him find it. With a grin, Esgal patted him on the shoulder and said, "Thanks to you."

Lim felt the blush rising in his cheeks. It was conceited to think such things in the privacy of his own head and embarrassing to hear someone else say them aloud.

"You don't have to thank me," he said again. "Any decent elf would have done the same if he could."

Esgal seemed to realise, perhaps from Lim's tone, that he'd embarrassed him, for he looked away again. After a moment's awkward pause, he asked, "So by getting me back home, you become a Swordmaster?"

Lim nodded, grinning. "Yes. Seregei said that despite the many idiot decisions I made, I completed what I set out to do."

"Idiot decisions?"

"Well, I thought that sending you off to ride home alone would be quite enough to do it." Lim looked at the floor for a moment.

Esgal frowned. "Then why did you?"

"Why did I what?"

"Send me on alone."

Lim blinked. "I told you: Winnowil couldn't go on doubly burdened for very much longer and they were catching up. It was the only way I could think of to get you home safely."

A grin started to spread across Esgal's face. "Even though you thought that would lead to your failing your Task?"

"I didn't just come looking for you in order to become a Swordmaster," protested Lim, wondering if Esgal had been thinking that ever since he'd learned that he was a Trainee. "I wanted to come and rescue you from the moment I heard from Seregei what had happened. Like I said, any decent elf would at least try to help you."

Esgal was definitely grinning now, and he once again laid a hand on Lim's shoulder before pulling him into a hug.

"Thank you," he said softly. "You may say I don't need to say it, but I can never thank you enough, my friend."

Lim hesitated a moment, then hugged Esgal back.

"It's all right," he said, smiling. "I just hope I never need to come looking for you again."

Esgal laughed as he pulled away. "If I'm recovered enough, can I come and see you take your oath?"

Lim raised an eyebrow. "Need you ask? You should be healed by then; it'll be a couple of weeks. Seregei said that we'd have to wait for my leg to heal before I could finish my initiation. I get the impression that a delay is pretty common."

Esgal nodded. "I imagine that Trainees are often hurt on their Tasks," he said softly.

Lim nodded. "So you're welcome to come, and I hope you can see again!"

"As do I," said Esgal fervently. "Do you yet know what your epithet will be?"

Lim chuckled. "Yes," he said. "Seregei said that he was impressed with how quickly I came home, and the fact that I run very fast was the thing that I always felt most proud of in my youth..."

Esgal poked him. "Come, my friend, out with it!"

"Swift. Lim the Swift."

4115245R00152

Printed in Great Britain
by Amazon.co.uk, Ltd.,
Marston Gate.